Hour of the Witch Spinners

By:
Scarlet Darkwood
&
P. Mattern

Chapter One

Larissa North Strondovan, sat on a colorful braided rug in her bedroom, viewing an open Book of Shadows. The book had been a special gift from her favorite neighbor, Dorenda.

"Use it to write down everything you learn, everything you know, my child, for your wisdom is greater than most." The older woman had looked around quickly before pressing the jeweled book into the little girl's hands. "This shall be our secret only. No one is to know what you write within its pages. Inside yourself there is great power. One day you will come to know it well."

On one of the empty pages, Larissa had scribbled a levitation spell in an unruly childish handwriting. Her confidence soared. Surely this time, the words were correct, after working on them for days. The girl viewed her surroundings with satisfaction, smiling at all the favorite stuffed animals bought by her adoptive parents, Rick and Amy Martin.

These animals were her prized possessions, and they would do her bidding, if all went as intended. Out of the pocket of her skirt, she drew her wand, another gift from Dorenda. The piece stemmed from a perfectly shaped branch of the willow tree in her back yard.

Dorenda helped select the perfect one, tossed the rough wood in her Vapors Cauldron, and recited a few ancient, well-practiced incantations. The cauldron hissed and blew out a cloud of steam, spitting out a finished wand. The woman held the piece a few seconds and smiled, stating with satisfaction, "It's a fairly decent working wand for a beginning witch."

Time to put her neighbor's words to the test. Larissa drew in a deep breath and recited:

"Erigo et maneat in loco!"

A light wind swept through the room. To her delight, the toys rose evenly into the air, six feet above her head. Each one spun in an easy clockwise rotation. Delighted, Larissa jumped up and down, clapping her hands. The spell had been a success, written all by herself. Time to show Dorenda.

Just as she ran toward her closet, Larissa froze in fear at the ominous tap, tap, tap of her mother's high heels coming down the hallway. The bedroom door swung open. All the stuffed animals halted mid-spin and crashed to the floor.

Amy steadied herself against the doorframe, gazing wide-eyed into the room. Larissa had barely replaced her wand and Book of Shadows into her deep dress pockets.

"Rick, where are you? Come here!" Amy scooped Larissa into her arms, holding her close. "Rick!"

"What do you want?" He joined his wife. An annoyed look covered his face.

"The poltergeists are back. We need another cleansing."

"Oh, come on. Seriously?"

"Do it. Call Ghost Eradicators. Now!"

Later that night, Larissa lay quietly in her bed, listening closely. Not a sound inside the house.

"Good. The coast is clear." She scrambled from her bed and ran to her closet. The floor was dusty, but in the back-left corner against the dark wooden flooring, she again noticed the odd golden circle with serrated edges giving off a soft glow. She'd often wondered how it had gotten there, and why anyone would paint such a thing on the floor of a small closet. She always meant to ask her parents or Dorenda about it, but somehow it always slipped her mind until the next time she saw it.

According to Dorenda's instructions, Larissa stood in the corner opposite the golden circle. Concentrating on the woman, she tapped her left foot three times on the floor and said, "*Lacus*."

In a blinding flash of white light, Larissa found herself standing in front of a blazing fireplace. She shook her head, regaining her bearings and breathing deeply. These transports always sent her stomach into a cascade of queasy flip-flops.

Dorenda leaned forward from her wingback chair, unperturbed, and handed the young girl a cup of hot cambric tea in a chipped bone china cup. "The uneasy sensations will ease in time, the more you become accustomed to transportation." The woman eyed her visitor with kind eyes. "I knew you were coming."

"It worked!" Larissa said. Her eyes glittered with excitement. "Exactly as I wanted—until Mommy came in and ruined everything." Her face clouded with the memory of it all. "Can't I tell them, Dorenda? Please? It would make things so much easier. Mommy and Dad think our house is actually haunted." The little girl's eyes widened with indignation. "They have no clue that it's just me doing what I love."

Larissa waved her hands, gesturing as if she held her beloved wand.

Dorenda sipped from her cup of tea, gazing into Larissa's anxious face before answering. As always, the lady considered the child's words.

"Your adoptive parents were chosen carefully, my dear, and they are wonderful people. A true blessing in a time of great need. Their lack of knowledge regarding your heritage and innate magical gifts protects them—and you."

The older woman sat up straighter in her chair and placed her teacup on a matching saucer. Larissa stared back, mesmerized by the glinting eyes in a face showing remarkable, stunning beauty for her age. Her skin showed almost no wrinkles, and her raven black hair, worn in an old-fashioned chignon, bore a few silver streaks.

"I will tell you now that there are those who have sought your whereabouts since you were a baby. Might I add that they would not hesitate one second to kill your precious family, as you know them, to get to you?"

A sober expression covered Dorenda's face. The young girl looked at her, drowning in a swell of emotions. The child had gravitated to her neighbor the moment they met. When the woman revealed her identity on Larissa's sixth birthday, everything made sense as to why.

"Auntie Dorenda, you don't need to remind me, but I can dream, can't I?" Her face brightened. "But what did you think of the levitation spell? You should have seen it!"

Dorenda's eyes twinkled with delight. She leaned forward, patting her niece's hand. "I think you're off to a good start."

~~Six Months Later~~

Amy sat fretting at the kitchen table, drumming her manicured nails on top. She stared out the window, watching Larissa, and mumbled, "I love that child as if I'd birthed her myself, but dear God, why do strange things happen when she's around?"

Those "strange things" had gotten worse a year ago when Larissa turned seven years of age. Amy sank back in her chair and swallowed a mouthful of warm coffee, remembering days gone by when life at least seemed normal.

She'd never forget finding the sturdy woven basket outside her front door. Snuggled beneath a pink woolen blanket rested a tiny baby. When the infant inside cooed, that was the day her and Rick's life changed forever.

Dear Mr. and Mrs. Martin,

It is with mixed emotions of heart-felt sadness and joy that we have placed this magnificent child in your care. We are aware that you desire such a blessing, but forces of nature have denied it.

You both have great love in your hearts. This baby girl needs that in her life, and we have determined that you shall have your wishes granted. Please present yourselves, along with the infant, to the office of Ignatius Grant, on 156 Firecrest Lane, Addyson, KS, and all the tedious details of this serendipitous adoption will be completed in full. One more thing, please bring the rattle on which you found this attached message.

Yours Truly,
Ignatius Grant, Esquire

She and Rick had studied the rolled-up parchment paper that had been attached to a baby rattle.

"Where on earth is 156 Firecrest Lane? I've never heard of it." Rick scratched his head.

"I'm not finding the place, either." Amy had looked over and over at the city map. "If we want a baby in our lives, this will be our only chance, and all we have to do is show up." She tapped Rick on the arm. "Do you know how hard adoption is? And a baby at that. This Ignatius-something-or-other makes it seem so easy."

"Kinda like magic, if you know what I mean." Rick laughed.

"This whole thing seems like something out of a storybook. A baby on the doorstep? Come on!"

Rick took her in his arms. "Let's just go with it. We'll find our way to Ignatius-something-or-other's office and get this whole thing done."

Amy gazed into her husband's eyes. "We're going to have a baby." She squealed with delight and hugged Rick.

Ignatius Grant's office hadn't looked particularly out of the ordinary when the couple arrived, but a peculiar air lingered about the place. A few law books lined the shelves inside the room, which most attorneys likely possessed in any office, but the other books created questioning glances between Rick and Amy.

The big question, why have books that looked older than Methuselah, and why the odd writing on the spines? They didn't look anything remotely familiar.

Stranger still, Ignatius Grant took the rattle they had brought with them and shook it, moving to different corners of the room as he did so.

She and Rick had watched, struggling to contain their laughter. But they knew Mr. Grant did his task with as much seriousness as any lawyer committed to verifying his clients and work. All they heard was the familiar sounds rattles made.

From the look on his face, Mr. Grant seemed to hear something else, altogether.

"There now, I believe we're all set," said Grant, sitting down at his desk. He opened a drawer and pulled out a pen and legal document. "Are you two prepared to take on the most important task of a lifetime? Being a parent is never easy. And some children are . . . How should I say it? Unique. Yes, that's it. You must always be prepared for that uniqueness. Never stifle creativity. Just remember that."

"Of course. Ever since we've been married, we've wanted a baby," Amy said. "Rick and I will be the best parents ever."

Ignatius Grant looked from one to the other. "Very well, then. Please sign on your designated lines, and this precious child is yours."

Mr. Grant must have liked nice writing implements because the pen from his hand flashed bright silver, momentarily blinding her. On the shiny surface, the small engraved letters "*sterling silver*" glowed briefly. In an instant, the pen looked like any ordinary one—except for the fact that her hand tingled the whole time she signed her signature.

The legal form looked like the same type of paper on the rattle. When Rick signed his name, he must have felt the same sensations because the look on his face showed one perplexed.

"We are finished." Mr. Grant placed the pen and paper back in the drawer.

"Can you tell us more about her, where this baby came from?" asked Rick. "Most people at least have some sort of history when they adopt a child."

Ignatius Grant stared at Rick, his eyebrows furrowed in thought. "No, there is nothing I can tell you, except that she's a child in need of a good home. The parents have disappeared, and no one seems able to state why. When I received the child, I had to find her a good and proper home." He smiled. "Now we have that settled."

"But—Mr.—" Amy stepped closer to the desk.

"Godspeed my friends. Take very good care of Little Larissa, who is extremely special. Oh, and there is one more thing. You are to never change the child's name for any reason. Woe be unto you if this is done."

Before the new parents could protest, the door to the office opened, and they felt an unseen force pull them away from the desk.

Amy put the memory out of her mind. She'd thought about the meeting with Ignatius Grant many times, trying to figure out the oddities that occurred in the house.

True to their agreement, Larissa's name remained as written on the legal adoption paper. No disobedience occurred regarding anything asked of them by Mr. Grant. So why all the ruckus and strange goings-on? Ghost Eradicators failed miserably. Even a priest from another state, one known for performing exorcisms, didn't work.

That exercise had been a total flop, like all the others before. Rick was poor support, wrinkling his nose every time he heard each descriptive occurrence.

When a new neighbor, Dorenda Soltaro, moved in next door, things settled down. But not for long.

"Mama, can I keep her?" Larissa ran inside, nearly knocking over Amy's coffee cup when she reached the table. The little girl held out a kitten with a black and white tuxedo-style fur pattern.

"Oh, honey." Amy shook her head immediately. "We can't have a kitty."

"Why not?" Larissa's eyes brimmed with tears. "The kitty needs a home."

"I know, sweetheart, but maybe it already belongs to someone else. They'll be missing her. You need to take the kitty back outside so she can go home."

"She said her home is with me." Larissa stamped her foot.

"Larissa!" Amy sat up straight. A flash of irritation radiated through her.

"Her name is Sophie, and she's supposed to be with me."

Amy opened her mouth to say something else, but the words wouldn't come. "Do you really want her?"

"Yes." Larissa's eyes flashed. "Dorenda says I need a special friend." The little girl smiled and hugged the purring cat.

~~Sixteen Years Later~~

In Nepal, deep in the Himalayas, a fortress stood tall and proud on the Makalu peak. The stone castle of Katharta lay nestled inside a circle of high thick walls. To the normal eye, the site appeared impenetrable.

The Hawthorne Enchanter Dynasty knew their luxurious stronghold was safe from everything—except other witches. Like all claves, family units with origins from the first cave witches, they constantly kept guard. Great covens and claves of the Magiverse with renowned specialty powers often warred with one another, vying for additional strength. Smart witches never let their guard down for long.

Inside Katharta Castle, the decor reflected a family connected to a long line of royalty. Expansive, elegant, and mysterious, this clave enjoyed a place where they basked in the trappings of their station and flexed their magical skills. Bright red carpets lined stone and wooden floors.

Ornate furniture filled the vast number of rooms. Meals prepared by specialty Mortal chefs titillated the palate and came served on plates of the finest porcelain and consumed with utensils passed down from generations. Goblets of gold and silver held copious amounts of wine on demand.

August Hawthorne, the clave's youngest male, sank deeper in the soft eiderdown mattress of his bed. The last thing he wanted was a rude interruption to his blissful sleep. He fought back, keeping his eyes clamped shut. With each passing second his irritation grew more intense.

No matter how hard he tried to block everything out, maintain control on all his senses, the loud tap, tap, tapping noises persisted. He forced one eye open to get his bearings and peered across the room. Behind the thick windowpane, he made out a small, annoying familiar shape. August groaned in disgust. This wasn't good at all.

Gently, he disentangled himself from the leg of his pretty sleeping companion, Fiona, who had curled around him like an octopus during the wee hours of the morning. Without a sound, he stuck his long legs over the side of the bed, wincing when his feet touch the cold floor. Neither Fiona nor her sister seemed immediately disturbed at his leaving.

The debauchery and play the night before left the threesome satisfied but exhausted. August smiled, his body perking up at the mere thought. The sisters knew how to please him in many ways, lavishing attention executed with skill and dexterity. They exceeded his expectations.

August headed straight to the louvered window and cranked it open. Outside on the ledge, a War Pigeon stared back, tapping its tiny foot with impatience. The look in its eyes showed smoldering anger; the beak shut with obstinance. The bird hopped in, ruffling its feathers and warbling in scolding tones.

"So sorry, dear fellow. How rude of me for not answering sooner." August stroked its downy head with his fingers. "But you can't blame a guy for having a good time, can you?"

The bird sounded off in another tirade of disapproval, sticking a claw from its foot into the young man's hand. The move didn't puncture the skin, but the force behind it meant business.

"A peace offering, you say?" said August, laughing. "I'd be most delighted to do that for all your trouble. You've come a long way, and in frightful weather." He walked over to a small carved table and from a copper tray, plucked off some large crumbs of shortbread left over from the previous night's meal.

"There you go, dear friend. I hope this will satisfy your hunger and anger. We can't be on bad terms, you know."

The pigeon swallowed down the crumbs and rubbed against August's fingers.

"I thought you might forgive me with such tasty morsels. Only the best when you come to our place." He glanced down and frowned. "I guess it's down to business we go. What have we here?"

The moment he untied the rolled-up message from the pigeon's ruff above its foot, August recognized the official colored parchment paper of the Hawthorne Clave. His remaining drowsiness left in a flash. This was no ordinary missive, but a summons to his Grandfather Jove's control room.

To a Mortal viewing the message, it looked like ancient runic script at best. Holding the parchment paper close to his mouth, August exhaled a soft breath over it. This action deactivated the protection spell placed over it by the sender, ensuring only he, August Hawthorne, could see it and not an enemy. Just as he expected, characters within the decoy message floated momentarily above the paper, glowing bright green:

Dearest Grandson,

Your presence is required at once. An event has transpired requiring immediate attention. Make haste.

Jove Hawthorne
Patriarch Hawthorne Clave

The letters vanished the moment he finished reading. Irritated, August raked back thick locks of wavy blonde hair from his shoulders and gazed at the sleeping young women in his bed. A mere glance, and his morning erection stretched out in front of him in all its resplendent glory. Fiona's lush white, dimpled bottom shined in clear view. Daisy's succulent breasts, with their perfect rosy nipples, teased him from the silk coverlets.

If he hurried, there was time to engage in another lusty romp and service them both. With a few quick strides, he hopped into bed.

***

Jove paced back and forth in the control room, fuming. Such a display of emotion was usually the norm for him, complete with furrowed gray bushy brows.

"Where is that boy?" he bellowed. "He was supposed to be here over a quarter of an hour ago." The old gentleman pounded a fist into his hand. "By the gods, I should have him whipped!"

"Here I am Grandsire." A cherry male voice called out from the arched entranceway. So sorry to annoy you with my tardiness, but you didn't give me much notice. I was . . . um . . . in the middle of something."

His Grandfather grunted in disapproval. "Hmph, in between two lily-white thighs, I imagine." The eyebrows flowed together once again in tandem with piercing black eyes narrowing into slits. "Sewing your wild oats and praying for a crop failure. That's what you're doing." He shook a bony finger at his grandson. "You really need to take up other hobbies, August. Your reputation as a Libertine has not escaped even my ears."

Undaunted the golden-haired youth vaulted neatly over a couch between the two of them and hugged the older man before drawing back.

"So what is this emergency? Which of the claves has declared war on us now?"

"Sit down, my boy." The old man pointed to a gilded ornately carved chaise lounge cattycorner to another matching one. "This is a serious matter, and it concerns you, of all people."

August sat up straight and paid attention. The former light-heartedness in him disappeared as if someone had flipped a switch. Instincts told him this matter was more than another skirmish for territories and power. The fact that his grandfather had summoned him personally, rather than any of his brothers, intrigued him more.

"I'm all ears, Grandfather Jove, Most High Ruler of the Hawthorne Clave." He lowered his head in a momentary bow of deference.

"Ah, August," Jove responded, shaking his head. "With a heavy heart, I must tell you that I have heard from the Glanarium Supremo, the highest council of witches of the Magiverse." The gentleman paused and stared at August."

"And?"

"They submitted a special assignment, seeking our help. This assignment, if you will, is one that will continue to rear its ugly head until resolved. It involves our family and another. After much thought and consideration, I have officially agreed that you will be the one to carry out and complete this special quest."

August paled at the words. He didn't want a special quest. Staying in the rich surroundings of Katharta Castle suited him just fine. Couldn't his grandfather simply cast a spell, do an enchantment, and be done with it, whatever the Council wanted?

"May I add," continued Jove, "that it won't be an enviable task. It will involve traveling to hostile locations, dealing with some of the most unscrupulous individuals in the Magiverse, and taking on risks no young witch in his prime should take on."

The young man tried maintaining his composure. From the look on Jove's face, he was in no mood for foolishness or protests. "Sounds somewhat interesting so far, Grandfather. But I must ask. Why did the you select me for the quest?

All my older brothers have much more experience in both casting and warfare. Fortuno is better than any of us when it comes to enchanting and casting spells. It is also a well-known fact that Lentis can draw a wand faster than anyone.

Capistro has the Ague Throwing gift. He is deadly accurate and can wipe out an entire front line of an approaching army with malaria. His fireballs do the trick quite nicely, too, if he wants to make his choices more precise. As for me, I have none of these skills."

His Grandfather leaned forward and clasped his grandson's shoulder with his large hand. His eyes showed deep sympathy.

"The Council selected you, mentioned you by name, August. That's why I decided I had to comply. Only current heirs are selected to find a solution to the problem plaguing our families. Part of the solution involves locating and returning a powerful relic to its rightful owner. Doing so will solve the great number of complications plaguing unity for generations.

"Oh, there is one other thing. You will not be alone on the quest."

At this announcement, August leaned forward to hear every word clearly. "Someone's coming with me?"

"Yes, dear boy," said Jove. "The person is Larissa North Strondovan. She is the heir and Remnant of a once-proud elemental witch clave. They have been shamed for a long time, ridiculed and nearly stamped out, all due to a feud with our family. But this particular heir could be the key to locating and returning the stolen relic to its rightful owner."

Before he could stop himself, August bounded to his feet, his cheeks blazing bright pink. "I've heard of them." He clenched his fists, struggling to keep his voice below a shout. "You can't possibly mean *that* family of Norths."

"Now, son . . ." The older man held out a hand.

"But Grandfather, we are the ones who helped in stamping out their line. And with good, righteous reason, I might add. They slandered and cheated us in a wand duel. They killed Uncle Clement. Have you forgotten that?"

August placed his feet in a wide stance and crossed his arms, glaring at Jove. He continued, "If they have fallen in power, if they have suffered from a stain on their reputations, it is more than justice."

Jove bolted from his chair and stood toe to toe with August, his face dark with anger. He shoved his grandson back down into his seat again.

"Listen to me. You have no choice. And for that matter, neither do I. And don't think I didn't try my damnedest to get you out of this mess." His words came out like the sound of roaring thunder. "You will put your prejudices and personal feelings aside and comply with the Council's request. Are you aware of the consequences if you don't? Do I have to spell it out for you?"

August stared up in shock at the towering figure of his grandfather. Whether or not he liked the situation was of no importance at all. Every witch who was anything knew that refusing a request from the Glanarium Supremo would result in severe reprisals.

Some witches who had dared to argue lost their tongues, their hearing, their faculties, or worse for the duration of their pitiful and diminished lives.

August got his breathing under control. Arguing would be futile. This whole ordeal was going to be a shit quest, and worse, he would be making it with a member of an elemental clave he had been raised to despise.

He cursed his rotten luck. There couldn't possibly be a worse assignment or companion.

Chapter Two

August left the control room. The more he thought about the dangerous task ahead, the more his anger roiled inside of him. Not even another lusty romp with Fiona and Daisy would tame the strength of emotions he felt right now.

Instead of turning down the hallway toward his bedroom, he decided on something else. During the sparring between him and Jove, he never once asked exactly what happened that he and this Larissa girl should find themselves in such a predicament.

Just thinking of the prospects of interacting with someone from the North Clave sent him into a virtual icy pit of pure hatred. August racked his brain, trying to recall what had transpired in history, what caused this so-called feud. It was a war, really, from what he'd briefly heard.

If someone asked him for an oration of the past events leading to his present situation, he couldn't do it. No one ever told him the details, and all these years he'd been too busy playing around and enjoying his family's wealth to care. If it didn't require his attention in the present moment, he didn't bother wasting his time inquiring about anything.

Farther down another hallway, August rounded a corner and descended a flight of stone steps leading into the bowels of Katharta Castle. Like all witches, he could engage in magic. The problem, he wasn't the most adept, as he'd noted to his grandfather. He didn't spend lots of time practicing. How would he stack up against Larissa North Strondovan?

Most witches didn't discriminate when it came to gender and magical skills. Most witches did discriminate when it came to skills pertaining to a type of magic. Claves and covens were known for their specialties, and families prided themselves on their heritage when it came to a special art in executing something.

The families passed it down through generations, keeping their training exercises a tight-lipped secret. If Larissa was indeed a Remnant, what had she learned in the magical arts, if anything? Her family wouldn't have been around to teach what she needed to know.

Frustrated, August rounded another corner, descended a smaller flight of stairs, and headed down a narrow hallway. When he faced the arched door of his choosing, his eyes scanned the carving on the wooden surface. It was nothing more than a simple square with a circle inside. No writing, no other identification. No doorknob or keyhole, either.

The symbol alone told him what he needed to know. "I guess I'll try my hand at scrying. Again." August grimaced and said, "*Locus fiora intuata.*" Nothing happened. He stared at the door. "I said, *locus fiora intuata.*" He called out louder, hoping the rise in voice might make the spell work better. Still nothing happened.

"Shit!" August kicked the door and was rewarded by a resounding shock. A tingling sensation shot up his leg. He cried out and rubbed his thigh. "What's the spell? Come on, I know this." He chided himself for not practicing so much on his magic.

With an a-ha moment dawning on him, he blurted out, "*Locus fuisset intuita.*" A faint sound of chimes filled his ear. The door glowed a soft, shimmering blue and silently swung open. August stepped inside, grateful he'd even remembered the spell at all.

The room measured twenty-five square feet, like most of the other rooms down this particular hallway. Each one contained a specific symbol on the door, noting the specialty inside. Each door opened the same way, but with a different spell just for that room. August opened the scrying room.

When the young man stood three feet past the door, it closed. In the middle of the room, he viewed with apprehension the gazing pool. Carved from a special marble imported from Italy, the interior of the pool was round, holding sacred waters from a long-hidden lake in the United States.

The exterior of the pool surrounded the inner area in a square layout. Quartz points lined all sides. Large dumortierite spheres rested inside the four inner corners. August couldn't remember the last time he'd been here. The longer he stood by the gazing pool, the more he relaxed. Combinations of quartz and dumortierite did that to one's disposition.

They also brought his focus into a sharper state. He looked around the room. If he didn't want to use the gazing pool, there were other options. In one corner stood a table holding an enormous clear crystal sphere.

In another corner, a small table held a large pillar candle. A round smoked mirror was stationed in the third corner, and in the last, nothing but a large cushion on the floor. Which would it be? Gazing pool, crystal ball, flame, scrying mirror, or ether?

Gazing pool it would be. August let out a sigh. No way he would consider the etheric method. Only advanced witches with a strong third eye used such a method without difficulty. When he seated himself on the cushion by the pool, a series of ripples raced across the surface. This was a good sign. The water scrying spirits had been waiting for him.

August took some deep breaths and concentrated. At last he mumbled a brief incantation that somehow popped into his head, praying it would work.

Spirits on high, do not lie. My request of you seems vast. Keep it clear, as if viewed by eye. Show me the distant past. Two beings fighting, I know not why, their reasons still unclear. Tell me all, tell me true. The answers I'll hold dear.

Ripples spread across the water faster. A thin fog formed and lifted. The water glowed green, switching to purple, and in the end, darkened to a deep gray. Wide-eyed, August watched with wonder and relief. His mind opened, settling itself on learning the answers, regardless of the truth and how knowledge of it would affect his mission.

Deep understanding was of grave importance. If a relic needed discovery and its rightful owner found, he must understand what occurred to the fullest. Even if he loathed the answer. The pool seemed to widen; the young man knew this was a better sign.

A vision would play before his eyes, like someone watching a movie. With any luck, the images contained sound. Another misty cloud arose out of the blackness of the pool. August watched and concentrated harder than he'd ever done in his whole life:

"What say you, Clement Hawthorne?" A young man postured in front of another, who appeared near the same age.

"What say you, Desmond Strondovan, you scoundrel? Am I not good enough for your beloved sister, Ciana? You think I'm worthless?

"There will be very few who has the worthiness to marry Ciana. She has great powers. You know this very well." Desmond turned his gaze to a woman who crouched beneath an oak tree. Fear lit her eyes. Her whole body trembled as she viewed each man.

"Have you forgotten that the Hawthorne Clave is renowned for its enchanting skills. And we're of royal blood, to boot." Clement brandished his wand. A light breeze sent his cloak waving in the air, creating a rather ominous figure.

"You don't scare me, nor your family," Desmond retorted. We're a mighty clave as old as the earth itself. We have power unmatched by most."

"You want to put your powers where you mouth is?" Clement had walked up close enough to Desmond, poking his rival's chest with his wand.

Desmond laughed. "Are you foolish enough to do such a thing? You'll not win." The man crossed his arms and glared back at Clement. He turned to his sister. "Ciana, you love this man so much you want to be with him? Give that family knowledge of your powers? You've lost your mind."

"Please, gentlemen, do not do this. Clement, my love, my heart, please do not challenge my brother." She turned away, stifling her sobs.

Clement's mouth dropped open, stunned. He walked over to the young woman and turned her face up to his. "Ciana, what are you talking about? Does our love not mean anything?"

Ciana glanced at Desmond and back to Clement. "My dear," she said, regaining control of her emotions, "let this go right now. Do not challenge him. We can work something out when others least expect it." She pulled Clement closer, gracing a quick kiss on his lips. "We can work this out."

"We'll settle this right now. Not later." He pulled away from Ciana and strode back to Desmond. "Right now. Come on, Strondovan, time to show what you're really made of. A wand duel. That'll settle it. The first one to land the other on the ground wins."

"Very well, Clement," answered Desmond, "if I win, you can't have my sister. If you win, I have no choice but to defer to your wishes."

Clement grinned with satisfaction. "All rules of the duel start the moment we pace off. Twenty-five paces, turn, and fire. Oh, and no cheating whatsoever. Witches High Moral Code in effect as always."

Desmond nodded and bowed. Ciana sank against the mighty oak and sobbed. The two men paced off, turned, raised their wands, and fired. Bolts of blue shot through the air. Desmond dodged the first one. Clement took a hit on the left shoulder.

He cried out, staggering backward, but regained his stance. Ciana gasped in horror and shielded her eyes. Both men paused, repositioned themselves again, and looked at each other head on.

Desmond narrowed his eyes and angled his head, determining the best location to aim the flash from his wand. Clement quickly blew Ciana a kiss and squared up his shoulders. Both men gestured in their own unique manner and the flashing commenced.

From Desmond's wand, a bolt landed on Clement's right shoulder, knocking him off balance. The return bolt from Clement struck Desmond's hand. His wand dropped to the ground. The man cursed.

"That's okay, Desmond. Pick it up and we start again. You think you've got the better of me with two good blows, but I'll have you yet."

For the next round, the two men lifted their hands, wands ready. Clement tried positioning his hand, ready to let loose. Nothing happened. He tried again. Numbness settled in, rendering him paralyzed. How odd. Before he could try again and fire his wand off, a blue bolt tinged in red came barreling through the air, striking him square in the chest. The man dropped to the ground and lay still. Ciana screamed and sprinted to her lover.

Desmond remain still, eyes narrowed. He waited a couple of seconds. That was strange. He didn't remember brandishing his wand quite that fast. He surely didn't intend to send a charge so amped up.

For duels, one only wanted just enough strength to knock an opponent down. "Get up, Clement. That one was a doozy, but it shouldn't have been that strong to knock you out cold."

"He's not moving," Ciana cried out. "Clement. Darling. Wake up." She smacked the man's cheeks lightly, trying to rouse him.

"Oh, for heaven's sake, sister. Are you sure he's not carrying on?" Exasperated, Desmond ran over to his sister's side. He knelt by the unconscious man. Placing an ear over his opponent's heart, he listened for a few seconds.

"He's dead, Desmond. You killed him." Ciana's eyes blazed with hot fiery rage. "You killed him. You cheated." She arose and stamped her feet. "You'll pay for this, you cheater." The angry woman waved a fist in her brother's face. "You'll pay for this."

Gripped with fear, Desmond stood transfixed. From behind the oak tree the shadow of a figure rustled, unseen. No one moved now. Desmond and Ciana stayed still as if they were mere statues.

The gazing pool rippled, turning back to its original clear water. August remained on the cushion, dumfounded. He rubbed his eyes and continued staring at the pool, thinking it might show more. It didn't. He rubbed his lip, thinking. At one time, a Hawthorne was in love with a Strondovan!

***

Inside a large super seven crystal cave, tucked away in the heart of Brazil, Larissa looked up from a large clear quartz sphere. It had been fashioned and polished to perfection, resting in the middle of one of the large rooms. Like August, she'd viewed the whole scene.

"So that's what happened between our two families, and why I must make this quest with August Hawthorne?"

"Yes," said Dorenda. She ran her hand through Larissa's long black locks, staring at her niece with affection. "According to the Council's orders, this problem will plague the Strondovans and Hawthornes until the issue is completely resolved. Your great-great uncle, Desmond, is thought to have broken the Witches High Moral Code. But he insisted that he didn't."

"What happened with Clement Hawthorne?" asked Larissa.

"He died." Dorenda frowned at the memory and paced the cave floor. "Nobody could rouse him, not even the most powerful witch in the Magiverse. Whatever happened to him was so strong it couldn't be undone."

"Do you believe Uncle Desmond? If he says he didn't kill Clement, then why doesn't anyone believe him?"

"My dear, in the Glanarium Supremo, a witch still has to offer some semblance of truth and it be believable. Desmond simply couldn't do it. After a careful investigation, the Council determine the case as static, unresolved."

"So their decision is to curse both families?" Larissa's eyes clouded. "That doesn't seem fair."

"It wouldn't be fair to unjustly punish a witch. The Council made the best decision they could. Put the onus back on the two families involved and let them work it out. Until the mystery is solved, each current generation will work together to help."

"They picked me and August, didn't they?"

"Dear girl, you two represent the current generation. It is the council's hope that you can resolve what happened or come up with a solution to rectify and resolve this once and for all. A plan that is not only acceptable to both families but blessed by the Council."

The older woman plucked at the girl's sleeve. "Bad feelings and unresolved conflicts fester for years, and those energy waves spread throughout the Magiverse, affecting many in the smallest way."

Larissa looked around the cave with wonder. "Why did you bring me here to this land, so far away from home? Couldn't we have done this at your house, in your cellar? You have everything down there."

"I wanted you to see your beginnings, where you came from. This is your family's cave." Dorenda's expression showed a hint of renewed excitement. "Part of your family name, North, indicates that you came from one of the elemental witch claves. Clave means a clan from a cave. All claves extend to the moment time and earth were created.

"You see, there are four elemental cave types corresponding to certain family lines, North South, East, and West. These caves also correspond to the elements, earth, wind, fire, water. Your Strondovan family line is a North elemental born from the crystal caves, and not all earth caves are crystal, let alone a super seven. There is only one of those."

Larissa smiled for the first time. "That does sound rather interesting."

"My dear, it is. It's something to be extremely proud of. The Norths are connected to earth. The Souths are connected to fire, the Easts to air, and the Wests to water. Your specific line being connected to the super seven crystal cave makes the Strondovan family one of the most heavily favored in the Magiverse."

"And we're in it now," said Larissa, looking up again for confirmation from Dorenda.

"We are where your Strondovan family originated eons ago. It has been here since time immemorial.

"Tell me more about the super seven. What is it and what does it mean?" Larissa viewed her surroundings, staring at the huge crystal points. They sent off an energy she'd never felt before, but immediately liked.

"A super seven crystal contains the following elements in one crystal: clear quartz, amethyst, rutile, smoky quartz, cacoxenite, goethite, and lepidocrocite. Quartz channels your soul's highest purposes and opens up your pathway to the spirit world. Amethyst is responsible for spiritual growth and transformation.

"Rutile conducts and amplifies energy. Cacoxenite is an awakener and connects intellect between self and all things. Goethite holds the blueprint of the universe and star systems. Lepidocrocite aligns and harmonizes energy while on the earth. It's everything. Thus, the reason it's highly favored."

"You've studied this all your life, haven't you?" Larissa picked up a small super seven crystal from the ground. A jolt of energy coursed through her, and the stone fell from her hand.

Dorenda chuckled. "It takes time and training to attune with the energies of stones, especially ones that have been in their original place and untouched. Super sevens are more powerful than the others. As for knowledge, you've been studying all your life too. That's why I came when I did, when you were very young. I made sure you learned everything I could teach you. And there's still more."

Sophie rubbed against Larissa's ankle as she dropped a crystal at her owner's feet. A few seconds later, she brought another one in similar shape and size. Both contained the characteristic look of the super seven, smoky brown with streaks of red, purple and some black and light brown colors.

Within minutes, a small pile of different colored stones lay in a heap next to the first two crystals.

"*You need these.*" The cat looked up and let out a soft meow. Her green eyes flashed.

"Your familiar is right, my dear," said Dorenda. You need these stones. It's time to fashion a wand much different from the one you've been using all these years."

Larissa stooped down, viewing the pile. "How will we make a wand with these? Do they end up in the Vapors Cauldron like the willow branch?

The aunt laughed. "No. This particular wand will have great power and must used with extreme care. We'll even create a special box so you can store the piece and keep it safe. Just so you know, the other stones of jasper, agate, aventurine, sodalite, just to name the few Sophie brought, are not native to this cave."

"Really? Where did they come from?"

"It wasn't uncommon for families to collect magical stones, talismans, anything that could add to power. Some of these stones were gifted to your family. Others were found and brought back here to be included in the family supply list."

"Just like your supply list at home, right Auntie Dorenda?" Larissa smiled.

"Exactly. You must start your supply closet because you are going to need it. For the quest with August, I will help you create a travel chest containing what you will need the most, including your new powerful wand."

"Any way out of this mission? Isn't there a cousin or some other North family member who would be more suited?"

Dorenda shook her head. "Unfortunately, Uncle Desmond's deed sent shockwaves throughout the claves, and your family's line was hunted down, killed, and separated because of it. You are officially known as a Remnant, which is unfortunately a blight on your ancestral heritage."

"That's so unfair," Larissa frowned.

"Life's not fair, even for powerful witches. Some who were more sympathetic and compassionate wanted to protect the North family line as much as possible. Doing so ensured the family line and its power wouldn't vanish into oblivion.

The Council agreed wholeheartedly. The desire is to unite it and bring back its full honor and glory. That's why you were put up for adoption, and Rick and Amy were selected as your parents."

Larissa added. "They have been wonderful."

"Yes, and they have helped in ways they can't begin to imagine. We knew that you may have a role to play someday, so we took the necessary steps to protect you and your adopted family. And we did the right thing. The Council's message named you directly as a participant."

"When do I meet this August Hawthorne man, and what do you know about him?" Larissa looked into her aunt's eyes.

"The Council will give the orders. We just follow. You'll learn more in good time, dear." The older woman reached for her niece's hand. "Let me show you the rest of the cave. These crystals and their power are a sight to behold."

***

Larissa answered her cell phone, wincing at the crackling sound blasting in her ear. Dorenda explained to her at length long ago that wireless technology worked poorly for true witches. Larissa still insisted on connecting herself to the modern world. She had learned that the aura or magnetic energy surrounding the body of a Magical was much stronger than that of Non-Magicals. Because magic was, in and of itself, wireless electrical energy more powerful than Wifi, it caused all kinds of interference.

Sometimes she received a light shock when she picked up a call. This call was from a young man she liked, so it was worth it. They met at Dorenda's house one day. He was the son of an old friend of her aunt's, off to study abroad, and had stopped in to get pointers on potion-making. Among her repertoire of magical talents, Dorenda was renowned for her potions.

"Hi Daniel," Larissa said. His warmth seemed to radiate through the receiver. "How are you? Did exams go okay?"

"They were beastly!" he replied with a laugh. "If it hadn't been for your Aunt Dorenda, I might have failed the Potions Exam. But I didn't call to talk about that. I called because I've been thinking about you. How are you? Really?"

"Well enough," Larissa said, feeling her face flush with pleasure. Daniel was a handsome witch, tall, well-muscled, with shoulder-length brown hair and twinkling eyes. "I've been thinking about you. Wish we'd had more time together before you left, you know?"

"I know. I feel the same way," Daniel said.

His voice held an irresistible tone, sexy and low. Larissa's libido rose, and a pleasant thrumming sensation filled her core. Daniel's voice had a way of touching her psychically, teasing at certain times.

Their connection upon meeting had been instantaneous. They only shared one furtive spontaneous kiss when left alone for a few minutes in front of Dorenda's fireplace. That one kiss assured her that their intense attraction was mutual.

Being around Daniel made her crave intimacies that she had only read about in her beloved romance novels. Every nuance that passed between them confirmed their feelings for each other. Her heart raced each time his arm slid around her when they sat together. A certain current ran between them when his hand brushed against hers.

She warmed at the touch of his thigh pressing against hers as they sat together, listening to Aunt Dorenda recounting tales of the famous witches and necromancers she had known. Larissa knew she and Daniel shared a bond. Magic and all its intricacies deepened their attraction.

His absence had created a longing within her, and she discovered shortly after he left how much she'd missed him.

"Listen," he said. His speech broke into her thoughts as though they shared them. "Remember that we promised to write?"

"Yes," Larissa breathed cautiously.

"Well, I'll be sending you missives through Pigeon Post, wherever you are. I know you are leaving to go on a quest soon. Your aunt filled me in."

Larissa sat up immediately, rather indignant. "Why did Dorenda share such sensitive information?" Her voice rose in alarm.

"Not to worry. Calm down. The news is spreading like wildfire throughout the Magiverse, so I would have known anyway."

"I thought that this mission was kept under raps. Mortals are nosy enough, but Magicals are just as bad or worse." Larissa sank back down on the bed.

"Listen, I want to warn you about something." Daniels voice lowered, sounding more intimate.

Larissa sat up again, listening. "What? Is it bad?"

"Just be cautious of your partner while you're on this dangerous quest. August Rhys Hawthorne is nothing but a rich playboy. Don't be like the others and give in to his false charms."

"Go on, Daniel. What else do I need to know?"

"Look, I know you are a sensible witch, Rissa, and nobody's fool. I just want to give you a heads-up, that's all. Oh, and he has a well-deserved reputation as a despoiler of young women as well as a magical lightweight."

"Are you sure all this is nothing more than vicious rumors?" Larissa chuckled into the receiver. Daniel's intensity hit her senses as rather endearing.

"I've heard it all too many times," the young man continued. "He has no bragging rights when it comes to skills in casting or enchanting, despite his family's reputation. No witch can vouch that he even possesses a skill set at all, so you will have to rely on yourself. Think long and hard about that."

Larissa giggled. It was humorous listening to Daniel take pot shots at August Hawthorne. So what if that man was lazy and full of himself? She had taken her abilities and her craft seriously the moment Dorenda mentioned them to her. No need for August, anyway. Inwardly she resolved to be civil, polite, and keep her distance from the spoiled witch.

"Do you hear what I'm telling you?" Daniel sounded a little annoyed.

"I hear you. I hear you. I'll be careful. But you'll have my back, too, won't you? Somehow?"

"Only as much as I'm allowed." The young man grew quiet for several seconds. "I care about you, 'Rissa."

"It'll be okay, Daniel. Really it will."

Deep inside, Larissa held some misgivings. Would things be okay? Taking care of herself would be hard enough without having to babysit an overgrown, petulant man child.

***

At four o'clock the following morning, Dorenda sent a signal.

***

In the dark wee hours before dawn, Larissa bolted up from a fitful sleep. Earlier dreams had shown her nothing but dark, unfriendly, gauzy images. Frightful creatures slipped in silence among the shadows of sleep, keeping always steady on her heels.

She jumped, clutching the bed sheets with a tight grip. There was no mistaking the tingling radiating through her body. Dorenda communicated many times this way, and Larissa learned through the years to pay attention. Her Aunt wanted something, but why this early?

On the dresser, something glowed. Curious, Larissa got out of bed for a look. She pulled a letter out of an unsealed envelope. The moment the page opened, words lit up:

Dear Mom and Dad,

Now comes the time for me to fulfill my destiny. For this I must leave a while. I can't tell you where I'm going because I don't know, and locations will change as I travel. You have fulfilled your requirements in being superb parents and accepting the information you were given from the beginning.

The time has come for you to know me for what I truly am. I would have liked to have explained it all myself, but time didn't permit. At an appropriate time, Dorenda, our beloved neighbor will tell you everything.

Do not try and find me. Such action could result in harm for all of us. Just remember that I love you both and want to thank you for everything you've done.

Love,
Larissa North Strondovan

Several words floated above the page, shimmering in a sparkling gold light. These were clearly not part of the note: *Get dressed. Everything else is packed and ready.* Larissa scratched her head. She'd never written the letter but knew well what it meant. From the way the paper and letters glowed, Dorenda surely had written everything on her behalf. The letter ended up back in the envelope, sealed and placed on a bed pillow. "I don't like leaving this way, but there's no choice."

Sophie meowed and brushed up against Larissa's arm. "Yes, of course I'm taking you with me. I'd never leave you for a single minute." She quickly dressed, took the cat into her arms, and headed to the special area inside her closet.

***

"I'm sorry it's so early, but we couldn't do anything without direct orders, anyway. They finally came." Aunt Dorenda stood waiting patiently by the fireplace. Several packed bags lay at her feet.

"Is it time?" Larissa asked.

"Yes. Did you place the letter where your parents will see?"

"Sealed and done after I read it. Saved me the heartache of writing myself."

"You'll have plenty to do on your own. You and August that is. We are going to Katharta Castle in Nepal. It's afternoon there already. You two will be properly introduced and the quest carefully outlined."

"You're coming, too, Auntie?" Relief flooded Larissa. Having her aunt around made matters so much easier. "I'm bringing Sophie."

"Perfect my dear. You'll need everything in your arsenal to succeed."

In the young girl's mind, it didn't matter how many eons had passed since the clave families had fallen out. She still felt as though she were venturing into enemy territory.

Daniel had warned her loud and clear about August Hawthorne, but she'd never heard anything negative concerning the Hawthorne patriarch, Jove. Apprehension held her in its determined grip.

"One more thing, my dear, before we take the Vanishport to Katharta. I want to give you something very important." Dorenda retrieved a small white velvet box from the pocket of her royal blue velvet traveling robe. She laughed at the surprise on Larissa's face and pressed the small box into the young witch's palm.

Lifting the hinged lid, Larissa's mouth fell open when she viewed the contents. "It's very pretty, Auntie. Thank you." She lifted the object by its delicate silver chain and looked up at her aunt. "The pendant looks like a tiny tuning fork."

"It is a special *fine* tuning fork for magical spells. It's called an Amplituner. It amplifies incantations and intentions with extra energy when you use it. Consider it a power booster when you need it most. But use it wisely and only when necessary, because it will wear out eventually."

Overwhelmed by the generous gift, Larissa kissed the older woman. "I'm going to miss you, Auntie."

"We best get going," Dorenda said, watching Larissa slip the Amplituner around her neck. "Lot's to do." The older lady closed her eyes and called out: "*Parata onerarium.*"

In the middle of the living room, a vague outline of a large tall box-like craft materialized into view. The icy blue dimension lines pulsed, growing brighter until the Vanishport fully consolidated.

Dorenda loaded all the travel gear inside. "After you, dear," she said to her niece.

Larissa stepped through the doorway and waited.

Chapter Three

"Ah, I see you've made it. I am Raju." Jove's head butler smiled when he saw the ladies. The dimension lines of the Vanishport had glowed pink, signaling a safe landing and the end of travel. The craft vanished. "Mr. Jove Hawthorne sends his apologies that he couldn't be here to greet you. Other urgent matters called for his attention."

Larissa stood still, blinking only her eyes. Over the years, she'd learned how to manage the bodily sensations when traveling by magic. Short distances weren't too bad, but a long trip like this one, by any standards of magic, was still long. The whole experience nearly sent her reeling.

She briefly stared around what must have been a receiving room. Other than a couple of carts, a row of cabinets along one wall, and a countertop with a sink, the room held nothing else.

"You must be Miss Strondovan." Raju handed Larissa a crystal glass filled with a bubbly clear liquid. "Something to help settle your stomach."

She sniffed a lemon scent from the glass and swallowed. The nausea disappeared in an instant.

"Miss Soltaro, shall I get one for you as well, or just a regular cocktail?"

"A regular cocktail. I've been doing this all my life." She smiled and added with a whisper, "She's still young and somewhat inexperienced in these things, but otherwise quite capable."

"I see." Raju nodded. "And you must be hungry, my little friend." The gentleman reached down and stroked Sophie's head. He walked to some cabinets, pulled out a small bag, and shook out a few morsels onto the floor.

"I will show you to your rooms, and then you will meet everyone."

"How long before she and August set out?" Dorenda angled her head in Larissa's direction.

Raju headed back to the cabinets. "Miss Soltaro, I don't know the details. Mr. Hawthorne usually tells me everything involving the family, but not this time. I and a few select staff are entrusted to oversee and provide for your comforts."

"Very top secret, I see." Dorenda took the cocktail from Raju.

"That it is, Miss Soltaro." Raju retrieved a rolling cart and on it placed all the bags his guests brought. "Please, ladies, follow me."

Larissa walked beside her aunt, holding Sophie close and gazing at the beauty around her. The opulence reflected pictures she'd seen in history books or described in novels. Her vision took in the hallways lined with chairs covered with rich brocade cushions. Tables held bronze statues and what must have been rare collections of books. Oil paintings hung on the walls.

The fact she'd be spending time in a place filled with history and magic sent her into heady excitement. Jove Hawthorne had done well for himself, amassing property and possessions. She thought about her biological parents. Were they so powerful at one time that they had nice things too? She'd asked Dorenda many times to tell her everything, but the older woman had said very little.

Equally dramatic in comparison to the décor was a pulsing energy flowing through the castle. Larissa's body felt it humming away at a happy pace, radiating through every nerve and muscle fiber. Her mood picked up dramatically as she seemed to fall into the natural rhythm of the place. For a moment her apprehension over the upcoming quest dimmed a little.

In a brief blinding second, Larissa saw a vision for herself that formed and evaporated just as quickly. The lingering impression left her a little uneasy, only because it seemed like she belonged here. Brushing away the notion, she tried concentrating on the present moment.

Her mind kept insisting that she didn't belong. This was Hawthorne's domain. Her future lay with her and whatever she wanted it to be, not based on a vision she couldn't quite tell if it were fact or fiction.

Her family and theirs were supposed to be at odds. There was no reason for her to feel quite at home in Katharta Castle. Larissa turned her gaze briefly at Dorenda. The older woman stared back at her, a sober look on her face.

Raju led the two women down another hallway, equally as breathtaking as the others. "Miss Soltaro, this will be your room." He opened the door to a spacious bedroom filled with fine oriental rugs and a canopied bed. A divan sat several feet away, in front of a carved ebony table. Books lined both sides of a large fireplace which held a glowing cozy fire. A crystal chandelier hung above.

"The bathroom is through that door over there on the right." The butler pointed to the far-right corner.

Larissa's eyes widened. From where she stood, her gaze landed on a marble tub. She sincerely hoped for a similar one in her room.

Raju continued. "The closet is over there. He pointed to a decorative carved door on the left side of the bed. "Lots of room for your clothing and bags." He unloaded three bags and placed them behind the closet door.

Dorenda nodded on his return. "What lovely accommodations. Jove Hawthorne is only too gracious opening his home to us."

"Your pleasure will be conveyed to him, Miss." Raju bowed in humility. "One last thing, the bell pull is next to the bed, if you need any assistance."

"Miss Strondovan, it's time to see your quarters." The man smiled and headed to the door."

"Are you coming, too, Auntie?" Larissa asked.

"Return here when you're settled in, and you can show me everything later." The older lady smiled.

Excited, Larissa followed Raju.

"We're not going far." On arrival, he placed a key in the lock and turned it. The door swung open.

Larissa gasped when she stepped inside. Sophie jumped from her arms and made herself at home on one of the chairs by the window. This room was decorated in soft celery-green and dusty-pink. The room was a little smaller, but the overall coziness mixed with fierce elegance suited her completely.

"You also have a walk-in closet, and here is the bathroom."

She followed Raju, feeling a small rush of disappointment at the lack of a marble tub. The porcelain claw-foot tub gleamed pure white, with sparkling fixtures. In one corner sat a copper Japanese-style soaking tub. Seeing this perked her up immensely.

"Feel free to use anything you may need. You can ring for one of us like your aunt." Raju pointed to the bell pull, also next to her bed.

"Raju, can you give us a schedule of events, what we can expect?" Larissa turned and smiled at the butler. "I wouldn't want to be late or miss anything important."

The man laughed. "We would be derelict in our duty should you or your lovely aunt miss anything. Please relax and leave the rest up to us." Raju placed the young lady's bags in the closet, bowed politely, and left the room.

For the next several minutes, Larissa prowled her quarters, touching everything, running her fingers over different types of wood making up the furniture and the textiles on the chairs and bed. Like Dorenda's room, this one also housed numerous books, which sat on a set of shelves lining a far wall.

Curious, Larissa wandered over to the books, fingering the volumes and reading the spines. Her pulse quickened. Many of them were about the subject of witchcraft, history of witches, spells, and how to fine-tune your inner witch.

Out of the corner of her eye, she saw a book move, easing closer to the shelf's edge. Every sense, including the sixth, perked up. Out of all the books in this room, why this specific one? Why so soon? She'd just arrived. But no doubt about it, the movement held her spellbound for a reason.

Dorenda taught her long ago to trust a gut instinct, and Larissa constantly followed through when something attracted her attention. To turn away or ignore the signs diminished any witch, and good ones never did, lest their magic weaken and their powers disappear.

The book kept moving until it rested on the edge of the shelf, nearly falling out. Larissa carefully grasped the volume, taking great care not to damage what looked like an antiquated tome. A tingling sensation coursed through her hands. She sat down at a narrow table a few feet away and opened the front cover.

The pages flew open, turning on their own until Larissa stared at a select highlighted paragraph. Mesmerized, she studied the text:

History of the Witch Spinners

As old as time itself, a select few, called Witch Spinners, hold a distinct and honored place in the kingdom of witches. A blend of half angel and half human, they are exalted and sought after worldwide. The Witch Spinners have been endowed with the gift of spinning a conjuring cloth, which is the catalyst for any creation the spinner desires. It must be used with great care, for its power surpasses all others. Spinning a conjuring cloth is a skill that cannot be learned, practiced, or honed by regular witches.

The words disappeared, sending the other paragraphs on the page scurrying back into place. The book snapped shut. Larissa let out a small cry of surprise. Without waiting for her to return it, the tome sailed back to its rightful place on the shelf and vanished.

The young girl sat back in the chair, stunned. She looked over at the chair by the window. Sophie's eyes gleamed. She'd seen it all too.

"What do you say, sweet kitty?" Larissa smiled at her familiar.

"*Information meant for your eyes only.*"

"That must be it." Larissa frowned and shook her head. She'd never seen anything like what she'd just read. And Aunt Dorenda had never mentioned it, either. "Maybe it's time to ask her."

The cat perked up at the open door, dashing from the chair and speeding out of the room like a flash of lightning. Larissa headed to her aunt's quarters.

***

Sophie sniffed the air, taking in all the strange scents of the castle. Good thing her owner didn't make a fuss when she felt the need to wander. And the instinct to wander, which earlier started out as a mild rumble within her, hit hard right now. Someone somewhere in the castle was talking about Larissa.

The cat tensed a moment, wagged the tip of her tail, and turned down another hallway. Yes, the energy here grew stronger. The psychic vibration from one area pulsed out in strong waves, fierce and bold. Passion infused every beat. Sophie purred. Just what she was looking for.

Not making a sound, the animal crept up to the door and sat there a moment, listening. Her tail wagged slowly back and forth, brushing against the fine carpet. No mistaking it, she had arrived. The cat stuck out her paw, testing the door. It moved a little. Someone must have failed to shut it completely. Sophie wiggled her head until she saw fully inside the room.

"You're not yourself today, are you?" The pouty-sounding voice came from Fiona.

August sighed, bouncing his foot rapidly on the bed. "Is it that obvious?" He glanced over at Fiona.

"Yes, it's that obvious. You've been acting strange for weeks now. What's gotten into you?"

"I've told you before, Fi, I can't say. It's kind of a personal matter."

"Like we haven't gotten personal before?" Daisy popped her head up from a cushy pillow and stared over her sister's shoulder. "We've pleasured each other in every imaginable way, but you can't tell us why the goblins have you tongue-tied."

"Pretty much." August grimaced back at Daisy.

Fiona sat up, not minding at all when the covers fell down, exposing a set of perky bare breasts. "It's another woman, isn't it?" She turned toward August, glaring at him a second. "You're trying to figure out how to tell us."

Daisy chimed in. "Is she the one you're going to marry, August, the new woman you're not talking about? You know you'll have to marry someday."

"Eee Gad! Listen how you two carry on, like a sad dog howling at the moon. Do you even hear yourselves?" In a wave of frustration, the young man threw off the covers, leaving his body bare to the two women.

They looked over him quickly and focused their attention back to the conversation, almost undeterred.

"If it's not another woman," said Fiona, "can you at least give us a little hint at what's nibbling away at you?"

"Can't hurt. And we promise not to say a word." Daisy reached over and kicked at August's foot with her own.

August adjusted his head on the pillow and bent a knee, trying to get comfortable. "Maybe I can tell just a little bit, but you have to keep perfectly quiet about it. Not a word to anyone."

"Cross our hearts," said Fiona and Daisy in unison.

"I'm about to undertake a special project, and it does involve a lady."

"I knew it." Fiona threw up a hand and looked over at Daisy.

"And," said Daisy, ignoring her sister.

"And she's someone I'm not interested in being involved with for this project, or any other for that matter. She's from a bad family, can't be trusted, and an overall bad, evil woman."

The two women said nothing but exchanged glances and turned their attention back on the young gentleman next to them.

"What are you going to do?" asked Daisy. "Don't you get a choice in the matter?"

"None whatsoever." The words came out of August's mouth as if he were spitting out poison. "If I could, I'd get rid of her myself."

The scene both captivated and infuriated Sophie. She pushed herself further until she was completely inside the room, sitting and glaring at the three people on the bed.

A brief strong breeze blew through the room, ruffling the curtains, tipping over a fire poker by the fireplace, and sending some loose papers on August's desk scattering to the floor.

The young man shot straight up out of bed. "What the hell?" His gaze fell squarely on Sophie sitting erect by the door.

"You," he said, scrambling from his bed. "How the hell did you get in here? You . . ." He pointed to the cat and ran forward, making a swift move to grab it by the nape of the neck.

Sophie growled and bolted out of the room, leaving no reward for August except a bump on the head when he crashed into the bedroom door.

"What was that?" Daisy asked, wide-eyed.

"I'm not sure, but I'll get to the bottom of it." August swore under his breath and shut the door, fully locking it shut. He knew the time left for him and his adored lady friends was quickly coming to an end.

***

"So it has finally been revealed to you who the Witch Spinners are." Dorenda sat in one of the chairs by her fireplace.

"The information came to me the moment Raju left. I was looking through the books, and there it was." Larissa leaned forward in the other chair opposite her aunt. "Why was I supposed to see that information?"

"All things are revealed to us in good time, dear." Dorenda fidgeted in her chair.

"Does this have anything to do with my family? Our family? You've never said much about them when I've asked. Is there a reason why?"

"Again," replied the older woman, "time reveals its secrets when a person needs to know."

"Auntie Dorenda, you knew my parents, our families. I don't see the harm in giving me some insight into who they were, what they did." Larissa's tone grew more resolute. "If I'm now aware of the existence of Witch Spinners, I think it's time for you to speak more freely."

The lady sat back in her chair, gazing into the fire. The reflection of the light danced in her eyes, giving her a more animated appearance than what she displayed.

"Perhaps you're right." Dorenda turned her face toward the young woman and smiled. "I kept quiet all these years to protect you, me, and our family. But the time has come to speak a little more freely, as you say."

"Tell me what you know." Larissa rested back in her chair, a steady gaze fixed on her aunt.

"You already know that you're a Remnant, as we've discussed before. That was the curse of the Strondovan family line, and your mother was affected when she married into it. I'm not a Remnant, technically, because I never married into the Strondovan family. But I'm still close enough by association where I could be targeted. I have to always be careful. At the moment, I have no idea where your mother is. I hope she still exists somewhere.

"When she married your father, those who were against the family successfully hunted them down and succeeded in splitting them apart. Your parents were forced away from each other and you. Any who were in direct blood relation or married a Strondovan faced the same fate.

"Each generation of children were placed with other families, many of them Mortals. When possible, a select family member was chosen to keep watch, such as I have with you. If there wasn't a family member available, then a benevolent witch from another clave assisted. It was important that all from the Strondovan family line learn of their heritage and hone their magical talents."

Larissa held up her hand to interrupt. "And the Council is the one who arranges all this?"

"Yes, my dear," answered Dorenda. "Again, the Council wants peace in the Magiverse. They hold no ill will toward the Strondovans. They just want to see an old perceived wrong rectified again."

"Was our family as powerful as the Hawthornes? Look at Katharta Castle."

"The elemental clave families were every bit as rich and powerful as the Hawthorne's who, by the way, are known as South Hawthorne. They are connected to the element of fire." Dorenda shook her head. "But poor Uncle Desmond ruined it for his family."

"Where do the Witch Spinners come in, Auntie?"

At this question, Dorenda became quiet, staring at the fire again.

"Were there any Witch Spinners in our family from either side? There has to be something, or else why would the book have revealed such information?"

The older woman drummed her fingers on her leg, considering her niece's question. "I've not shared this with anyone until now, only because I haven't quite figured everything out."

Larissa sat up straighter in her chair. "Figured what out? What have you been hiding that is so secretive you didn't even share it with me?" A hurt expression covered the girl's face.

"Don't take it personally at all, my dear. Again, I kept quiet for safety. But here is the secret. I have come close many times creating a conjuring cloth. If I could discover what it is I'm missing, I would be a full-fledged Witch Spinner."

The girl's eyes widened. "You're a Witch Spinner, and part angel too?"

"Not quite, but almost, if I ever create a full conjuring cloth."

"When did you discover this? And what does all that have to do with me?"

"I'm not sure where you fit it, if at all. Perhaps you may meet a spinner on your quest with August. As for learning this myself, it was revealed to me in a dream. Many times my dreams are prophetic, other times instructive. It depends on what the message is I need to learn or be aware of. The suggestion came from a being I've never met, but the face was beautiful to behold. When I woke up, I felt a compelling urge to learn this skill, nothing I've felt so strong before. So I've been studying ancient tomes, trying to learn all I can." Dorenda frowned. "But I can never find all the information. Pieces are missing, and at times I feel like I'm going in circles."

"Is this something we could discuss with Jove Hawthorne?"

The aunt shook her head lightly. "I don't know. Let me think about it. If I decide to bring it up, I'll be the first to do so. I'm still not sure how much they can be trusted, and I know they feel the same about us."

"Fair enough," answered Larissa.

Both ladies turned their attention toward the door, watching as a sheet of parchment paper slid easily from underneath. Larissa promptly got up from her chair and returned with the sheet.

"It looks like we're scheduled for dinner with the Hawthornes in two hours." She glanced up at her aunt.

"Good. Enough time to rest and prepare."

Back in her quarters, Larissa bathed and selected an indigo dress to wear. Carefully, she replaced the amplituner in its velvet box for safe-keeping and opted on wearing a garnet and faceted quartz necklace. In her wavy dark hair, she pulled back a side lock on either side of her head and fastened them in place with a pair of clear Herkimer diamond cabochon clips.

"*I saw him. August.*" Sophie brushed up against Larissa's ankles.

"Where?" Larissa stopped her dressing routine and stared down at her familiar.

"*In his room. And he's every bit as awful as Daniel said. Two girls in bed with him. When he saw me, he came after me, ready to strike.*"

"Did he hit you?" Larissa's cheeks turned scarlet.

"*I'm fast. Got away before he could think twice. But he's ill-tempered and arrogant. Oh, and another thing. He'd like nothing better than to be rid of you. Watch out.*" Sophie winked at her owner.

Larissa cocked an eyebrow. "He wants to be rid of me, does he? All I can say, dear Sophie, is that he better watch out. I know my magic is much stronger than his. Sounds like he hardly gives his potential magical talent any thought."

"He's going to be a piece of work. He'll try your patience. I got tired of him in the few minutes I was in his room." Sophie turned away and headed back to the chair by the window.

***

The banquet hall in Katharta Castle displayed magnificence, with its tapestries, candelabras, sterling flatware, and crisp embroidered table linens. In one corner of the room, a harpist sat plucking a tune reminiscent of olden times.

Dorenda and Larissa were escorted to one end of the table, which could easily seat fifty people, had there been guests. The head setting was reserved for Jove Hawthorne. Settings for Larissa and Dorenda were on his left. An empty space was for August, on Jove's right.

Both ladies sat eyeing each other, waiting patiently. Dorenda, usually calm and confident, sat staring at the table with pursed lips and hands resting neatly in her lap. Larissa's eyes darted all around the room. Her stomach clenched at times, and her mind raced. She thought of everything and nothing.

The gravity of her situation started seeping into Larissa's head, instilling fear inside her. If Jove and Dorenda couldn't give much guidance, it would be left up to her and August to fill in the blanks. From what Sophie had told her, the odds immediately didn't look good.

A male Nepalese staff member stepped behind Jove's empty chair. He called out in a loud, crisp voice, "Attention, all. Announcing the entrance of Jove Hawthorne, most honorable patriarch of the South Hawthorne Clave.

Larissa and Dorenda glanced at each other first and moved their gazes to the main entrance of the banquet hall. A tall, formidable older man stood, clothed in a rich suit of deep navy blue, white shirt, and a brilliant red tie with the family coat of arms embroidered on the front. His polished fine leather dress shoes made soft pitter-patter taps against the stone floor.

He smiled cordially and acknowledged the two ladies as he walked to his chair at the head of the table and took his seat. "It's a pleasure to serve as your host, my dear ladies. Welcome to Katharta Castle."

Dorenda spoke up first, while Larissa smiled and nodded at Jove's greeting. "I speak for both of us when I say thank you for your fine hospitality. It's a privilege to meet you and spend time in such an elegant domain."

The staff waited a few seconds and called out again, "Attention, all. Announcing the entrance of August Hawthorne, grandson of Jove Hawthorne, most honorable patriarch of the South Hawthorne Clave."

More quickly than she'd intended, Larissa jerked her gaze towards the entrance and watched as a man near her age, striking in looks, and a magnificent mane of shoulder-length honey-golden hair, walked towards them. His stiff countenance lent him an air of aloofness and self-righteousness.

August held his head high, not glancing a second at the guests seated at the table. His amber eyes reflected a tumultuous war brewing in his head. The rosy pink lips spread out in a grim line across his face.

Larissa watched Jove's expression, which displayed a hint of annoyance at the young man entering the room. Like his grandfather, August waited for the staff to pull out his chair before seating himself resolutely, looking like he was waiting for his own execution. Jove gave the signal, and the wait staff busied themselves in bringing out the first course.

"I hope you find the meal palatable. We reserve our best dishes and ingredients for honored guests such as yourselves." Jove smiled at the two ladies.

"A man of such impeccable taste will surely provide a most delectable meal. Thank you for sharing it with us." Dorenda bowed her head in Jove's direction.

August sat with crossed arms, not concealing the expression of annoyance made with his eyes. Larissa stared at him. His sheer beauty created an odd feeling deep within her. While emotions on the surface hinted at immediate disdain, something deeper stirred. She didn't know where it came from nor why it occurred at all but brushed them away as a mere distraction.

Dorenda ventured first in asking a question. "August, have you been on any fascinating journeys? Surely you have some interesting stories to tell." The older lady smiled.

Silence filled the room. August acted as if he hadn't heard. Dorenda sat patiently, glancing from Jove and back to the young son. Larissa detected a slight movement from Jove, and August let out a startled grunt.

With a grudging look on his face, August answered, not fully looking at the dinner guest across from him. "No, I have not, nor do I have anything to tell." He turned his face back towards his plate.

Jove's lips twitched. His eyes glistened with internal anger. He turned to Dorenda and forced a smile. "You'll have to forgive my grandson's behavior, Miss Soltaro. I have a suspicion he's nervous about the impending task before him."

"You may call me Dorenda, sir," said the aunt. "I don't doubt one minute the anxiety these two children harbor."

"And I will be Jove to you from now on," answered the patriarch. "I'm hoping that after dinner, we can all sit down and devise a plan to help get these two started."

Jove turned to Larissa. "I'm fully aware of your situation and would like to see everything rectified. But I must ask. Has your aunt schooled you well in the subject of magic?"

"My aunt is the most capable of teachers." Larissa beamed at the older lady. "At the age of six I cast my first spell. I use my wand all the time and have learned and created all kinds of spells. Whenever I need to see her, I have a special area of my closet where I go and am transported immediately."

The older man's eyes lit up. "How impressive, young lady. You sound like you're turning into a capable witch. I'm so glad to hear it." Jove made a move with his foot, forcing another grunt from August and sending the young son into another round of annoyance. "Isn't that good to know, August? You'll have a worthy companion."

"Splendid, sir." The words came out of August's mouth, stiff and venomous. He stabbed at his plate and shoved a fork laden with food into his mouth.

Larissa's heart sank. This quest was going to be extremely difficult.

***

Jove, August, and the two women sat inside a luxurious study. Jove pulled out a fine pipe and puffed intermittently, sending out an intoxicating rich tobacco scent infused with cherry. August had already downed two glasses of wine and poured a third. At that point, Jove motioned for the staff to remove the bottle and place it by him.

Larissa sipped on a rich almond-tasting liquor. Dorenda held a steaming cup of fine Arabic coffee. An assortment of confections lay in finely decorated china plates on an exquisite gold-tone cart.

"My two fine ladies, it's time to discuss the quest in more detail. We need to have a clear focus on what is needed."

Dorenda asked, "Has the Council not given any hints on how to progress, where to look, any pointers?"

"None." Jove stared across the room, his lips pulled in a grim straight line. "It's been my knowledge from history that the Council doesn't step into matters unless they have to. They leave it up to the parties involved."

"I've educated my niece on what occurred, to the best of my knowledge."

"And I have educated my grandson as well." August's face colored at his grandfather's words.

"If only we could talk to our ancestors. That would be key." Larissa spoke up, looking from Dorenda to Jove. "They would know everything, or not."

Jove's eyes sparkled. He continued staring at Larissa as he puffed his pipe. "I think you just solved the problem on where to start."

Dorenda's face lit up in a smile. Larissa beamed with pride. August grew sulkier.

"Everyone, follow me." Jove got up from his chair.

***

Jove led the way to the bottom of Katharta Castle, the same place where August saw the wand duel in the gazing room. The room entered by the patriarch and his guests was located several doors down from the one his grandson used before.

"This, my good friends, is our Location Room. In here, we can map out just about anything."

In the middle of the floor stood a large table. File cabinets lined one wall. On another, rows of pull-down maps hung in neat order.

The older man turned to Larissa and wrapped an arm around her shoulders. "You, dear, gave me a wonderful idea on how to start this mission."

August bristled at the scene, watching his grandfather cozy up to the young girl and her aunt. What on earth could this girl possibly say to start anything? She was a Remnant, an orphan, a hand-off.

"Dorenda, do you want to have a gander at it? Are you and I tracking on what Larissa said?" The man's face glowed with excitement.

"I'm thinking," said the aunt, "that if one is to try and consult with ancestors, one needs a medium or channel to do it. Someone who is skilled in such arts."

"Unless one is a channel themselves." Jove looked at Larissa. "Are you a channel, my child?"

"I am on some things sir, but that's not a strong skill of mine. I've never tried rousing the dead, for sure. That's frowned upon, isn't it?" Larissa gazed at the gentleman head on.

Jove considered her words. "Yes, it usually is. However, there are times it has to be done. I'm thinking this is one of them."

August stifled an audible yawn, avoiding everyone's eyes when they stared at him.

"Did you have something to say, son?" Jove scowled in the young man's direction.

"We need a Witch of Endor, like Saul had in the Bible." He nibbled on a hang nail, looking bored. "Too bad that was thousands of years ago. She's definitely not around today." He shrugged and stared up at the ceiling.

"Thanks for playing, son, but no cigar. If you spent more time on honing your magical skills instead of being a smart ass, you might actually come up with some brilliant ideas yourself." Jove turned toward the women. "You'll have to excuse my bad manners, but I'll warn you now, my grandson can be difficult at times."

"I thought August's suggestion was wonderful," said Dorenda. "Jove, what do you have in mind, since it's true that such a witch doesn't exist anymore."

The older man struck a thoughtful pose. "Places may change, boundary lines move, buildings are built and destroyed. But the place never really goes away."

Dorenda nodded. Larissa listened to Jove. Out of the corner of her eye she caught a glimpse of August on his cell phone texting someone, blowing silent kisses at the screen. Her stomach lurched in disgust.

"And here's another thing," said Jove. His face lit up with a triumphant expression. "The Witch of Endor still lives."

Even August put down his cell phone and joined the women in staring at the older man, wide-eyed as if someone had shocked them with a jolt of electricity.

"She has descendants, no doubt. We really don't know that she didn't have offspring, married or not." Dorenda snapped her fingers. "Or better yet, there is a coven committed to her legacy, a group of mediums whose skills lie, fortunately or unfortunately, in the extreme dark arts."

"My dear Dorenda," said Jove, "you've said it. There is an order that exists in the place where Endor used to stand. They are called Order of the Onyx Night. They were formed to honor her legacy."

"Do they still awaken the dead?" Larissa asked.

"They do," answered Jove. "One has to know about them. Our conversation spurred my memory. Like you said, tasks involved in summoning the dead are usually avoided."

"We will have to go where Endor stood, won't we?" Larissa stared at the maps on the wall.

"Ah, that you will, my dear girl," said Jove. He walked over to one of the maps and pulled it down. It showed a map of modern-day Israel. He walked down to the far end of the wall and pulled down another map showing old Israel. "*Ipsas*," the man called out.

Larissa watched with wonder as a copy of each map, outlined with fiery gold, lifted and floated to the table, settling easily one on top of the other.

"Let's have a look, shall we?" Jove headed toward the table, where Dorenda stood waiting. "August, will you be joining us?"

The sullen young man pushed himself away from the wall and lingered several inches behind the women and his grandfather.

Jove pointed to a place on the map, a spot between Mt. Tabor and Mt. Moreh. "Here is where Endor would stand today. Of course, it's not going to look anything like what it was in the time of Saul."

"Where would we find The Order of the Onyx Night? Do they have an office on the site where old Endor once stood, something we would recognize as their place?"

"*Ostende Order of the Onyx Night,*" Jove called out.

On the map, a small point burned brightly. The name of the order lit up in black letters and floated a few millimeters above the map.

"Ostende loco coordinata," Jove stated. Location coordinates lit up: Endor Village: Latitude: 32° 37' 32.34" N; Longitude: 35° 22' 11.57" E.

Larissa's face brightened with a smile. "*Liber sombrarum.*" A book appeared in her hands. "I must write those coordinates down in my Book of Shadows. August and I will need that information."

August's face reddened in disgust. "You forgot to call for a pen. Shall I assist?" He snapped his fingers. "*Calamus stilus.*" Between his fingers, he held a thick hollow reed with an old-fashioned metal nib fastened on the end. His face wrinkled into a frown. "That's not what I wanted."

Jove and Dorenda stifled their smiles, trying to remain solemn.

"*Calamum scriber,*" said Larissa. In seconds, she held a simple modern writing pen. She struggled to keep from laughing as she saw August's eyes nearly pop out of his head from anger and embarrassment.

"Sorry, I got my words mixed up. It happens." He looked away and stared at his cell phone again.

Quickly Larissa jotted down the information for Endor.

"Those coordinates should get you to the boundaries of the city, or at least where it used to be." Jove looked over the girl's shoulder at the page where the numbers were written. "In 1948, the area was depopulated and left in ruins. War does that, you know." His face sobered.

"Any idea on how to find the Order once she's there?" asked Dorenda. "What if they don't meet anyone, or no one has heard of the Order?"

"*Ostende optimo linea Ordinis,*" Jove called out.

A throbbing line appeared on the map, lighting a path from Mt. Tabor to Endor. The following sentence hovered in mid-air: This way is the only way. It follows the old.

"What does that mean?" asked Larissa. She looked at Jove and Dorenda.

"I'm thinking that this route shown to you must be followed exactly. No matter what changes have been made now, you can only follow as the way existed in olden times." Dorenda looked at Jove.

"You're aunt's right." The older man frowned as he studied the map. "I'm thinking that there is a spell around the Order's location, to keep intruders and prying eyes out."

"How will they let us in?" Larissa asked. "There wouldn't be a point of having an order if they couldn't serve some purpose."

"They may be extremely selective on whom they assist," said Jove. "Let's give this some more thought tomorrow, and you set out the day after."

Larissa's pulse sped up. Once they had this part solved, there was no reason for stalling longer. For the first time the heaviness of this quest set hard on her thoughts and her being. August acting like a stubborn fool put more pressure on her than ever.

Jove rolled up the maps after Larissa made some quick sketches in her Book of Shadows. The map on the table vanished after she drew the last line. The young girl headed quietly back to her room. Dorenda kept quiet, watching her niece disappear around the corner. August, acting as if nothing had transpired, skipped merrily off to his own quarters.

***

Larissa breathed a sigh of relief the moment she shut her bedroom door. Fear sank in deeper, chilling her to the bone. She slipped off her clothes and turned on the faucets of the Japanese soaking tub. Perhaps a long hot soak would relax and stir up her mind again. There had to be a way to summon the Order once she and August reached their destination.

The fact that neither Dorenda nor Jove had any ready ideas disturbed her deeply. Whom else could she ask? She sank down deeper into the hot water and closed her eyes.

At once she awoke with a start. Had she fallen asleep that fast? The water surrounded her, lukewarm, almost chilling. She scrambled out of the tub and slipped on a robe.

Sophie sat upright in the chair by the window. The cat's mouth trembled. Her teeth chattered, and from her throat, a series of high-pitched chirps. Her gaze locked onto something outside the window, but Larissa didn't know what.

A few seconds later, it came, a series of tap, tap, taps. The more she tried ignoring the sound, the louder and more insistent they came. Sophie pawed at the window, frantically trying to open it. The cat let out a long, drawn out meow.

"You want me to open the window, Sophie?" Larissa opened the window, surprised when she saw a pigeon sitting on the ledge, its feathers ruffled against the cold. Around one of the feet, a rolled piece of parchment paper.

The bird let out a series of chirps, inching closer to the window. "You want to come in, little fella?" Larissa tapped on the inside sill. "What are you?"

"*It's a War Pigeon,*" Sophie said. She sat close to the bird, which didn't seem afraid of the cat at all, but instead, had hopped inside and nestled close against her soft fur.

"For what? Are we having a war I'm not aware of?"

"*It's a name these birds were given. If you don't want another witch hijacking your messages, then use one of these pigeons. They will deliver information safely to the right person.*"

"Who would want to send me a message that secretive?" Larissa furrowed her brow and freed the parchment when the bird lifted its tiny foot.

Another series of chirps attracted Larissa's attention. "You want what, sweetie?" She looked around the room and spied a light fog surrounding a small cabinet door built into one end of the bookcase. Curious, she walked over to it. From inside she pulled out a small bag of chopped bread. "I think this is what you're wanting." She unfastened the bag and poured out a few morsels. The bird gobbled them as if it were starving.

"*What does the message say*?" asked Sophie. She hadn't budged from her place on the sill, where the bird remained steadfast, refusing to move.

"It's from Daniel." Larissa smiled. "He promised me he'd write." She read the words:

"*Dearest Sweet Rissa,*

No matter the outcome of this quest, just be aware that we know each other deeply on a core level. I have learned that I can tap into you and your experiences when my intent is strong enough. Watch out for August Hawthorne. You could be in great danger if you're not careful. He's not happy about you. As for contacting the Order of the Onyx Night, you will locate an old well in the city. It is ten miles from the northern coordinate. Write your wish to see the members on a piece of parchment, fold it twice, blow on it thrice, and toss it into the well. My studies will serve both of us!
Much fond thoughts,
Daniel"

"Oh, my." Larissa sat down, looking at Sophie and the pigeon. "How did Daniel come up with such advice?"

Sophie flicked her tail and answered, "*Jove and Dorenda may know a lot. They're older. Of course, they would. But don't underestimate the powers of a young witch who happens to be top of his class. There are witch wonders in the Magiverse, and he may be one of them.*"

"You may be right about that, sweet Sophie." Larissa stroked her cat. The pigeon perked up and pecked on the window. "Fly well my friend." Both owner and cat watched until they no longer saw the bird.

From the opposite wing of Katharta Castle, August stood looking out his own window. He'd seen the pigeon land at Larissa's sill. The sight of it angered him beyond words. His blunder in the map room earlier still stung his ego.

"Who is sending that girl private messages? And why? I knew I couldn't trust her." He pounded a fist into his hand. "Damn them. Damn them to hell!"

Chapter Four

The Vanishport stood ready. Its blue outline glowed in the transport room of Katharta Castle. Raju made sure all was in order, while Jove and Dorenda stood in silence, grim looks on their faces. Larissa stepped inside and waited by her two bags. One held clothing and some food, and the other held her magical supplies, including a box holding the super seven wand she'd crafted at Dorenda's house. The memory of fashioning the piece burned in her memory as if it were yesterday.

The sterling silver rod of the wand provided a perfect backdrop and channel for placing all the stones she'd selected, with the super seven crystals topping both ends. Through her hands, she felt the sheer vibratory power of her beloved new piece.

Following Daniel's instructions, she made sure to pack parchment paper and writing pens, along with various herbs, crystals, and ceremonial oils. The Amplituner lay tucked away safe in its box. Her magic arsenal was more important to her than clothes and personal items.

August, sullen the whole time, slipped through the boundaries of the Vanishport and waited on the opposite side of Larissa. Raju dutifully placed a couple of bags by the young man's feet.

Jove took a moment and peeked inside the craft, Dorenda at his side. "Do you think you two will be able to do this and not kill each other?" He glared at August. The young man pursed his lips and said nothing. His eyes flashed with resentment.

Larissa spoke up, "Mr. Hawthorne, I'm sure August and I will work out a solid plan for fixing this dilemma."

The patriarch smiled at the young girl. "My dear, may a cloak of magic surround and protect you. You will be the pride of the Hawthornes and Strondovans. The Glanarium Supremo will not have known such a powerful witch as yourself, if you solve this curse."

"Don't forget our talk from yesterday," Dorenda added. "There could be more at stake than just a mere feud. My instincts are suggesting more."

"Auntie, I'll get to the bottom of it. You'll see." Larissa blew a kiss to her aunt.

"Just remember," said Jove, "We're as close as a spell, if you need to contact us. And don't forget the War Pigeons, if your messages need more secure handling."

At the mention of the word War Pigeons, August's face reddened. He turned a set of smoldering eyes toward Larissa. The girl ignored him, but she'd not missed his look or the emotions displayed by his behavior.

"Sir, I believe the two are ready to go. You cast the spell for the location coordinates so they arrive where they need to, yes?"

"I did, Raju." Jove spoke to Larissa. "The way will not be easy, and you will have to follow the path exactly as outlined. There are no shortcuts or deviations."

"I've got it all down in my notes, sir. Not to worry." Larissa pointed down to one of her bags.

"Your aunt and I will be extremely worried the whole time. Make no mistake about that. Godspeed, my dear." The older man blew a kiss toward her. "And you," he said to August, "mind your Ps and Qs. You will not disgrace this family."

"Yes, sir," mumbled August.

Larissa looked at Jove and Dorenda. Her heart nearly broke as she viewed her aunt wiping away a tear with a floral handkerchief. The breath caught in her throat. The Vanishport was ready for travel. A strong energy surged through her, and all went black.

***

Consciousness inched its way back into Larissa's body. The lines of the Vanishport glowed pink and disappeared altogether. Another long trip completed. Larissa took a deep breath, willing herself not to heave everything from deep inside her stomach.

August wasn't so lucky. When the craft disappeared, he knelt on the ground and vomited a couple of times. Larissa turned briefly away. Part of her felt a little sorry for him.

"It's hard to get used to long trips. I've taken a few of them myself, and they nearly get the better of me every time," she said.

The young man wiped his mouth with a shaking hand, quickly glaring up at her. After wretching one more time, he stood up on wobbly legs. "Where do we go from here?" His voice came out in raspy breaths.

Larissa looked around. For miles she saw dirt roads, lowlands, fields, and old dwellings built into the mountainside in the distance. Everything looked abandoned, lonely, nothing like the vibrant past with a strong history. The air swirled around her, hot and dry.

She opened her magic bag and pulled out the Book of Shadows, where she'd sketched out the path. "Your grandfather set the Vanishport coordinates to land at the latitude and longitude values the map showed us."

Studying the drawing in more detail, it was clear that the start of the path leading to the Order wouldn't be reached quickly. Several miles lay between the starting point and where the two found themselves in the present moment.

Daniel's message had been added to the page, face-down so the contents weren't readily seen by prying eyes. And Larissa felt them, August's gaze burning in her direction as he walked closer to her for a look at the book.

Larissa snapped the book shut and placed it inside her bag. Between viewing the sketches and her friend's message, the old well would be miles from the coordinates. Would she approach it first as the start of the journey? He hadn't given that many details.

As an answer, a gust of wind blew up. August and Larissa shielded their eyes from the dust. She pulled out a scarf from her bag and draped it over her head, wrapping the ends around her neck. Intuition told her to take the dirt road a few feet away and follow it.

"Wait a minute," August called out. "Just where in the hell are we going? Care to let me in on your plans?"

"We're going to start walking until we find an old well. When we get there, we'll figure out the next steps." Larissa turned back around, focused on the dirt road in front of her.

"An old well? Who said anything about a well?" August picked up his bags and ran forward, catching up with his companion.

"Let's just say it came to me in a flash of intuition before we started."

"Intuition my ass." August grabbed her arm, whirling the girl around toward him.

"Let go!" Larissa jerked away. "Touch me like that again, and I'll turn that arm of yours into a useless pole."

"I saw it." August's voice came out through clenched teeth. "You got a message from one of the War Pigeons."

Larissa's face blanched. She said nothing.

"Who was it? Who sent you something so private that Pigeon Post was needed?"

"Why were you spying on me?"

August let out a surly laugh. "Spying? On you? I wouldn't waste any time of day watching you. It just so happened I was looking out my window, trying to enjoy the scenery for a moment." He leaned close to her ear. "The wing where you stayed was right across from mine."

"Taking a break from your bed wenches? I'm surprised." Larissa grinned.

The expression on the young man's face turned into unadulterated fury. "You make another comment like that, and I'll . . ."

"You'll what?" Larissa laughed. "Flub the dub on a spell? That's okay. We all do it sometimes. Happens to the best of us."

Without another word, August jerked up his bags and headed toward the road.

"You're going in the wrong direction," Larissa called out. She landed on the road and walked the opposite way. "Coming with me? There could be bandits out here."

August stopped, whirled around and glared at her.

"Face it, my magic is better than yours, whether you want to believe it or not."

***

It was difficult going up Mt. Tabor. Larissa grew tired of August's steady stream of running commentary. It ran on, droning and never dissipating like an annoying swarm of gnats.

After he stumbled and twisted an ankle, both found sturdy sticks to help them walk. The incline of the mountain made for rough going. A lush pine forest surrounded them, and Larissa stole a moment to enjoy the scent of the trees. She even stopped to hug one. When an access road came into view, they thought luck had turned for the better.

Taking the road would bypass steep elevations, making travel much easier. No such luck. The moment their feet touched down, it all disappeared, leaving nothing but the ragged pathways of old. The two had no choice. A path was set, and they had to follow it no matter what.

"I still fail to see why we couldn't have traveled some other way than on foot," August said. A complaining whine rang in his voice. "I mean we could arrive there in a matter of seconds. At this rate, it will take hours, maybe days."

Larissa stopped in her tracks. Even though both had been briefed on the curiosities their pilgrimage would entail the day before they left, it was obvious that August hadn't listened. Either that, or he was an idiot who couldn't retain anything. She was inclined to believe the latter.

Turning to him, she struggled to keep her voice calm, in spite of her rising ire. "We were told before we left that to reach the Order of the

Night, anyone traveling by magic will never arrive. Their location is under a powerful protective spell.

"This keeps unwelcome visitors at bay, guards against sudden witch attacks, and assures that only those truly seeking their guidance and wisdom will wind up in their presence. And we have to follow the path just like the maps outlined. Period. Get it?"

"No reason to get snippy," August told her. His face displayed a baleful look. "I have to ask, are you on your period or something? I was told you were vivacious and charming. I'm still waiting to experience that side of your winning personality."

It took everything inside Larissa to not use one of her signature Tae Kwon Do moves and scissor-kick her unruly companion back down the slopes.

"That was rude, August," she yelled. "And since I'm the only one who seems to know the way and what to do, I suggest you keep your forked tongue quiet."

Angling her head slightly, she asked, "By the way, do you actually practice magic? I'm only curious because I've seen very little evidence of the skill your grandfather Jove told me you have. Now there's a true wizard. Your grandfather, I mean." Larissa stared off a moment and smiled. "Just standing in his presence, I could sense his power. Strong. Vibrant. Consuming." Her gaze landed back on the young man, glaring at him. "You, however, not so much."

August looked up from a few feet below with a look of surprise that quickly turned to a cool appraising look. "Well, there is this." He closed his eyes.

A rustling sound came from the right and left sides of where they stood. Larissa felt something slither across the toe of her sturdy leather boots. A wave of hissing filled the air. In a moment, they came from all directions, in all sizes and colors, the variegated patterns visible even in the forest shadows of Mt. Tabor. Snakes.

"I didn't know you were a Trem Serpant," she said. The sight of the snakes surprised her. The fact that August contained the gift of Snake Summoner surprised her more. "But being a Trem Serpant is an inherited skill, isn't it? Not one you have to study, right? You're just born with it."

August glared up at her warily from beneath his errant mop of curls. "Yeah, so?"

Larissa sighed. She knew he understood her implication and was just daring her to spell it out. He had no idea who he was messing with. As far as she knew bluntness was an inherited trait from her natural parents, and her adoptive family expressed the same trait too.

"What I am saying is that it is a gift. Gifts are like a "gimme". They are different than the spells involved in the craft. You didn't have to study for it, perfect it, or hone it. You probably just discovered it one day."

The two stood eyeing each other for several seconds.

"Supernatural gifts are useful. I'm not saying they aren't. But I've yet to see you come up with something clever since we've started that might help us out. That's what I'm talking about."

Larissa could feel him bristling.

"Are you calling me wandless?" His facial muscles tightened. "For just a moment there I sensed an implied insult."

She shifted from one foot to the other, looking back at him. His face was flushed. Annoyance flashed in his eyes.

"Clearly you own a wand and know how to use it." She said, a wry smile on her face. "In modern times, being able to cast without a wand is considered more than a throwback technique. In some circles it is considered an acceptable method.

"But the Glanarium Supremo has determined that the highest skill levels can only be reached through study and practice, combined with inherent power and keen focus. All the great Magicals throughout time, going back to the days of the Norsemen, rose to levels of power based on these principles. It's just an inarguable fact, August."

August grumbled under his breath in reply, and Larissa turned before he could see her satisfied smile. Among the many failings of his personality and personal habits, despite his high-born Hawthorne witch genealogy, he seemed to her as nothing more than the black sheep of the bunch.

Even in their short time together, she had noticed how poor his wand hygiene was. She saw where it wasn't in a protective box when he'd opened his bag once. Did he even know to wipe it off after use, say protective spells over it, or speak to it?

It was a damn shame such an admirable monarch like his grandfather Jove Hawthorne had to rely on this grandson to carry out such an important mission. Larissa had instantly liked and admired Jove Hawthorne, and something had passed between them the day she had been presented to him. She knew instinctively that he was counting on her to keep August straight, and it was obvious her task was going to be huge to that end.

After ascending another mile, they stopped by a clear running stream to eat and drink. Larissa had packed a roll of PanPan, the traditional staple for traveling witches. Out of politeness, she offered some to August. He waved it off, flipped the tab on a Lite beer retrieved from his bag, and leaned back against a rock, unwrapping what was obviously a sandwich from a local restaurant in his area.

To the unspoken question in her eyes he said, "Preservation spell. That way I can dine on food I brought for days."

"Oh," she said, primly munching on her PanPan. Usually she enjoyed the light airy taste and the way it filled her up, but she had to admit a scrumptious tasty sandwich would have satisfied a hungry appetite much better. It saddened her, somewhat, that he'd not offered her a bite like she did with her food.

Neither said a word as they ate. Larissa would have liked conversation, get to know August better, but she held back. Her ears had already been treated to a hearty dose of his biting sarcasm. No need for inviting more.

A soft breeze cut the heat, and rest energized them better than expected. The hike had been slowed down because of carrying bags containing their only worldly possessions as they strained against the altitude of the mountain.

When they'd finishing eating, the pair trekked the remaining distance to their destination. Larissa braced herself mentally for the challenges ahead. Her body already fought fatigue, and her mind had started to cloud slightly.

Much to her surprise, they reached a set of 999 narrow hand-hewn steps cut into the side of the mountain, spiraling up to the top. Nothing more than an extra deterrent to the unworthy. Those steps only stretched out the trek that much longer, and needlessly by any other standard.

August seemed to have a complaint for each one he scaled. When they finished that exercise, the two traversed several more miles. During the whole time, he occupied himself singing annoying songs, the kind drunken young witches sang in the Cervisios, drinking pubs in every major city reserved especially for witches.

Most of the lyrics contained off-color words. Though August had a decent singing voice, she much preferred his endless complaining. Larissa tried ignoring him as he belted out a bawdy tune:

Yon a youth under an elm
Pining for a maid so fetching
Laughing eyes and auburn hair
Ripe for catching and for bedding
Never stay with her my son
Though she beguiles with many pleasures
She hides a dagger in her bosom
And will take all of your treasures!

The air had cooled somewhat as they reached the summit of the mountain. When they arrived at the top, her eyes widened. There could be no mistaking what she saw. A cylindrical shape stood four feet out of the ground. Some of the top had weathered away, breaking off altogether. It had to be the old well Daniel mentioned in his message.

Excited, Larissa ran toward it, forgetting momentarily the weight of her bags. She peeped over the edge. Nothing but blackness inside. A few small rocks lay strewn at the base. She picked up one and tossed it inside. A soft far-away splash emanated from deep inside.

"Why are we stopping here? Something special about it?" August came up to her, out of breath, and dropped his bags.

"Remember that old well we talked about? We're here."

August narrowed his eyes. "What do we do with it?"

Larissa didn't answer but reached in her bag and pulled out a slip of blank parchment paper and a pen. She racked her brain, thinking. How would one address the Order in such a convincing way that they would let you in to see them?

"What are you trying to do?" August sidled up to Larissa.

"We have to write a note to the Order, asking if they will see us. I'm not sure what to put down on this paper." Larissa tapped her pen against the blank sheet.

"I'd just be simple and honest about it. Tell them who we are, why we're here, and we wish to seek their expertise." August shook his head. "Don't over think it."

For once the man made some semblance of sense. Just like he'd done in the first place, mentioning the great witch in the map room at Katharta Castle. Larissa penned the following:

To The Order of the Onyx Night:
From: August Hawthorne, Grandson of Jove Hawthorn, Patriarch of the South Hawthorne Clave and his companion Larissa North Strondovan of the North Strondovan Clave

Esteemed Members,
In accordance with the Glanarium Supremo, we have been tasked with a quest to find a special relic and return it to the rightful owner. History suggests that our ancestors would be the most appropriate ones who can direct us in our mission.

We humbly beseech your expertise in summoning them for a brief moment to assist in such an important quest, as their input may be valuable and restore order in the Magiverse.

"I see nothing wrong with what you wrote," said August, peering over her shoulder. "How do you propose to get it to the members?"

"From the instructions I received in a dream the night before we left." Larissa folded the paper twice, blew on it three times, and tossed it inside the well.

August's face wrinkled with exasperation. "Cut the bullshit and just say you got the instructions from Pigeon Post. It's not like I don't know."

Both stood transfixed. A sound issued from the well, like the sound of a thousand voices singing out a note in unison. It rang forth from the well, strong, full, charged. At that moment, a gust of wind picked up and a blue sky turned dismally gray. Thunder sounded in the distance. Lightning flashed.

"Ugh, and now we have to face rain?" August looked up in disgust.

"Look." Larissa pointed to a pigeon flying out of the well. "It's got something in its beak." When the bird landed on the wall, she reached out and retrieved the paper. The bird flew away.

"I guess we'll either continue with Plan A or move on to Plan B," said August pointing to the note. "What does it say?"

Larissa read out loud the following:

Traverse down the mountain and into the valley. You will see the light.

"That's it? That's all the direction they'll give us?" August swiped his hair back and gazed around him. Panic lit his eyes. "We're not sure how long it will take us. It could be dark by the time we get there." The sun already shone its position of late afternoon.

"I think going down will be easier. We've eaten and rested some. Lucky for us they even considered our request at all." Larissa picked up her bags.

Going down was not easier. The trails were slick and rocky. The young couple held on to trees and banks of the trails as they carefully wound their way down without careening to the bottom. Larissa slipped on a stone and slid a few feet on her backside. To make matters worse, August didn't seem intent on helping. He passed by her and kept walking.

She stood up and brushed herself off, noting with dismay the small tear she felt in the back of her jeans. A mending spell should fix it once they had a free moment. For now, all she could do was keep walking. Every moment counted.

The forests of the mountains lessened as the two descended near the base. When they reached the bottom, the valley stretched out before them. There were dwellings and farmland scattered all around.

On one side of the valley, Larissa noted some cliffs. From the look of the rocks and crevices, there surely had to be some caves there, perhaps unexplored, abandoned. A perfect place for witches to hide and do their work undetected. The way up was more treacherous than the mountain.

August stood staring in the same direction. By this time, the sun lay on the horizon. Several more minutes and the grey tones of evening would set in.

Larissa's eyes scanned over the stones. She'd not considered any location in the valley itself. Her instincts supported the decision. Her mind seemed to set into a trancelike state as concentration set in. Where was the light the note mentioned?

"Over there," said August, his words tinged with excitement. "Look." He tapped his companion on the shoulder, pointing.

On a far distant cliff, a golden light shone from an opening in the rocks.

"Are you sure, or is it your imagination?" Larissa squinted her eyes, staring.

The light disappeared and quickly returned, flashing like someone flipping an on and off switch of a lamp.

"That's it." August reached for his bags again. "It can't be anything else." He turned and looked over the valley, viewing some of the lights twinkling in the distance. "The original Witch of Endor was found in a cave. There's no reason to suspect the Order wouldn't choose the same to continue her work. If it worked then, it will work now."

"How do we get up there without breaking our necks?" Larissa's breath came faster. "And it's getting dark. We'll never make it."

"Oh, wow. Look at that," August whispered.

A hundred yards away, a winding staircase lit up out of nowhere. It led directly to the entrance where the golden light shone.

"They're not making this easy one bit. That's a mighty long, twisty staircase."

"It's better than rock climbing. Let's go." August headed toward the stairs, moving with speed like his life depended on it. Larissa followed, moving as fast as possible despite the horrible backache setting in.

The steps were narrow, winding sharply, and slippery as if someone had applied a thin layer of oil just for the spite of it.

"I think I'm going to be sick," said Larissa. This is making me so dizzy." She stopped a moment trying to soothe a queasy stomach.

"I agree. Those witches are trying us out to the nth degree. Now I understand why worthy ones make it." August swallowed hard, catching another breath. "But we have no choice but to continue taking the stairs."

He pointed behind Larissa. She looked around and let out a scream, nearly toppling over. The remaining steps behind them had disappeared, leaving nothing but a drop to sure death. With a quick grasp of the handrail, she caught herself before slipping entirely off the step. Her bag of clothing, unfortunately, had dislodged from her hand and was lost to the ground below.

With dismay and a chill of fear, she saw the beginnings of a smirk on August's lips as he stood perfectly still, watching. Mouthing a silent prayer and a quick personal protection spell, Larissa continued upward. Her bag of magical items remained with her, and that was the most important. Clothing and food could be replaced.

The spiral of the staircase ended as it neared the cavern entrance. Larissa's gut clenched. A sharp warning flashed through her body. There was one more test. She knew it.

"August, stop."

"What?" Annoyed, he turned around, scowling. "We're here."

"Your life depends on it. Stop."

The young lady barely slid past her companion, taking care that neither fall in the process. Bending over, she studied the third step from the entrance. No mistaking it. A thin glaze of ice covered the surface. Worse, the step also appeared detached on one side. Stepping on it would lead to a loss of balance, sending one careening down the cliff.

Larissa unzipped her bag and pulled out the beautiful newly crafted wand. Moving her hand with steady motions, she made a counterclockwise sweep toward the entranceway.

"*Videtur*," she called out.

Immediately a rune appeared, along with a message in Sanskrit, which she was readily able to translate:

Enter worthy travelers
We entertain the best
But first ask for the welcome mat
Provided for our guests

"*We have arrived, O Order of the Onyx Night. We humbly ask for the welcome mat and safe entrance to your site,*" Larissa answered at once.

In front of them, a scarlet carpet appeared and floated down over the remaining treacherous steps. She motioned to August, who watched in awe and silence, and quickly stepped upward into the dark interior of the cavern.

"I can't see a damn thing in front of my face," August remarked, finding his voice again.

"Stick close behind me, then," Larissa whispered.

Total darkness pressed around them from all sides. The pair moved forward, blind. Disorientation set in followed by overwhelming panic. Another test, even though they'd made it inside the cave. What would help dispel the darkness and fear? She remembered the amplituner and clutched her bag tighter.

Knowing a good enough spell for providing light in darkness wasn't the problem, but for this type of all-consuming darkness, the amplituner would strengthen it. But she didn't want to waste its power if there were other options.

Behind her came a soft click, and a thin stream of light streamed over her shoulder.

"Flashlight," August said cheerfully. "I always travel with one. I find them essential, actually."

"Well, the joke is on you because as you can see, it's not helping." Larissa knew her tone sounded ungrateful. He had tried to help. "That puny thing barely penetrates this cover of darkness. I can barely make out three feet ahead."

She looked down, and her stomach lurched. They appeared to be walking on nothing, no visible path, only more darkness below her feet. Dizziness set in again. Her gaze shifted forward.

Without warning, a strong wind whipped from behind with a force so powerful that it lifted the two off their feet, propelling them forward as though they were nothing more than mere human cannonballs.

A glorious light blazed through, bright enough to blind them until the glare diminished to a comfortable level. At first glance, Larissa wondered if they were in a sanctuary of some kind. The ceilings stretched endlessly high. Wisps of clouds floated above her head. Beyond that, she viewed the stained-glass apex of the central cathedral ceiling. The colors of faceted glass were brilliant in color. They glistened in shades of red, purple, magenta, and deep azure blues. On the panels of glass, scenes depicted witches, starry skies, full moons, and even planets.

She and August stood, taking in the sheer grandeur of the place. Their eyes turned to the entire central portion of the room. Rows of seats, resembling church pews, sat arranged in tiers along both sides.

A high altar stood in the front with the symbol of the Septimus hanging above it. The image showed a round circle of lapis. Gold lines divided twelve sections representing the houses of the zodiac. In a section showing the seventh house, an emblem of a blazing sun shimmered in gold.

The vision stunned her. Larissa had anticipated dark caves with flickering shadows dancing on the walls, like what King Saul may have experienced during his fateful meeting with the original Witch of Endor.

Today, she and August would stand in the presence of the line stemming from this elusive being. According to Jove, The Order of the Onyx Night were the greatest oracles still existing in the modern world. They made either fabulous allies or horrendous foes. Politically they chose to remain neutral.

As the pair stood entranced, bright candelabras flared up. Members of the Order entered from alcoves on opposite sides of the altar. Their hooded robes resembled cloister garments, all in deep magenta tones, with the Septimus symbol embroidered in heavy gold thread on the breast and each shoulder.

Three of them stepped forward and pulled back their hoods. To her surprise, Larissa stared into the faces of two women and one man. They resembled nothing like the ancient beings she expected. The womens' faces, though not young in appearance, held every bit as much beauty as her own dear Aunt Dorenda. The male's face showed handsome features, with a squared jaw and strong cheekbones.

"We pay homage to you, most, esteemed oracle among Magicals," August said, kneeling as he spoke. Quickly reaching up, he pulled Larissa down to her knees. "We are honored to be in your presence and thank you for your generosity in allowing us to meet with you."

Impressed with August's ceremonial grandeur, Larissa bowed her head in deference, her mind racing. When had August picked up any couth or manners? She hadn't detected any as they traveled on their quest. This was the same man who appeared to delight in her near mishap on the stairs to the cavern.

While Larissa floundered mentally in coming up with something proper to say, the witch in the center of the three came forward, taking her hand, assisting her to a standing position.

"Dorenda's niece," she said. The ancient voice sounded like dry leaves rustling in a glorious chilly autumn. "Of course. I would recognize those eyes anywhere. All the North Elementals have them." She pressed the young lady's hand in hers with warm affection. "Welcome my dear. We have been waiting for you."

As she embraced Larissa, August struggled to his feet. Out of the corner of her eye, Larissa spied his disappointment at not being greeted first by the Order.

The witch turned, acknowledging the young man with a warm, sincere embrace.

"The grandson of Jove," she said. "I would recognize you anywhere as the Hawthorne heir."

Chapter Five

The witch stepped back and viewed the young pair in front of her. "My name is Shahar."

"I am Aviya, " The other female stepped forward, smiling.

"And I am Haran," said the male witch.

Haran turned and walked toward the altar, where Aviya led Larissa and August.

In unison, the three witches faced the congregation, which responded, "We are the Order of the Onyx Night. Welcome." The members seated themselves in the pews.

"O Strondovan and Hawthorne, you have shown your worthiness," said Shahar. Her voice filled the room as she spoke in clear enunciated tones. "We seek to assist in your endeavors. Our Order wishes to know why you are here."

Larissa, for once, looked to August for guidance. With a quick smug grin on his face, he focused his attention in the direction of the pews.

His voice rang out with confidence and authority, stunning Larissa yet again. "Esteemed Order, it is our wish to speak to our ancestors. As the representatives of the current generation in our families, we have been tasked by the Glanarium Supremo to settle a family feud and return a valued relic to its rightful owner."

The witches in the pews sat still. They all had pulled back their hoods, like their leaders.

"Do you have specific ancestors in mind?" asked Haran.

"We do," answered August, still addressing the witches.

"How many?"

"Three."

Shahar spoke again. "O Strondovan and Hawthorne, you have presented your request to our order. We shall deliberate and determine if we can assist." She held her hands out and spoke, "You may go." The congregation stood and filed out of the room.

Aviya told Larissa and August, "You will stay with us until your task here is completed. Our accommodations are comfortable and soothing to the spirit. All bags will be delivered to your rooms. In the meantime, please follow me."

Deep within the caverns, a wondrous world emerged in all its earthly glory. Winding walkways led to other chambers. Waterfalls fell in some places. Small lakes and pools dotted the internal landscape. Even the sun managed to pour in its light and power through openings in the earth above.

"I'm taking you to a special section of our dwelling that is only for guests. There is a common area and hot and cold springs for relaxation. We have areas for practicing magic if you need to do any special work." Aviya led August and Larissa several yards down a winding trail before it turned upward again.

"Do you have many guests?" asked Larissa, breaking her silence for the first time.

"We have a regular small flow of guests. Many seek our expertise. Only a few make it."

"Have people died by accidentally falling off the last step, or failing to see the tricky third step from the top?" Larissa scowled at August, who happened to look in her direction.

Aviya laughed. Larissa stopped walking, stunned.

"Come my dear," said the older witch. "we may refuse to serve unworthy ones, but we have no desire to harm, let alone kill, anyone. When someone falls, they land on our catch net, which is a special force field that catches the body and gently lowers it to the ground. The unhappy witch simply has to go back from whence they came or try again. Just so you know, if a witch tries again, we always change the test."

August stared back at Larissa. She tossed her head, snubbing him.

"How do you get these lovely plants and flowers to grow underground like this?" August ran his finger over a shiny striped leaf.

"Magical horticulturists. They specialize in propagating the right species of foliage for this environment. Spells designed just for botanicals do wonders, you know." Aviya patted August on the back. "We're so glad you like them. They brighten up the place immensely."

Larissa watched as other witches passed. What did they do, and where did they go in this place? She did see various chambers that looked like shops or work rooms. Each member had their own quarters, no doubt.

"And here we are." Aviya rounded a corner, leading them into the space of a large landing area lined by what looked like the entrance to three chambers. She pointed to the middle chamber. "Mr. Hawthorne, this will be yours. And Miss Strondovan, you will take the one on the right.

"We're right next to each other?" Larissa asked.

"Since you are companions on a quest, it is best to keep you together, don't you think? You may need to discuss the particulars of your plan. You'll have the common area. Come, I'll show you."

The older witch walked past the other room beside August's and led the pair on a side trail that descended a little from the current level they just left. Several yards down on the right was an alcove with cushioned seating, a table in the middle, and some artwork on the stone walls. In the far corner stood a wooden table and chairs ensemble. Soft lighting filled the area.

Across from the room came the sound of a waterfall. Larissa took the liberty of wandering to the other side of the trail across from the room and looked over a stone railing. Streams of water fell from a great height to a pool below. A rush of cool air brushed across her face. Lights lit up the area in strategic places, showing off plants and benches. Down below.

"You can venture down there if you like," said Aviya.

August sauntered up next to Larissa, at which point, the young lady casually stepped away from him and stood by Aviya on the opposite side.

"How do you get down there?" Larissa asked.

"Just follow the trail. It ends there. It's so beautiful, and energizing." Aviya pointed to other chambers past the common area. "Those are magic rooms we talked about earlier. They only lock from the inside."

The three witches walked back up to the landing.

"Room keys are in the doors. Please take them with you while you are here. Replace them when you leave. Meals are served in the common room. The schedule is posted on the inside of your bedroom door."

"How do we know when we will summon our ancestors?" asked August.

"I or Haran will come and take you to the summoning room. It's a special place that has its own area separate from our rooms and yours. Conditions have to be ideal for such delicate procedures."

August nodded.

"If you need me or Haran, call out our name and clap three times. Either of us will be delighted to serve. We will come within minutes." Aviya smiled. "I leave the two of you to your own counsel." The witch bowed lightly in humility and walked away.

"Seems simple enough, I guess." Larissa watched until Aviya disappeared down the trail.

"I hope it's not too long," said August. "I don't fancy staying here for days on end, no matter how comfortable."

"The members seem nice so far."

"True. But I'm already feeling a tad claustrophobic, probably because we can't make it to the outside world as easily now." August looked around. "Didn't realize how much I adored weather."

"I'm going to my room. If we're needed they will direct us." Larissa headed toward her room.

"What do we do to assuage boredom?"

"Figure it out. Not sure how easy it will be to find bed wenches, here." With a grin, Larissa turned the key and disappeared inside her room, leaving an irritated August standing by himself.

The young lady stared around her room in wonder. Her bags, true to Aviya's words, lay near the bed, including the one she dropped on the way up. She immediately loved this room in its own way as much as she enjoyed the quarters at Katharta Castle. Hand-woven rugs lay across sections of the dirt floor. Sconces with burning flames lit the room.

A simple bed held a down mattress with silk coverlets and thick pillows for sleeping. The nightstand next to the room held a candle lamp and a tray of fruit and nuts, along with a small carafe of water and a glass.

The bathroom was simple, earthy, complete with fluffy cotton towels, a jasper tub, and faucets that allowed the downpour of hot water from a spring somewhere deep in the caverns. A toilet and copper sink finished off the décor.

Larissa nibbled on some fruit. Like Katharta Castle, a small simple bookshelf sat in one corner of the room. To think that the Order had created such a wondrous world away from prying eyes so they could do their work for others, no matter how dark or otherwise shunned.

As she studied magic throughout the years under Dorenda's tender tutelage, she often wondered if somehow there wasn't benefit to the dark arts, in a twisted sordid way. Contrast of good and evil clarified choices and likely consequences.

In her mind, everything had its part in the world, an order that truly made some semblance of sense when looking at everything as a whole. Normally she would jot some entries into her Book of Shadows, noting some of the experiences on the way over Mt. Tabor and upward to the caverns, but that could wait until later.

She wanted to check out the area with the waterfall. Something about it called to her, as if the rushing water whispered her name. Larissa stepped outside her room and locked the door. August was nowhere in sight, which brought on immediate relief. Other than his admirable pomp and flair in front of the Order, the rest of his behavior had been nothing but irritating and disheartening.

"Larissa? Larissa Strondovan?"

A male called out from the direction of the other room next to August's.

Surprised, Larissa looked in the direction from where the voice came. Her eyes narrowed as she processed the identity of the speaker.

The young man strode toward her, his lips pulling into a wide, jubilant grin. "What are you doing here?"

"Dennis?" Larissa's eyes widened. "What are *you* doing here?"

"I'm on a mission," he said, looking around.

"Oh?"

"Hey, let's go somewhere and talk." Dennis wrapped Larissa in a warm embraced lasting several seconds.

In Dennis Fagen's arms, Larissa experienced a sensation of sweet nostalgia. Her heart raced as she remembered the moment she and her friend declared themselves committed to only each other. They met when he came to her town for a secret gathering of witches. Him living in a town an hour away didn't stop them at first, but in the end, driving time and busier schedules drove them apart after a year.

Holding hands, Larissa and Dennis walked past the common room and followed the trail just as Aviya directed. The air cooled as they neared the bottom.

Splashing water from the falls sounded louder. A cat darted across the path, zig-zagging its way into a cluster of small shrubs. It wasn't the only one Larissa had seen after they left the cathedral area. Cats seemed to be a fixture in the caverns.

Dennis selected a cozy spot opposite where the falls hit the pool. A thick grove of plants and trees blocked the sound a little better. He pulled Larissa down next to him on a stone bench.

"I've missed you, what we had," said the young man. He continued holding Larissa's hand, staring into her eyes.

"I think about you too. We had fun, didn't we?"

"I never thought we'd meet here. What's up with you?"

Larissa thought a moment. How much should she reveal to her old boyfriend? "A call from the Glanarium Supremo. I have some family business to take care of."

"You ever find your real family, Rissa? We talked about them some, you know."

"Nope. It's almost like they've become nothing more than a fantasy. I have nothing that shows me what they look like. No story about who they were or what really happened to them."

Dennis gazed at her, nodding at intervals. "Are you going to look for them, see if they're dead, maybe?"

"I'm hoping the Order will allow me to talk to some ancestors, but not my parents." She stared at the ground. "I never thought about asking just to see if they were dead."

"I'm here to see if they will let me talk to Marguerite de Chantalle. She is one of the greatest supreme witches."

"I've heard of her. Wasn't she noted for some unorthodox practices, though?" Larissa studied her former boyfriend. He had always seemed on the up and up. Why would he want to talk to someone like Marguerite de Chantalle?

"I think," answered Dennis, "that a superb witch needs to know as much as possible, including what we know as the dark arts. Knowledge is power. I only plan to use anything I learn for the highest and greatest good. "I'm a white witch, as you are." He pressed her hand in earnest. "Unless you've changed?"

"No, I haven't changed." She chuckled. "Though you have to admit that our coming here at all is not the most orthodox, either. But I see your side too."

"Hey, Rissa, any chance we could have a second try? Maybe see what we could do to make things more amenable or easier this time around?" Dennis leaned in so close his lips almost brushed against hers. "We could be so good together, you and I. Our magic would be a wondrous combination. Nothing could stop us."

Larissa watched her ex with interest. It wouldn't have taken much convincing at another time and place, but somehow she'd moved on, taken different paths and held different interests. This quest foisted on her and August was a game-changer, and there was no getting out of it.

"Dennis, hate to break it to you, but our time has come and gone, I believe."

"There's another, isn't there? Do you like him better? We were a dynamic team. Just because our time was limited doesn't mean we weren't the best."

"I'm in a situation I can't get out of. It will be sure death if I do. But we were pretty good together back then."

"Can I kiss you, Rissa, for old time's sake? If there's not another, it shouldn't be a problem."

Larissa thought a second. It had been a while since she'd been properly kissed, especially with Daniel away at school. And the earnest look in Dennis's eyes touched her greatly. His skill in kissing had measured pretty high in her book, from what she remembered.

"Yes," she said.

The young man leaned close, placing his lips tenderly on hers. She opened her mouth, accepting his warm, eager tongue. Her mind shot back in time when their love for each other blossomed, sweet and innocent. After a few moments, Dennis ended the kiss. A soft smile lit his face. A small fire of passion glowed in his eyes.

"Maybe we need to go back," he said, "They'll be serving dinner soon."

The young couple retraced their steps toward the rooms, stopping at times to run their fingers through the water, touch a flower in one of the beds, and to stroke a cat that walked by. At one point, Dennis coaxed Larissa into a quaint little dance they used to do at parties, taking the lead while she followed. He kissed her again when they finished.

From behind a set of bushes, August looked on in mild interest. He had seen and heard everything.

***

During the middle of the night, Larissa awoke to a rustling sound on the pillow next to her. The brush of something furry against her cheek sent her bolting straight up in bed. She switched on the light.

"*Miss me?*"

"Sophie!" Larissa hugged her cat, kissing it several times on the top of its head. "Did Auntie Dorenda finally let you come?"

"*That was hard work, getting her to let me do it. I mewed enough.*" The cat rubbed her head against Larissa's cheek.

"I knew she'd give in with enough time."

Sophie sat on top of Larissa's legs, staring straight into her face. "*Watch what you say and do. Someone has their eyes on you.*"

"Someone here?"

"*That odious playboy in the next room.*"

"What?" Larissa's heart pounded faster. "What are you talking about, Sophie?"

"*He saw everything.*" Sophie walked off her owner's legs and curled up into a deep sleep on the bed.

Larissa turned off the light and lay back down. She thought about her time with Dennis. Had August been spying on them?

In the next room, August lay in bed, tossing and turning with fitful dreams. The touch, sweet cherubic lips, soft hair. The kiss. That captivating little dance. The fog of dreams touched down again, turning the young man's visions into a mumbled, jumbled, senseless string of visions. Ah, the lovely Fiona and charming Daisy.

August smiled, half awake. In a half-lucid haze, he reached between his legs and released all his pent up, frustrated energy.

***

Dennis had gone. Larissa intuitively sensed the sudden emptiness. A clock on the wall shone eight in the morning Israel time. To make sure her hunch was right, she slipped out of her room and moved toward his door. After a few knocks with no answer, sadness washed over her. A chance to say goodbye and wish him well would have been nice.

Had her old boyfriend been summoned during the night or in the wee hours? When would the time come for her and August to have their meeting?

"Good morning, dear Strondovan."

Larissa turned her gaze in the direction of Haran coming toward her. "Did the gentleman in this room leave? If you're at liberty to say."

"He did, hours ago. The time for his summoning encounter came, and he immediately left after it was over." Haran's face displayed a warm smile. "His choice. Not ours. We would have been more than glad to have him stay a little longer to make plans or gain other advice if needed."

"I see." Larissa's heart sank. "Do you know when we might be called for our summoning engagement?" She glanced at the sound of August coming out of his room. Quietly, he approached.

"I'm glad both of you are here," said Haran, gazing at the pair. "Your appointment will be in two hours. A little shorter notice than we like, but we are sometimes at the mercy of the ones being summoned. It gets trickier when we're preparing for more than one soul spirit."

"Anything we need to do in preparation? And isn't it a little early?" August asked.

Haran answered, "The spirit world is active this morning, as they sometimes are. They make their presence known before work and other preoccupations fill our minds for the day." A warm smile lit up the witch's handsome face. "As for preparations, quickly bathe and dress in clean clothes. These actions show purity and intent. Bodily cleansing clears away negative energy that might affect the outcome of the summons."

"I guess you better get started," Larissa blurted out, turning in August's direction. "You need all the cleansing you can get."

Her words were met with a big scowl from her companion.

Haran said nothing but watched with interest. "In two hours, I will return and escort you to the summoning chamber. Let's hope for the best outcome, shall we?"

Larissa and August both nodded.

The older witch bowed his head lightly and turned away, retracing his steps.

Without another word, Larissa whirled around and headed back to her room, leaving August in front of his, simmering with irritation.

Two hours later, Haran returned as promised, knocking on each door. The couple followed him back through the cave. At an intersection of trails, the older witch turned right. The path meandered deeper into the heart of the caverns. The air grew a little cooler and draftier. Larissa sensed a change in pressure.

Deeper inside, the surroundings seemed unusually quiet. Larissa knew they were far from alone. The ambience held a charge to it, full and pulsing. There were fifth-dimension spirits in these caves. They swirled above her head, watching. At times they flew past her.

She watched August momentarily. He seemed quieter, more pensive. Did he feel the same charge, the same energy? From the overall look of him, he seemed mostly like his usual aloof self.

Down, down they walked. The trail turned from dry to wet. A drop of water fell from a stalactite above. Larissa jump at the cold drop hitting her in the middle of the head. She let out a yelp. Arms extended, she struggled for balance as she nearly slipped.

Haran, with his quick reflexes, rushed to steady a swaying body. August turned and stared at the two, his face emotionless. He did nothing nor asked Larissa if she was okay. Haran's eyes narrowed and his face tightened with disapproval.

"If you wish, hold on to my arm. We're nearly there."

Grateful, she latched onto the older witch's arm and walked carefully until the three entered a large cavernous area. Larissa looked around, noting clusters of stalactites and stalagmites scattered all over. Straining her eyes, she made out what appeared to be more rooms behind the formations.

Haran spoke again, "We will take this trail, which leads us over there." He pointed in the direction. The three moved onward until they reached a door built into the rock. "We enter here."

Larissa's heart raced. Serious things happened in this place, everything discouraged and almost forbidden. Was she ready for such an experience? What would she ask Desmond, Clement, and Ciana?

Haran opened the arched wooden door. "Step inside but move no further until I give the command."

The area was dark, except for a blazing fire in the middle. The scent of sandalwood and frankincense filled the air. On first glance, Larissa couldn't quite determine the size of the chamber. As her eyes adjusted, she made out two circular rows of robed members sitting around the fire. An aisle split the circle, leading to the center.

Shahar and Aviya stood near the fire, two chairs placed between them. Both women wore black dresses and purple robes. Each wore a headband covered with an assortment of gemstones. A small table holding supplies sat a few feet away from the women. Haran led Larissa and August to the center, where Shahar took Larissa's hand and guided her to the chair nearest Aviya. Haran indicated for August to remain standing.

"Welcome O Hawthorne and Strondovan." Shahar's voice rang out in full clarity. "We have deemed your request not only worthy but necessary. We have patiently waited for your arrival, though your presence does not negate the need for showing worthiness, just the same.

"It seems the Magiverse is plummeting ever farther into darkness. Evil is wrapping its tendrils around us. None knows the means to stop it. There are as many unanswered questions as answered. In accordance with the Glanarium Supremo, it has been decreed that you two are the chosen ones to solve the mystery and restore order. To fail is to let the enemy win. And there is an enemy."

The witch's words indicated a tall order for the two young people. Larissa watched August's face. He stood tall and erect, gazing blankly into the fire. Did he feel anything at all? Shahar's formal announcement held a chilling message, and it set her on edge the moment the words left her mouth.

Shahar continued, "To engage in a summoning of the deceased is the gravest circumstance encountered by any witch who finds themselves with no other choice. Thus the reason we determine worthiness up to the final moment. O Hawthorne, heir of Jove, you will be first to submit to the test of worthiness."

Haran had returned to the table, leaving August standing alone. The older witch picked up a crystal carafe and filled one of two glasses with a small amount of clear liquid. Larissa knew on instinct that it wasn't water, though water was often used in ceremonies.

August stiffened on hearing Shahar's words. With reluctance he took the glass from Haran. He stood still as if thinking about what to do or how to get out of this predicament. Larissa watched with dread.

"Go on, Hawthorne. Drink." Shahar's order came out commanding and firm, but not unkind.

The young man licked his lower lip, hesitating a second longer. He brought the glass to his lips and downed the contents in one swallow. August shuddered. A breeze rushed through the chamber. The fire snapped, sending a trail of embers floating upward.

Larissa gripped the sides of her seat. Her gut clenched. August didn't look well at all. Her companion's face turned red. Helpless, he lifted a hand to his mouth. He turned way, heaving. Haran rushed forward, handing him a brass bowl. August couldn't fight the situation any longer. He gagged and spit into the bowl. Larissa averted her gaze.

The members watched in silence. Haran took the bowl from August and gently turned him toward the fire once more.

"What say you, Hawthorne?" asked Shahar. "Are you worthy to complete this quest?"

August nodded. The look on his face suggested otherwise. His lips pulled into a grim straight line and his jaw tightened.

The witch's expression changed to a skeptical one as well. Her eyes glittered as sparks seemed to fly between them.

"You didn't handle the serum well. Word of your Libertine lifestyle, unbefitting a grand and noble heritage, has also reached our ears. Can you explain yourself, August?" Shahar's voice took on a kinder more personal tone.

August stiffened at the sound of his first name.

"Well . . ." He shifted from one foot to the other. His demeanor didn't match the grandiose manner shown in the past.

"Is that all you have to say? 'Well' is not an answer. The Order of the Onyx Night demands an answer." Shahar stood still and waited.

The young man, wiped a hand over his mouth, thinking. "Perhaps I do indulge from time to time." He glanced quickly at Shahar and Aviya and back to the fire.

The two women nodded lightly in unison.

"What can I say, honored members? I love life and everything it offers. There are great things to be enjoyed in the world, and I partake when I can. It would be a waste not to."

"Young August," said Shahar. The tone in her voice matched the one she used on the couple's arrival. "It is true. The world is full of fanciful things. Great beauty, curiosities that fill one with wonder. But it's also full of vice and trickery. Things aren't always what they appear.

"Pretty trinkets lose their ability to hold interest. Good looks fade. Sweet dispositions grow bitter on a whim. And then there comes the time when one must take up the sword and do battle. That time has come for you and your lovely companion. What say you?"

The members stayed still, eyeing August. Larissa watched him flounder again.

"I say that I will perform any task to the utmost of my ability." He glanced at Shahar and Aviya and on to Haran.

The sound of Haran's masculine powerful voice filled the room. "How will you do your utmost when your magical ability is at nearly the level of a beginning witch?"

August winced at the question but said nothing.

"How will you do your utmost when you have no regard for your companion, her well-being, or her life?" His words came out loud, indignant, adamant.

Larissa's mouth dropped open. August's gaze fell to the floor. Nothing was heard but the light crack of the fire. He shook his head, speechless.

"You will answer, August," said Shahar. "Or this mission will end before it gets started. You will be the shame and disappointment of your family and the Magiverse."

Aviya spoke up, "What would you tell the Glanarium Supremo?"

"She's a Remnant." August lifted his head, gazing at the three witches. His eyes glowed with anger. "Her family is loathed and despised since one of her ancestors killed one of ours. My family has hated hers from then on. I thrill knowing her family was dismantled and gotten rid of." The young man shuddered, looking distressed.

From what Larissa surmised, August looked as if he were about to heave again.

"I despised this quest when it was proposed. I despise her," he continued.

A gusty breeze sailed through the room, rustling clothing and fanning flames. August brought a hand to his mouth once again, crumpled over, and turned away. Haran rushed over with the brass bowl.

Larissa closed her eyes. The sound of her companion's discomfort nauseated her. Now she'd heard the truth, how this man really felt. Relief consumed her. Knowing potential pitfalls was one thing. Learning that someone loathed you without going on anything but history hit hard. Old prejudices died harder.

The hate had been instilled in August from birth. She remembered how kind Jove had been to her and Dorenda. Charming, accommodating, inclusive. The patriarch had given her family a chance once they met. August had not made the transition. Would he ever? But now she knew for sure where he stood concerning her and the past.

August wiped his mouth with the back of his hand. Emotionless, he gazed at the fire. After several moments, he glanced over at Shahar and Aviya.

"How do you feel, August?" asked Shahar.

"I feel nothing at the moment," the young man answered. His words came out in a low mumble.

"You have been cleansed, purified by the serum. It pulled out the darkest within you, released your deepest thoughts concerning the current matter. There will be difficulties ahead, but the bindings to your pure hate have been loosened and stripped away." Shahar smiled. "There is nowhere to go but onward and upward in your journey. Please be seated."

Haran escorted August to the empty chair. Extending his hand to Larissa, he led her to the same place by the fire.

"O Strondovan, heir of Roman—for that is your father's name—you will now submit to the test of worthiness."

Her father's name had never been uttered in her presence. Even Dorenda had kept quiet about the history surrounding her family. The young lady reached for the glass pushed in her direction. Without encouragement, she drank the contents, swallowing easily. Strange, she thought. Why did the liquid taste like some of Dorenda's best jasmine tea? If offered another glass, she'd gladly accept.

"What say you, Strondovan?" asked Shahar. "Are you worthy to complete this quest?"

"Yes, I am. I will do all in my power to solve the riddle that has plagued the Hawthorne and Strondovan families. I will attempt to restore order where there is chaos. I will attempt to restore light where there is darkness. It is my wish that my actions benefit both families and the Magiverse."

"Well spoken, my beautiful child." Shahar smiled and bowed lightly in Larissa's direction. "Though you were ripped from the arms of loving parents, your family scattered, and many destroyed, you diligently studied magic and your place in the Magiverse. You have evolved into a more than capable witch, using spells and personal abilities appropriately when needed."

Haran spoke up, "But your companion says he despises you and the quest the two of you will undertake. How do you plan to manage?"

"Like I have since the moment we started out. Pushing my tolerance level while trying to be helpful at the same time. Like I did on the third step from the top before we were granted entrance to your humble abode. I will still guard his life. We are to accomplish this mission together, not apart."

Larissa looked at the members and at the three leading witches. She also glanced briefly at August, who kept his gaze on the fire.

"You have spoken well, my dear," said Aviya. "Are there any here who doubt either of these two, who say that this mission needs to be reconsidered by the Glanarium Supremo?"

No one spoke up.

Shahar lifted up her arms. "Then we will begin our summons."

Chapter Six

In a small brass bowl, Haran added a mixture of lavender, sandalwood, gardenia, and frankincense, grinding them enough to bring forth the oils within the herbs. Close to the fire he placed the bowl on a small metal stand. The heat sent the fragrance wafting into the air. Larissa closed her eyes and inhaled the scent.

She had been led back to her seat next to August. He didn't acknowledge her, nor did he flinch when her arm accidentally brushed his. What would happen next? What did deceased spirits really look like? The biggest question looming in her mind was what to ask them, should the elder witches allow questioning.

Shahar, with outstretched hands and face turned upward, spoke an invocation. "O souls who have departed this life, you have returned to your resting place marking the level of evolution you attained while you lived out your existence on this material plane.

"Our request for a brief return disturbs your sleep, your soul cleansing. For this we extend our requests with humility and respect. Though we know you may not contain extraordinary knowledge, no more than when you departed this life, you still hold answers we need for our life on this material plane. For this reason, we request your presence."

Aviya spoke up. "Our suffumigation has been prepared with great care to detail, a special blend of herbs for summoning each spirit today. It is with high hopes they will answer and join us. It is our stronger hope they impart knowledge that will be of great use to those who seek the advice."

Haran tapped a mallet against a metal singing bowl, sending out a crisp, clear ring. He spoke, "Our first spirit, we call on the entity once known as Desmond Strondovan. Hear our call. Receive our vibrations. Come to us, we implore you." The mallet hit the singing bowl once again.

Larissa's heart pounded in her chest. Involuntarily, her eyes moved to August's face. He stared back at her, expressionless. The air grew suddenly cold. She shivered. No one moved. Shahar, Aviya, and Haran stayed still, standing with their faces turned toward the ceiling, eyes closed.

A small rumbling issued from the fire, sending a blast of embers upward. One loud crack sent Larissa nearly jumping out of her seat. She tightened her lips together to keep from screaming. August sat motionless next to her. Did nothing disturb him? She watched in horror and awe as a swirl of white, bluish smoke trailed up and away from the fire.

Larissa sat up straight, eyes on the smoke that swayed to and fro, tendrils trailing and moving until the form of a man stood where she and August declared their worthiness. A quick glance at the members showed nothing, no excitement, no fear. They sat motionless.

The young lady stared harder at the form, noting what appeared to be a tall handsome man in more antiquated clothing. He wore a dignified look on his face. This was the spirit of her ancestor, the first time she viewed anyone from her family, in any form. Did her father resemble Desmond in any way?

"I am the entity known as Desmond Strondovan," the figure spoke. "For what reason do you disturb my sleep?" The voice came out firm, resolute.

"O good Strondovan," said Shahar, we have a descendant of your family with us today. She has been tasked with a special quest stemming from the duel you had with a Hawthorne clave member. She wishes to ask you some questions."

Haran walked around and escorted Larissa to a spot a few feet away from the form. Her body quaked as she walked. Part of her wanted to faint. Would she be able to talk?

"You may speak," said Haran, whispering in Larissa's ear.

She gulped, clenched her fists, and tried settling her mind enough to remember what she saw in the crystal sphere. "Dear Uncle, can you tell me why you were so against Ciana's relationship with Clement? What was going on at that time?"

The ghostly figure remained quiet several seconds, wavering. At one point it appeared that Desmond would fade away for good. Larissa held her breath.

The spirit form spoke at last. "There was evil at work. All in the Magiverse knew it. A fight between light and dark. Unholy unions feed the darkness, strengthen it. Precautions were necessary. Darkness must never prevail."

"Nothing can hurt you now. Tell me the truth. Did you kill Clement? Your descendants are paying the price for your folly."

"No folly or wicked deed came from me. Something else released the last charge from my wand. I know not what it was nor whom it was."

Larissa started to ask another question, but Desmond's spirit evaporated. She gasped.

Haran placed his hands on her shoulders. "He will not speak further. You shall return to your seat." He led Larissa back to her place next to August. When he returned to the fire, he struck the singing bowl with the mallet.

Shahar spoke, "We thank you, O Strondovan. May your words assist your descendant and her companion."

Haran prepared another brass bowl filled with balm of Giliad, anise, and dried carnation. After placing the bowl in its stand near the fire, he tapped on the singing bowl as he did with Desmond Strondovan. "Our second spirit, we call on the entity once known as Clement Hawthorne. Hear our call. Receive our vibrations. Come to us, we implore you." The witch tapped the mallet against the singing bowl.

Another blast of cold air filled the chamber. The fire hissed, popped, and roared with energy. Whitish blue tendrils of smoke left the fire, writhing into the form of a man who was dressed similarly to the one before him.

"I am the entity known as Clement Hawthorne. For what reason do you disturb my sleep?" The voice held an authoritative tone.

Shahar answered, "O good Hawthorne, we have a descendant of your family with us today. He has been tasked with a special quest stemming from the duel you had with a Strondovan clave member. He wishes to ask you some questions."

August arose, avoiding eye contact with Larissa. He followed Haran to the fire and stood with his shoulders squared. Larissa watched with a twinge of envy. When this man stood with resolve, he made an impression.

"You may now speak," said Haran.

"Dear Uncle Clement. Why would you ever consider entering an unholy union with a Strondovan?"

Larissa cringed. She knew her companion's question was meant as insult to her and the Strondovan family, but like it or not, the question had seared itself into her mind as well. Why would someone risk their life in a duel to marry someone else?

The image briefly loosened into nothing but a thick band of smoke but quickly resumed its shape once again. "Who said anything about an unholy union? Blasphemy that you suggest such a thing." The voice thundered throughout the chamber. Members of the Order shifted in their seats.

Clement's nephew kept his cool. "My sincere apologies, dear Uncle. Can you tell me why you loved a Strondovan woman?"

"Who wouldn't love a Strondovan, boy? The family is revered, renowned. It would be any man's privilege to marry a woman from that family. Royalty belongs together."

August's jaw tightened. Dismay brewed in his eyes. He wrapped his arms behind his back and gazed at the image of his uncle. "What was so special about Ciana?"

"She has a great skill, one that means ultimate power and goodness. Our Hawthorne line has the power to activate it. Alas, there are others who also have her powers and others who have ours. But there is only one destiny."

"And what might that be, dear Uncle?"

The image of Clement Hawthorne stood in full force for a second and his lit form vanished as if someone had pulled a lamp plug from a wall socket.

"He will not speak further. Please return to your seat." Haran led August back to his place beside Larissa.

With outstretched arms, Shahar said, "We thank you, O Hawthorne. May your words assist your descendant and his companion."

In the last brass bowl, Haran mixed a blend of dittany, heather, and sweet grass. After tapping the mallet against the singing bowl, he called out, "Our last spirit, we call on the entity once known as Ciana Strondovan. Hear our call. Receive our vibrations. Come to us, we implore you." A sharp chime sounded.

All eyes focused on the fire. Several seconds passed. The air rushing through the chamber hadn't changed. The fire continued burning normally.

Haran narrowed his eyes and spoke the invocation again. At the last chime sounding from the singing bowl, the fire at once turned a bright blood red. The members of the Order gasped in surprise. Confused, Larissa looked at the three lead witches. They stood staring, eyes wide and mouths open.

Shahar and Aviya glanced at each other. Haran turned his attention back on the fire. The red color dissipated, leaving the orange flames dancing and waving as before.

Aviya spoke up, "This is a sign. It means one thing. The entity known as Ciana Strondovan is not among the dead."

Murmurs from the Order filled the room. For the first time, Larissa and August turned and stared at each other, perplexed. He shook his head and turned his eyes back in the direction of the fire. If Ciana wasn't dead, where was she? The bigger question, how would she still be alive after all these years?

***

Larissa sat on the same bench she and Dennis occupied the night before. This time the sound of falling water didn't sooth her. She reviewed the latest events that transpired in the summoning chamber. Both Desmond and Clement seemed intent on sharing little information, just enough to fan the flames of burning curiosity.

And Ciana. The red flames meant she still lived. How would she locate her great great aunt? The fact that she had been alive for longer than a human lifespan suggested more about this mysterious family member of hers. Ciana could possibly answer questions that Desmond and Clement refused.

"A penny for your thoughts." August dropped down on the bench beside Larissa.

The young woman looked at him, startled.

"I'm sorry. Was this space saved for lover boy?"

"Excuse me?"

"Can I kiss you, Rissa? For old time's sake?" August snickered.

"You're disgusting." Larissa turned away. Irritation shot through her like a bullet out of a gun.

"That was also a charming little dance you did. I'm slowly beginning to appreciate your talents." August leered at her with mock interest.

Larissa jumped up from the bench in a huff.

"Wait. Sit down." The young man grabbed her arm and pulled her back down beside him.

"Let go of me, you vile—"

"Sit down. I want to talk."

The earnest look on August's face indicated he now meant business. For the first time, his words compelled her to obey. She jerked her arm from his grip and scowled.

"I'll start over. Have you been thinking about what we saw earlier?"

"Of course." Larissa turned her nose up in a haughty display of superiority. "I'm surprised you've given it another thought. And since you despise me so much, why do you care what I think?"

August's face colored. He scratched his head in a moment of embarrassment. "I have to admit, Uncle Clement's words floored me. And seeing you with an old flame." He looked directly into his companion's face. "What do you Strondovan women possess that gets men hot and going? It must be good." His eyes glittered with interest.

With lightning speed, Larissa shot out her hand, aiming at August's face. His quick reflexes intercepted her move. "My bad. Again." He let out an exasperated breath.

"That was uncalled for, August, you despicable wretch. I've had enough of you and your hateful ways." Her face flashed with a heated expression of anger.

"Honestly, my dear, it was a sincere question, not meant in the way you took it."

"Oh, really? How am I supposed to take it?"

The two stared each other down for several seconds.

"Royalty belongs with royalty. I'm your equal and better. At least I'm not a beginner witch." Larissa wrenched her arm free and sped quickly away, heading back to her room.

August sat brooding, watching the waterfall. This exchange was a missed opportunity he would have to recoup later. The thought of it filled him with frustration. He and this fiery young lass would have to get past years of his prejudices. The serum may have loosened his hatred, but he and the Strondovan woman still had a long way to go.

***

"Clement Hawthorne said royalty belongs together. I'm assuming Ciana was royalty?" Larissa sat in her room, staring intently into a smoked glass scrying mirror. Sometimes she used it for gazing purposes instead of crystal spheres. Many times, she and Dorenda used it to communicate.

They liked this method over modern computer communication apps. No electricity, man-made signals, or other technology. Just good old-fashioned astral-type projection. And no risk of any tech company snatching the information and storing it. The images in the mirror were mostly flawless and clear. The sound came through even better.

"As your journey unfolds, I feel more comfortable sharing more information with you. I never said anything before, but your family was royalty. They are on par with the Hawthorne clave."

"That was obviously dad's side of the family. What about you and mom?" Saying the word 'mom' in reference to anyone other than Amy felt strange to Larissa.

"Your mother and I came from a line of evolved witches on our father's side. Lucas Soltaro married Rose Fairmeade, who came from a long family line of high-level metaphysical practitioners. The skill and backgrounds from our parents blended nicely into offspring who naturally excelled in the supernatural arts."

"Can you tell me anything about my natural mother, your sister?"

Dorenda sighed, staring upward in thought. A light smile played across her lips. "As little girls, your mother Eleanor and I were quite the mischief-makers."

"Really?" Larissa sank back in her chair, eyeing her aunt with surprise. "I have a hard time seeing you as a mischievous person. You're always so warm and sweet, with some humor at times, but intent on what you do."

"Ah, my dear. The passing of youth and tragedy strip away carefree thoughts. Don't get me wrong, we played hard when we wanted to, but that didn't negate the fact that your mother and I studied and practiced our witchcraft with diligence. We went at everything with a certain gusto. Our father loved us so much, just like our mother."

"What did my mother look like?"

"Just look in the mirror, dear, and you will see a close resemblance. Your dark hair and eyes and pale skin look a lot like her. Some of your facial features, nose, mouth, smile, resemble your father, Roman."

"Did you like my father? Tell me about him." Larissa shifted lightly in her seat.

"Roman was strong-willed, but kind. He adored your mother—and you. Your father also had dark hair and eyes. His face held intense, piercing eyes and a determined expression. It was as if he looked deep into your soul. He was quite handsome, and when he smiled, very few could resist his charms."

"I take it that he and mother were capable witches?"

"Very capable. Your father had high standards. He would never have considered your mother for a mate if she didn't have strong talent in the arts."

"Why were they not able to fight off those waring against them? And didn't they have family to help?"

"My dear, there are others in the Magiverse who are just as strong and capable as your parents. At some point, it becomes a matter of wits and cunning as much as pure magical power. You must keep in mind you're a Remnant, one of the last survivors of a family line. So there aren't many of you.

"I was devastated when your parents were dispersed. I have no idea if they are even alive or not. I was not at home when our family—your family—was invaded, but in another town attending a special witch's convention. Your mother declined coming with me, vowing we would enroll in another one in the future."

"How did you hear about what happened? What did you do?" Larissa's eyes widened with interest.

"A War Pigeon delivered the message. I knew the moment it landed outside the window of my room where I was staying that something bad had happened. The sight of that bird filled me with profound dread. I'm not sure who sent the message because the sender didn't identify themselves. That's how secretive everything was.

"I didn't dare tell anyone, though news spread quickly. In the middle of the night, I slipped out of town and made my way to your neighborhood, next to Rick and Amy. I had been given orders from the pigeon that I must follow instructions to the letter, or risk being wiped out myself." Dorenda's voice faltered, and she brushed away a tear from her eye. "I never got to tell your mother that I loved her or say good-bye."

"Any other family members survive? Surely there are cousins or other aunts and uncles."

"Your mother and I were the only ones from Lucas and Rose. Your father had two brothers and a sister. Very nice, indeed, they were. Noble-looking, carried themselves with pride, and extremely apt in the arts of witchcraft and metaphysics. One brother had two sons. The other brother had a daughter and a son. The sister had two daughters."

Larissa smiled. "I have cousins, uncles, and aunts. I'd love to meet them."

Dorenda held up her hand. "Larissa, please keep in mind that they could be dead. We don't know how many or if any, but the fact is we don't know."

"What about other relatives? Don't you and mom have cousins? My dad, what about him?"

"We do, but I don't know what happened to them." Dorenda leaned forward, looking at her niece with earnestness. "Dear, you and August need to find out what happened to your family, our family, on both your mother and father's side. It's important so darkness will not prevail. The Strondovan and Hawthorne families must unite. It's the only way."

***

August seated himself across from Larissa at the dining table. He studied her expression. Was she still mad from their earlier encounter? The young man still couldn't wrap his head around the fact that his Uncle Clement adored Ciana Strondovan. Surely Larissa's aunt had to have been much more amenable and pleasant than her niece.

"Do you think we can get through dinner and not have one of us losing our temper?"

"Can you speak to me without being sarcastic or odious?" Larissa's face bore a hard expression of determination.

"Look, I'm doing the best I can, considering I'm battling years of—shall I say—ingrained teachings." August displayed a forced smile.

"You better end that battle quickly, because I'm not tolerating any more of your nastiness." Larissa shot him a warning look. "Not where my family is concerned, even if I've never met them personally."

The server brought the pair their dinner. August smiled and nodded, mouthing a polite thank you.

"I'll do my best. Be patient with me, though." He picked up his fork and downed it into a succulent piece of roast chicken. "You know we can't stay here, right?"

Larissa grimaced. "No, I guess we can't. Has anyone said anything to you about us leaving?"

"Not yet, but I think we need to approach the leaders with our plan and move on, wherever that is." August closed his eyes, enjoying the taste of his food.

The wine served was even better. He watched his companion as she ate. So dainty and polite. She looked extra pretty tonight, wearing a sapphire blue dress and a strand of pearls around her lean neck. She had pulled her hair in a lose bun on top of her head, fastening it in place with a matching pearl clasp.

He changed his thoughts immediately. Uncle Clement may have had his weaknesses, but August would be damned if he'd fall prey so easily. "I'll ask again, what do you think about what we heard in that chamber? Neither of our relatives shared much. And we still have one at large."

The young lady sipped some wine, meeting his gaze directly. "I have a sneaking suspicion that we'll continue getting bits and pieces of information as we go. None of this is going to be easy or quick."

"Then we have to ask the right questions. It's the only way."

"Any brilliant ideas? I'm racking my brain, and I'm not having much luck. Do you think Haran, Shahar, or Aviya might know?"

August stared into Larissa's face. "I think we need to figure this out for ourselves. The Order can help with summonings. I'm not sure they like giving advice. That's not what they do."

Larissa turned up her nose with brief indignation. "I disagree. They might have some ideas on some wise people we can talk to."

Sophie came trotting into the dining room and headed toward her cat bowls of food and water. "*I have an idea on what you need to do next.*"

"And what's that?" Larissa turned toward her familiar.

August arched his eyebrows. He didn't have a familiar himself, but he knew many witches did. Silently he watched his companion and her pet.

"*I've been doing some research. You need to solicit the help of an ancient deity.*"

"An ancient deity?" Larissa frowned. "Oh, come on, Sophie. Ancient deities were nothing more than myths, archetypes for psychological concepts or aspects of living."

"There are truths behind those myths. Besides, many of those deities were representatives of higher advanced beings. The least you can do is tap into that knowledge. It's there, you know." The cat said nothing else but focused on her dinner.

"An ancient deity," mumbled August. "If we can summon the dead, why not ask help from a god or goddess?"

"You actually like that idea?" Stunned, Larissa turned in August's direction.

"It worked in ancient societies, I suppose." August shook his head. "I never thought I'd take advice from a cat, but we don't have anything else right now." He met Larissa's gaze. "There is a force behind requesting help from universal power. All witches and people versed in metaphysics know this."

"Any ideas on where to find a handy god or goddess?" Larissa swallowed a bite of food, watching August with mild interest.

***

August sat on his bed after dinner, ruminating over the conversation with Larissa. They had already exhausted one means of trying to gain information from family members. Ciana needed to be located, and fast. Her information would be vital to resolving this whole issue between the Hawthorne and Strondovan families.

The other burning question, why would darkness prevail if he and Larissa failed in their mission? Shahar said there was an enemy, but what or whom was it? August turned toward his bag of magical equipment. A vibrating hum came from inside.

"What the hell?" Curious, August opened the bag, digging around until he found the source of the sound. He pulled out a quartz crystal sphere, the size of a baseball. Another round of strong vibrations sent waves of tingling up his arm. "Geeze, hold on, for fuck's sake." He cursed while fumbling for the stand resting deep inside the bag.

"What do you mean 'hold on'? And watch your language." The face of a man appeared.

August nearly knocked the ball off the stand, he was so stunned—and skittish at the sight of Jove peering at him.

"Miss your old man?" Jove's lips pulled into a big smile. "You're a cantankerous cuss, but I surely do miss you."

The young man laughed. "Grandfather, to what do I owe this wonderful surprise? And whether or not you believe me, I miss you too. Are you calling me home? Perhaps this quest thing has been recalled."

"Ah, young man, hold your tongue. No, the quest isn't called off. As a matter of fact, that's why I'm checking in on you. How did everything go?"

"Very interesting, and then nothing. Clement and Desmond held their information tighter than a poker player holds his winning hand to his vest. And Ciana is still alive."

"After all this time?" Jove's face wrinkled with a perplexed expression. "That's the strangest thing I ever heard. But pay attention. There's something special about her."

"Why didn't you tell me the royalty status of the Strondovans?"

"Hmm?" The older man shook his head. "I thought you knew that from historical orations concerning our family. You need to pay attention, boy. And another thing, mind your Ps and Qs. Lighten up on that girl. She's a fine one." Jove smiled again.

August wrinkled his nose in disgust. He shared what occurred during the summoning and also what Sophie had suggested.

"And that's just why I've contacted you. I have the name of the next person who can help you on your quest. And Shahar is right, there is an enemy out there. Their power must be stopped."

"Any clue to who the enemy is?" August lay on his side, gazing at Jove through the ball.

"I've got a sneaking suspicion it's another clave. I just can't put my finger on which one. They've done a good job keeping secrets, but you and Larissa are about to blow their cover."

"What if we fail, Grandfather? Or become vanquished in the process?"

Jove shuddered. "Don't say things like that, son. Negative words stem from negative thoughts, and then you'll surely have disaster. If this clave gains total power, we will all be steeped in ignorance, distrust, and our magic will be snuffed out. Witches will lose their importance, their power. We are responsible for maintaining and guarding the magical arts and the dimension that allows it to work. We feed it with vitality, passing on knowledge and history to the younger ones.

August nodded in thought. "Where do we go next, Grandfather?"

"To the source of ancient power, my boy."

Chapter Seven

Remington Allwine sat at a carved antique wooden table inside a handsomely decorated apartment in Cairo, Egypt. He gazed at the young man and woman sitting across from him.

"To what do I owe the pleasure of such wonderful company?" His voice came out soft and warm, with the Egyptian accent of a native speaking fluent English.

August appraised the man with great interest, noting the close-cropped head of black hair, piercing dark eyes, and full lips. "My father, Jove South Hawthorne, sent us here because he said you could help us with a certain matter."

"Ah, it depends on what you are seeking." The older man paused a moment. "May I get you some wine, coffee, anything to eat? You must be tired after your journey."

"Coffee would be wonderful," said Larissa, smoothing out her skirt. The travel and hot air of the city left her dripping with sweat and limp hair. Nevertheless, she needed a drink that would perk her up.

"Wine for me, if you don't mind," said August, smiling.

"Wine and coffee will be served." Remington rang a sterling silver bell resting beside him on the table. A servant appeared from the kitchen. "Wine and coffee please. And serve the best for our guests." The servant nodded and sped off. "Now, my friends, tell me what it is you are needing."

"We need the assistance of an ancient deity." Larissa spoke first, much to the chagrin of August, who looked at her with a mild frown.

Remington sat back in his chair and folded his hands neatly in his lap. The light in his eyes danced with glee when he heard the young woman's statement. "And if you don't mind my asking, why do you need the assistance of a god or goddess?"

Just as Larissa opened her mouth to speak, August interjected, "My grandfather was the one who recommended this and that we see you. He also provided the name of the specific deity we need." He spent the next several minutes informing his host of the details of their quest.

"What foresight your grandfather has, young man." Remington sat up straight and leaned forward on the table. "It is important to choose the right deity, and they must be approached with great sincerity. So many tourists come and visit, making pilgrimages to the temples. Some are sincere, others not as much. But none of them truly have access to the gods. They just think they do." The man smiled at his last statement.

"If you don't mind my asking, Mr. Allwine, your name doesn't sound Egyptian. How did you come into your position in such a land and working with deities, of all things?" Larissa tilted her head with a questioning look on her face.

Remington laughed. "I don't mind you asking at all. My father and I were born here. My grandfather was born in England to Egyptian parents who migrated there. He changed his surname from Alawa, to Allwine before migrating here. Said he did it to have anonymity while respecting his English heritage."

August spoke up, "From what my grandfather says, you inherited a great gift."

"Mr. South Hawthorne did his homework very well indeed." Remington nodded toward August. "It is true. I am a descendant from the last dynastic line of the greatest high priests that ever lived in ancient Egypt. On my father's side, of course. I do not practice the witching arts, but I dabble a little in the metaphysical realms."

"You do more than dabble, good sir," said August, squaring up his shoulders. "You are a hem-netjer, the one who draws the bolt from the sacred rooms of the deities. Only someone worthy would have such a gift."

The older man bowed his head with humility. "And I can open the door to any of the deities you wish. My family lineage fills me with great pride. To show my deep appreciation and respect for such a pedigree, I use my divine skills in making passkeys so I can continue the service work of my ancestors."

"Would you be willing to make a passkey for us?" Larissa asked.

"And how far is the Temple of Hathor from here?" August sipped the wine brought to him by the servant. "My grandfather recommended that particular goddess."

Remington laughed again. "You see, here's where it gets interesting. The deities do not reside in their so-called temples."

Larissa and August sat stunned.

"So where are they, really?" August finally spoke up.

"They reside in a place so secret, no one knows the whereabouts. Even I do not allow you to see the location, if I agree to create a passkey at all. Only the worthy will get a key."

"We were worthy in the eyes of The Order of the Onyx Night," said Larissa. Her voice held a twinge of indignation.

"My dear, that is an extremely well-respected reference, and thus the reason I would entertain your request." Remington smiled wider, showing a set of large white teeth.

"Wouldn't my grandfather's knowledge of you at all count for something as well? Not everyone knows who you are or what you do." August glanced with a bit of apprehension in Larissa's direction. "We are royalty, she and I."

"All very well and good, my friends. May I add that I have created passkeys for others who were also of royal lineage or noble bloodlines. Not only witches have received these special keys, but also metaphysical practitioners and regular people who don't specialize in anything."

"What will it take for us to gain a passkey?" Larissa asked. "Is there a cost? I'm sure we can pay." She exchanged glances with August.

The older man chuckled. "There's a cost to everything. I'm no different. But once you enter a deal with me, you will fulfill it or . . ." He paused, considering his words.

"Or what?" asked August, sitting straighter in his chair.

"You die. Simple as that." Remington watched his guest intently, sipping brandy from a snifter. He closed his eyes momentarily and savored the taste.

"Have you ever killed anyone?" Larissa's face showed alarm.

"My dear, let's not dwell on such negative thoughts. We want things to be amiable, don't we?" Remington dismissed Larissa's words with an absent wave of his hand.

August squinted at his host. "Okay. We know what happens with failure. Can you tell us the cost?"

"Not until you enter a solid binding agreement with me."

"But we don't know what your cost is, or if we could even pay it." Larissa's words grew shriller.

"Dear lady, what would life be without the occasional gamble? It makes living that much more exciting, don't you think?"

"This is do or die. It's not that exciting," Larissa retorted.

"Depends on one's perspective." Remington swallowed another swig of brandy. "From my perspective, I find it rather jolly. You will, too, if you succeed." The smile faded from his face. "You and your friend either come up with another plan and be on your way, or you follow through. It's simple. Only two choices, my friends." He flashed her another quick ingratiating smile.

"One other thing I forgot to add," said Remington. "If you choose to leave here without a binding deal, you will be cursed in the most horrible way."

Larissa and August glared at Remington.

"You are cheating us. No one ever said we were damned if we do or damned if we don't when it came to asking you for help." August clenched his fists in anger. "Is this what you do? Trap poor unsuspecting people?"

"Oh, come now, Mr. Hawthorne, you definitely won't be damned if you succeed. These misfortunes that will occur if you don't do not come from me."

"How's that?" Larissa asked. Her lips showed a grim line of unhappiness.

"You see, my friends, to fail at a task is to incur the wrath of your desired deity. Death is their response. They want the purest of the pure soliciting them, someone who will stop at nothing to win.

"To simply walk away from me only annoys them, trifles with their patience. It shows a lack of sincerity. Their curse on you is a reminder to always go at things with a purpose and with pure intent. They don't like people who waffle back and forth. Simple, really."

August scowled at Remington. "No, not so simple. And we really don't have a choice at this point."

"There are always choices, my friend. You must decide which of the poisons you find less bitter." Remington's lips pulled into a wide grin. "Not the best choice of words, but it gets my point across. I'm sure you understand."

August stared at Larissa. "We're screwed."

***

"I can't believe we're on a wild goose chase for a prized phurba." August looked at Larissa as they dined in the restaurant of their hotel later that night. "And how in the hell are we supposed to find its owner, this Gamal Emara fellow? That wretch didn't even give us a clue or any information."

The meeting with Remington Allwine left them with a sour taste. The older man had stated his request and added that he was under no obligation to share anything more. Both remained silent during the walk from his house back to their hotel. He'd offered them a fine dinner at his place, but of course they declined.

"I would never have thought a humble hem-netjer would have been so sneaky." Larissa pouted.

August turned his gaze toward the ceiling, thinking for several seconds. "Missing the opportunity for a passkey to Hathor wouldn't have served us well, either. We're witches. We can deal with most anything. Have we forgotten that?"

"Have you forgotten that I am the one with the strongest powers? To this day, I still don't know what you have." Larissa scowled at the young man.

"Are you going to keep rubbing my nose in that?"

"I really think you need to let me help you hone your magic. I could do it, you know. Share some things Aunt Dorenda has taught me."

"I have tricks up my sleeves. And for your sauciness, I'm not going to tell you what they are. I'll just save them for when we need them."

Larissa let out a huff of disgust. "Good thing I have a few tricks myself—for when we need them."

August stared at his glass of wine. "First of all, why would Remington want a phurba from Gamal Emara? For someone who makes passkeys to deities with every power in the universe, I can't imagine what a phurba would do for him."

"It must have a power like no other. Something that the gods and goddesses can't do—or won't do."

"Have you ever used one, Larissa?" August rested his chin in one of his hands, gazing at his companion.

"I haven't. With all my magic abilities, I barely understand what they're used for. What about you?"

The young man shrugged. "Grandfather has some locked away for his collection of magic tools, but I've never seen him use them." He wasn't about to tell her that he'd sneaked downstairs one night and tried his hand at using one.

All he wanted was to enhance a woman's interest in him, before Fiona and Daisy came on the scene. Instead of conjuring love, he managed to call forth a bunch of hopping toads. He spent a good twenty minutes before he finally discovered the spell to get rid of them.

"We have to start bright and early tomorrow. We only have a couple of days." Larissa savored a bite of her meal once the server placed a steaming plate on the table.

"I'll see if I can determine where to find this man, and his mysterious phurba." August relaxed a moment and focused his attention on the plate in front of him.

***

In his hotel room after dinner, August sat on his bed, staring at the leather travel bag holding his magical tools. What would be the best way to find Gamal Emara? The old-fashioned method would be the best way to start. He checked his cell phone, doing an Internet search. No luck. He grabbed a phone book and spent a few minutes looking through it. Again, no luck.

Frustrated, August had one last way, and that was via candle magic. He rummaged through his bag and pulled out a silver candle, a candleholder, and a white cloth. Setting everything up on a desk, the young man at last sat in the faux leather chair. This would be his altar setup.

"Hone my magic, she says," muttered August. "I'll show her." He concentrated his gaze at the wick, snapped his fingers, and uttered the words, "*Par Lux.*" The wick caught fire. August smiled. It didn't hurt that he used this spell quite often, lighting the candles in his bedroom when Fiona and Daisy came to visit.

The next part would be the hardest. An invocation that would connect with the person he wanted. August sat for a moment, mesmerized, watching the flame dance on the wick. At once he fell into a trance-like state. Searching deep in his memory for the spell, he concentrated on Emara's name. *"Light of flame, light of all, find the one I wish to call. Call him loud, call him clear. Tonight I reach a willing ear."*

He gazed long and hard at the candle flame. His mind opened, cleared of distractions. The tiny firelight swayed and rocked, pulling in will and desire. August sat up straight when he viewed an image forming within the flame. A small, yet distinctive, outline of a man formed, details more vivid the longer the flame danced.

August's pulse quickened. *"Where can I find you?"* He repeated the question several times in his mind. The man's faced peered back from the flame, a smile on his lips. This outcome was exactly what August wanted. *"Where can I find you?"*

From the flame, a wisp of smoke formed the answer. *Khan Al Khalili.*

"Where in Khan Al Khalili?" August posed his question, concentrating on each word.

The smoky words dispersed. In its place, another answer. *Find my stall.*

"Which one?"

"Look for the ankh."

Before August could form another question, the flame went out, sending soft tendrils of smoke spiraling upwards.

"Damn!" The young man clenched his fists. "This trip will get the better of us before we even get started." August pulled out his cell phone and spent a good hour studying the history and location of Khan Al Khalili. Intriguing, at best. A trap, at worst.

Earlier that evening, inside her room, two pillar candles burned on the desk, creating the only light. Larissa sat nude in a lotus position on her bed. She wore bracelets of rose quartz beads on each wrist, and over her shoulders, a large white chiffon ceremonial scarf encrusted with amethyst, lapis lazuli, and clear quartz. Dorenda had lovingly fashioned it for her, hand-sewing each bead on the fabric. After completion, she and Dorenda passed a sacred flame over the piece, infusing it with blessings and power to the user.

Earlier Larissa had bathed in water with rose oil added. Afterward she smudged the room with a sage bundle to purify the area and create a sacred space. In the space in front of her sat a quartz generator. From a crystal pyramid-shaped stone, four equally clear quartz points jutted out, equidistant, around the middle.

She used this piece for more powerful sessions, drawing from the amplified energy that could manifest from or reach out through the ether. Placed beneath the generator was a piece of blessed parchment paper with Gamal Emara's name written in pink ink.

Remington had placed them in a life or death situation, and his cavalier blamelessness infuriated her still. Emara must be on her and August's side. Period.

Placing her hands over the generator, she closed her eyes, taking in three deep, cleansing breaths, holding each for several seconds, and exhaling. Her hands tingled with a warm heat that grew to hard throbbing pain. Larissa pulled her hands a little higher to dissipate the energy. She smiled. So far so good.

In a low clear voice, she stated her invocation, "*To thee I call, O Gamal, a sincere intent request. Come to me. Talk to me. Acknowledge my behest.*"

The air grew charged, cooling down several degrees. The flames on the candle tops gyrated and flickered. One of them snapped like a well-stoked fire. Larissa's gut tightened. A few inches above the generator, a ghostly outline wafted into the shape of a man. The figure towered over her.

Excited, Larissa looked up, making eye contact.

"To what do I owe your earnest call, charming lady?" A voice sounded off in a low whispery tone. The man's lips pulled into an amiable, interested smile.

As seconds passed, his body had become abnormally dense, but still remained ethereal enough to remind Larissa that Gamal Emara's presence only showed in astral form, nothing more.

"I thank you for such a speedy response, good sir." Larissa glanced down, all at once acutely aware of her nudity. She'd performed ceremonies like this in the past, but it was only with her and Dennis when they wanted to converse and be present in a more personal manner, though they remained far away from each other.

"Do not be ashamed, dear one. Appreciating the human form is what I do best." The man bowed his head in a show of respect.

"Who are you and what do you do, Mr. Emara?"

"Perhaps it is only appropriate that I ask the first question. Again. Why have you called me?"

"Remington Allwine gave us your name."

Gamal's figure shifted into a kneeling position so that he and Larissa nearly stared at each other. He chuckled. "The hem-netjer, Remington Allwine, eh?"

Larissa nodded.

"You know he's a scoundrel, yes?"

"I kind of guessed that. I still can't figure out how a man like him possesses such a special gift."

"My dear," answered Gamal, "you know quite well that it is the nature of the universe to be impartial. His intent is strong, whether for good or evil. Besides, he practices well his divine gift. So he will never lose it."

"This is life or death. My companion, August South Hawthorne, and I will die if we don't give him what he wants."

"True, unfortunately. And I take it you are needing me to help with something, correct?"

"Yes. Would you be willing?"

"Let's talk further, physically. Come to Khan Al Khalili tomorrow. I will be in my stall waiting for you and your friend." Gamal moved his right hand in a few spiral motions and placed the product of his materialization on the bed. "Wear these when you come. Simply follow as you are led. That is all." Gamal Emara vanished.

Beside the generator lay two golden ankh pendants, each an inch long and hanging from simple black silk cords. Larissa picked them up. The gold surface of both flashed with a magical light of their own. Holding them filled her with both excitement and apprehension.

***

By noon, August and Larissa had taken the metro and sped along the busy streets to Khan Al Khalili. Larissa eyed with wonder all the buildings and residences she viewed through the windows, the unique architecture, geometric patterns worked into stone constructions, lofty towers rising from mosques, the age of it all.

She sank back in her seat, filled at once with gratitude. All her travels abroad had left parts of themselves deeply imbedded in her soul. Every place she had visited held great, unique beauty, and the luck in being able to see much of it overwhelmed her at once. Thoughts of wandering through the markets, seeing the sights, smelling the smells enticed her. Dorenda had told her about this place years ago, suggesting that if her niece had a chance to visit for any reason, take it at once.

"Hey, quit daydreaming." August punched Larissa's shoulder, intruding on her moment of pleasure for such a grave task facing them.

"I'm not daydreaming, thank you." Her face showed him an irritated scowl. "And don't touch me like that. It hurts."

"So sorry, my delicate flower. I'll try to be more gentle next time I touch that tender skin of yours." August let out a breath of disgust. "In case you forgot, we're not going on a jaunty shopping spree. From the grin on your face, you'd think we could just dally all day as we please."

"You know, August, I don't know how I ever managed without you bossing me around. It's a wonder I can get out of bed on my own every morning."

"If it hadn't been for me, we wouldn't be on this bus right now. You'd still be in bed snoozing away."

Larissa blushed. August had her on that one. She hadn't gone straight to sleep after her brief conversation with Gamal Emara.

"What on earth tired you out to such a degree?" August viewed her with a tiny bit of disdain.

"Doing my homework, my good man, which is probably more than I can say for you." She lifted her face in a display of righteousness.

August chuckled. "Don't patronize me, my dear. I do my homework well enough. You'll see."

"I bet I do mine better." Larissa winked at him, a seductive grin gliding across her lips. "And I'm not your delicate flower or your dear. So stop patronizing *me*." She turned her view toward the windows again, taking in the sights.

"God, you're impossible." August shook his head and focused his attention elsewhere.

The bus pulled to a stop several minutes later. Larissa and August stepped down, checking out the area around them. Men walking together. Women walking and conversing. Many wore hijabs. One lady wore a full face covering, with only her eyes showing. Children walked with their parents. One lady several feet away fed a cat some cheese as she passed it.

The smell of food filled the air. Larissa took in a deep breath. She'd love a good cup of coffee and a pastry. The heat already played havoc with August's hair, fluffing it out like a lion's mane. In the bright sun, his head seemed to gleam like the finest gold. For a brief moment, she saw the handsome looks for what they were with a young man like him. Virile, strong arms, and a firm chest. When he caught her looking at him, she turned away, feigning interest in something else.

"We need to look for the sign of the ankh." He nodded his head with authority. "It could be anywhere. Over a doorway, on a building, perhaps a figurine. Anything."

Larissa narrowed her eyes, listening and acting as if August's words were the most important in all the world. "Or we could use these. I think it would take the guesswork out of everything." She reached in her purse and pulled out the two golden ankhs, dangling them in front of him.

August's eyes grew wide. For once he stood speechless. His cheeks reddened.

Larissa tied one of the pendants around her neck, watching with glee at her companions dumbfounded face. "Allow me." She reached around his neck, quickly tying the cord holding the other pendant and securing it in place. "There, it actually looks nice on you."

"Where in the hell did you get these?"

"Gamal Emara." Larissa fluttered her lashes, noting the bemused look on August's face.

"Okay. He gave us necklaces. That doesn't tell us anything about where he could be. This marketplace is huge."

"The ankhs must have power, or he does. Our wearing them will help us find him."

"Let's start walking then. Maybe we could ask some people. Surely someone has heard of him."

August led the way with Larissa following. The young woman paid close attention to her intuition, noting her feelings and if she felt compelled to move a certain direction in and out of the rows of vendor stalls. The line of tables rambled endlessly through the streets.

They sold everything here. Jewelry, clothing, scarves, pottery, antiques. A time or two, August pulled her along when she paused too long at a table. Young handsome men tried luring Larissa to their tables.

They seem to undress her with their eyes, smiling and motioning her in their direction. She moved along, casting her gaze on other vendors, gravitating to stalls run by women. August and Larissa continued wandering up and down the rows. He still looked for a sign. She waited for some sort of magnetic pull toward an unknown destination.

Something at once felt strange. Larissa stopped walking. August did the same. Both looked down. During their walk at some point in time, the young man had taken his companion's hand in his, holding it with a sure grip.

Their eyes met. Larissa tried pulling gently away. August persisted, refusing to let go. In that moment of recognition, it happened.

Chapter Eight

"Ah, I see you made it." Gamal Emara's face lit up in a smile when Larissa and August reached a table at the end of a row stationed in the heart of the marketplace. The man pointed to their entwined hands. "You see, when you work together, anything is possible."

"Yes," Larissa answered. She introduced herself formally and pulled her hand away from August's loosened grip, while staring into the vendor's face. He was better looking than August, better than many of the men she'd seen on the streets. His short dark hair held a smooth sheen, with bangs swept neatly away off his forehead.

A pair of mirthful glittering black eyes teased her, and thoughts of being held in his arms sent a rush of heat inside her. Out of the corner of her eye, she noted August staring at her with a smirk.

"You have a lively assortment of items for sale," said August, turning his attention back to the vendor.

In Emara's stall, Larissa viewed the body oils used for enhancing romance, health, and vitality. She caught a whiff of the perfume oils sitting in a small shelf beside her. One shelf a few feet away held candles of all colors with love affirmations on the label. One table held several books on how to please your partner. Figurines related to love and relationships dotted the stall. In the far corner, a shelf held large pillows of different sizes and shapes and colorful bedcovers.

"What is your specialty, Mr. Emara? I remember asking you that last night when we briefly chatted." Larissa quickly glanced at August, trying to catch a view of his face.

"Now I will answer your question." Gamal bowed his head in affirmation. "I am a tantric magician, my dear. Love and sex are my specialties."

Larissa's face went blank. August smiled and let out a sound of approval. "We seem to have some things in common, Mr. Emara."

"With all due respect, Mr. Hawthorne, we do not." Gamal's lips pulled into an amiable, easy smile.

The smile faded from August's face. In its place, a flushed set of cheeks and a clenched jaw.

And you, my charming one," said Gamal, turning to Larissa, "are more delightful in person. You have had some passion in your life, no?"

Larissa blushed. "There have been one or two, I suppose."

Gamal leaned in closer to the young woman. "You feel deeply, love deeply. You just haven't uncovered your true full potential in that arena yet. I predict you will have an able partner—once he is fully trained." He cast an eye on August and back to Larissa. His eyes lit up, and his lips pulled into a knowing smile.

"Are you able to talk to us more about why we need you?" August asked. He spoke as if he'd not heard Gamal's words.

"I will be more than glad to talk to you, sir. I'm always glad to be of service. It's what I do best. Serving others, you know."

"How quaint. Good to know." August nodded and looked away at some of the oils on the table.

Larissa's eyes moved with an expression of exasperation at August. "Do you have a lot of clients, Mr. Emara?" she said, turning to the man in front of her. "You mentioned being a magician. Is that for entertainment purposes, or are you a real witch?"

"I am a real witch who functions with real magical capacities, not just those illusion techniques you see on TV—though I can do those too." He laughed.

"When would be a good time to talk more, alone?" Larissa asked. Her gaze remained locked on to Gamal's face. He seemed to peer into the deepest aspects of her soul. It both tantalized and frightened her. It left her with a feeling of vulnerability, a brief loss of control, a feeling she'd never experienced before with someone, not even Dennis or Daniel. It also sent a jolt of excitement through her.

His smile lightened. The animated glint in his eyes shifted to a look of intent interest, one that contained an aspect of sincerity rather than unbridled lust.

They both turned and viewed August, who stood staring at them with an air of confusion.

He pulled out a scrap of paper and a pen and quickly scribbled something on it. "Come to this address at five o'clock. "We'll talk more in my home." Gamal bowed his head again and turned toward a customer who came up to the table.

***

"Why were you holding my hand?" Larissa asked August.

They sat at one of the tables inside El Fishawy, one of the oldest cafes in the city. They had an hour and a half to kill before heading off to Gamal Emara's residence.

Mirrors on the walls, antique furniture, and dark paneling formed a linear backdrop for tables traversing a colorful patterned floor. Anyone who was someone and those who weren't filled the café from beginning to end. The ambience allowed for intimacy while allowing an immersion into the diversity of people who frequented the establishment.

August sipped some hot coffee, thinking. "I honestly have no idea."

"Seriously? How could you not know something like that?"

"It was crowded, a lot going on. I don't know. I wasn't aware of anything until we saw Gamal, and he mentioned it. Besides, why didn't you say something?"

Larissa bit into her pastry and brooded while she ate. "I think something happened once we held hands. Like we had to do it, or else. We were under a spell."

"You think so?"

"That was the catalyst. And the ankhs were merely ID badges so he'd know who we were for sure."

"Speaking of ankhs, where's yours?" August wrinkled his brow. "I didn't see you take it off."

"You're not wearing yours, either." Larissa pointed at his neck.

Both touched the hollow of their throats and sat open-mouthed with shock.

"How strange they would disappear like that," said Larissa.

"He's a magician, witch, something." August waved his hand absently. "I guess the charms served their purpose. It's not like you or I wear them on a regular basis, anyway."

"We're going to find out a lot more when we meet with him." Larissa's face lightened a little. "I like him. I trust him way more than that Allwine guy."

"Humph." August stifled a laugh. "He had the hots for you. That much I know. See, you Strondovan women have that—"

"Would you stop it? Don't start with that again, or I'll leave you sitting here."

"Oh, please." August's face showed impatience. "You won't make it far, being a woman and all." He held out his hand in response to Larissa's ready protest. "We're not in the United States. We're in countries where men truly are dominant. Like it or not it's the truth."

"Men are dominant in the United States too. I don't kid myself thinking everyone is equal."

"And that's what is so wonderful about being witches. We are equal. It's only the level of magical power and the ability of the magical arts that separates one from another."

Larissa grinned. "Well, then, that makes me dominant where we two are concerned." She leaned her head back and laughed, harder when she saw August's scowl.

"Enough." He sipped his coffee in silence while Larissa finished her treat.

"What do you think Gamal is going to do about the phurba?" Larissa asked, glancing at the clock on her cell phone.

"He's not going to hand it over. That much I can tell you. But I have a sneaking suspicion, whatever happens, it's going to involve something we don't like. I feel it in my bones."

"Ten more minutes and we go. Good or bad, it will be time to face the music."

***

The walk to Gamal Emara's house was not far from the marketplace. They passed another mosque and a long line of homes before reaching the magician's residence. Larissa and August entered a stone building, hiked up a set of dark winding stairs to his apartment on an upper floor, and knocked at his door.

"Welcome, my friends." Gamal smiled, graciously motioning for the pair to enter.

Larissa at once liked his apartment. A spicy perfume scent filled the air. Neat, comfortable, the place held an assortment of antique furniture and a fine collection of oil paintings, which included several nudes of males, females, and couples. One cabinet held the oddest collection of erotic figurines. Her eyes locked on to the pieces, viewing them with interest.

Gamal smiled. "Let me show you some of my favorites." He led August and Larissa to the cabinet, slipping his hand inside and pulling out a figure of a reclining couple wrapped in an embrace.

Larissa stared at the detail. The piece, made of fine porcelain, showed vibrant hues. The man and woman were semi-clothed, with the woman's breasts revealed. From beneath the drape on the male, an erection showed. The facial expressions showed deep desire as the couple stared at each other.

"Why do you like that piece so much, Mr. Emara?" August asked.

"I like this one because of its subtlety. The positioning of the couple, the looks on their faces, and the emotion captured in the eyes say it all. You see the love, and if you look deeply enough, you detect the desire. It runs deep between the two."

August glanced up at Gamal. "Do you have such passion for all your pieces, or just this one?"

Gamal turned and gazed at the cabinet. "Each piece holds something special for me in the way of tantra. Each one represents an aspect of maleness or femaleness. Each stage, the beginning, middle, and the end of the tantric sutras."

"Can you tell us a little about what you do?" asked Larissa.

"I teach couples how to fall in love again, how to truly understand intimacy and how it unites us all spiritually."

"How so?" Larissa tilted her head with interest.

"My dear, Tantra teaches one how to use spiritual principles and teachings to enhance spiritual excellence. When there is the union of masculine, feminine, spirit, and earthly matter, there is spiritual bliss and non-duality. It also embraces both spiritual development while satisfying natural desires simultaneously."

Larissa stared at Gamal, entranced by his words. Even August stood still, listening with great interest."

"Go on, Mr. Emara. We'd like to hear more," said August.

Gamal smiled graciously. "As you wish. In Tantra, the goddess Shakti and Lord Shiva are honored, as they represent the grand union, the indestructible force of two energies that sustain all.

"With Tantra, one expands and weaves together the polarities of male and female and brings them together as one. And do you want to know what is interesting about Tantra?"

Larissa and August gazed at Gamal, wide-eyed. "Yes," they said in unison.

"It's really not about the sex." Gamal grinned, locking his gaze on the couple standing before him.

"Oh," said August. His face lost its animated expression. "So what is the point?"

"The point is focusing on connection and not so much on the final outcome." Gamal winked. "You know exactly what I mean." He stared at the confusion on August's face. "Come now, Mr. Hawthorne. You love women. Have you ever had a favorite person with whom you just wanted to connect, savor the moment, try to make it last forever? Of course, in your case, I'm assuming attaining spiritual heights wasn't on your mind."

August frowned. "True." He lowered his gaze. "But yes, there have been brief moments when I wanted something to last a little longer."

"Sometimes, Mr. Hawthorne, we get too caught up in the heady goal of achieving brief satisfaction, thinking it is the end all be all, the true ultimate bliss, when it is nothing more than a quickie. In Tantra, it's not about achieving that. It is about sustaining and holding out."

Gamal turned to Larissa. "Any questions my dear?"

"No, sir." Her voice came out as a tiny cracked whisper.

"So tell me. How can I be of service to such a charming pair? Something tells me you didn't come here to see my collection of erotica." Gamal placed the figurine back in the cabinet and motioned for them to sit on the sofa. He settled down into one of his cushy armchairs and gazed at his guests, taking time to study their features in more detail. Though they looked tired, the beauty of their faces captivated his attention.

The girl's face displayed fresh youthful skin, bright eyes and kissable lips. Underneath her clothes, he detected a sensual body with the perfect hourglass figure. Her male companion's looks didn't fail to please, either. He admired August's lean sinewy body, strong elegant facial features and a head full of brilliant wavy hair.

"Mr. Emara, I'll get to the point," said August. He relaxed against a large over-sized cushion. "Rumor has it you own a prized phurba."

"Rumor?" Gamal winked at Larissa. "Hmm, a phurba." Gamal closed his eyes in thought. "I own more than one, you know." He nodded in satisfaction.

August raised his brows and quickly glanced at Larissa.

"Do you have a favorite, Mr. Emara? You have a favorite figurine. I would think if you own more than one phurba, you would surely have a favorite among those too."

"Do you understand the powers of such a tool?" Gamal rested his chin in one of his hands, relaxing further in his chair. "Witches have many magical tools they use. Usually phurbas aren't on the list."

"I'll admit I've never used one," said August. "My father has some."

"And you never asked him about them?" Gamal's face contorted into a look of shock. "But then again, your father, if he's a truly knowledgeable witch with such a collection, would only discuss the phurba with someone worthy of the information."

Larissa grinned, lightly punching August's arm. He frowned in response.

"Come, let me show you my collection. I'll explain more what they do."

The pair followed Gamal through his apartment to the far end, where three rooms were stationed. The décor here didn't fail to please. The dining area held another array of antiques, tables, chairs, and a matching china cabinet and buffet. The hallway consisted of hardwood floors, like the rest of the apartment. Area rugs took the place of carpet.

Art on the walls consisted of more nudes and depictions of ancient deities, all in the form of oil paintings and lithographs.

"You enjoy collecting don't you, Mr. Emara," said Larissa. "Your apartment defines you well."

"I'm so glad you enjoy it." Gamal stopped briefly, turned to the young woman, and smiled at her. "All I have brings me such great joy, and it brings me greater bliss when others can appreciate the beauty of the pieces as much as I do."

August watched Gamal and Larissa. He slowly shook his head. Those two had chemistry. He felt the energy between them. The charge cracked and sizzled in its sixth-sense way, in that extra dimension where only witches and seasoned metaphysical practitioners could discern.

It wasn't so much that Gamal and his companion seemed to get along well (and that Gamal had taken every opportunity to slight him, with Larissa cheering on), but it disturbed him deeply that a certain awareness had crept into his psyche. Why did he care if Larissa and Gamal had that special chemistry? He'd seen the looks on their faces. The magician studying Larissa far too long. Larissa staring back like a schoolgirl in love, struggling to act casual as if they talked quite often.

"Mr. Hawthorne, are you going to join us, or are you going to study something else in the hallway that appears to have captured your attention?" Gamal called out from the room at the end of the apartment.

"So sorry. I'm coming." August shook his head and sped forward, stepping into a luxurious bedroom that rivaled his own. He stood rooted on the floor, stunned. "What a magnificent room."

"It serves me well." Gamal grinned and strode to a large armoire in the corner. He removed a key from a small porcelain box on the back of a shelf. "My phurbas are locked up. They are powerful, and I take them out only when needed."

Larissa and August watched closely as Gamal unlocked a bottom drawer and removed a large black box. They moved toward the bed, where their host opened the box, motioning them to come closer.

Inside, five phurbas rested in their compartments lined in red silk. Two of them were crafted of metal at the bottom, with the tops showing fine enamel carvings. He picked up one of them, holding it reverently in his hand. The three-pronged blade end glistened in the sunlight brightening the room.

"Gold?" asked Larissa.

"Yes. Pure metal. No alloys. The other is silver. The blades are used to destroy demons." Gamal rubbed his fingers on the top end, caressing the surface of a face that looked like a dragon. Rotating the tool, he displayed the other faces. One was in the likeness of a male. The other, a female. "And the round end is used for blessings."

August eyed the box with great interest, noting stones of labradorite, black obsidian, and nephrite jade. They also contained the carved blades at the bottom, while the tops denoted intricate carving within the stone. A round ball had been carved on top, denoting the end for bestowing blessings. "The gemstone phurbas are quite lovely. Is one more powerful than the others?" He turned his gaze to Gamal, waiting for an answer.

Gamal's eyes glistened with pride. "The stone pieces are also quite powerful. And yes, there is one more powerful than the others."

August caught Larissa's gaze and quickly focused back on the magician. "Which one would that be, Mr. Emara?"

"I think the one made of labradorite would surely be quite powerful." Larissa spoke up. Her eyes shined as she gazed at the stone phurba resting in the middle between the others.

"You guess correctly, my fine lady. You know your stones and magic well, do you not?" Gamal surveyed the young woman.

Blushing, she spoke up. "I know that labradorite protects against those who wish you ill."

"And it also protects you against those who desire you as a love object but become scorned when you don't reciprocate their interest."

Gamal glanced over at August.

"Don't look at me, sir. I have absolutely no desire for her at all." The young man grinned, looking quite proud as he uttered his declaration.

The magician said nothing but narrowed his eyes in thought. He looked from Larissa to August and back to the young woman. "And these are my phurbas. But you mentioned earlier that you need something from me. We still have not answered that question yet."

Larissa rubbed her lower lip, thinking. "We want your prized phurba, the one that is the most powerful of all. The one that will defeat the destroyer of light."

The look of anticipation disappeared from Gamal's face, leaving him bearing a stone-cold expression.

Silence filled the room. Larissa stared deeply into Gamal's eyes. August gazed at the floor in silence.

"Let us return to the living room," Gamal said after a few seconds.

The magician spent several minutes making and pouring coffee for him and his guests. "I think it would be helpful if you told me the whole story. Why do you need my best phurba?"

August and Larissa informed Gamal of all the events that had transpired until the present, described their quest, and ended on the subject of the phurba once again.

"How do we meet Mr. Allwine's request so we can have a passkey made, ask our questions of the deity, and get out alive? We're stuck, Mr. Emara." August tapped his fingers on his knee.

"To what lengths would you go to have it?" asked Gamal. His eyes glittered with new light. "The labradorite phurba is extremely powerful. It is the one that vanquishes the destroyer of light. It would only be used in an extreme time of need."

"So you would give it up? How did you get it to start with?" Larissa met Gamal's gaze and sipped from her coffee cup.

"I came into its possession in a most unusual way. It would take too long to go into detail." Gamal finished his cup of coffee, and stated resolutely, "And if you want it you shall have it."

Both Larissa and August gazed at Gamal.

"And, said August, "the price is . . .?"

"There will be a price. There always is." The magician smiled in a gallant way, appearing very pleased with himself for making such an offer.

"What do we have to do for the phurba?" Larissa sat on the edge of her seat.

"You will give me your lives." Gamal sat back in his chair, watching his guests.

Larissa and August exchanged glances.

"So you're no better than that rascal hem-netjer, are you?" August scowled and sprang from his seat.

"Hold on, Mr. Hawthorne. Not so fast." Gamal raised his hand and sent out a bolt of light blue. The flash hit August squarely on the chest, stunning him a few seconds. "Please take your seat, sir. There is no reason for alarm. Perhaps I chose my words poorly." He watched as August staggered back to his seat.

"If you don't wish to kill us, what do you mean by giving you our lives?" Larissa asked.

"I am much older than both of you by thirty years. Like most people, I value youth and everything that goes with it."

"And you want what, exactly? How would we be able to help in any way?" The young woman lifted her chin, staring hard at the older man sitting in the large easy chair.

"Simple," said Gamal. "I want ten years of life from each of you." He folded his hands in his lap and smiled at the couple.

Larissa's face blanched.

August, who had finally recovered, spoke up, "That's preposterous. How would we give you that? You can't transfer age from one person to another."

"Ah, but I can," said Gamal. "I've found a way. It's my secret. Will you do what I ask, or not?"

"We have no choice," said August. "We're trapped like fish in a net."

"Come now, Mr. Hawthorne. You make this all sound so bleak and unappealing. You and your lovely companion will only be in your thirties if you do this. That's not so bad, is it? I will get some of my youth back. I'll be back in the same age range as you." He grinned, sank back in his chair, and let out a relieved sigh.

The couple on the sofa said nothing, sitting in deep thought. Their faces held morose looks.

"There really is no way out of this, even as witches, is there?" August looked at Larissa, hoping beyond hope she would think of something."

"Anything we'd do would destroy our path to fulfilling our quest. Just when you think you're a quite powerful witch, there is always someone who is stronger and better, more cunning. It's just the way it goes. Besides, the Glanarium Supremo is the highest law in the Magiverse. It has rules like Mortals have." Larissa stared back at August.

"Tick tock, my pretty friends. Will you tarry here all day and night trying to decide such a simple matter?" Gamal sat up straight and gazed at both of them with a sober look on his face. "Believe it or not, I'm on your side."

"Exactly what does this involve, Mr. Emara?" A dejected expression covered August's face.

"Glad you asked. Mr. Hawthorne, please follow me."

Larissa sat still, watching as August and Gamal slipped toward the hallway. A door opened and closed. She strained her ears, listening for any sound. All was quiet within the house, except for the soft ticking of the clock on the mantel of the fireplace.

Ten years of her life sapped away from her at once. How could this be? The best years of her youth torn from her, all for the sake of a phurba she didn't know how to use. What would she look like ten years older? What would August look like?

At once, she wanted to run away, hide, perhaps return to the super seven crystal cave of her family, her ancestors. What would she do there? Larissa held her face in her hands and wept softly.

Chapter Nine

Gamal led August to one of the rooms and closed the door behind them when they stepped inside. August looked around, taking in the environment. He and the magician stood in what looked like a spare bedroom, complete with an antique bed, and a simple bureau with a matching vanity dresser and mirror. A tall lamp stood in one corner of the room. Only the evening sun streamed through the windows.

"And this is where a lot of transformation will be happening today, Mr. Hawthorne. Are you ready? I am."

"Easy for you to say," August looked toward the door.

"I assure you this will not be a painful process. It will leave you a little fatigued, but you'll recover quickly." Gamal held out his arms toward August. "Shall we begin?"

"Mr. Emara, surely there is something else we can give that you would find equally beneficial. Don't you think?"

"Name three things, and I will gladly reconsider my offer."

August racked his brain, thinking. What would a tantric magician want? What did he or Larissa have to give other than their youth? Of course Gamal would want youth. Everyone always wanted it. He closed his eyes and thought some more. A spell, secret wisdom? Did Jove have anything he might be willing to exchange?

He jumped at the sensation of Gamal grasping his arms at the elbows. His eyes shot wide open in surprise.

"Let us begin, Mr. Hawthorn." Gamal smiled easily. "Please, place your hands around my arms like I've done yours."

Reluctantly, August obeyed. He couldn't fight this situation any longer. A feeling of dread filled his soul.

Gamal closed his eyes and softly spoke an incantation.

"From you to me youth doth pass, my years will slowly dwindle. Round and round, new age is spun, like fiber from a spindle. May age's wisdom serve you well. I made use of mine. May both of us see benefits from this exchange of time."

A surge of energy swirled around August, nearly throwing him into a claustrophobic state. Through closed eyes he saw all the colors of the rainbow. He struggled to catch his breath. An onslaught of dizziness nearly sent him collapsing to the floor. Gamal tightened his grip for assistance and support.

August saw his life passing in front of him, visions of when he was a little boy sitting at Jove's side, the first time he cast a spell that worked, the first girl he ever kissed. A loud roaring filled his ears. Fear gripped him. At once he sensed his former energy being sucked away. The vitality he had moments ago seemed to dull, leaving in its place a new feeling of fatigue.

"We're finished," said Gamal, loosening his grip. "Look in the mirror. He led his guest to the dresser.

The reflection took August completely off-guard, leaving him with a wobbly feeling. His face held a few heavier lines around the mouth and eyes. Youth's softness had faded, leaving a more hardened look, though not unpleasant.

"You age quite nicely." Gamal grinned.

"And you were quite handsome when you were younger." August's words came out in barely a whisper.

"Ah, but I have ten more years to remove. Not meaning to sound too arrogant, but I was quite a nice-looking man in my prime." The magician stared into August's face. "We all long for youth, to capture that part of us once again when we are older and suddenly find ourselves reflecting and longing for the past. But I also have the wisdom of the years I just lost. I didn't forget anything. You will have subtle hints of inner wisdom you didn't have before, as if you lived those lost years but still have yet to live them."

August narrowed his eyes, trying to understand Gamal's words.

"It's rather complicated to explain. Just know that there is good in every season of our lives, and it is up to us to make the best use of it." He led August to the bed and pushed him lightly down. "Sit here for now. I must attend to your companion."

"You mean sap the life right out of her." August mumbled the words under his breath after Gamal closed the door. He swiped a hand over his brow. This would take some getting used to, aging rapidly all at once. What would Fiona and Daisy say if they saw him now?

Gamal stepped up to Larissa. She barely acknowledged him when he offered his hand.

"Come my pretty one. Don't despair. I sense you have wonderful genes, and you'll be beautiful at any age. Your friend did quite well."

"Is there anything else I can offer you, other than years of my life? How would renewed youth make a difference in the long run for you? Haven't those opportunities that occurred in the past long gone?"

"Clever question my dear one, but new opportunities always come up. Being younger, I would simply take advantage at that time. There's never a shortage of things that happen."

"Can I perhaps give you something rare?"

"And what might that be?" The magician smiled. "Fair warning, your companion has already tried this with me a few moments ago. He wasn't successful."

Larissa thought hard before an idea popped into her head. It was a long shot, but it might appeal to Gamal. "Perhaps I can put you in the possession of a conjuring cloth." She smiled. "It would be a wonderful item to possess."

Gamal stepped back, appraising the young woman with interest. "Do you know how to spin this cloth? I've heard of it but have never met anyone who could create one."

"I don't know how to do it myself, but I have an aunt who is learning how. Somehow she inherited the ability, but she hasn't perfected her skill enough to produce a finished piece. Yet. Couldn't this be an IOU of some sort? I'm sure she will learn in time."

"My dear, you make a worthy appeal, but we could be chasing rainbows. Your aunt may never be able to perfect the skill. The fact that she is able to attempt it speaks volumes, though." Gamal's eyes sparkled with delight at the conversation. "She must have angelic traits to even begin to work on something as noble as spinning a conjuring cloth." He studied Larissa harder, reaching out and stroking her hair. "It's possible you may have inherited some of those traits. Have you ever thought about that?"

"At times. But I haven't felt compelled to try, if you want to know the truth. I just learned what Witch Spinners are."

"Keep in mind what I'm telling you. To spin a conjuring cloth is a rare gift given to the lucky few. And you can't teach me such a skill no matter how hard you try."

Larissa cast her gaze to the floor. Her only option of saving herself faded in an instant.

"Come, my dear girl. Follow me." Gamal took her by the hand and pulled her along with him until they reached his bedroom.

A look of horror crossed her face. "Why would we come back here? I can understand you keep certain magical collections stowed away, but why bring me back to your personal space?"

"Because this is where I choose to do my work with you personally. But fear not. My intentions are honorable." Gamal led her near the bed and lifted her face up to his. He stared deeply into her eyes.

Larissa immediately sensed herself being drawn in. Her mind, little by little, went blank and focused on nothing. Previous fear and worries dissipated. She barely heard Gamal softly speak the incantation he used with August. His hands felt warm and strong encircling her face.

When his lips met hers, she didn't feel any immediate emotion but noted the warmth and softness of his kiss. Deep inside something in her rebelled, wanted to pull away, telling her this shouldn't be happening. The determination, eagerness, and steadfastness with which Gamal applied himself slowly and assuredly pulled the years from Larissa.

Like August, she also had closed her eyes and now saw all the colors of the rainbow. Her head seemed to spin, sending her into a bout of dizziness threatening to land her on the floor. Gamal wrapped one arm around her waist, keeping contact with her face using his other hand. The kiss grew more intense with the magician slipping in his tongue and softly placing it on the roof of her mouth.

Larissa's life also played out in her mind, with visions of her as a young girl learning magic from Dorenda, playing in the backyard of Amy and Rick's home, seeing herself at her sixteenth birthday party. A brief darkness filled her mental sight, wiping away the former scenes, and she nearly startled at the image wavering before her eyes.

It was of a woman reaching out to her with open hands. Through the haze she locked her vision onto the woman's eyes. What a beautiful face, if only she could see it more clearly. The woman smiled and beckoned with her hand. Larissa wanted to go, though she couldn't imagine why. Who was this being she viewed through the fog?

As the vision of the strange woman faded, Larissa sensed the years piling themselves on her through Gamal's kiss, one that should have been sweet and desirable, but filled her with a certain bitterness. Her body didn't feel quite as spry as it had moments earlier. The change felt somewhat subtle yet blatant at the same time, leaving her confused and loathing what had happened.

So much had happened in a short amount of time. Her calm normal life had been turned upside down. She had been thrown with a companion who didn't have her best interest at heart, and both had to solve a riddle, a quest that had not been of their making. She let out a sigh. Thinking too much seemed tiresome right now.

"We are done," Gamal whispered in her ear.

Larissa opened her eyes and stared up into the most handsome face. In his thirties, Gamal posed a striking figure. His eyes didn't hypnotize her any longer, but they held an allure, nonetheless.

"You're every bit as beautiful." The magician stroked her cheek. "The most important, you're a smart, kind person, and a more than capable witch. Nothing will decrease your value or contribution to others or your family. You are most worthy."

"Do you always try and flatter women this way?" Larissa's words came out in a tone of great sadness.

"Look in the mirror." Gamal led her to his.

Fearful, Larissa forced a glance at her reflection. She saw the age, a face with youth stripped away. The eyes held not only sadness but a look of fatigue. Her face held a twinge more fullness to it. Her beauty had not faded but deepened with the caresses of age.

"Follow me." Gamal pulled her away from the bed.

"But what about the phurba?" Larissa resisted slightly.

"You will get what I promised you. As cruel as this exchange seemed, I will not be crueller and add dishonesty. But there is one last thing that must be done. Come with me."

"You didn't mention anything about us having to do more than give you the best years of our lives." Her eyes filled with tears.

"My dear, you've completed a hard part. Nothing will change that. But in order for me to give you the phurba, there is one last task. I did not wish to overwhelm you with too much."

He overcame the resistance and led her to the room where August waited. When they entered, he jumped up from the bed. His eyes widened when he saw Larissa. Both stood gazing at each other, speechless.

"I still say you two are the most beautiful people. More beautiful than average couples. But I know this is a shock to your system and psyche. You'll get used to it. As for me, I thank you two from the bottom of my heart.

Larissa spoke to August. "He wants us to do one more thing before he parts with his prized phurba."

August showed a look of pure exasperation. "What on earth could you possibly want from us now? And you didn't mention us having to do anything more to get the phurba. This is cheating."

"My good man, I never cheat. I just make good use of opportunities when they come around. You should learn to do the same." Gamal glanced from Larissa to August.

"Then out with it, Mr. Emara." August's face turned pink "What crazed thing will you have us do now?"

Gamal led Larissa close to August and placed a hand on each of their shoulders. "You two will have an intimate moment together. I determine how and for how long."

August and Larissa's mouths dropped wide open; their eyes filled with horror.

The magician tilted his head back and laughed. "My goodness, you would think this was worse than giving me ten years of your lives. This should be the easy part."

"You're a sick, sordid man, Mr. Emara. Do you know that?" August's face filled with a fury that worried Larissa. He had attitude, but what would he be like filled with pure fiery rage?

"Come, Mr. Hawthorne. Is your mind always leaning in a certain direction? I hope your new-found age cures you of some of that nonsense."

"Just what would you have us do? Perform right before your eyes? Would that make you feel better?" Larissa scowled.

"My dear," replied Gamal, "it would not. I have no desire to watch things of that nature, though I've seen some interesting things in my day. But like I told your friend, what I really do and teach is not about sex as you two think of it. What I teach leaves you with deeper understanding, not just a main end goal. If you'll permit me, I'll tell what you will do."

Gamal pulled Larissa by the arm. "Come. I need you to change into something else. You, Mr. Hawthorne, stay right here."

Larissa's heart pounded so hard in her chest she swore she'd pass out then and there. "Change into what? My clothes are just fine."

"No, they aren't. Trust me on this." The magician whirled around, facing her. "You two must trust me. Everything I do is with a purpose. Contrary to what you might think, it's all noble."

Inside a cozy bathroom, Gamal stood before an ornately carved closet door. The geometric designs in the wood made no connection in Larissa's brain, but she sensed intuitively that they held an ancient metaphysical meaning. She watched intently as he closed his eyes, held out his hands, and mouthed an incantation. Her ears heightened in their sense of hearing, but it was no use. Gamal shielded his words well.

When he finished the spell, a sound of a bell chimed in the air. He flicked out his fingers toward the door and pulled it open. From a shelf he pulled out a red, sheer kaftan, a set of matching lacey high-top panties, and a bra.

"You'll remove your current clothes and put these on. Be quick about it, because I'm sensing Mr. Allwine's urgency to get what he wants, and you are on a deadline." He grinned wryly at Larissa. "As a magician, I'm none too shabby in my intuitive abilities. Meet us back in the room." Gamal left.

Frustrated, Larissa stared at the lacy garments, determining one last time if there was a way to get out of this predicament. Should she summon Dorenda? Even Sophie would do, but the cat had returned to her aunt after leaving Endor. She held her head in her hands for a minute, eyes closed, thinking hard.

The image came to her again, in fuller force this time than the one she had when Gamal stole her youth. The woman's face shone with greater detail, with a beauty that nearly took Larissa's breath away.

"What do you want?"

The lips on the woman moved. "*Do it.*" She held out her hands in an imploring manner. "*Do it now.*"

Larissa wrinkled her brow. She opened her eyes and stared at the red garments. A new resolve flooded her. Her power and will came through in fuller confidence. No matter what, she and August would get through this quest, one way or another. Gamal had already said the task at hand would have the best intentions. He hadn't harmed them thus far.

The loss of youth would sting for a while. Resigned, she slipped off her shoes, stripped, and put on the garments Gamal had materialized. They fit her perfectly. She gazed at herself in the mirror and winced. She'd never worn lingerie like this for anyone, not even Dennis or Daniel, though the thought had crossed her mind more than once.

Slowly, Larissa headed back to the room, embarrassment threatening to send her running to Gamal's bedroom and locking the door, as if it would have done any good. Both men looked at her and stood when she entered. She avoided their gaze, heading straight for the bed and sitting on one corner, hands folded neatly in her lap.

"Ah, Miss Strondovan. Shy, are we?" Gamal's voice rang out in a cheery tone. Larissa didn't answer. "Very well, then. I think she needs a little time to adjust, don't you agree, Mr. Hawthorne?"

Silence.

He turned to August and grinned. "Excuse me, did you hear my question?"

"Um, yes." August shook his head, tearing his gaze away from Larissa.

"Very well," continued Gamal, "you're next Mr. Hawthorne, but you don't need anything quite as lovely as your companion."

August's brows wrinkled. His lips turned down in displeasure. "And what would you mean by that, exactly?"

"I need you to strip." Gamal stepped back. "Now. And only down to your tidy whiteys, or whatever fancy jock attire you have under your clothes."

Horrified, Larissa turned her eyes toward the men. She watched August's face turn bright crimson.

"Come now, Mr. Hawthorne, I hear you have quite a reputation. Stripping down to your briefs should not pose a problem—unless you aren't wearing anything? Of course, I wouldn't think less of you, if that were the case."

August's jaw tightened. Slowly, little by little, he pulled off each piece of clothing. Larissa couldn't help herself but watched with a mix of interest and a twinge of nausea rumbling in her gut. Her head was within seconds of exploding into what she knew would surely be a horrid migraine. And she'd never been plagued by health conditions.

When August stood in nothing but his underwear, Gamal motioned for him to sit on the bed. "Come. I want both of you together. Miss Strondovan, I think you've warmed that corner up enough. Sit closer to Mr. Hawthorne, please."

Reluctantly, Larissa scooted within a few inches of August.

"Very good." Gamal folded his hands together in front of him. "You two will engage in a body massage, thirty minutes each."

The two looked at Gamal, their mouths open in surprise. Their eyes narrowed in anger.

"Nice. You two seem so excited. See, that's progress." Gamal chuckled and continued, "After that, you two will recline on the bed in each other's arms and gaze into the face of your partner. This you will do for seven minutes."

August rubbed his forehead. "Is there a reason for this? Is there something else we can do for you to obtain that infernal phurba?" His lips tightened in frustration. "Maybe wash dishes, do your laundry, clean up your apartment? Anything, really."

Gamal cocked his head to one side, studying the man on the bed. "Tell me, do you two loathe each other that much?"

Larissa and August glanced at each other and back to Gamal.

"Yes. We're not necessarily that fond of one another." Larissa shuddered, emphasizing her dislike. August shook his head.

"How do you plan to be successful in this important quest if you two can barely tolerate each other?"

"We have magic and a purpose. We'll get through." Larissa's face showed cold determination.

"You will find yourselves in some compromising situations. Danger will surround you. Trust and loyalty are everything in this. Never mind love, which wouldn't hurt if you had just a little, at least some compassion on a general level." Gamal opened his hands for emphasis. "You two must develop some respect and sincere care for each other. It's imperative, or you will be destroyed. This is where I come in to help. I have every desire to see you succeed, as well as the Magiverse."

Gamal stood directly in front of the pair. "When I leave this room, you will hear a bell chime. Begin the first exercise at once. It doesn't matter who starts. On the second chime, switch up. On the third, perform the last exercise. I will come in when time is up for everything." He turned around and immediately left August and Larissa alone.

The sound of a chime filled the air.

"Oh, god!" August held his head in his hands. "Ready or not, here we go."

"I'll do you first." Larissa stood up.

"That sounds so kinky." August looked at her, a half-smile on his lips.

"Like you haven't done kinky before? Two women at the same time sounds kinky to me."

August's face colored. "You know nothing about me, so don't even go there."

"I know enough. So be quiet and let's get this done." Larissa had already started massaging August's shoulders and the back of his neck.

"Damn, woman. That feels so good." He closed his eyes and let out a soft groan, craning his neck from one side to the other. "Hey, have you ever given what's-his-name a massage? You know, your old boyfriend, the one we saw at Endor."

Larissa answered with a swift sharp pinch to the back of August's neck.

"Ow!" He turned his gaze to hers, scowling. "It's an honest question, and a fair one. So don't get rough with me."

"If you don't shut up right now, I'll make your massage a living hell."

"Enough, you two. Keep it kind and pleasant, or no phurba for you." A voice bellowed out in the room, but Gamal had not returned.

Larissa stopped. She and August gazed about, startled.

"Hell! He's listening to everything we're saying. Probably watching us, too, the kinky bastard." August let out a yelp when an electrical shock bolted through him. A flame of blue flashed out. The jolt was enough to mean business, but not enough to harm.

"Shh! Quiet. He knows exactly what we're doing and saying. We're not getting out of this, August." Larissa's voice turned into a calm and soothing tone. "Let's just do what we need and move forward. Maybe a good workover will improve your disposition." She smiled sweetly at him.

He let out another groan, eyes closed as a passionate expression filled his face. "I gotta hand it to you. You know how to work those fingers. And might I add, you're really pretty in that red outfit." When Larissa paused, he took the opportunity and stretched out on the bed. "I also want to say how pretty you look when we have dinner. Great taste in clothes and jewelry." August opened his eyes and winked at her.

"You're so tight." Her fingers moved over his arms and legs. "Just let yourself go." She spent the next several moments rubbing in circles, clockwise, on his abdomen. "Your hair is beautiful. Thick, and a beautiful honey-golden color." When her hands landed on his thighs, Larissa noticed out of the corner of her eye that August had responded in his own way to her touch. Everything she needed to know showed in a strain against his briefs.

She averted her eyes. "I've been meaning to tell you how I admire the way you conduct yourself in front of others, how well-spoken and regal you are."

"Grandpa Jove taught me well." His lips pulled into a lazy smile. Without instruction, he flipped over so Larissa could massage his back.

Her eyes took in the sight of his skin and muscles. August was a beautiful man, without a doubt, age and all. The thought of what they had to give up set in full force once again, and she focused with all her might to try and shove the depression of it all to the farthest recesses of her mind.

The sound of a chime filled the room.

"Your turn." August sat up and slid off the bed.

"Any way you want me?" Larissa asked, staring into his face.

"You any way is beautiful to me." August's eyes shot wide open. He glanced around in confusion. Gathering his wits about him, he cleared his throat and added, "Any position you want to start with is fine." He motioned for her go lay on the bed.

Larissa lay on her back and closed her eyes. August positioned his hands around her face, massaging gently over the cheek bones and forehead, followed by the sides and back of her neck. He worked his way down to her feet, moving in the same manner she had done with him earlier. When the bell sounded again, August had finished rubbing over her back and calves.

"You ready for this next part?" He asked her.

"As ready as I'll ever be, I guess."

Both of them lay on the bed, propped up on their elbows, staring at each other.

"I don't think we're doing this quite right," said Larissa.

"Maybe like this?" August reached out and took her in his arms, pulling her close.

"That's it." Larissa blinked a few times and landed her gaze on his face.

August stared at the woman in his arms. He hadn't found touching the soft skin and gazing on her striking form totally unpleasant at all. She was truly prettier than Fiona and Daisy. Her regal manner and witchcraft skills added to the new appeal. For the first time he wondered why the feeling of loathing had consumed him before. She was a witch, bewitching, skilled, smart, and bold. At once Fiona and Daisy and all the women he'd had before paled in comparison.

Larissa basked in an overwhelming sense of warmth, a warmth and strength that exuded from August's strong embrace. His face radiated elegance and handsomeness. He bore his royal heritage well when the need called for it. His magical abilities could always be refreshed and practiced. Is this what women felt when they were with him in his bed? The ones Sophie, her familiar, had mentioned?

"I see you survived." Gamal entered the room, a wide smile on his lips. "Feel better, my friends?"

The pair broke free from their gazes and stared at the magician standing at the foot of the bed.

"Do we get our phurba now?" asked August.

"Please tell me you thought of other things during these exercises, and not on the phurba."

"We managed, Mr. Emara. But we really need to get the phurba and go. Perhaps we should be grateful you even considered giving it up at all."

"And perhaps that phurba was never mine to keep?" Gamal angled his head, eyes fixed on the couple.

Larissa sat up, her face contorted with surprise. "What exactly do you mean?"

"Come. Follow me." Gamal turned around when he reached the door. "Oh, you may dress into your regular clothes. Meet me in my bedroom when you're done."

August and Larissa met Gamal once again in his private quarters. He pulled out the collection of phurbas he'd shown them earlier and pulled out the one made of labradorite. "You will give this one to Mr. Allwine." He handed it to Larissa. "And this one, you'll keep for yourself to use when the time comes to fight the forces of darkness." He stared at the two. "And the time will come. Just know that."

The couple watched as Gamal headed to a corner, removed a tall standing lamp, and pulled up a door in the floor. August raised an eyebrow and exchanged glances with his companion.

"Here you are, my friends. The phurba you will not, under any circumstance, give to Mr. Allwine. He has no business with it." Gamal opened a black velvet box. Inside lay a triple Grade A phruba made of labradorite.

"But won't he know?" asked Larissa.

"Remember. He's not a witch. Other than creating passkeys, he has no magical powers at all. How would he know?" Gamal stared back at the perplexed look on Larissa and August's faces. "Listen, he's an avid collector as much as I am. The only difference, I use what I collect. He likes to think he has power by ownership. Ownership may be nine tenths of the law, but that's as far as it goes, really."

"Mr. Emara," said August, "thank you for giving us what we need. You've, in essence, saved our lives. For that we express our gratitude." He bowed his head in respect toward the magician.

"You have been entrusted to save all our lives. Your task is great. The one who gave me this phurba left it to me for safekeeping until I could give it to you, the rightful fighters of darkness. It will make sense to you the more you progress on this quest. I am not at liberty to say much of anything else."

"Very well, Mr. Emara," answered Larissa. "We thank you."

Gamal escorted his guests to the front door. "I am always at your service if you need any guidance."

When Larissa and August disappeared from sight, Gamal returned to his room and replaced the standing lamp over the space where the prized phurba had been removed. An apparition appeared before him. He didn't seem surprised in the least upon viewing the astral image.

"To what do I owe this wondrous visit, my good lady. And might I add, you're as ravishing as ever."

The lady smiled graciously in return. "You always were one to flatter, Gamal." The expression on her face turned sober quickly. "You did give it to them, didn't you?"

"Of course, my good lady. You entrusted me with it, and I delivered. But I do wish you would tell me more about where you are and any information that I could use to help. I sense you're in distress."

"Knowing the phurba is in the correct hands relieves me more than anything. All secrets will be revealed in good time, dear Gamal. And might I add, you're looking rather dashing tonight."

"Gamal blushed. "Thank you."

The lady quickly vanished from Gamal's sight. Inside a room far away from sight, she sat back on her soft cushions and spent time between brooding and celebrating August and Larissa's new possession. "They must guard it carefully and use it wisely," she said softly to herself.

Chapter Ten

Remington Allwine beamed with glee, turning the labradorite phurba over and over in his hands. Flashes of green, gold, and teal shone as the light hit different areas of the stone. He caressed the surface, cooing with admiration. He viewed Larissa and August.

"This piece is more magnificent than I ever imagined. You paid a price for this, didn't you? You look different than before."

"Thank you for stating the obvious, Mr. Allwine," said August. Irritation filled his voice. "I think we're ready for a passkey to the temple of Hathor. How long will it take you to make one?"

"As you wish. Keys are made on location." Remington excused himself and disappeared for a moment. On returning, he stated, "Follow me, please."

August and Larissa followed their host through his apartment, down a hallway, and to a door at the end. A flight of narrow stairs led down to a dimly lit garage. Remington motioned for them to enter the back seat of a limousine.

Following August's command, Larissa entered first. When he settled in beside her, Remington closed the door and locked it from the outside.

"It's pitch black in here," said Larissa.

"Yes, is it—and watch where you put your hand." August grasped her wrist, which had somehow found its way to the upper part of his thigh.

"Sorry. I can't see a thing."

"Stay put and don't move. Our hem-netjer doesn't intend for us to see where he's going. He mentioned this temple being in a secret place."

"The only reason I'm half-way trusting him is because of your father. Otherwise I'd think he's a cook and a fraud."

"Come now, Miss Strondovan, do you think that's a nice thing to say about someone who is allowing you admittance to the deity of your choice?"

Remington's voice cracked through a speaker in the back area of the car.

August and Larissa jumped at the sound.

"You can hear us?" Larissa frowned.

"Of course, my good friend. As you have quickly discovered, I have blackened the windows in the passenger area. Everyone experiences this who goes to my temples."

"Has anyone ever not made it to the temples?" August asked. He grunted when Larissa elbowed him in the side.

"I hope you're merely joking with that question, Mr. Hawthorne," said Remington.

"Trust me. I'm not joking in the least, and I mean no offense, either."

"You gave me what I asked for. I will give you the key to Hathor. I keep my promises."

Larissa let out a sharp squeal as the car lurched forward. When Remington made a sharp turn, she nearly tipped over into August's lap. Instead of a rebuke, he slid his arm around her shoulders, holding her close to him for support as the car moved forward several more seconds, ending with a few sharp turns, and continued onward.

Without warning, a faint glow of light lit up the back area where they sat. August looked at his companion in surprise. She placed a finger on her lips, indicating he remain silent. Closing her eyes, Larissa mouthed an incantation. The windows lost their opaque blackness. The glass swirled with tones of light and dark grey, expanding and retracting until they allowed a colorless view of the outside surroundings.

Remington continued driving, oblivious to what was happening in the back of his vehicle. August clapped a hand over his mouth. He stared at the woman beside him. She smiled back. With a finger, she wrote in the air a message to him in green light: *One way mirror.* The pair continued the ride in silence. Larissa made mental notes on where they were heading.

The area they were in was more desolate. Buildings had become sparse. The general population number had dwindled. Businesses were scarce. People didn't gather in large numbers like they did in the more populated areas. Traffic didn't clog the streets. Marketplaces didn't exist here.

Remington turned down a street and drove to a building that looked much like a lonely old abandoned store. A curtain blocked the front window. The simple wooden door had curtains covering the pane of glass in it. He continued around the side and to the back. A black garage door opened, and he slowly maneuvered the vehicle inside. The door rolled down immediately.

"Play it cool," August mouthed to Larissa. She nodded in agreement.

"We are here, my friends." Remington opened the back door of the car, smiling amiably.

August slid out, followed by Larissa. The garage to this building was every bit as dark, dingy, and mysterious looking as the one at Remington's apartment. How could a non-assuming building be home to deities and their respective temples? Something didn't make sense.

"Follow me. Stay close behind. Do not wander off anywhere without permission." Remington viewed his guests with a stern gaze.

"This looks like nothing more than an old building. Where would a person wander off, pray tell?" August looked askance at the hem-netjer.

"Has anyone ever taught you that looks can be deceiving, Mr. Hawthorne?" The priest grinned. "Don't let my humble building fool you in the least." He motioned for August and Larissa to follow.

The three headed toward a door, climbed a set of long narrow dark stairs, and passed through another door at the top.

Inside, the building didn't look like anything out of the ordinary. Across from the door appeared a large open room. Had it ever been used for anything? Other doors could be seen several feet down the hall.

"This way, please." Remington beckoned his guests toward the left of the door from where they emerged.

Larissa inhaled deeply. Somewhere in the overwhelming scent of musty air, she detected the unmistakable tinge of an exotic incense or resin she couldn't readily identify. Where did the other trace of odor come from? "Is this building used for anything else?" she asked.

Remington turned around toward his guest. "Anything else?" He laughed. "Nothing other than what it was designed to do. The façade is nothing more than what it is. A cover, a disguise, really. It has changed over the years due to wear from the elements. But this place is secret. On the outside, an ordinary shop or office building. On the inside, however, something different altogether."

August and Larissa exchanged glances, narrowing their eyes at each other in confusion. They said nothing else but followed their host to the opposite end of the hall. Remington turned to the left side of the wall and stopped in front of a large embroidered tapestry with a large figure of Baphomet.

On the four corners gleamed golden ankhs fashioned from metallic threads. The work of art held a certain charged energy. The androgyne goat gazed straight on at the viewers. On Remington's face, the characteristic smile lit his countenance.

"I take it you know the true meaning of Baphomet?" he asked.

"The truly initiated or witches who follow the path of light see this creature as representing the ultimate universal balance of opposites, complete unity, a symbol of astral light, the basis of magic and resulting enlightenment."

"Did you memorize that out of a book you read?" August lifted his brow in amazement at Larissa, grinning lightly.

Remington chuckled. "Do you know something different, Mr. Hawthorne. Perhaps you could . . . oh say . . . enlighten us?" He tilted his head back and let out a laugh that filled the hall.

August squared up his shoulders. "Speaking of opposites, this creature also has its opposite where symbolism is concerned. It's use and understanding dates back to the Knights Templar, who learned from the Arabians, according to history. The black magicians of Atlantis perverted its meaning for their own gain, greed, and power. That has continued through time, resulting in many seeing this human goat as the figure of Satan. One only has to see an inverted pentagram to fully realize which ceremony our so-called Baphomet is being used."

Larissa's eyes widened at August's retort.

"Well, Mr. Hawthorne, I'm impressed. Between the two of you there is wisdom. Very comforting to know. But let us proceed. Time is running out. Hathor grows impatient."

He turned toward the wall. When he touched the tapestry, the fabric rippled, a chill filled the air, and the flame on top of the goat's head burst into life, sizzling tendrils of fire dancing, wavering back and forth. The goat inhaled, exhaled, blinked it eyes, and sat still. Larissa and August stared at it, mesmerized

Remington grasped one side of the artwork. With one swift motion of his hand, he sent it sailing to one side, revealing a carved wooden door.

"Hathor is down there?" Larissa asked softly.

"Every deity is down there, my dear lady." Remington turned around, his eyes gleaming with pride. "You are about to behold a wondrous vision. Only those who would dare ask for a chance to speak to a deity would come to me and end up here."

"And once again, how do we gain a key? You still have not answered that." August shifted from one foot to another, visibly impatient.

"All will be revealed in good time. You will see." Remington's face sobered. "Have you thought about what you wish to ask Hathor?"

Larissa and August exchanged glances.

"We have our question ready," said Larissa. Her face held a steely expression, with set mouth and flashing eyes.

"Very good. only one question can be asked to the deity, you know. Make it good." He smiled and opened the door.

August quickly showed Larissa a look of exasperation, shaking his head with a knowing look in his eye.

"Are you coming?" Remington stopped and turned around, viewing the pair with a stern eye.

"We're right behind you, sir," replied August.

The narrow staircase of stone led down to the bowels of the building. At the end, a soft rosy light glowed. Larissa and her companion used the walls for support, stepping gingerly as they descended. When they came to the main landing at the end, Remington stopped, allowing his guests to catch up. From where they stood, intersecting hallways stretched right and left, with another set of stairs continuing forward from the landing.

"We have seventy rooms. This covers the major Egyptian and Greco-Roman deities. There are three intersecting horizontal hallways with ten rooms on either side. We are at the first set of halls. To reach Hathor, we must go to the last intersection."

August stroked his chin in thought. "This seems so small to hold such a large number. Temples are usually elaborate, elegant, mysterious, filled with symbolic art."

Larissa lightly punched August's arm. "Aren't you forgetting that we do our work in small rooms? Our bedrooms. In your case at Katharta Castle, you have spell rooms. No offense, but I'm sure they aren't elaborate. They allow you to do your work with the tools needed. That's it. Nothing more, nothing less."

Her companion scowled.

"Exactly, my dear lady," said Remington. "Please don't forget, my friends, that it's not the elaborateness of a temple or even the things in it. It's what's inside you. Your own divinity inside that desires to be unleashed once awakened. If you are as advanced as you claim, second ring magic, and maybe third, is what you use. Am I not correct?"

"You mean changing our inner nature to affect the outer world, and then at best, calling on etheric beings or assistance to work with worldly and personal realities." August shot a smug glance in Larissa's direction.

Remington's face brightened. "Exactly. Mr. Hawthorne, sometimes you amaze me."

"And just what is that supposed to mean?" August clenched a fist.

"Nothing more than a feeling I get when I'm around you. Your lady friend seems vibrant, a learned witch, a scholar when it comes to magic and the supernatural. You, on the other hand, possess some knowledge. But I strongly suggest you put your talents to use. You do have them." Remington winked at August and continued.

Firelit lanterns along the walls burned with hot orange flames, casting eerie shadows on the white marble floors. Along the ceiling, illuminated by a special lighting system, a backdrop of indigo showed shimmering constellations, interspersed with colorful mystic symbols. The walls held more symbols and flattened scrolls with strange writing within gilded frames.

"This is rather amazing, the more I see of it." Larissa stopped briefly to admire one of the pictures on the wall.

"I have enjoyed working in this space since the moment I started my mission." Remington also paused, gazing up at the ceiling.

"You are not a witch, Mr. Allwine, but do you study metaphysics in any way? Are you a member of a hermetic order?" August faced Remington. "I would think someone with your job might dabble in the alchemical arts."

"I am a seeker, Mr. Hawthorne, but again, I have no supernatural powers like you and your lovely friend. All I can do is continue my work. The only power I have is to make the passkeys."

They reached the last intersecting hallway and Remington turned to the right and continued walking. The doors to the temples appeared made of bronze. On each one, an embossed figure of the deity for that temple shone on the dark surface.

"There are no doorknobs," Larissa said.

"Good observation," Remington answered. "Thus the reason for my special passkeys. The creation of these keys is the only so-called magic I do. The key I create for a person is used only by them the first time to enter the temple. Once it's activated, it disappears."

"No person uses the same key twice?" asked August.

"Not at all, Mr. Hawthorne. Every key created, even for the same temple, is different."

"As you'll see, the key is not a physical key at all." Remington closed his eyes a moment, savoring his own words. "A beautiful system, one as old as time. It's said that the gods of Olympus created the system."

"Or perhaps some advanced beings we like to call extraterrestrials? You know the ancient gods and goddesses were most likely high-level space creatures." August grinned at Remington.

"You could be right about that, sir." The hem-netjer grinned back. "But the essence of those beings and their wisdom is housed in this space we're walking through now."

When the three reached the last door at the end of the hall, Remington stopped. "We're here. Hathor awaits." He pointed to the door.

Larissa moved in closer, eyeing the embossed image of a cow's head topped with a magnificent set of horns. She nodded slowly. "That's the symbol of Hathor, indeed."

Remington turned and viewed the pair waiting with him. "Are you really ready? What you're about to do is quite important to your mission. Remember, you only get one question."

"Is there a time-limit on how long we can be in there?" asked August. "There seems to be a beat-the clock aspect to everything we do, lately."

"Oddly enough, no." Remington wrinkled his brow. "But here's what's interesting. Once the deity is finished providing its answers or wisdom, you're truly done. They will not speak or add anything more. There is no reason to remain any longer in the temple. The time aspect takes care of itself."

"Shall we begin, Mr. Allwine?" asked Larissa. "We don't need to take up any more of your time, and we don't want ours to run out when we're right here at the door." She smiled, swiping away a lock of her hair that had fallen out of place.

"As you wish." Remington motioned for August and Larissa to stand back a little so he could have some space. He turned toward the door, holding out both hands, palms upward. "*Magnum digni enomu ven. Pro lavelum domini sum.*"

Larissa and August watched with amazement. In Remington's hands a broken purple outline of a key shone, sparkling in his hands. The purple changed to green and on to gold, leaving a solid key. He held it in front of the face on the door. A rush of wind surrounded them, dissipating as quickly as it came. Larissa shivered. With a soft swoosh, the door opened a few inches.

"You may pass, my friends." Remington stepped aside. "Here I will leave you, only to return when you are finished."

The pair said nothing, glancing at each other before August ventured the first step inside. Once they stood past the door, it swished shut with a startling rapid speed, leaving them trapped inside a room twenty-five by fifteen feet.

In the corners stood four large fluted columns of malachite. The floor shone of polished stones of picture jasper, interspersed with green Russian serpentine, reminiscent of a field. An arched ceiling, sectioned with beams of copper, had its quadrants painted deep navy. Faceted quartz crystal orbs, resembling stars, had been embedded into the backdrop of blue, shooting out flashes of light that gave one the impression of a clear, starry night.

It was the statue against the far wall that sent them in a state of awe. A twelve-foot-tall Hathor stood gazing straight ahead. The lower body, resembling a human woman, was made of polished ebony, with a robe of gold. In one hand she held a shimmering golden ankh. Her headdress consisted of two long shiny black onyx cow horns with a stone sphere of flawless bright carnelian resting between them.

The most striking aspect was the face, which showed that of a cow with large intent eyes. Something within them held a soulful look. Her feet were bare, and she sat in a simple throne of green moss agate stone.

Larissa's voice came out in a whispered hiss. "We didn't ask how to get out of here once we got in."

"Nope. Forgot that part. But I'm sure our deity will be only too kind to show us the way." August eyed the statue with wonder. Grasping Larissa's hand, he walked slowly toward Hathor, never taking his gaze away.

"Truly beautiful," murmured Larissa.

Both she and August stood fully in front of the deity, marveling in the simple construction and quality craftsmanship that someone had gone to great lengths to create.

"No, don't . . .!" August cried out, attempting to intervene. Too late.

On impulse, Larissa had reached out and touched the ankh. Before their eyes the statue came to life. Hathor stepped from the throne. The body diminished in size to a six-foot tall human. The cow face slowly morphed into that of a dark-skinned woman with the most flawless skin and shining eyes. Her cosmetically adorned face showed brightly painted eyes and a soft pearly sheen illuminating the cheeks. A light smile rested on her pink glossy lips. Her ears remained shaped like those of a cow, but with the skin of a human. Simple large bright blue turquoise studs pierced the top of each ear. Rows of thick black braids draped from her head, flowing onto the golden robe over her long tunic-style dress. The beauty of the goddess left Larissa and her companion breathless.

"To what do I owe this visit?" said Hathor.

August found his voice first. "O great one, with beauty and brilliance rivaling a thousand suns, we are two humble witches on an important mission. We wish to seek your advice."

"Then state your business, please." Hathor's voice was straight-forward, but not unkind. The warmth brewing behind her eyes and the softness of a smile lingering on her face disarmed the seekers, who had anticipated a haughty and stern demeanor.

"We need to know . . ." August's expression went blank. For once, he stumbled in his verbiage.

He and Larissa had been so busy completing tasks for Remington and Gamal, trying to beat timeframes, that they had failed to reach an agreement on what would be asked of Hathor.

Hathor studied August with an intent gaze, licking her lower lip with a certain air of impatience.

Larissa spoke up, "O Great One, we need to know more about the strange beautiful woman who comes to us in visions. She seems in earnest, like there's an important message that needs be told. Her eyes are full and imploring. We can't help but suspect she's someone of great importance. She keeps showing herself."

August's eyes popped wide open. His mouth opened in protest but shut tight when Hathor spoke.

"Dear girl, your forbear wishes to make herself known. She's seen the sun and moon of many days and nights, far more than an average person." Hathor's face clouded a moment in thought. "She's hiding something of great value. As always with those having a thing of great value, someone is after it. They have limited her power, but not totally."

The goddess placed an arm around Larissa and one around August. "That dark force is after you. Be vigilant. Be wary. It follows you, seeks to destroy you. There must be unity. The scattered pieces must be found and put together again." She nodded toward Larissa. "Those pieces belong to you, my dear, and they will help prevail against the darkness."

A smile lit up Hathor's face. "And that is all I can offer."

August and Larissa stood silent, stunned at the deity's words. A rush of air passed through the temple, and Hathor motioned toward the door. "You must go now. Find the pieces."

The door had opened, showing a glimpse of the hallway. Just as the pair turned to leave, the deity detained August briefly. "I also know what is in your heart and what you strongly desire, young man." Her lips pulled into a sly grin. Two small polished copper mirrors with bone handles in the shape of her likeness materialized. She handed them to August. "You will figure out what to do with these," she whispered in his ear.

Remington came within seconds down the hallway and escorted his guests to the limousine. "I take it all went well with Hathor?" His voice rang out in the back. Larissa had invoked her spells again, to the oblivion of the man driving.

"We made it out alive. That's all that counts," August replied.

"Come now. You sound like it was a most harrowing experience." Remington chuckled. "Everyone makes it out alive. Did she give good advice? Anything that I can help with? Perhaps expand on regarding her suggestions?"

"She covered everything beautifully. I don't think anyone could outdo her, really." Larissa glanced over at August, shaking her head with exasperation. He acknowledged her with a light smile.

"Very well, my friends. Please know that, although we seemed to hit a rocky spot working out the details, I am truly at your service."

The hem-netjer dropped them off back to their hotel after a long ride in silence. When he returned to his apartment, he walked to the hiding place to where the prized phurba lay hidden and removed it from a special storage box.

"You are most beautiful. Those two witches may not have shared anything with me, but I'll get the information I need one way or another. I have sources." His eyes shone as he rubbed his finger over the surface like he'd done before. He stared long and hard at the piece, turning it in all directions just to see the different colors glinting off the stone. Remington murmured to himself. "The top for blessings. The bottom for ridding the enemy. And the enemy is light. It's harsh. It burns. There's no place to hide in the light."

He gripped the piece tighter in his hands. "In darkness there is peace, a place to hide and ponder. Darkness cloaks and protects. It's comforting. And there is truth in darkness." He smiled.

The happy expression faded from his face. For some inexplicable reason, the phurba grew hot between his fingers, the heat growing so intense, sparks emanated from it. Remington yelled out in pain and closed his eyes in a blinding flash of light. The prized phurba fell from his hands, crashing to the hardwood floor, shattering in pieces. What had once been a shimmering fantastic piece of crafted perfection now shone black and pitted. The phurba was destroyed forever.

In place of the broken pieces, tendrils of smoke appeared, swirling, swaying, and thickening until the astral image of Gamal Emara appeared.

"Good evening, my dear Mr. Allwine. And how are things going for such a wonderful hem-netjer as yourself?"

"What do you want Gamal? I demand to know what happened to the phurba. One minute it's fine. The next it's—"

"You were never to have had such a powerful tool as the phurba, a special one in particular."

"But you made a deal with those two who worked on my behalf. You cheated them and me. That's dishonorable. It goes against common decency."

Gamal laughed. "Like you care about common decency. That phurba was only intended for the right people who will use it when the time comes. And if my instincts are right, that day is coming soon. You'll no more gain or wield power then than you do now. You're barely worthy enough to do what you earned through birth only."

"Then where is the real phurba, Gamal, you cheating snake?" Remington clenched his fists and glowered at the magician.

"It's with the rightful owner. Better than being with a fraud like you." With these last words, Gamal vanished. Along with him, the remnants of the phurba vanished too.

The hem-netjer sat on one of the fine chairs in his room, brooding. A chance at true power had eluded him. How would he explain what happened to the ones who were counting on him? Remington narrowed his eyes and cursed. There would be payback. Details remained murky, but there would be hell to pay for what happened.

***

August sat alone in his room after he and Larissa had eaten dinner. He had bathed in a special fleur de sel salt bath to cleanse not only his body, but his aura as well. With deep meditation and reception to psychic messages, he opened himself up to the impressions entering his mind. Taking note of them, he stepped out of the tub and dried off.

Laying a dry towel on the bathroom floor, he gathered his ritual equipment for this ceremony, placed everything in proper position, and lowered himself into a lotus position in front of a mirror he'd conjured up on his own. A large pillar candle burned. Beside the mirror sat a small bottle of personally crafted ginseng and celery oil, along with a tiny bottle filled with some of the same oil.

In the candlelight, he viewed his shadowy reflection, noting the hair hanging in damp ringlets around his face and shoulders.

The musculature he once had showed softer beneath the skin, less pronounced. He gazed at his face, wincing at the harder lines and the twinges of fullness around the jaws. Vitality had not been what it used to be. His balls cupped a flaccid cock. Quietly he plucked up the tip, working the sensitive flesh between his thumb and forefinger. August smiled, concentrating his mind on the sensation and the way he felt as he slowly touched himself.

From the main bottle of oil, he poured a generous amount into his right palm and worked the solution into his skin, feeling himself become erect. He closed his eyes, working himself with more conviction. Images flooded his mind. Concentrating on those, he kept working his flesh, focusing on keywords that had been given to him by divine instruction.

A light breeze filled the room, sending the flame on the candle gyrating in seductive motions. Shadows flickered and danced on the walls. August glanced at the mirror, focusing harder on the images and words, the spell, feeling with full force the ache in his cock, a tightening in his balls. With a firmer grip, he rubbed and pressed in those erogenous areas, sending his body into an exploding orgasm.

He rested his head back, groaning softly, letting his body ride out the spasms overcoming him. The images dimmed; the words receded to the corners of his mind. With one finger, he gathered up some of his ejaculate and added it to the tiniest bottle. After quickly topping it with a small cork, he gently tipped it back and forth so his essence mixed with the oil.

Using his other hand, he rubbed the remaining fluids of passion into his own skin. The first part of this spell ritual was completed. Whether or not the rest of it would work left him a little nervous and trembling slightly.

This would be one of the most profound things he'd ever done. It could work wonderfully or backfire with dire consequences. August cleaned up the bathroom and proceeded to prepare the main room of his quarters for the final part of the ritual.

Chapter Eleven

Larissa sat on the edge of the bed next to August in his hotel room. The scent of sage filled the air. Two large candles burned on each nightstand on both sides of the bed. "Are you sure this is going to work? And where did these come from?" Her brows wrinkled in skepticism as she moved a finger over the small object in her hand, studying the intricate details.

August grinned over at her. "A gift from someone special. I've spent time on learning this ritual. But I need your full cooperation."

"And just what do I have to do? It won't be too strange or obscene, will it?"

"We do what needs to be done, or none of this will work."

She rubbed her chin in thought. "Any repercussions that you know of?"

"No. I tried getting the answer to that too. But that doesn't mean anything. Even if there is no direct backfiring, there is always human nature, revenge." August grimaced. "That's how that whole thing goes, you know?"

Larissa nodded. "Okay, here's to trying. Right?"

August got up from the bed and switched off the lights to the room, leaving nothing but the candlelight filtering across the walls.

He said, "I've done the first part. It's you who will undergo the second part. After that, we take these and stare into them, like scrying when we use a crystal ball." He held up one of the tiny mirrors Hathor gave him. "And it's very important that we focus hard on our desire, the one we discussed when you first came in. Got it?"

"I've got it." She watched August move in beside her.

"We need to strip down to our underwear, at least. Unless you want to do this nude, which allows the clearest transfer of energy."

"We'll keep our underclothes on. I'd feel better."

"I'm going to put some oil on you, a special one that I made up for this ceremony."

"What's in it?"

"Just a base carrier oil and some ginseng and celery essential oils."

"That's it? Anything else?" Larissa stared intently at August.

With a straight face, he answered, "That's it. Just the things we need to get what we want." He cleared his throat. But I have to put this special oil on two areas."

"Like where?" Her eyes widened with uneasiness.

"The top of your pubic area and on each breast."

"That's three places."

August tilted his head, eyeing Larissa. "You know what I mean. Breasts count as one unit."

"You have to do it? Or could I just do it myself?"

"I have to do it. It's an energy transfer that occurs from me touching you. After that, there is only our joining hands while holding the mirrors Hathor gave us.

She let out a sigh of resignation. "All right then. Let's do this. I just hope you're not leading me on."

The pair stripped down to their undergarments, pulled down the bedspread and sheets and slipped in beside each other.

"I'll make this quick." August opened the tiny bottle of oil, tipped it, and applied half of it on Larissa's breasts, slipping his hands under her bra. How soft her skin was, supple, resilient.

"You can go a little faster, if you like." Larissa's faced showed a trace of annoyance.

After rubbing a few more times on the second breast, August applied the remainder of the oil on the top of Larissa's pubic area, moving diligently.

"Don't go down any further." She moved his hand back up at little.

"Sorry. It's a little dark in here."

"I'm sure you're used to finding things in the dark."

"Listen, smarty, don't blame me because the ritual calls for certain things. I'm just doing my job." August had moved his lips close to Larissa's ear.

"I get it. Are you finished with that oil? This whole thing is making me nervous."

"I am." August placed the empty bottle on the nightstand. He took up his mirror and watched Larissa position hers. They joined hands and gazed into their mirrors. He uttered the following incantation: "*Venimus ab iuventus. Non revertetur ad iuventus.*"

The flames from the candles had grown abnormally brighter after August's spell. Their reflections were a little easier to see. Larissa let out a whimper. August groaned. The grip of their hands tightened.

Still they didn't remove their faces from the front of Hathor's mirrors.

A tingling sensation filled both bodies, burning into intense heat the stronger it evolved. Despite the discomfort ripping through them, August and Larissa breathed heavily, forcing themselves to keep their eyes on their reflections. A bright flash of light emanated from the mirrors. Larissa let out a quick scream. August jumped and grunted. At once, they dropped back on the pillows and sheets, closing their eyes, losing consciousness. The mirrors fell beside them and vanished.

***

Gamal Emara stood looking at himself in the bathroom mirror. "Something is happening." He glanced toward the astral projection of the lady.

"That's what you get when you take advantage of situations. I told you where to find the phurba, how to hide it, and to whom it goes. You did well until you simply couldn't resist temptation."

"Ah, my dear lady, I meant no harm. Can you blame me?"

"Yes, I do blame you. You are a worthy tantric magician from a noble line who practices your art. Very skilled and clever. Youth is tempting, but how could you forget the beauty of age? Humans may not look their best, but their mind and experience are most worthy."

"Nobody cares about a beautiful mind." Gamal frowned in the lady's direction. "I had to have that one last opportunity. You must admit I was quite the looker, yes?"

"A handsome person is a looker when he makes the right decisions, does the right things at the right time. You took advantage and fell in a moment of weakness."

Gamal let out a groan and shuddered. He grasped the countertop of the bathroom sink struggling to steady himself. In a quick fit of nausea, he vomited. The lady looking on grimaced but didn't break her gaze.

"Let it all out, Gamal. And don't transgress again."

The magician gasped, taking in a deep breath. "I think you're right about that." He sputtered out the words between hanging on to the counter, gagging, and taking hard breaths.

"One more thing you must promise me."

"And that is?" Gamal wiped his mouth on a towel.

"You are not to harm those two. You are not to exact revenge."

"What can you do? I get a strong sense that you can't even save yourself from whatever it is that has you. I sense it, feel it. Won't you please tell me?"

"Ah, my dear Gamal." The lady smiled. "There are limitations, and then there are limitations. I'll leave it at that. Don't try and cross me. Remember, we're on the same team."

"You have my word. I did rather like those two." Gamal looked in the mirror and groaned at the reflection of his former age. "It was good while it lasted, even if for a very short time."

***

Larissa and August sat in her hotel room early the next morning, enjoying breakfast via room service. Her face held its former youthful glow and bright beauty. She stared at August. Though he was comely in his older age, his young visage held the handsome good looks she found difficult to merely dismiss and place in the farthest recesses of her mind.

He was radiantly attractive. And why did she hurry him along the night before when he clearly didn't mind touching her, acting like he relished lingering longer over her more private areas? His fingers were strong and sure in their movements, not rough or careless. Heat radiated through her cheeks, filling them with a pink glow at the thoughts racing through her head.

"I'm just going to say it," said August, placing his coffee cup on a saucer. "We look fantastic. Do we not?" His lips pulled into a wide smile.

"We do." Larissa smiled back. "How did you pull that off? What a feat of magic. To reverse a powerful spell cast by such a magician as Gamal Emara? Ballsy, to say the least."

August swallowed down a bite of toast. "It was ballsy. I'd be damned if I was going to let that Gamal guy screw us over. A Hawthorne will not be taken advantage of."

"But how did you find the spell? It's not like you go around using magic all the time. I've yet to see any gallant display of it—until now, anyway."

He looked indignant. "You're a magic snob. Anyone ever tell you that?"

She cast him an expression of amusement and sipped her coffee.

"Heavy-duty research and strong desire didn't hurt. But I did it. That's what counts," continued August.

"You put something else in that oil. I felt it. It tickled a little when it touched my skin. I demand to know everything that was in that concoction you used."

"You demand?" August laughed. "You get more hoity-toity by the second. I'm not telling because I already told you."

Larissa shot out a bright orange current from her finger, smiling with satisfaction when it landed squarely on the young man's hand.

"Damn!" The forkful of eggs benedict dropped back on the plate with a loud garish clang. He glared at her. "Fine. Along with the carrier and essential oils was another ingredient from moi, yours truly. Consider it a personal touch." Grinning, August added, "Didn't mind a bit. It was for a worthy cause."

She narrowed her eyes, lips parting in horror.

He leaned in. "Listen, don't get your knickers all knotted up. It was part of the ritual. I had no other choice."

Her face lightened with a slight grimace. "You'd be wise to step up to the plate more often than you do. I hope you have as much strong desire to complete this goose chase we're on so we can get on with our lives. And I can get my family back."

She looked at her companion from across the small table where they ate. "That's what Hathor meant by the broken pieces, isn't it? I need to find my family and bring us all together again."

"Sounds that way to me." August buttered a biscuit, slathered it with jam, and took a bite.

"We have to talk to the lady."

"And that's another thing I want to ask. Who in the hell is this lady you mentioned to Hathor? I've not seen a lady anywhere."

Larissa fluttered her lashes and grinned. "You see me every day."

"Oh tosh!" August put his biscuit down and glared at her. "You really try my patience, you know that?"

"And you mine. But remember what our goddess told us. Unity. And what did our crazy tantric magician try to do? Unify us. That's just too many people telling us we need to get our act together, 'together' being the operative word."

August let out a light huff and drummed his fingers on the table.

"Besides," she continued, "you seemed all lovey dovey last night."

"I already told you. I had a job to do. There was nothing more to it."

"Hmph!" Larissa turned her face up in disagreement.

"This unity thing is going to kick both our asses." August focused his attention back on his food. "If I could find a spell to end this quest, I'd do that in a heartbeat too."

"Has it not occurred to you that the better we work together and put our minds and magic to good use, it might further our cause? I've tried finding a way to end this, and nothing is coming to me. You may have scored one with your stunt last night, but I'll wager you can't sustain a running streak." Larissa kicked him lightly under the table.

"Would you stop?" An annoyed look covered his face. In retaliation, he held out his palm toward her, eyes glinting, lips uttering a barely audible command. Instead, a blast of wind knocked over the small vase of flowers and condiment shakers on the table, toppling them to the floor. August sat, wide-eyed with dismay.

Larissa laughed and gazed at the floor. "Hate it when pretty flowers and salt and pepper go to waste. Hate it worse when a magic spell is mucked up." She laughed again. With a snap of her fingers, the items on the floor returned to the table as if they'd never been touched. "There, much better. And just so you know, I really appreciate you getting our youth back."

The two finished their meal in silence with August sulking the remainder of the time.

***

At the El Fishawy café, August and Larissa sat once again, contemplating their next move.

"We need to reach the lady," said Larissa. She stirred a small spoon in her espresso cup.

"You mean Ciana?" August narrowed his eyes as they fixed intently on Larissa.

"My forebear? Yes, it has to be her. There can be no one else. And it makes perfectly good sense too."

"As a Nephilim, she could live a much longer life than us mere humans—and witches." August leaned back his head, staring at the ceiling. "She didn't show up at Endor because she's still alive. You're right, it has to be her." He sat up straight and leaned in toward Larissa. "She's trying to get our attention. Your attention mostly. You're her niece."

Larissa fidgeted, biting quickly at a nail on one of her fingers. She glanced around and back to her cup, tapping her fingers against the porcelain surface. "There's something I have to confess to you."

"Who is he this time?" August grimaced.

She shook her head vigorously. "No, silly. It has nothing to do with a man, but something my aunt told me while we were at Katharta."

"Well, do tell." The young man rested his head in one of his hands and listened intently.

In a monologue lasting several minutes, Larissa revealed to August what she had read the night they arrived, including what Dorenda had told her.

August's eyes shot wide open. "If Ciana is part angel, and Dorenda is compelled to . . . and some beautiful woman appeared to her too . . ." He shook his head in disbelief. "Do you know what the genetic probability is that you . . .?

Larissa held out her hand. "I don't have a drive to create anything like what Dorenda told me."

"You've never tried once you knew about this? Even just a little?"

"We've been nothing but on the move. No, I've not tried."

"Surely we can summon Ciana." August's face held a look of determination. "If she's appearing to you, we can reach her. I say we meet in one of our rooms tonight and do it. A calling ceremony."

Larissa let out a light squeal. Several people turned in their direction, looking at the pair in surprise. August scowled with embarrassment. A cat's head popped up from under the table and faced its owner.

"Sophie!" The young lady, with as much discretion as possible, cuddled her familiar close and kissed the animal between its ears. "What are you doing here?"

"Again, I've come to help."

"Why do we have that furball with us again? We'll get thrown out if management sees." August voiced his disapproval through clenched teeth.

Sophie took the liberty of quickly turning around and hissing in August's direction. The man waved her away with an expression of disgust.

"You have no respect for familiars, do you, August? I would think as a witch you'd know better. Don't you have a familiar somewhere lurking around, a toad, perhaps?" Larissa flashed him an indignant look.

"Maybe I don't need anything. I can rely on myself."

At that statement, Sophie turned again and let out an eerie audible human laugh in his direction. August sat aghast, shuddering at the sound. "God, you're a creepy furball."

Ignoring the comment, the cat faced her owner, resting her head next to Larissa's ear. *"You need to go to the Hall of Winds. Everything will be revealed there."*

"The Hall of Winds?" Larissa looked at her familiar, perplexed.

The cat insisted. *"All secrets are heard there. If you really listen."*

Cocking an eyebrow, Larissa asked, "And to whom are we supposed to hear when we go there?"

With a twitching tail, the animal answered, *"The very person you're trying to reach, of course. Who else would it be?"* Sophie seemed rather impatient and dug her claws into Larissa's shoulder. She flinched. *"You must go there immediately. Time is of the essence."*

"It's always about time, isn't it?" Larissa's lips puckered with irritation.

"Listen, don't dawdle. Go to the Hall of Winds. When you reach the Cavern of Music, you will hear. But beware. Don't let the music distract you. It's a trap. You must listen to what's between the music to receive the flow of information. If you become entranced by the music, you are lost forever. You'll never get out."

The cat ducked her head back under the table and disappeared.

"Did you hear that?" Larissa stared at August in surprise.

"Unbelievable." August shook his head and rubbed his eyes. "Do we even know where this place is? Have we ever heard of it?"

"We have to go there now," said Larissa. "Sophie says so. I can ask Aunt Dorenda if she knows anything about it."

When the pair finished their espressos, they left their table and headed back to the hotel. At a table a few feet away sat a young man reading a magazine and sipping coffee. His ears, tuned in with a heightened sense of hearing, had picked up on the conversation between August and Larissa. He pulled out a small notebook and pen and made a few quick notations.

On the magazine page he had been reading, the man tapped three times on a large central image with his index finger. A face of another gentleman slowly steadied into view.

I know their next location. On top of the image, the first man wrote the message.

We'll be ready. Go there and prepare. Follow the directions we give you. The reply came across the image in glowing yellow letters. The magazine owner nodded, closed the pages and left the table.

***

"So she's the one who visited me in my dream." Dorenda's image and voice emanated clearly from the large quartz crystal ball. Sophie sat quietly, perched on the older woman's shoulder.

This time, August and Larissa sat in her hotel room with the rock sphere placed between them. They had informed the aunt of everything that had transpired in Egypt.

"Can you tell us anything about the Hall of Winds?" asked Larissa. "Where is it? Any pit falls, things to be aware of? What do we need to listen for?"

The older lady remained silent, thinking for several seconds. At last she spoke, "It's located in a remote area in the region of Colorado, and it's not the famous cave you hear about there. It's actually in a dimension apart from but still near that cave."

"Another dimension?" August enunciated his words and sat up straight, staring closer at the crystal ball. "Does the Vanishport even go into other dimensions? We've never used it for that kind of travel before."

Dorenda answered. "The Vanishport can reach those special dimensions. There is a spell used specifically for that kind of travel. The Vanishport can take you there and the Vanishport can take you away to anywhere else you need to go. That's the beauty of using it."

"Auntie, why the Hall of Winds? If Ciana can show herself, why couldn't she send messages in other ways without having to go to such an odd place?"

"Ciana is using the Hall of Winds because it's the only way she can communicate directly without anyone hearing her message. I've never visited it myself, nor do I know of anyone who has. What I know is only what I've heard through lore. It's a tricky place. The spirits who inhabit it love to hold visitors captive if they can. They will try and fool you, lure you in with their sounds."

August finally spoke up. "Dorenda, is there any special magic tools we need to take with us or certain spells we need to know, other than for our transportation means? Apparently Hathor informed us that we are being watched, followed."

"I would say Hathor is right, but I would have thought you and my niece would have known that the moment you left Katharta Castle."

The young man's face colored briefly. "We haven't noticed anything blatant, but you're right. That doesn't mean the dark forces haven't been around."

"Larissa," said Dorenda, "take the amplituner with you. If it becomes necessary, you can use it. The Hall of Winds is a good place to use this tool because it has everything to do with sound, whether it comes from you or another source."

Her niece nodded. "I'll take it with us."

Dorenda added, "Again, be on your guard. I'm getting a bad vibe about you and August going there. The dark forces, whatever or whomever, are getting stronger. The Glanarium Supremo has noted this in their recent messages to us.

"Aunt Dorenda," said Larissa, "has my mother tried communicating with you, or my father? If Ciana is doing it, why aren't other family members doing it too?"

"No. Ciana has only shown herself to me on the one occasion, like I shared before. Showing herself to you is becoming more commonplace, it seems, and she's not appearing to August. I also agree with Hathor. Something or someone has limited her in some way. Nephilim have strong powers, and for her to be using The Hall of Winds is rather disturbing."

"We'll head there tomorrow," added August. "Keeping an eye out for the bad guys will be a number one priority."

Dorenda smiled. "My dear man, please guard my niece. Both of you will need to call on all the powers in your possession."

"Will do, Auntie. Have a good evening," Larissa waved to her aunt. The crystal ball went dark.

"This should be interesting." August grimaced. "Another dimension." He scratched his head and sighed. "What will that be like?"

Larissa sat silent in thought for several seconds. "Couldn't be much different than being on this plane we're on, the third dimension. I don't think we'll be going to a full fourth dimension, like going to another constellation or galaxy, perhaps."

August snapped his fingers. "Maybe it's a three-and-a-half dimension. Something in between. You know." He gazed at Larissa.

"We may feel different or a little woozy until we get used to it. But enough about that. We need to think about Ciana. Maybe we can ask her things we didn't or couldn't ask Hathor."

"First, I think it's important we try and find out where she is and who has her. And why?" August nodded, speaking softly as if to himself. "The second will be trying to find out about your parents. Your family is scattered, so getting them together is going to be harrowing, at best."

The young man stared at his companion. "How does it feel to think about finding your parents, Larissa? Do you ever think about that? Do you miss them?"

"I think about them all the time. I'll admit it's a little nerve-wracking to think about seeing them face-to-face. Will they like me? Will I fit in? How will I react? Those sorts of things. They've been nothing more than a fantasy until now."

"Of course they'll like you. You're their daughter. And you're a remarkable witch." August waved her away, chuckling. "Maybe Ciana can give some real clues on how to start looking for them. Or maybe clarify just exactly what we are looking for. We still don't know for sure what it is that got stolen."

Larissa rubbed her lower lip in thought. "I'm beginning to think I know what we're looking for."

August perked up, his eyes glittering.

"I think whomever has Ciana took a conjuring cloth she'd made."

Chapter Twelve

The Vanishport landed at the edge of a wooded strip outside a charming old Victorian house. The Scarlet Bugle Bed and Breakfast looked just as quaint in person as it did on the website. A cobblestone walkway led to the house. Pristine, colorful flower gardens added elegance and charm to the property.

August and Larissa had immediately fallen in love with the place and booked a king bedroom, lucky enough to snag the last space before "No Availability" popped up for their chosen date. They carefully glanced around, making sure no one saw them, and ambled up the steps. Upon entering the house, two cheerful inn owners greeted the pair. August and Larissa officially checked in and marched up the polished wooden steps, bags in tow.

"What an adorable place." Larissa plopped down in an oversized, stuffed chair after placing her bags by the bed. "Being back home feels so good."

"I thought your home was in Kansas." August helped himself to the bottle of wine sitting on a Queen Anne-style table by the window and poured himself and his companion a glass of rich chardonnay.

"After where we've been, anywhere in the States is home to me. There's an energy here, a strong pulse of life from people who know how to live, how to have a good time. It's a place for the best of everything."

"Before you wax too poetic, we need to find a way to the cave tomorrow." August sat down at Larissa's feet.

"So what'll it be? Vanishport or hire a driver? Maybe we ask the owners if they have a shuttle service." The young lady tilted her head back for a sip of wine from her glass.

"Let's hire a driver. It keeps us away from the crowds." August picked up his cell phone and started scrolling through the listings.

Larissa jumped at the vibrations emanating from her phone. She read the text message.

"*Where are you*?" The message was from Daniel.

"*Colorado. Where are you*?"

"*OMG Me too! :O*"

"*Call me*." Larissa waited for the phone to ring. "Hey, what are you doing here?"

"I've missed you."

Daniels's smooth voice filled her ear. Larissa's heart skipped a beat. It had been too long since she'd heard that wonderful sound.

August glanced up with a wrinkled brow. "Who is it?" he mouthed.

Larissa shook her head at August, and focused back on Daniel. "You still didn't answer me. Why are you here? Of all places, I'd never expect running into you in Colorado."

The man didn't answer immediately.

"Daniel? Are you still there? Can you hear me?"

"I'm here. What town are you in?"

"Manitou Springs."

"Too cool. So am I. Came for some sight-seeing and relaxation. Maybe we can do something together. Wouldn't that be great, Larissa?" His voice came out seductive, tempting.

Larissa fell against the back of her chair. "Um, I don't know, Daniel. I've already got plans, and I can't really change them, if you know what I mean."

On hearing the name, August glared up at Larissa, a perplexed look crossing his face. "What the hell?" he mouthed at her again.

The young lady ignored him. "Maybe we can meet somewhere else some other time?"

"Where are you going that's so important?" Daniel asked.

"I'm going on a cave trip. You've heard of it, I'm sure. Don't have all the details worked out just yet."

"I'm doing some caving myself. If we're going to the same place, why don't I swing by and pick you up?"

Larissa thought a moment. It could work. She could let Daniel do his thing once he dropped them off, and then she and August could do their thing. Simple. "I don't see why not."

August scowled and shook his head. His face bore the emphatic expression of a solid no.

"Yes, come around twelve thirty. That'll be a good time. Here's where I'm staying." She provided the address. After a few more streams of conversation, the call ended.

"Just what the hell was that all about? I don't want friends or friends of friends anywhere near us. We have a job to do."

"Don't think I don't know that, smarty." Larissa scowled back. "It's a . . . friend of mine. Yeah." She nodded, trying to convince herself with the words trickling out of her mouth.

August groaned. "Oh, god, no. It's not just any friend, is it? It's a boyfriend. I know it is. Has to be." He held his head and wiped his eyes in a show of fatigue. "Can you please call him back and cancel? Give any excuse. Blame it all on me, if you have to."

"No, I won't. Stop getting so uptight every time there's a man involved." Larissa took another swig of wine. Good lord, she needed another glass, if she and August were going to banter like this the rest of the day. "He's giving us a ride to the cave."

"What?" August's eyes nearly bulged out of his head. "You can't be serious." He stood up, hands on hips, and frowned. "He's not coming with us. He can't."

"Chill out, August. He'll go his own way. When he sees you with me, there's nothing else to do. I'll tell him that we have some other plans, and that's that."

"It's never as easy as 'that's that.' There's always more. And what excuse are we going to give him?"

"I'll think of something."

Daniel stared at his phone, smiling. He pocketed the device and walked back to his hotel. Later that night a companion dined with him.

"Everything set for tomorrow?" asked the friend.

"All set. We feel everything out. Play it nice and easy." Daniel savored a bite of his food. "When we reach the cave, I'll go inside and meet you."

The friend nodded. "And then it's watch, wait, and follow, right?"

"Yep. We need to find out who they're meeting and what is said. Gather as much information as possible. It's the reason we're being sent in the first place."

***

At twelve thirty sharp, Daniel arrived at the front entrance of The Scarlet Bugle in a rental car. August and Larissa walked out of the inn.

"Great place. I like it." Daniel grabbed Larissa in his arms and kissed her while August watched wide-eyed in disbelief. "Gosh, I've missed you so much. You just don't know." He hugged her again tightly, kissing her a second time.

Larissa threw her arms around him. "I've missed you too. I think about you every day," she whispered in his ear.

August silently opened the passenger door and slid inside. Larissa rested in the seat up front next to Daniel.

"Have you seen much of Colorado?" Daniel put the car in gear and drove off.

"Just got here last night, so no." Larissa felt a warm heat all over when Daniel reached for her hand, holding it in his.

"I hear this cave is something else. Has a lot of other activities to do if you don't want to cave it for the day. And I didn't get your name." Daniel glanced in the rear-view mirror.

"Name's August."

"My bad," said Larissa. "I should have introduced him."

"August, do you ever go spelunking?" Daniel asked. "This is my first time."

"No, can't say I have. Should be good." August sulked in the back seat, watching Daniel and Larissa cozy up to each other as much as they could in a moving car.

"These are some incredible mountains. Would you look at the size!" Larissa turned her head in all directions as they drove, taking in the gargantuan rocky peaks dotted with trees. Layers of rock showed through, displaying colors of rich brown and sandy tones. A brilliant blue sky blazed above.

Daniel answered, "The United States has beauty everywhere, and Colorado is known for just that.

"August, is this your first time to the States?" Larissa called back, craning her neck toward the back seat.

"Yes." The young man didn't elaborate further.

"Where do you live, August?" asked Daniel.

"I live in Nepal"

"Cool. Never been there. You like it?"

"Works for me." August turned his gaze toward his window and took in the scenery.

Daniel and Larissa exchanged glances. He squeezed her hand tighter. "I wish we could visit the cave together, but I already got tickets with a buddy."

"Oh, somebody I know?"

"No, he's a friend from school." Daniel kept his face expressionless and added nothing more.

"August and I will be fine. But I'll miss you." Larissa rubbed her thumb over the top of her boyfriend's hand.

August asked, "Are we almost there?"

"A few more minutes, buddy, and we'll be there." Daniel kept his eyes on the road and sped along. When he reached the entrance to the park, he found a spot and turned off the engine. A large building stood proudly on top of a high mountain cliff.

The three walked toward the building. August surveyed the different activity courses set up outside. He tapped on Larissa's shoulder. When she turned around, he pointed to one of the courses.

Taking her cue, Larissa said to Daniel, "I think we're stopping here for right now. He wants to check out the adventure courses first."

Daniel lifted his brows in surprise. "Oh, okay. I'm heading on in, then. Text me later."

"Will do." Larissa smiled and tilted her head back as Daniel kissed her lips. He nodded toward August. "Nice to meet you. Have fun."

August offered a polite nod in return, saying nothing.

Larissa watched Daniel head off. She turned around and scowled at her companion. "You couldn't have been more congenial, could you, August? Just your usual delightful self."

"I am delightful. At least some people think so." August made a googly face at her. "We'll wait until lover boy is completely inside, and then we make our move to the Hall of Winds." He scratched his head in thought. "Have we figured out how to access this dimension?"

Larissa let out a sharp screech. A pigeon crashed against her, fluttering to the ground. August looked down in dismay.

"What do you know, it's a War Pigeon," he said.

The bird shook its head trying to regain its bearings. It hopped up on its two feet and waited.

"Let's see what this note says." Larissa gently removed the tiny piece of paper, scrutinizing the writing. "It says to follow him." She looked at the bird, meeting its gaze. "Are you going to show us the entrance into the Hall of Winds?"

Several quick sounds from the bird confirmed the question, and it flew into the air. The couple followed the bird, dodging people and making their way to the far side of the building. August steadied Larissa as she stumbled on a larger stone that had rolled onto the pavement. In a blinding flash, they both found themselves in a large cavernous anteroom.

From inside the main building, Daniel and his companion stood together off to one side, ignoring everyone passing by and blending in with other park goers. Together they focused on the ScryView in Daniel's hand.

The friend smiled. "Looks like they're in. Are we ready?"

"Ready," said Daniel. "We keep our distance, pay attention to detail, and do what our commander tells us. Simple. You got that?"

"Uh-huh." The other young man nodded, a sober expression covering his face.

"Let's go." Daniel snapped his finger, turning off the ScryView and placing it in his pocket.

"So this is the other dimension." August took in a deep breath and looked around.

Round holes, a foot in diameter each, had been carved into the rock. They lined the full circumference of the room. A blustery breeze whipped through the area, sending clear notes of different pitches filling the air in a straying symphony of unrelated sounds.

Larissa narrowed her eyes, listening with her head angled to one side. "It's rather pretty and haunting, yet it's not."

August didn't answer but seemed intent on listening to the sounds.

"Hey, did you hear me?" Larissa spoke louder and tugged on his sleeve.

"Hmm?" He focused his gaze on her, blinking several times to clear his head. "It's rather interesting, don't you think? You know what else? I hear things in the sounds."

"Like what?" Larissa's face contorted in disbelief. "I don't hear anything. At least not yet."

"Very alluring." He smiled. "It's like something or someone is calling out for me."

"We have to get out of here and move on. You can't stay and listen to that all day."

The pair took a hallway leading out, choosing it because they sensed a pull in that direction.

The amplituner rested inside Larissa's blouse. An energy emitted from it, sending a light tingling sensation running through her throat. Without thinking, she sung out a note, sustaining it loud and clear. August came to a sudden stop and glared at her.

"What's with you?" he asked.

She shook her head in an indication for him to keep silent and belted out another note. The wind in the hall rustled louder. Somewhere in the distance a sing-song voice answered back. She sung out another pitch. A sound came through in reply.

"It's as if you're trying to call someone, and they're responding," said August. His eyes widened with wonder. "Keep doing that, and we'll follow the direction of the voice." He quickly eyed his partner. "You are sure it's safe to do this, right?"

"Of course, I'm sure. I feel it. I sense it." Larissa whispered in his ear. "She who must not be named is calling out to us."

"Mmm." August nodded and kept walking, motioning for her to keep singing.

The passage narrowed and widened, twisted and turned. More holes lined the walls. Breezes whipped by, sending a haunting melody throughout the air.

Larissa had briefly stopped her monotone notes, following August. They came to an intersection and paused.

"Which way do we go?" He stopped, confused.

"Let me try singing again." This time Larissa let out a series of chillingly beautiful sounds, reminiscent of European-styled tunes of old.

August stared at her, amazed. His eyes glittered with interest. They both turned their heads to the right. The same voice answering them previously sounded out again. As they started walking, August let out a grunt.

"What was that?" Larissa stopped and grabbed his arm.

"The hell if I know." He scowled and fluffed his golden mane of hair back in place. "Something hit me." The young man rubbed his head. "I wonder now if we're being fooled."

"Yes, what Aunt Dorenda said. The spirits. Remember?"

"Exactly." August tightened his lips together. He stood, gazing at Larissa's blouse. Slowly he reached out and spread the top portion open, exposing her throat.

She jumped, warding off his hands. "What do you think you're doing? This is no place to—"

"Shh," he answered. A soft smile tugged at the corner of his lips. "I'm wondering if you don't need to put this to good use." He rubbed his finger over the amplituner.

Her mouth opened, annoyed at his forwardness. "I was just going to use it, so I'm one step ahead of you."

"Hmph. Then why didn't you have it out and ready to start with?"

"You have to use this wisely. Auntie said so. It doesn't last forever."

August answered, "We won't last forever in here, either, if you don't start using that thing." He ducked quickly and frowned. Another rush of something unseen brushed over his hair.

Larissa gripped the amplituner by the end, closed her eyes, and hummed out the primordial vowel sound, ancient as time itself. Her lips curled into a perfect O. The higher pitches she sang out before turned into a lowered tone this time, strong and beautiful.

She listened intently, moving in the opposite direction toward the other hallway. August followed, glancing back one last time as the melodic voice called out from the distance.

"Keep walking. I heard her. It's a soft whisper, but I know for sure it's not what we heard before." She looked at August. "Someone was playing tricks on us."

Though there were other halls branching off from the one Larissa and August walked, they kept straight, never veering. When he wanted to linger and hear the notes filtering through the hall, she grabbed his arm and pulled.

"Do not, under any circumstance, stop and listen, August. You'll be the death of us yet, or yourself, at any rate."

"I'm stronger than that. I know when I'm being duped, so it shouldn't hurt to at least enjoy myself a little." He frowned at her.

A cold blast of wind burst through, nearly knocking them down. Larissa let out a quick scream. August swore.

Holding the amplituner between her fingers again, Larissa piped out a high note, sending the wind to a sudden halt. August stood still, listening. Neither said a word. Nothing moved.

"Run. Follow me." Larissa ran ahead, August tearing off after her.

Within seconds, they came to a small flight of rocky stairs. When they landed on the first step, a blue light lit up the walls. A horrendous cacophony of wails blasted all around them. In pain, they covered their ears.

Larissa angled her head toward the far wall of the stairs, indicating they continue the descent. As they moved, a crackling sound emitted as the wails reached an unbearable crescendo. In one last valiant effort, the amplituner came into play. From Larissa's throat, another soprano note split the air, sending the deafening sounds into another round of silence.

"She's down there," said Larissa, quickly picking her way over the stairs.

"You can hear her? Why can't I?" August cursed when he nearly sprained his ankle on an uneven step.

"She's limiting who can hear her. For safety, no doubt. So don't take it personally."

"How can I not take it personally? We're in this together. And I'm a South Hawthorn clave member, I might add."

"Trust me on this one. Let's go. There's not much time."

They reached the bottom of the steps and found themselves in another large room. Holes in the floor lined the perimeter of the space. Breezes wafting over them sent out more melodic tunes, a little higher in octaves than the first room in which they landed on arrival.

Larissa stopped, looking all around her. A quick flash of white light glanced off the walls of a hall on their left side. "This way," she said.

The two sprinted forward, August following her lead. At the end of the hall, they stood before a narrow opening in a rock wall. They looked at each other and slipped inside, ending up in a round stone room. The air held sounds of light crackling, much different than what they'd heard earlier.

"Now what?" murmured August.

"I listen. So be quiet." Larissa put a finger to her lips.

She closed her eyes, concentrating on nothing but the soft whisper filling her ears. A light wind twirled itself around her, but no sound came from it. The whisper she heard came from a distant place, not where they were now. There was no astral projection of a figure, but merely the movie-like images flickering through her mind, like the visions she first experienced at Gamal Emara's apartment.

The vision came in colors of black and white. Larissa focused intently as they formed in greater clarity. She saw her, the most beautiful creature she could imagine. Long tendrils of light flowing hair, soulful eyes, and cherubic lips.

"*You have come at last, my dear*." The woman's eyes gleamed with emotion. Her lips pulled up in a radiant smile.

"Are you Ciana, sister of Desmond North Strondovan, lover of Clement South Hawthorne?"

"*I am none other than that of whom you speak. I am your great great aunt, Ciana. I asked you here to the Hall of Winds because we can speak in secret, unencumbered.*"

"Dear Auntie Ciana, where are you? And how is it that you can be alive so many years?" Larissa's heart pounded with excitement. Speaking to her ancestor who held all the clues to her long-lost world created strong emotions. The questions in her head swirled in a topsy-turvy bundle.

The lady glanced around quickly before answering "*There is little time to talk. So many questions and answers to go along. You must know that he seeks to destroy you and what is yours.*"

"Who? Do I know him? Have I ever met him?" Larissa tuned in more intently, fully shutting out her immediate surroundings.

Ciana continued, "*The one who really killed Clement has me now. You must find your family and ready yourself for battle. Time ticks away, my dear.*"

Larissa held out her hands in despair. "I don't even know where to begin. What happened to my parents? Where are they, and how would I recognize them as my own?"

"*My darling niece, once you and the South Hawthorne heir officially accepted this quest, the entities who wished to help put themselves on notice, on guard. They will come at the most opportune times. Their wisdom will be beneficial. Never forget that. But also know that not all are trustworthy.*"

"I think I've already discovered that. But what are you, and what other advice do you have? Can we talk again?"

"*I'm a witch spinner, a Nephilim. We can only communicate when I am able. My powers are now limited due to him, the dark one. You must take back what was taken from me.*"

"And what was that, dear Auntie?" Larissa tuned in full force. The answer from Ciana was one of the most important reasons for her and August being selected for this quest. The answer would also confirm or refute her present suspicions.

"*The item you must retrieve is a . . .*"

The vision evaporated. All went dark in Larissa's mind. Panic set in with a suffocating grip. Her inner eyes searched, hoping for any means necessary to get Ciana back. But nothing worked. Larissa sensed an enormous loss the moment her aunt disappeared. She still didn't know where Ciana was nor any new clues on how to contact her family. The fact of almost learning what the special item was, only to have the woman vanish at the most opportune time, caused Larissa much frustration.

The young lady pounded a fist into her other hand. "Ohhh! So close yet so far." Her eyes opened, and she saw nothing but the room again, with its stone walls engulfing her. The crackling sounds continued as before. To her surprise, she was alone. "August?"

No answer.

Cold fear set in. What happened to him? She ran to the opening and landed in the hallway, looking frantically for her companion. Had something or someone finally absconded with him, held him captive somewhere? Worse yet, had something harmed him?

"August!" Larissa's eyes filled with tears. "Where are you? Answer me." Her screams ricocheted throughout the hall, slamming back against her ears in a desperate haunting echo. She shuddered.

The music of the winds picked up again, their sounds moaning and dreadful in their appeal, moving and sounding off with urgency that matched Larissa's emotions. One thing for sure, August must be located. She would never leave the Hall of Winds without him. It wouldn't be allowed. Worse, a part of her psyche felt his absence acutely. A hollowness set in, a pain of emptiness creeping all over that surprised her.

Frantic, she retraced the paths taken earlier. Her mind whirled. Where would he have gone? Dorenda's words came back, chastising her for being so careless. They should have created a means of staying connected while meeting with Ciana. This whole ordeal would have never happened if only they had been more thoughtful.

Larissa stopped a moment, breathing hard. The last vestige of energy vibrated from the amplituner, heating her skin. Using it would be the last time before its power died for good. Closing her eyes, she grasped the end and amped up her inner listening. A high-pitched hum filled her ears. This sound came from a higher frequency. It didn't match the crackling sounds from the room she recently left nor the cries of the wind.

The sound resonated with a certain energy, strong and direct. It talked to her, pulled her through hallways she and August had not explored. Deeper into the interior she walked, sometimes running when she felt compelled to do so. At once, a sharp sting permeated her thumb and forefinger. Larissa cried out in pain. The amplituner ignited into a rainbow of flames, disintegrating into nothingness, taking the chain along with it.

Soft grey and pale blue lights that had lit her way disappeared. Larissa found herself shrouded in darkness, rooted motionless to the floor. Her mind went blank. An ominous sensation reared its ugly head, creating an unexplained dread. The wall on her left flashed with a blinding white-blue light. She raised a hand, shielding her eyes from the burst of pain. A blast of cold air sailed through the hall.

It took several seconds for Larissa to digest the vision, one so awful she nearly collapsed. Encased in the wall, sealed in thick clear sheets of ice, stood August. His form remained motionless like a statue. Lifeless eyes and a face void of expression suggested certain death. Larissa let out a scream, the shrill pitch speeding throughout the cavern. The lady crumpled to the floor, hitting it with a dull thud.

Daniel and his companion stood gazing from a hidden vantage point several yards away.

Dennis spoke first, "That took a lot of work. Looks like we finally got them. Now what?"

"Give me a second. We have to handle this the right way, or else we're toast." Daniel closed his eyes and raised his hand toward the direction of August and Larissa. Immediately a blinding flash of white light, coupled with a deafening explosion, filled the hall.

Chapter Thirteen

The older lady gazed at her clear quartz crystal ball. She chortled with delight. Mirth filled her eyes. "Oh, no my dear boys. You don't 'finally got them'. Not by a long shot." She threw back her head and belted out a hearty laugh. "You two were quick, though. Had to be on my toes. But you won't outsmart an old broad like me. No, you won't, my dears. Most important, you will not win."

Her face sobered with an intent expression. "Now, my job is just beginning." She closed her scrying session, uttering choice sacred words and cleansing the ball before placing it lovingly on a shelf.

***

From a secluded chateau tucked away in Rouen, in the Normandy region of France, a young man scowled at a female crouched in the corner of a small dismal gray room. The sole narrow window begrudgingly allowed a slice of afternoon sun a quick slip of fading rays through the dusty pane.

"You try my patience, Ciana." The man paced back and forth, casting glances at his prisoner. That's what she'd been to his family since the day his ancestors captured her in the clearing that fateful day Clement South Hawthorne died.

"Try all you want, but you'll never get anything from me." Ciana turned her face away in defiance and disgust.

"Oh, really? We'll see about that. You may be a Nephilim, but you can be worn down. Don't forget the human part of you." He turned and leered into her face, forcing a meeting of the eyes. "Perhaps I need to try harder. All these years of work trying to get you to do this one thing, and you still won't come through."

Ciana pursed her lips and closed her eyes, hoping to shut out his voice and the mere look of him. He was intoxicatingly beautiful. A walking picture of physical perfection. But that didn't deter her in the least. She'd stay true to her goal or wither away in this slip of a room on the lower-most level of an extraordinary fine house.

A house that looked much like the one she and her brother Desmond occupied in their glory days, days when she and Clement South Hawthorne loved each other with reckless abandon and passion. Together they had made a pact, one that fulfilled a destiny for the North Strondovan and South Hawthorne dynasties. All had gone according to plan until the moment that odious wand duel occurred. That was also the last time she'd seen her family, for she'd been unceremoniously whisked away to France.

"I have the fire that's needed to ignite this, activate its powers." The young man waved a wide strip of cloth in front of her. The fibers sparkled with an inner light, ready for the unleashing. "But this one won't work. Remove the spell you've cast and be part of a ruling power for all eternity. We can be partners in this."

Ciana's eyes moved in a display of irritation and impatience. "You are not the only one who carries the igniting flame. How many times do I have to remind you of that? There are others who have the same powers."

"But I want to be the one who finishes this, the one who sets it free to work in all its radiant glory." The man postured once again in front of her. "Besides, my family is well-deserving of a union with you and your abilities. We can't create such wonders as this, but we could do great things with it."

"You and yours are intent on nothing but power, utter destruction, and ruination." Ciana's face clouded. "Power like mine runs only in a few select witch families, and we take great care in choosing who activates the power of what we create."

The man looked hurt. "Are you listening to yourself? Really, one's perception of destruction and ruination is another one's power to create and do great and wondrous things. That's not bad."

"Mark my words," said Ciana, "I'll not remove that spell, nor will I share any information on how the piece you have in your possession is created. You stole it from me, plain and simple. You killed an innocent witch and allowed everyone to believe a lie about what really happened." Her eyes narrowed in anger at the man. "You and your family are despicable."

The young man squared up his shoulders. "Just know one thing, Ciana. I am more than aware that you're trying to communicate with your descendants. Your beloved niece and her lothario boyfriend should have been mine right now. Those two foolish young witches failed to intervene properly this time in the Hall of Winds. They will get an earful by the time I'm done with them.

"You don't fool me. I sense everything you do. Trust me on this, my family and I will prevail." He turned on his heel and marched out of the room, slamming the door behind him.

Ciana grimaced as she heard the key in the lock. She whispered, "Your family's time is coming to an end. The Magiverse has grown weary of your meddling and greed for power. The glory isn't for you, but for the North Strondovan and South Hawthorne claves." She turned her gaze upwards, clasping two delicate hands together. "It's been written in the cosmos. The Glanarium Supremo acknowledges it. It will be done."

***

Larissa's head pounded. Her eyes slammed shut the moment sunlight struck them. "Oh," she moaned. Her body dropped back down on the ground. Something in her head said she needed to get up right away, but memory failed as to the reason why.

"Hey."

She jumped at the touch of a hand on hers. Larissa ventured another attempt at opening her sluggish eyes.

"You okay?" August had stretched out his hand.

"Mmm," she answered. "My head is killing me." In a surge of energy, the young lady sat straight up, eyeing her partner. "I thought you were dead."

August squinted back, confused. "I don't know what you mean. Why would I be dead? Though I guess either of us could go at any time." He shook his head and stared back at her. "Where in the hell are we?"

"No clue." Larissa gazed all around, blinking to clear her vision.

The land around them blazed brilliant green, rising up and flowing downward in a series of rolling hills. Trees dotted the grass. The sweet scent of wildflowers filled the air. They seemed to have landed in a meadow.

"What happened to you when I was talking to Ciana? We finished. You disappeared. And then I saw you in . . ."

August said nothing, staring at her as if she'd lost her mind.

"You have no idea, do you?" Larissa frowned.

"It was noisy in there, confusing." The young man shrugged. "Besides, I wasn't part of the club, remember?"

Larissa wagged her head with impatience. "Oh, for Pete's sake! When are you going to stop that pity party of yours?" A light grin pulled at the corners of her mouth. "It was the music, wasn't it?"

"It most certainly was not."

"It most certainly was," answered Larissa. She imitated her companion's deep tone of voice, chuckling afterward. "You couldn't help yourself, could you? Had to listen. Couldn't resist."

"Give it a rest." He pulled himself up with a loud groan. "I suggest we get on with it to wherever we're supposed to go, need to go. Hell, I can't even begin to imagine where we are."

"Yoo-hoo, my darlings."

Larissa and August turned their heads in the direction of an older woman walking toward them. A wide smile lit up her face, and she frantically waved two neatly manicured hands.

"You're here, now, safe and sound. How delightful." Her voice came out in a high-pitched sing-song tone. The wind had ruffled her grey and black-streaked hair in a tousled array around her head. She swiped wayward strands away from her face. "I hope the fall wasn't too hard on you? The Hall of Winds can try the best of us."

She stood in front of August and Larissa, spending most of her time surveying August. "You're just as handsome as I've heard about in stories."

Larissa stared at August, who blushed. He answered, "I'm sure I don't know what you mean." He glanced at Larissa and back at the lady. "As a matter of fact, why would you even hear of me at all? And who are you? Where are we?"

The lady's laugh matched the tone of her musical-sounding voice. "I am the ever-illustrious Greta Marvo. At your service." She brandished an arm in front of her and bowed lightly before the two, who stood with their mouths agape.

Larissa snapped a finger. "I've heard of you." She glanced at August with a smug look.

"I knew one of you had surely heard of me." Greta's eyes sparkled with delight. "Takes a minute, though, doesn't it?" She fluttered her long black lashes in August's direction. "You have quite a reputation, young man. Do you really live up to it? I'm very curious about that."

August stood speechless, his cheeks turning scarlet.

Larissa gazed at the two with a cocked eyebrow. "It's a pleasure to meet you, Miss Marvo, but can you tell us where we are?"

"My dears, you are in no other place than land of Nag Wanthei. It is in the dimension between Earth and the Outer Band of Dreams. Only true witches can come here, either of their own accord—or perhaps brought here by an inhabitant, like myself." She displayed another one of her captivating smiles. "We can't have people pretending they are witches by merely claiming they are. That's just not the way it's done."

"You brought us here?" asked Larissa. "Why?"

"You were in trouble," answered Greta. She pointed to August. "And you, my sweet." The woman shook her head and clucked her tongue. "You were in a bad way."

Grinning, Larissa reached out and punched August on the shoulder. "Told you."

August scowled at her, rubbing his skin. "That's going to leave a mark."

"You know there were two other witches in the Hall of Winds, don't you?" Greta glanced between the two young people.

"Wouldn't there be other witches who needed to go there or wanted to?" asked Larissa. "It's a big place. I don't think I'd considered there not being others."

August asked Greta, "You saw them?"

Greta nodded. "I had to intervene, or you two would have wound up somewhere else. Not a good place, either." She motioned for them to follow her. "The two of you can sojourn at my cottage. It's not far from here. We can talk in more detail over tea and something delectable to eat. Sound good?" Her lips pulled into another smile.

"I think we'd be delighted to take you up on your offer, if you think it wouldn't be such an inconvenience to a gracious lady like yourself." August bowed lightly.

Larissa close her mouth, after opening it to lightly decline. Her facial expression clouded.

"Then follow me. We'll take that trail over there and follow it all the way to my place."

***

Larissa sat at wooden table in the most charming cottage she'd ever seen. In her lap sat Greta's strange, beautiful cat, with light chocolate brown fur and ears in the shape of bat wings. Since the animal wasn't her familiar, all she could do was stroke the tantalizing silky fur and lose herself in its haunting pale blue eyes. Greta had insisted August help her in the kitchen.

"Did you miss us, or are you enjoying Sousoin's company?" Greta had slipped up to the table and placed a hand-painted tray of mouth-watering finger sandwiches in the center. August followed behind and moved to Larissa's other side, placing another tray of tea and accessory items beside the first one. "Help yourselves, dearies," said Greta.

"I'm still interested in what made you rescue us." Larissa had deposited Sousoin gently on the floor and helped herself to some food and tea.

"I'll gladly tell you. I'm known for keeping up with current events in the Magiverse. I had heard that you two were the elected ones to right an old wrong."

The lady sat up straighter in her chair, picking up Sousoin and placing the cat in her lap. "I'm extremely intuitive, and when I get something strong roiling in my gut, I pay attention, because I like to help when I can. And I knew I could be of service. Felt it in my bones." She winked at August. "I grabbed my crystal scrying sphere and spent the good portion of an hour watching." She shook her head. "I didn't like what I saw. Very ominous. Something was going on, and I couldn't get my head around it."

August and Larissa stopped eating and listened, wide-eyed.

"The longer I watched, the more I began to put some elements together. I saw energy orbs, two of them. They hovered so very near the two of you, following at every turn. When you slowed, they slowed. When you ran, they sped up."

"Greta," said August, "how come Larissa and I didn't sense what you did? Being witches, there's no reason why we wouldn't have."

The older lady tapped her fingers on the table. "Because the orbs were cloaked. I could see them barely through my special ball. Whomever were following you, they made sure you couldn't sense them in any way. Besides, when you were conversing, the natural static in that room cloaks everything."

"They were with August and me when I spoke to . . .?" Larissa sat motionless, stunned.

"I know to whom you were speaking," Greta whispered. "It's your great-great aunt, Ciana. I was able to channel some information, but I had to work hard to tune in to her frequency. She picked the perfect place to converse with you."

"I didn't learn a whole lot. No time."

"She's being held captive. I can't get the exact location, but it's on the Earth plane. I'm receiving impressions that Ciana's in Europe. You can take that to the bank, I tell you. My premonitions are usually correct."

Larissa's mouth fell open. August raised his eyebrows.

"I just can't pinpoint exactly where, but I know it; I sense it."

"Can't you pin down a country, city?" asked August.

"I've tried. My mind suddenly goes blank when I do. It's like there's an interference of some kind."

"Greta, where would I even begin to look for my family? They are scattered, you know. What exactly happened? Aunt Dorenda is either closed-lipped or she really doesn't know. She claims she doesn't know."

The older lady grew quiet, staring into her cup of tea. "Don't know how to say this, or even if I should, but I'd be doing you a terrible disservice if I didn't."

August sat back, his eyes glittering with interest. "So out with it."

"It may be that Dorenda knows more than she's letting on. Not sure for what reason she'd hide something. Maybe for safety. Maybe for something else."

Larissa frowned. "She's been my only family since I was little girl. Why would there be something going on with her?"

Greta shook her head and poured another cup of tea. "Again. Don't know." She looked over at Larissa. "My dear, people can fool you. Even family." The lady leaned closer toward the young woman. "Even those we trust absolutely."

"She's taught me everything I know," Larissa continued.

"I'm not taking anything away from her knowledge base or her skills, my dear. Everything may be on the up and up. Just be aware. That's all I'm saying."

"What about where to start looking for the Strondovans?" asked August. "No one seems to have any information on that."

"That's a mystery for everyone. But I'm inclined to disregard the old saying that you can't go home again."

Larissa and August stared at the older woman in surprise.

"I'm just saying," continued Greta, "that sometimes the best place to start looking is the place where they may have left. But that's just my opinion. I don't know anything for sure."

Later that night, Greta showed Larissa to her room.

"Thank you for letting us stay here. We'll get our bearings, figure out what we need to do next, and then leave you in peace." Larissa glanced at the neat bedroom, which was every bit as cozy at the rest of the house.

"Good night and sweet dreams, my dear." Greta smiled and left.

August stood outside the cottage, gazing at the garden behind the house. He breathed in the sweetest scents.

"Ah, there you are." Greta's sing-song voice blended in with the night. "I've tucked your friend away for the evening." She sidled up to August.

"Oh?" he answered.

"Yes. But I must confess, I sneaked in a sleep spell when she wasn't looking or thinking about anything in particular. Had to get it right."

The young man looked confused. "I would think we're tired enough without a spell."

"The truth, my sweet, is that I've been dying to have a moment with you all to myself. Your friend is charming, and most beautiful, but I wanted her out of the way temporarily."

"Why would you want that?"

"Come with me. I want to show you something special." Greta looped her arm through August's and led him to the far end of the garden. She pointed to a set of plants. "Would you look at that."

August squinted, peering through the darkness. Greta had placed strategic lighting through her garden, but he still couldn't see.

"We'll have a closer look." She pulled him along.

"Oh, my goodness." August clapped a hand over his mouth. "I don't think I've ever seen those before. Are they real, or have you been up to something naughty?"

Greta threw back her head and laughed. "Nothing naughty, but they are powerful, and yes, they are real."

"What are they?" August stared, mesmerized, at the plants, which looked exactly like a man's private member.

"They resemble the tropical pitcher plants on Earth, but these plants don't consume insects. On the contrary, my dear, they spur creativity, insight." She whispered in his ear. "They also help a little with . . . well, you know what I mean." Greta raked a fingernail over his arm.

August gazed at her, a new heat filling his cheeks. The flesh awakened between his thighs.

"Let's move a little more to the center of them. I want you to feel the full effect."

He followed, walking carefully to avoid crushing one of his hostess's prized plants.

"Now, my sweet. Close your eyes." Greta placed her arms gently around August's shoulders.

The young man closed his eyes. "Anything special I need to do?"

"Open yourself. Receive," the older lady whispered in his ear.

The top of August's scalp tingled, radiating through his entire head. His ears filled with a light tinkling sound. The space between his thighs throbbed with a new ache. He took in a deep breath, trying to focus back on the top of his head.

He opened his eyes lightly until he could see through the slits. All around floated wisps of white fluffy-like floaties, each ending with what looked like a tiny hard brown pointed seed. The vision reminded him of dandelions when one blew the soft puff of white from the stem. What surprised him most was the fact that they issued forth from the plants.

"Those are ideas, darling, full and brimming with potential." Greta cooed softly in his ear.

August closed his eyes again. What idea would touch him, enter his being? He relaxed a second, clearing his mind. A momentary sharp prick struck the top of his head. He let out a soft grunt. "I felt that."

"And that is the idea. It came to you. Keep it safe and use it when the time comes." Greta pulled on his arm. "Now come. Follow me."

Inside Greta's bedroom, she and August lay in a fine bed with an ornate carved wooden canopy overhead. She had pulled the pale silken gray drapes about the bed, leaving them cocooned inside. A colorful floral light from the wall burned above them. The older lady had lit a stick of spicy exotic incense before they both had stripped naked and climbed into bed.

"I've never been with someone like you," said August.

"You're nervous too. I can feel it." Greta smiled and caressed his cheek. Older ones like us get a bad rap. That's so unfair, darling." She sat up and leaned toward him. "We have all the experience. A lifetime of it. We know what you want, what you like. Most of the time, anyway."

August's eyes almost clouded from the hard ache pounding away between his legs. His cock stood at attention, and he lay back shamelessly, displaying his nudity and assets before Greta, before the eyes of a crone. But she was no ordinary crone. Her face held a haunting beauty, tenacious, elegant, refusing to yield completely to the passing of time. Or perhaps it was the spell of Nag Wanthei, the land of enchantment that gently took in the wave of dreams drifting from the Outer Band.

He let out a soft groan. Her tongue lapped at his taut flesh. The ache pounded harder. A set of nimble fingers squeezed his nipples. Sheer bliss raced over him like a burst of lightning in a summertime storm. Greta had straddled his legs. August closed his eyes as she held the most sensitive part of himself deep inside of her. Her muscles contracted and relaxed around him. His heart pounded with excitement. The older lady smiled, her eyes blazing with emotion. She brought her face close to his. August inhaled the light odor of mint as she kissed him tenderly on the lips.

Early the next morning, Greta, August, and Larissa sat at the table filled with steaming coffee and a light, savory breakfast Greta had prepared. August said little, avoiding Larissa's pointed gaze—and Greta's self-satisfied smile. His body still thrilled at the thoughts of what occurred the evening before.

"I'd love nothing better than for you two delightful people to stay longer, but I have received an order from the Glanarium Supremo that I must send you on your way. I've been instructed where to drop you off."

Larissa said, "The Glanarium Supremo? I thought they had abandoned us for good." She grimaced and sipped some of her coffee.

"Oh, no, my dear. They step in when they need to. Sometimes in the other dimensions, such as Nag Wanthei—or even The Hall of Winds—it can be a little precarious going from one plane to the next."

"Have we heard of where you are dropping us off? And where we will be headed?" August finally spoke.

A smile lit Greta's face. "You will be back on the Earth plane, but inside the remotest parts of the interior of the planet. Many witches are well familiar with the area, but so are other beings, many of whom are not the nicest. You'll have to watch your back."

"I'm sure we'll be fine." Larissa answered. "We're none too shabby when it comes to magic."

"Oh, yes. I remember August and the Hall of Winds. The ice . . ." Greta shook her head. "Never mind. Yes, I'm sure you two will be fine."

***

Larissa and August stared at the cavernous landscape before them. Dutifully and as promised, Greta had used a powerful incantation, sending them to the border area of Tonaea.

"So this is what it looks like deep inside." August mumbled in awe.

"Pretty magnificent, yeah?" Larissa stared out across, noting how massive everything was. The cave at Endor, though fantastic, seemed claustrophobic and rather dark in comparison. She glimpsed large bodies of water. Lights from the legendary crystal cities blinked far in the distance.

She turned to August. "We're to follow this path. It will lead us farther below. The great city way out there is not for us right now."

"Remind me to come back here when this quest is completed. I've got to see what it's like down here, out there." He pointed off to the distance.

"Mind you, August, that the civilization of beings down here isn't anything like us above. They're more elevated in nature. Only ones who are highly evolved can function and be accepted in this world. We're far away, on the outskirts, so we may run in to some bad folk who don't know any better.

"We're good," said August. "It's not like we want to hurt people. We may have our flaws, but oh my, you're such a prude."

"I know how to behave and mind my manners. And I know my history. Now let's stop blabbing and get started. Have your defense spells at the tip of your tongue. Greta has already given us a heads up."

August led the way, Larissa following. They wound their way deeper into the earth, watching carefully as they moved. The road leading to their destination was solid and well-constructed for a place so remote.

"Greta said we'll continue until we reach a lake," said Larissa.

"And I guess we'll figure out what to do once we get there? Just like that?" August snapped his finger.

"We'll find instructions. She said so."

Something rustled to the right and left of them. Larissa gasped. "What was that?"

August came to an abrupt halt. "Beats the hell out of me. We haven't seen anyone or anything on this road to nowhere."

A strange war cry split the air. Larissa turned around and let out a shriek. A large malodorous being with a nasty, leering, disfigured face lumbered toward her. She raised her hand toward the creature, who was none other than a member of the Dwandee, a notorious troll tribe she'd only read about in witch books. The pictures she saw long ago had made an indelible impression in her mind.

"*Occideratu ignisis*," she yelled. From her fingertips, streams of charged blue light flashed across, hitting the troll and searing it into nothing but a pile of dust on the road.

"*Et obliterata*," cried out August. His hand came down on the head of another troll member, sending the creature slamming against a jagged wall of rocks. The trolled turned into a bright orange light and vanished. "That'll show you, you infernal . . ."

"Who destroys my men?" A deep voice boomed a few yards ahead. Walking towards August and Larissa was a troll much larger than the others who had surrounded them.

The troll leader stepped closer. "Who are you and where are you going?"

August scrutinized the troll, who wore a purple mantle trimmed in gold. On its head rested a golden crown studded with sparkling gemstones. He didn't look much better than his inferiors, but his face wore a solid expression of authority.

"We're on our way somewhere, minding our own business. We mean no harm," said August. His voice came out strained as he tried to feign politeness.

"You have no business here. You either turn around and go back from whence you came, or I take you and your pretty concubine to my place." He turned to his men, who joined him in a round of laughter.

"Listen here, you foul-mouthed, low-life piece of trash . . ."

Larissa's mouth dropped open in horror. The troll king narrowed his eyes, surmising August with great interest.

"You are a most arrogant man, disrespectful, and foolish." Without another word, the king held out a massive club-like staff and aimed it straight at August. "*Cunthu arimore morante nu*." A blinding flash of white light issued forth.

August slumped to the ground. Larissa screamed. The troll king smiled, eyes blazing, and stared with a lusty smile in the young woman's direction.

Chapter Fourteen

August awakened with a start. His long muscular frame sprawled across one bench of a rowboat. As his eyes adjusted to the phosphorescent gloom, he saw Larissa doggedly rowing, oars in hand, sleeves rolled up, as she coolly appraised him. An eerie mist shrouded the waters they traversed, hanging in cloud-like wisps all around them. The hazy curtain seemed spectral and foreboding, reaching out like fronds from a spider's web.

"Where'd you get the boat," he croaked. His mind struggled to remember how his encounter with the troll had ended.

"This boat was a gift from your ardent admirer, one Marvo," Larissa said. An icy tone filled her voice. She turned up her nose in disgust. "I was loath to accept it, but under the circumstances I felt we had no choice. It was waiting at the bank."

"Admirer?" August echoed the word in a slightly scoffing voice. "Not likely. I mean she is a lovely lady and all but old enough to be my grandmother."

"Great grandmother is more like it." Larissa corrected him with a sniff. "And her age didn't seem to bother you the night she . . . never mind."

"I don't believe you 'Rissa," August said. He ignored his companion's last comment. "Why would she send a gift? How would she know exactly where we are at any given time to know what we need?"

"Well, she is a prominent crystal gazer, which you would have known, if you ever bothered to research the backgrounds of your fellow witches. And of course, I found this . . ."

Larissa stopped rowing and touched the oar loop, from which a large gift tag hung. She tore it off and shoved it under August's nose

"To handsome August Hawthorne. A gift from your admirer, Lady Marvo," he read aloud. "You can't deny that it was a timely gift, can you?" He bore a slightly defensive tone.

"Humph," Larissa responded.

"And I might point out that we can't seem to go anywhere on this sacred quest of ours without running into one of your ex-boyfriends. Also, I find it funny that none of them have come up with anything useful that can aid us in any way. All they seem to want is to play tonsil hockey with you. Are you a virgin, by the way? I'm ever so slightly curious, and I keep forgetting to ask you."

Larissa flushed at August's audacity.

"You might do well to learn a few lessons, August, an important one being to keep a civil tongue in your head. The reason you find yourself waking up in a rowboat is because the last thing you did was insult the troll king. You're lucky to be alive. I barely warded off the wretched tail end of his Testudo Graeca spell by nanoseconds. Knocking you out cold was a first start. He was continuing full force just to finish you off."

August stared at her. "Really? What the hell? What happened? I do feel a bit heavy and inflexible." He glanced at his arms. "Did he turn me into a turtle?"

"Not quite," Larissa replied. She fought back the smirk creeping over her face. "But you were very unattractive for a while with your green complexion. And, of course, the scales. Your eyes didn't change much, still dark and beady as they usually are."

August's face showed a slightly injured look, which she chose to ignore.

"Anyway, after your complexion started returning to its natural color, and your huge tongue shrank back into your head, you were talking in your sleep as though you were having a conversation with someone. Do you remember anything about that?"

August sat up straight, agitated. "Yes, yes," he said. "I was conversing with someone about the Legend of the Four Vanished Claves. I had the impression that I was speaking with the ghost or spirit of one of my ancestors, and they were trying to tell me something."

Larissa erupted in a fit of laughter. "Nice try, August. Every self-respecting witch knows that there have always been four Elemental Claves. I wasn't born yesterday."

August studied her for a moment.

"What?" Larissa demanded.

"I'm trying to figure out why your Aunt Dorenda never mentioned them," he said slowly. "I can only guess that she wanted to shield you somehow."

"From what, exactly?" Larissa asked, instantly annoyed. "If you have any evidence to the contrary, please feel free to share it. Although I have to warn you that I am predisposed not to believe anything you might offer in the way of explanation."

Instead of continuing to speak, August reached in his pocket. After retrieving a tiny book, he waved it in the air, back and forth, until it had grown to standard size.

The title, in worn gilt lettering was, *PERRIGINE'S ENCYCLOPAEDIA OF WITCHLORE: With Historical Footnotes*.

August's self-satisfied smile when he handed it to her was almost more than she could bear. But curiosity overcame her irritation, and she stopped rowing. Taking the book, she held it across the palms of her hands and uttered a finder spell that Aunt Dorenda had taught her.

It wasn't a complicated spell, but it was good for finding lost keys and cell phones, and also for locating subjects of particular interest in reference books. When the pages opened of their own accord, she looked down and began reading intently.

After a few minutes had passed, August said loudly, "Well?" He still had the superior expression lingering on his handsome face. "Am I right, or am I right?"

"It would appear so." Larissa sniffed, committing the pages to mind. She had always valued her photographic memory, which served her well in several close calls. "But not everyone accepts Perrigine as an unimpeachable source."

"Yeah, only intelligent witches," August said with a scoff. "You can believe what you like. And I hate to be the one to rock your sheltered little world, but you need to be aware of certain salient facts as we continue our journey. Namely that we aren't the only ones seeking the sacred cloth. It does exist, and it is the powerful sort of magic relic that witches kill for.

Even if we accomplish our mission, our victory might be short-lived unless it reveals its secrets willingly."

"I am aware of that, but we need to know why it was created to begin with. There are a lot of unanswered questions." Larissa frowned at him, taking up the oars once again. "Do you mind helping me row now, lazy boy? We have drifted a bit. If we get too close to the shore in these parts, no telling what might happen."

"Geography was never my strong suit," August commented. He fixed both oars in the rowing locks and rowed in unison with Larissa. "Exactly what dangers are we avoiding by keeping on course? Snakes, maybe? It seems they might inhabit these waters. This seems more like a swamp than a lake. And what's with the cloud cover?"

"That's actually natural rather than enchanted," Larissa told him. "And snakes might be the least of our worries. Look over there for a minute." She finished with a nod of her head. "See anything unusual, August?"

He looked over to the far shoreline, intermittently visible between the fog and the low cloud cover.

The clouds seemed to momentarily thin in the direction he was looking. Staring harder, he saw what appeared to be a large bed of thick reeds edging the shoreline. They were much larger than any he'd seen in the regular swamps and bogs that he'd explored when he was a child. These tendrils extended to the size of a man's fist at the base and stretched up over six feet high to their tips.

The end of the tips opened like pinchers, and he could see needle-sharp teeth inside. Their whiteness stood out in the gloom. As he observed with interest, a small grey hapless bird landed on one of the ends. In seconds, the poor creature was surrounded, torn apart completely, and devoured. A piteous final squawk signaled the end to its horrid demise.

"I suppose they eat men too," August remarked.

"You think?" Larissa shot back.

They rowed in silence for less than a minute before she spoke up again.

"August stop staring at my boobs, you moron!" she said. Her annoyance reached a high pitch. "What is wrong with you? In casual company, you exhibit none of the social graces you seem to have when we are introduced to powerful witches. How would you like it if I stared at your package the entire journey?"

August threw back his head and laughed, his chuckles reverberating and multiplying in their watery surroundings.

"Oh, please, be my guest." He disengaged one hand from his rowing and gestured toward his crotch with an exaggerated flourish. "I think my stallion and his companions like to be admired, in fact. Go ahead, knock yourself out Larissa."

"Just stop it, or I'll hit you with this oar hard enough to break your nose," Larissa said.

"Haven't you ever heard the expression, 'a cat may look at a king'? August said with a baleful look. "I need some scenery, something pleasant to look at in this dismal gray place. And I've been meaning to ask you. Are you wearing a bra?"

With a red face and a determined look in her eye, Larissa stood up in the boat and pulled one of the oars from its lock. Steadying herself, she prepared to slam it over August's head.

But before she could, a shadow swept over her. A loud buzzing sound filled the humid air.

"Oh, for Godsakes," August said. He looked up, scowling. "What fresh hell might this be?"

Circling the two witches were a pair of the largest dragonflies they had ever seen, with wingspans over eight feet and ominous heavy, pulpy-looking bodies.

"Don't move!" Larissa said in a loud whisper.

Just as she spoke, one of the creatures swooped down low. She ducked quickly, avoiding contact with it.

August had dropped his oars and held a wand in one hand and a pistol in the other.

"Enchanted or real? Enchanted or real?" he muttered to himself. "Just not sure."

In the next second, one of the huge insects dove straight toward him, moving in close. He raised his weapon and fired.

It immediately fell, landing in the bottom of the boat, where he proceeded to stamp it to death. The bottom and instep of his boots ended up covered in grayish gore.

Larissa struggled with the second dragonfly, which had its spiny hairy forelegs tangled in her hair. The beasty insect was intent on pulling her upward, despite attempts to bat it away with an oar. August recognized immediately that she was in greater danger of knocking herself out by accident than of landing a blow on the flying monster.

He shot it down like he did the other. Though his aim found purchase, the gory creature still gripped her hair. She tumbled backwards as it fell behind her.

"Get it off. Get it off!" she shrieked.

Standing over her, sweating profusely, August pulled a trusty sword from his side and brought it down on the farthest section that separated her hair from the insect.

She sat up immediately feeling her hair, from which a good several inches had been unevenly hacked. Her beautiful hair, her crowning glory, was now much shorter.

"My hair!" she wailed. For the first time she sounded like a child, which surprised and amused August.

"Just look what you did!"

August stood and looked on, nonplussed. "I did what had to be done, Larissa. It nearly carried you off," he said tersely. "And don't forget that they are incredibly smart carnivores. It would have eaten you alive."

"I hate you, August Hawthorne! Now, help me get these dragonfly carcasses out of the boat. I think we're nearly there!"

Larissa had been right, August admitted a few minutes later, after they both resumed rowing. Even with the cloud vapors, they both saw a sandy beach up ahead and beyond it, the open entrance to an incredibly large cavern. A cavern as big as an airplane hangar.

Together they disembarked and pulled the boat up on the sandy beach. Aside from a few small birds, some ferns and nettles and a rock or two, the area seemed deserted.

"I don't feel as though I'm quite up to meeting anyone," Larissa said. She fussed as she tried securing what was left of her hair up in a bun. "I don't like introducing myself to important people unless I look my best."

August took in her appearance. Their time together at Gamal Emara's awakened something in him, though he'd almost rather die than admit it. In spite of everything, Larissa was beautiful. Her complexion seemed to glow luminously in the dimness of the fog-shrouded shoreline. Her eyes were bright, and her lips were, he decided, the exact color of crushed strawberries.

He had an unnerving overwhelming impulse to kiss her but knew if he tried, she would likely kick him in the balls if he did so.

"You look fine," he told her. He surreptitiously adjusted the front of his pants, which had grown uncomfortably tight for some reason. "I'm sure whomever we're supposed to meet will find you as beautiful as we all do."

"Hah!" she scoffed, "I know you're saying that to try and get on my good side after hacking off my hair, but it won't work, August. If my Aunt could see how much of my hair you sacrificed, she would take a blade to you herself. She might even geld you." Larissa uttered the last comment with emphasis.

August thought the idea of Aunt Dorenda trying to geld him was amusing but stifled a laugh. He knew Aunt Dorenda was far too composed to carry out such an act. But Larissa might. For all her airs, she had a hair-trigger temper that rivaled his own. He knew better.

They were nearly to the entrance when August placed a protective arm in front of Larissa and brought a finger to his lips. He had felt as though someone was watching them since they'd gotten out of the boat, but now all his instincts were on alert.

With all his self-indulgent behaviors and faults, August had nevertheless inherited some of his Grandfather Jove's preternatural instincts, one of which was sensing imminent danger. He wasn't wrong.

Claw-like appendages shot up from underneath both he and Larissa, rising from the sand at their feet and capturing their ankles in an iron grip before yanking them down into the shifting sand. What once seemed a solid shore spun directly beneath them both, blasting fine sprays of sand into their faces as it dragged them downward.

When the sand ceased shifting, they found themselves buried up to their necks and unable to move.

"I have guests!" They heard a booming voice echo from inside the cavernous entrance. They craned what was visible of their necks toward the sound, trying to see the owner.

Emerging from the entrance, accompanied by a writhing, twisting entourage of river snakes, came The Lord of Lakes, Tiberinus.

He stood over them. His beard was the only portion of his face not overshadowed by the deep hood of his long cloak. He gestured to the carpet of snakes at his side and behind him to stay back.

"Announce yourselves." His stern, commanding voice rang out. He looked down on them with a face showing great skepticism. "I received no word that I was to have visitors today. Did all your pigeons have the flu?"

"We . . . um . . . did attempt to notify you of our coming," August said in a relatively calm voice. His claustrophobia was kicking in, and he was having a devil of a time trying to catch a deep breath while impacted in the wet sand. "I apologize, Sire, for our rude and unanticipated presentation. I am August South Hawthorne, Grandson of Jove South Hawthorne and heir to our clave.

May I present Larissa North Strondavan. She is also a coven heir. She is the niece of high witch Dorenda and possesses many gifts."

"Gifts?" the tall figure repeated. "I believe I am acquainted with both of your families. Elemental Witches, aren't they? Also known as the last of the Elementals, if I remember correctly. There were originally nine families, you know, not the current five that have survived."

The seashore shook. Larissa found herself propelled upward in a whirlwind of sand. She stood, remarkably dry, on the solid surface, only she was barefoot.

"My boots!" she cried out, staring down at her bare toes. Her eyes displayed an imploring look at the Lord of Lakes.

Lord Tiberinus looked like any other wizard, except the blue cloth comprising his voluminous hooded robe, which seemed to be in constant fluid motion like the lake waters.

"My pardon, young Larissa North Strondovan," he said, bowing slightly to her. "If you will step a foot or two to the side of where you are standing, I shall retrieve your boots immediately."

Larissa did so. Another sand whirl appeared with her boots revolving at its core. Within seconds, the sand whirl had spit the boots out and descended again into the surface of the shoreline.

"Thank you," she said, shaking them out and putting them back on her feet. She gestured over to where August's head was poking out of the sand. "Are you going to release my traveling companion? I believe you know his grandfather, Jove South Hawthorne."

"Yes, I do know of the Hawthorne Clave. This witch with his insolent head poking out of the sand at my feet is a non-favorite of mine, though I hold his Grandfather Jove in some esteem. His reputation has preceded him, my dear. I am half inclined to leave him where he is and let the tide take him."

Larissa looked over at August, who had gone strangely silent. She wondered what bargain she could make with the Lord of Lakes so that he would release August. There was also a part of her that enjoyed his discomfort immensely. After all, August had always lived in a careless, rebellious and selfish manner. It was almost poetic justice that he should suffer this indignity.

The Lord of Lakes moved until he leaned over August, who suddenly looked frightened.

"If I release you from the sand, will you promise to comport yourself in a manner that does your Grandfather proud, young Hawthorne?" he asked.

Larissa noted the undulating, wavering image of the moon decorating the back of Lord of Lake's cloak.

"I will Lord," August said. An attempt at bowing his head resulted in hitting his chin on the unrelenting sand holding him fast.

"Ah, well then, in that case," Tiberinus said with a sigh.

August was propelled upward a tad more violently than Larissa had been, which resulted in him shooting up from the sand like he'd been released from a cannon. He uttered a cry and fell from a height of six feet, hitting the sand hard.

Larissa covered her mouth, concealing a smile. Tiberinus sighed again, snapping his fingers. The sand cyclone formed one last time, spewing out August's boots. One of them landed squarely on his head as he lay prone on the shore.

"There you go," the Lord of Lakes said cheerfully. "Come now. We have much to discuss."

Larissa was surprised to see that the hangar-like interior of the cave led to a set of immense iron doors. They swung open, revealing an interior that seemed like the lobby of a glitzy hotel. It was lit by chandeliers of pure carved crystal rock. She could tell that they emanated a light generated by supernatural means.

"I expect you both must be famished," Tiberinus told them. "My servants will show you to your quarters, and you will join me and my other guests for dinner in half an hour sharp. I will see you then."

The pair recognized the throng of servants who joined them as Washlings, creatures long thought to be extinct, and who had existed eons ago. They were roughly humanoid creatures with webbed hands and feet and seahorse heads. They were highly intelligent.

Their speech was extremely high pitched and painful to human ears, so they were mute most of the time in deference to their witch and warlock superiors.

The Washlings appeared to be mostly female; their gender was hard to discern at times. Larissa had heard from ancient folklore that they were able to reproduce on their own without a partner.

They were on a tight time frame. As she stood looking in a full-length mirror in her room after the shower, Larissa admitted to herself that she was tired of wearing the one fancy dress she had packed. Unfortunately, she couldn't materialize one out of thin air without expending a lot of personal energy. Most of that had evaporated after rowing for hours and being buried up to her neck in sand. However, she knew that the situation could be improved.

"*Mutatio*," she shouted.

All the while, a crystal-clear image took root and stayed in her mind during the spell. It worked instantly. The blue dress changed to a deep rose color studded with sparkling rhinestones. Seed pearls dotted the neckline and sleeves. A contrasting sash in luxurious black velvet wrapped around the waist of the gown.

Smiling and nodding in satisfaction, she whipped around, the remainder of her hair making a graceful arc in the air. In the hallway she was surprised to run smack into August.

"Well, well, well," she said, surprised at his renewed appearance. "I see you clean up nicely, August."

"As do you," he answered. His eyes traveled down to her abundant cleavage prominently exposed at the top of the gown's neckline.

"I'm up here, August." she said sharply. "How is it that you manage to ruin a decent start to every conversation between us?"

"I know," he said. Their eyes met. As they walked together, he smiled and chatted amiably. "You really shouldn't make such a display of your . . . um . . . assets if you don't want them admired. Some men are leg men. Others prefer a tight derriere. I have always been a breast aficionado myself. I mean they have so much going for them, don't they? They are wonderfully round or banana-shaped, with areolas and nipples that just beg to be teased and sucked. Yes, definitely a breast man. I bet our Lord of Lakes, Tiberinus, might be too. Did you know that he is rumored to have over a thousand children?"

They had arrived at the grand dining hall. Music from a Washling orchestra played in the background. As they approached the dining table, Washling servants in uniform served hors d'oeuvres. The pair noticed extra guests. Larissa's heart nearly stopped when she saw them.

Chapter Fifteen

There were three extra persons sitting at the table, two women and one gentleman with long black hair that flowed over his shoulders. His face was in profile as he chatted with their host, but Larissa couldn't stifle a gasp when she saw him.

He seemed to notice her at the same moment. With elegant movements, he rose, came immediately to her side, and lifted her hand gently to his lips.

"Larissa, lady of beauty and heir to the spinners, it has been far too long!" he said with gallantry. August's face held a look of consternation.

He also turned briefly and acknowledge August with a cool, polite nod. "The Hawthorne heir, August. I don't believe we have met, but I must say your reputation precedes you."

August flushed. Turning to Larissa he asked, "You know this fellow?"

"I am Edouard Anguis, heir to the Anguis Clave, grandson of the Dragon Priest, Clavius and son of Priscilla the Beautiful." The striking dark-haired man stared back.

August noted the stranger's incredible height, taller than he was even at six feet two inches. He immediately straightened up to appear equally as tall.

Larissa's face was pink with joy. "August this is one of my oldest and dearest friends. We met in Ecuador years ago when I was on a vacation with my aunt. We met the Sabine Sisters, one of the oldest covens in South America, and they shared some of their knowledge of ancient potions."

Edouard led Larissa over to a seat at the right of their host, Tiberinus, and next to his own at the table. The Lord of Lakes nodded to August and gestured to a seat on his left, which August took unwillingly. He never liked being surprised, and meeting yet another acquaintance of Larissa was something unexpected.

"Edouard and his family know just about everyone worth knowing in the Magiverse," Larissa said, smiling around the table. "And I believe these gorgeous ladies are his younger sisters, Malevolinda and Carnetta. Did I recall your names correctly, ladies?"

"Oh, Yes." Malevolinda, the dark-haired sister, responded with a gracious smile. "My sister and I are happy to see you looking so vibrant, Larissa. Please give our best to your Aunt Dorenda next time you see her. Lovely woman. She was able to help Carnetta with her dizzy spells."

Dinner was served. As expected, most of the fare was harvested from the chain of lakes surrounding Tiberinus's dwelling place. Rainbow trout, snails, perch and smallmouth bass were presented on steaming trays. Lake oysters prepared several ways—in stews, fried, and raw—were also on the menu.

The Lord of Lakes prepared a toast and made the customary offering before the meal began. At last, all were free to eat their fill.

Larissa found she was ravenous. From what she viewed from across the immense carved abalone shell table, so was August. Even the slight embarrassment of having Edouard compliment her on her appetite didn't deter her. She focused solely on the delicious repast.

Between the seven-course dinner and dessert, Tiberinus declared a break so that his guests could use the restrooms and enjoy a walk around the cleverly constructed halls and common rooms within the cavernous space.

August waited until he saw Tiberinus engaged in conversation with the Anguis heir before approaching Larissa.

"Who is that guy to you, Larissa?" he said. "No, wait. Don't tell me. It's another one of your boy toys, right? I am really curious now. Is there anywhere in the entire world we can go and not run into one of your boyfriends? Or have you managed in the short time you have been in existence to have spread your favors over the entire planet?"

Larissa experienced the now all too familiar sensation, an itching in her right palm. The only relief would be to smack the sarcastic expression right off August's face, but the last thing she wanted to do was to create a scene.

Instead, her entire body ached to be in Edouard's arms. The attraction between them had never wavered, and now she felt a magnetic pull to be pressed up against his magnificent physique. It was the ancient attraction of Light and Shadow, and she found him irresistible.

Also, she didn't wish to displease the Lord of Lakes. She had a premonition that he might offer them something that might save their lives as she and August continued their journey.

"My private life—in particular my private life before you and I began this quest—has been and continues to be none of your business."

August raised his left hand and counted off her boyfriends on his raised fingers. "We just ran into Dennis at Endor. And then there was Daniel, who took us to the cave when we were in Colorado. Now we have bumped into yet another of your ex beaus. I mean, honestly, what am I to think? I had you figured for a good girl. Now I'm not so sure you haven't fooled us all.

"Not that I'm judging. Oh, no. Far be it for me to question the impetuousness of youth. I have quite the reputation as a libertine myself. But I was thinking unless you are diddling yourself while I sleep, I think maybe we should hook up. Use each other.

Become . . . what's the term? Oh yes. fuckbuddies. You should think about it. I am not a kiss and tell kind of guy, and I think it would relieve you of some of that bitchy tension you are always giving off. You seemed okay at Gamal Emara's. I have a point, you know."

At that moment Edouard Anguis, his white teeth in sharp contrast to his ebony skin, called her name. As she turned, Larissa purposely drove her heel into August's ankle, drawing blood.

August ruefully bent and rubbed his injured ankle, wiping the blood with a kerchief. He kept his eye on Larissa as she joined the tall, dark, and handsome Anguis heir. Edouard had his arm around Larissa's waist, holding her close. For her part, Larissa seemed quite comfortable with the familiar gesture.

Keeping a straight expression was difficult when inwardly, he felt a certain indignation he'd never felt concerning her. The ferocity of his feelings mystified him. He couldn't figure out why he cared so much about who Larissa saw or her past or what she was doing with Edouard. Why should he give a flying fuck?

He was still pondering his unexpected feelings when he felt a small hand slip into his. He looked down. Edouard Anguis's fair-haired sister, Carnetta, had taken his hand in hers and was smiling up at him.

"Good Lord!" he exclaimed. The words had slipped out by mistake. During dinner he had failed to notice that the young lady, apart from being incredibly fair in sharp contrast to her siblings, had crimson irises.

"Oh," the young lady said softly. She let out a light giggle. "I see you just figured out that I am an albino. It makes sense, doesn't it? I am the only fair-haired Anguis in my family."

"Your eyes," August murmured. "I'm sorry that I am staring, but they are unlike any I have ever seen."

"Yes. I am the white sheep of the family." She giggled again. "I was born albino. It seems that one of our own is born albino in each generation. We are called 'Praedita', the Gifted Ones. We are special We have certain abilities that the others don't."

"I just bet you do," August said. He moved closely to the mysterious young woman. Her hair was silver white, as were her eyebrows. She had an unbelievable figure with full breasts pouring over the top of a gown as crimson as her irises, a tiny waist, and full hips that swayed when she walked.

"Tell me more about yourself, Carnetta. What kind of special abilities do you have?"

"I can see the future," she said. "Both the immediate future and potential futures that appear in an array because of the free choice factor."

August smiled. She disarmed him. He was close enough to smell her scent and be captivated by it. Her skin gave off an aroma of both myrrh and amber, with a tantalizing undernote of female musk.

"And I can see that we will be fucking later, in a closet, you nasty boy." She said all this in a casual tone. She no sooner finished her seductive declaration than August felt his cock growing rigid, making his pants feel uncomfortably tight.

"I saw a closet on the way here," he said, glancing around to make sure all the other dinner guests were engaged. "I think I remember where it was."

They turned, Carnetta's hand still in August's, and exited quickly. Four feet outside of the dining hall stood the door to a linen closet, which was situated between two posts. August turned the handle, relieved when the door opened.

He had barely shut it when he felt her hands clawing at his clothing. She loosened his belt. His cock sprang forward of its own accord. Carnetta turned down the top of her gown, exposing a set of fine breasts. They were as immense as he had imagined. To his surprise, when he leaned forward to suck a nipple, it was fully large as one on a baby bottle. Inflamed further, his finger sought the treasure between her lily-white thighs.

"Fuck me, August," she said in a throaty whisper. "Fuck me as hard as you can."

August hoisted her up, letting out an animalistic noise as he slid his cock into her wet cunt. He realized that there was more going on than his pumping action. It seemed to him that her pussy was actually tightening around him, squeezing at the same time he was fucking her.

They kept at it, hard and determined. In seconds, he came like a stallion. Before he had finished ejaculating, Carnetta pushed him away and dropped to her knees, greedily sucking and swallowing his semen. She turned a smiling face up to his when she finished, exhaling a loud sigh of content. Her eyes sparkled like a thousand stars. "That was so good."

Strains of music floated down the hallway. The pair hastily buttoned up and arranged both their clothing. They assumed a casual expression.

"How do I look?" Carnetta asked. "Do I look like I've been fucking?"

August stared at her, amazed how perfectly calm she was. Her breathing had returned to normal. Their tryst still lingered within him, and he found himself a little breathy still from the heavy exertion.

"You have a little bit of something right there, at the corner of your mouth," he said.

"Oh." Carnetta stuck out her tongue, licking the drop of remaining ejaculate clinging to the edge of her lips.

"My first course." She closed her eyes briefly and smiled. I hate to waste a drop. You are delicious, August. I am just sorry my greedy little cunt got most of you."

Hardly anyone noticed when the couple returned to the table. Larissa and Edouard seemed to be engaged in intense conversation, oblivious to everything around them. When the fabulous flambé desserts landed on the table and were lit to an enthusiastic applause from the guests, the couple never took their eyes off each other.

After sharing personal stories and confidences, Edouard Anguis leaned close, whispering in her ear, "I never should have let you go, Larissa. In all the time that has transpired since our first meeting, I have never met a young woman or witch who comes close to you."

His declarations moved Larissa deeply, filling her with a sense of satisfaction. She had often thought about Edouard over the years, wondering what he was up to—and why he never contacted her. It wasn't in Larissa's nature to chase after a boy. Her Aunt Dorenda had always told her that as the most beautiful and talented of the Strondovan Witches of the North, she should take her time and choose her boyfriends carefully.

In fact, her aunt had often repeated that on the entire planet there was likely no male witch that was Larissa's equal.

"There isn't one young scalawag anywhere who is a worthy equal to you, Larissa." Her voice would brim with pride. "Not one."

"I'm glad you love me so much," Larissa would respond, "but Auntie, I will have to choose one of them anyway or die an old maid. Wouldn't you like some grand-nieces or nephews to dandle on your knee?"

The longer Larissa sat close to Edouard, the more she was convinced that she had found her true equal, both in physical beauty and magical prowess. Not only his ridiculously handsome appearance but also his voice drew her in. She could listen to him talk for hours. Here was someone at last in whom she could confide, reveal the secrets of her soul, and surrender her body in the heat of passion.

Because of his passionate personality, he approached everything full throttle. Music, the arts, potion-making, fine food. He also learned how to pilot a passenger jet, something witches didn't generally do, since they found and used natural portals or created ones of their own.

A servant interrupted her intense conversation with Edouard by presenting a silver tray under her pert nose. On it was a War Pigeon.

"We found the bird squawking just outside the entrance to the abode," the servant told her. His voice came out in a harsh nasal tone. "Apparently a message for you."

Larissa resisted the urge to clamp her hands over both ears, diminishing the Washling's unpleasant voice. She nodded graciously, thanking the servant and untying the rolled message from the pigeon's leg. The bird immediately began pecking at the crumbs left over on Larissa's dessert plate without waiting for an invitation.

"Rude little thing," Edouard commented, glaring at the bird, "Shall I take it outside?"

"Oh please, just let her have the rest of my dessert," Larissa murmured "Poor dear must be famished, I'm sure."

Larissa looked at the message that the pigeon had been carrying and frowned.

"It's from Daniel," she said aloud. "He said he's been following our progress and keeping in touch with Aunt Dorenda while I have been away. He misses me of course. Part of this is in a code we developed between us."

She glanced up at Edouard, immediately wishing she hadn't revealed that last infobyte. His eyes had lit up in a show of keen interest, displaying something strange in his overall demeanor. A bolt of uneasiness flashed through her, and she couldn't understand why.

"You don't say," he said smoothly. "Mind if I have a look at it? I used to be a decent code cracker even as a child. I have a penchant for deciphering codes, you might say. I also have skills as a cryptomagist.

"Let me try and decode it. With a little luck I can use a spell that will cause the meaning to rise up from the paper in your language of choice and hang in the air for fifteen seconds. In the past, I have found that is sufficient time to glean its meaning."

Larissa smiled and shot Edouard a brief look of admiration. But a gut instinct warned her to be cautious. "I can read the rest of it later. Right now, I am completely worn out from today's journey. Besides, it's probably some cute little reminder not to forget him."

"Is this your boyfriend who sent you this missive? He must have decent skills to program the pigeon to bring you a note. This realm is protected by deep magnetic fields emanating from the abyss-like center of the lake. It often confuses any creature flying over it. It is amazing to me that your War Pigeon found you."

A twinge of irritation shot through Larissa. Why would Edouard be asking so many questions about Daniel? Others' curiosity about her friendships with young suitors was never appreciated. Friendships went under the category of private business. However, since he had offered to help her with the coded message, she decided to lighten up a little. Would he be able to crack the code she and Daniel created just for each other?

"Daniel is a friend. He is very close to my Aunt Dorenda. We've spent many hours together over the years."

"I see," Edouard replied. He grinned and shook his head. "I suppose I shall have to get used to the idea that you have many admirers. It's not like I can't seem to be captured by your charms myself."

Before she could protest, Edouard, with a practiced hand, took the small paper and placed it on the table between them, waving his hand across it. It unrolled and lay flat against the tabletop, fresh and neat as though it had been ironed. The words were clearly legible. He whipped out a slender collapsible wand, snapping it to full length with a single shake.

"*Appeariatro bonum parragast, finitum revelare verbis*," he said in an authoritative voice. Dust drifted upward from the paper. The following phrase appeared in the air, so clear that they both were able to read it.

"Beware of snakes, dear girl. Not everyone who invites you into their nest is your friend."

"How very curious!" Larissa exclaimed. "It's almost a riddle, isn't it?"

"It is, indeed," Edouard replied.

Larissa swore she saw a glimmer of recognition in his dark eyes. The light grin on his lips caught her attention most. "Why Edouard, I believe you might have an idea of what Daniel meant. If you do, please clue me in."

Edouard's expression sobered. He shifted his gaze until he looked her in the eye. In a serious tone he said, "It reminds me of something I once heard before. Let me research it a bit to make sure, and I promise to share after I do." His eyes glittered anew as he gazed into her face. "I would never want to mislead you, Larissa my sweet."

Larissa smiled up at him. She rationalized in her mind. Of course he would be careful to fact check before he proffered an opinion. That was one of the qualities she admired most about him. He wasn't feckless like some of the young men she had known (August immediately sprang to mind), but he was deliberate and careful. In her estimation, Edouard was more mature than most male witches.

After the meal, Tiberinus motioned to August and Larissa that he wanted to meet with them privately. Flanked by Washling bodyguards, they moved into another cave-like chamber. It was nicely furnished, with a large desk that appeared to have been carved from a single piece of quartz. Veins of amethyst and feldspar ran through the rock walls.

Tiberinus gestured to the two seats in front of his desk. When the couple seated themselves, he sat down.

"You are here seeking my help, but I am loath to give it, I must confess." he said. "I have no quarrel with either of you, but having lived a few centuries, I naturally have a long memory.

"I am afraid neither of your claves have been kind to us Wizards of the Lakes. This is why I hesitate. We used to be known as the Laken Magicals and were well-respected by the rest of the powerful mages of old. However, it has come to my attention that we share a common enemy, and that casts a different light on the matter. I am, of course, speaking of the Devoratrix."

A shudder ran through August and Larissa at the mention of the name. That was a clave rumored to be behind the deaths of several beloved wizards and many of the natural disasters and wars that had visited the temporal world in modern times. Their origins went back to the beginning of time, it was said. Their rituals were obscenity itself, and the names of those involved with their secret society were shrouded in mystery.

But the most horrifying aspect of their organization, verified by thousands of witnesses who had somehow survived their attacks, was that they ate human flesh.

"I know of whom you speak," August said, "and I'm sure that Larissa does also. But we are not venturing near their clave as far as I know. Even if we were, we would be most foolish to attempt to take them on. Their magical prowess is legendary."

Tiberinus stroked his beard, contemplating August's words. He leaned forward. "My oracles have seen that you two, the heirs, are destined to confront them. They are hidden in plain sight. Your encounter with them is inevitable, I am afraid.

"Because I have foreknowledge of this, I have discovered a way that you can be useful to me. One of their high Magicals, is a necromancer by the name of Svapada. When you encounter him—and you will—I want you to bring me both his heads. He is a cojoined being, you see.

"They say he has three legs, three penises, and can walk up walls with rapid speed. You must be on your game and attack from three sides. I suggest you find another companion adept with a sword."

Larissa looked over at a frowning August. "You said the Devoratrix are hidden in plain sight. What did you mean by that?" she asked.

"My dear young witch, must I spell it out for you? They are a clave within a clave. They have assimilated and are protected by one of the most revered and well known of the witch claves."

August seemed to recover somewhat from the information overload. He had no idea if the Lord of Lakes was being truthful or just playing with them. "If we agree to kill this Svapada, what will you give us in return that will be of such value that we would gladly risk our lives fighting a three-legged cannibal?"

"I will show you," Tiberinus said. He sighed, stood up, and turned around. The pair watched closely as he waved his greenish overly long fingers in the air. At first, nothing seemed to happen. As they watched longer, they viewed the Lord of Lakes parting the air as if it were a heavy drape, pulling it apart to reveal a golden armoire.

He opened a drawer at the bottom and let out a sound of excitement, removing what appeared to be a rolled piece of black velvet cloth.

"Ah, there you are my beauty!" he murmured. "Inside this cloth, I have something for our efforts. You will need this special tool for your quest. It is valuable and will serve you well. He replaced the velvet bundle back in the drawer. When the drape fell, the armoire was no longer visible. Tiberinus turned to the pair and smiled. "Do we have a deal?"

"By the way," August said. "what did this Devoratrix do that you have singled him out for execution and commissioned Larissa and I to be your assassins? It might help us to know."

"Well, August, I am surprised you haven't guessed." The Lord of Lakes chuckled. "The bastard miscreant ate my wife!"

Chapter Sixteen

This time August propelled the boat carrying him and Larissa down another underground waterway. Earlier, Tiberinus had no hesitation in pointing him in the right direction.

"Go down that tunnel. It's a good ten miles long. When you round a bend, you only have several yards to go before you'll hit a patch of dry land. Anchor your boat securely and walk the remainder of the tunnel to the end. It's a dry path that leads to the outside world."

"And then where?" August had asked, frowning. "Surely we won't be on a wild goose chase, will we?"

"My son," answered Tiberinus, "why would I send you on anything of the kind, especially when I want restitution for my beloved deceased wife. And she was a very good one." He nodded with enthusiasm. "When you reach the outside, walk straight across a small field until you see the white rock. It has an opening. Enter and continue until you see something."

"That's it? Keep going until we see something?" Larissa frowned now. "Not meaning any disrespect, but I have to agree with August. This really does sound like a goose chase."

"My child, why do I have to keep spelling everything out for you?" Tiberinus leaned his head back and laughed. "Nothing is a goose chase. But that rock is really an entrance into the cave where the Devoratrix hold their sordid rituals. I've checked my scrying sources. They are holding a ceremony today, and Svapada is leading it. So you must make haste."

The Lord of Lakes shooed them away with the wave of his hands. "Go on, you two young, earnest witches. Bring me what I ask, and I'll give you something to add to your arsenal." He smiled a toothy smile. "I won't disappoint." With a wavy whirling motion, he shifted up and out of sight.

"Well, this is a fine kettle of fish," said August. "My arms are killing me. How much farther?"

"Oh, for heaven's sake, August, you've only been rowing for twenty minutes." Larissa let out a huff of disgust.

"It's ten miles. That's going to take some time rowing manually."

Larissa sat up. "Then let's just sail our way through. Tiberinus said to make haste, so we'll do it. Can't afford to miss anything noteworthy once we finally see something."

August laughed.

"*Solvit.*" The young witch held her hand upward. A long pole with a sail shot up from the middle of the boat.

"You're turning dear Greta's gift into a sailboat?" August asked.

"Your precious Greta was useful with this gift. I'll give her that."

"She had other gifts too," August blurted out.

Larissa sent an orange flash of light in her companion's direction, an electrical charge that landed on his hand.

"Damn!" The man yelped in pain. "Would you stop doing that every time you get saucy?" The oar he held burst into flames. He cried out again, casting the useless tool into the lake. "Now we're an oar short."

"Who needs it when we have this? "*Ventus!*"

August gasped and wobbled to one side. He steadied himself with one arm. A cool rush of wind sailed down the tunnel, landing squarely against the new-formed sail. The boat sliced down the water

"There, much better." Larissa smiled with satisfaction. "Should have thought of this the first time, but now we know where we're going—sort of."

A couple more sails were added. August guided the boat down the tunnel. His sailing skills, learned in cities with warmer climes, served him well. The air grew cooler in some areas. Eerie whispers on the tunnel breeze filled their ears like ominous messages sent from an unseen force. A force that somehow knew to where the pair traveled. Larissa and August rode in silence.

A rock tumbled from once side of the tunnel wall, clattering haphazardly into the water with a dull plop. A wet drop from somewhere above splattered on Larissa's head. She stifled a cry of protest, wiping at her hair. August's eyes darted all around, squinting at times for a better view.

He swore there were figures lurking behind some of the rocks and in between crevasses. Moving shadows proved confusing. Were they figments of imagination or something to really fear? Preferring not to alarm Larissa, he kept his concerns to himself. Tiberinus had given them a lantern to light the way, a witch light that illuminated stronger than an average Mortal beam.

After what seemed like sailing forever, they landed on the patch of land Tiberinus had mentioned. August guided the boat to a far side, where he barely saw a lone post sticking out of the ground.

"We're here," he muttered.

Together, they anchored and tied off the boat. Each one climbed out, steadying themselves against a floor of shifting soil comprised of sand and pebbly gravel. Something unidentified slid across Larissa's foot. She clapped a hand over her mouth, stifling a scream. August grunted, trying desperately to move his feet and scramble away from a creature that was hellbent on wrapping itself around his ankle. Where did the awful pest come from?

"We're not safe here. Let's get moving." He pulled himself past Larissa, struggling as he placed one foot in front of the other. The soil buried his feet up to his ankles. He glanced at Larissa, who seemed to be sinking little by little. "Grab my hand. Let's go. It's now or never."

Without a word of protest, she grasped August's hand, squeezing as if her life depended on it. The two made an agonizing trek across the makeshift beach, one that looked like a scene out of a dystopian horror novel.

"I don't think whomever or whatever it is that controls this part of the lake wants anyone coming around." August grasped Larissa's hand tighter.

"Ya think?" she said, glaring at him. "And to think I let you talk me out of finding a third person with a sword. Tiberinus suggested that. Why did I listen to you, instead?"

"Because we're more than capable witches," August replied. "We'll get this."

"I'm a capable witch," mumbled Larissa.

August stopped in his tracks. "Don't start with me, or I swear I'll dump you here and go by myself. I've come through when we've needed it. You just don't want to admit it."

She shuddered and spat. "God, what's in the air here? I'm nearly choking on heaven knows what."

"Make a brighter light." August pointed up at the etheric orb that looked like its energy level was on a wing and a prayer before sputtering out.

"I'm getting drained creating things. Make an orb yourself, since you allude to your skills being on par with mine."

She let out a screech and jerked her hand out of August's. The vibrating current running through her created a heat so strong she feared she'd spontaneously combust.

"Two can play that game, sister." August narrowed his eyes. A corner of his lip pulled up in a wicked sneer. "I did perfect a weak area of my *Hominem Fulgur Percutiens* skills.

August called out, "*Lux in via*." A dusty blue haze filled the tunnel, brightening until the pair had to shield their eyes.

"Okay, I believe you. Can you turn it down a little?" Larissa cried.

"Better?"

"Much. Oh, my god!" Larissa gazed around. "Would you look at that."

At intervals, insects resembling a cross between horseflies and scorpions flitted through the air, landing on the walls and scurrying away into the darkness.

"Let's go," said August. "And no more fighting, or we're toast."

The two rejoined hands and dragged themselves through the tunnel for what seemed like a good hour. At the end, they saw the natural outside light peeking through.

They stepped into a hazy field that stretched all around them. Something in the scenery held a feeling of desolation. No building or human could be seen. No trees, flowers, or ponds, either.

"There it is." August pointed to a far bank directly across from where they stood. As Tiberinus had described, a large rock fit snugly against a rise of earth.

"I don't see a door. How are we supposed to . . .?" Larissa pursed her lips. "I get it. To the casual outsider, it looks like a regular rock. But we know better."

August led the way. "Time for our best opening spells."

"Do you think we get so many tries before something awful happens?" Larissa asked.

"Geeze! Probably?"

Larissa nodded. "Good to know these things just in case. Remember, Tiberinus said the Devoratrix are master magicians. You know they're not going to let just anyone in."

"And how many people do you think just happen to wander here? This place looks like nobody ever comes around. Who would find it?"

"What spell are we going to use?" Larissa pulled at August's hand. He glanced down and pulled it away.

"Let's see once we get there."

The stone was a large white agate boulder. August ran his hand over the smooth surface.

"You know what agate really is, don't you?" Larissa spoke up.

"Hmm?"

"Agate is formed from volcanic rocks. Usually," she continued.

August stared at her, eyes narrowed in concentration. "Go on."

"This boulder is created out of fire."

"And?" he asked, tapping a foot with impatience.

"Don't you see, August? Fire. Fire is used in ceremony. Fire can also be used to reveal spells, codes, secret things."

The young man's eyes widened. "And fire, when revealing secrecy, is rarely used alone—when revealing secret things."

"Precisely." Larissa smiled. "And when rock really heats up, it becomes molten, liquid. It flows, moves, shifts."

August, murmured, nodding his head, "Mmm."

Larissa kept speaking. "I will do a spell to liquify this rock, more or less. You do a fire spell. We do it at the same time. It will be the closest thing to mimicking volcanic action. On a really simplified scale, if you know what I mean."

He smiled. "I like it. But how on earth did you come up with such a notion?"

She stopped a moment. "It's a feeling I'm getting. I'm thinking this through, only because the Devoratrix, being a cunning lot, would want an extra layer of protection just to make sure no one can hack their door."

August stepped back, surveying his companion. "You know, you may be smart, but I refuse to believe you're that smart. Coming up with something as new-fangled as this?"

Larissa squared up her shoulders. "Maybe I read and study more than you do. If you'd studied science and ancient spells and magical decoding like I have, you might not find my idea so implausible. Besides, the old texts talk about this sort of thing. You got any better ideas?"

"Do you feel that?" August whispered.

"What? Oh!" Larissa sucked in her breath. "I do now. Like a tiny earthquake beneath our feet." She looked up at the sky. The haze had deepened.

"Something's going on, and I don't know what it is, whether it's natural or has something to do with the Devoratrix and their ceremony."

"Let's just try my idea. Can't hurt. You go first, heat things up."

August grinned.

"Not that, you ninny!" Larissa kicked his ankle. "No time for wise cracks."

"Let me think," he said. Closing his eyes and stretching his hands toward the boulder, August uttered, "*Aperto igne. In quo.*"

"*Liquifiet. ostende ianuam.*" Larissa called out her spell immediately after his.

They both concentrated. August opened his eyes, watching. Larissa gazed at the stone, trance-like. The ground beneath them rumbled again.

The stone sweated. Droplets of water trickled over the surface. August and Larissa focused harder, reviewing their spells not aloud this time, but mentally. A light mist formed in front of the boulder. The surface turned translucent, thinning to a near water-like texture, revealing a shadow of a door.

"Now!" cried Larissa.

She and August made a run for it, dashing through the door. The instant they cleared the threshold, the stone turned back to its former state.

"Shit," muttered August, "we'll have a hell of a time getting out of here."

Together they hugged the side of the wall, carefully picking their way down an incline. Crude steps had been carved of volcanic lava. Torches lit the way. In silence they walked, looking behind them and all around for good measure. The winding steps led to an intersecting hall.

The two stopped short before continuing further. They stared at each other. August looked at Larissa. She put a finger to her lips and plastered herself against the wall, inching closer to the end. Slowly moving her head forward around the corner, she barely viewed the right side of the intersection. Her blood ran cold.

A Devoratrix guard had been stationed in an alcove a few feet away. Smaller torches burned on either side of him. Unlike Svapada, this being looked more human. His skin glowed a light dusty green. A thin layer of greasy gray hair covered his head. He wore a dark trench coat-style uniform and held a long sword by his side.

Larissa thought a moment on how to snuff out this guard. Too late. He moved away from the alcove and headed straight toward the intersection. "Look out," she whispered to August, pushing him roughly back into the hall.

"What the . . ." August pushed back with indignation.

"You, there," the guard called out. "How dare you enter here."

"*Ut pulvis*," Larissa called out, flicking her fingers in the guard's direction.

The Devoratrix turned into dust and showered to the ground, leaving behind a cloudy stink.

August with his mouth agape, stood looking on at the spectacle before him. "Holy hell! That was magnificent." He punched Larissa lightly on the arm in approval. "Fucking impressive."

"I rather like it myself. Great way to rid yourself of something pesky." She pointed to the left of the intersection. "This way."

Winding their way down a lava-paved trail, they found themselves standing before another entrance. But this wasn't made of stone. Nor did a cloth curtain cover it. Larissa shrank back in horror. August's face turned cold and emotionless.

A bed of pit vipers trailed from the top, stretched out full-length. More stretched out, twisting and gyrating from the sides. Their tongues flicked, and their eyes glowed a bright ruby red. Walking through it would be sure death.

"Might be another good time to try that spell you . . ." August choked on his words.

Larissa gasped, horrified. One of the vipers had sped from its place in the curtain formation and wrapped itself around August's neck, squeezing the life out of him. Worse, two more slithered in their direction. She said the magic words as before, aiming toward the curtain. The vipers were no more, crashing down in a heap of dust.

Turning toward August, she freed him of his attackers, sending them to the same fate.

"Are you okay?" She ran to August's side, rubbing his shoulder.

"Took your sweet time, didn't you? I thought I was a goner." He scowled.

"Had to get rid of the source first. They were starting to come quicker than I could knock them off. I'm fast, though." She wrapped her arm around his and gazed up to his face.

"Thank you," said August. "Really." He glanced down at his arm.

Larissa pulled away, embarrassed. "We've just begun. No telling what we're going to find."

They walked through the entrance and continued until the hall opened and revealed a large amphitheater. Larissa and August gazed below at the figures. There were at least fifty Devoratrix surrounding a table made of wood. Strapped to the surface, a woman lay crying out in fear. Or was it pain?

They had stripped off her clothing, leaving her legs lay splayed wide open with the help of two fasteners on either side of the table. One of the Devoratrix had been leaning over one of her breasts. He quietly handed over a set of pinchers toward the leader at the head of the table.

August and Larissa watched in agony as they realized from the blood trickling from the woman's breast that the nipple had been unceremoniously snipped away.

"Ah, a tasty amuse-bouche." The voice came from none other than Svapada himself. He popped the flesh into his mouth and smiled as he chewed. Within seconds he'd swallowed what had been handed to him. "You must hurry and do the other one to feed my second mouth. It longs for the taste of flesh from such a sweet tender one as this." He eyed the terrified woman lying on the table.

Larissa winced. Svapada was just as Tiberinus had described. Two heads that looked similar to the guard she'd killed earlier. But the guard didn't have this type of body she studied in fuller detail, this total freak of nature or magic. Svapada had also stripped off his clothing, showing the three legs with three penises, which were engorged and sticking out like fat prongs on a coat rack.

Two Devoratrix assistants stood on either side of their leader, manipulating the two penises he bore between either side of his middle leg, while he fondled the third penis standing out above it. The remainder of the beings, also naked, pleasured themselves as they watched.

Larissa turned briefly away in disgust. From her quick view of August, he was not amused or interested in the least, but stood stupefied and disgusted at the scene unfolding before them.

"Before I indulge in another bite, I must first do this." Svapada moved closer to the woman, working the penis above his middle leg solidly inside her. The woman bucked, moaning in discomfort. "Quite a nice fit." He gazed down at her. "I must surely be your first, am I not?" With a smile, he caressed her flushed cheek with his finger. The woman answered with another cry of anguish, straining against her fasters. Svapada said nothing else but moved with a slow, even rhythm, savoring the moment. He finished with a grunt. "Now, for the other one. My second side hungers."

At the touch of the pinchers against her other nipple, the woman screamed.

August whipped out his wand, uttering the words, "*Pallio zeli. In secondo.*"

The woman vanished.

A rumble of surprise and dismay filled the air. Svapada's eyes glowed yellow, the color shown in Devoratrix when they were enraged.

The crowed looked up at August and Larissa, giving off another sound of disapproval.

"Seize them!" Svapada yelled.

"We're in for it. Get ready," said August. He mobilized into position as four Devoratrix charged toward him.

Larissa wasted no time in using the same spell that killed the guard and snakes. It had worked fine, was quick and easy, and did the job in no time. She uttered the words and successfully reduced a group of Devoratrix to ashes.

Just as she called the spell out a second time to wipe out more, the vanquished ones materialized back to life. Each one carried a sterling silver wand and headed toward her.

Rough hands grabbed her from behind. She let out a blood-curdling scream as a group of Devoratix pulled her to the ground. When she felt her clothes being stripped away and hands moving between her legs, Larissa screamed August's name.

August had barely enough time to use his special Acidum Pulveris spell, killing off the revitalized Devoratrix once and for all. How he barely remembered this special concocted spell taught by Grandfather Jove was short of a miracle. He dodged figures right and left, using it, until he landed closer to Larissa.

With his wand and the spell, her attackers shrieked as they sizzled and burned, turning into a blistering bubbling mess before drying up and hitting the ground. This approach worked wonders because having the skin burn, bubble, and melt away was a most painful way for Devoratrix to die. The acid ensured they could not rejuvenate. They may have been formidable Magicals, but their skin was tender as a newborn babe's.

August hauled Larissa to her feet. "Stall them. I'll finish them off." He let out a yell and ducked, barely missing what would have been a decapitating blow from a Devoratrix sword.

Larissa decided she would mix her well-worn spell with a *Gelida*. This mixture of incantations froze the dust form in place, giving August barely enough time to finish them off before they morphed back to life with more weapons. After dodging swords, blasts from wands, and fireballs, the two witches left the Devoratrix enemy on the amphitheater floor in a soupy, smelly puddle.

August and Larissa stood looking around, breathing heavily. They turned their head in the direction of clapping sounds coming from the left side of the amphitheater. Larissa shrieked. August went pale.

Svapada clapped his hands and wiped away a stream of blood from his lips. "Most beautiful display of spell-casting, I must say. Quite clever too." He filled his mouth again, chewed, and swallowed. "What are you staring at?"

In front of him lay the woman, dismembered, with eyes staring cold and lifeless at the ceiling.

"I couldn't let such a tasty delight go to waste, now could I?" The Devoratrix leader smiled. "Besides, I'm a little insulted that you thought I couldn't crack your cloaking spell. Come on Hawthorne, roasting my men alive was pretty amazing, but you really need to work on your cloaking skills. But then again, I wouldn't have had such a delightful meal."

"You fucking son-of-a bitch." August leapt forward, sailing into the air toward Svapada. He landed beside the woman, but the Devoratrix was not there.

"Over here, Hawthorne. You really must be on your toes."

August clenched his fists. The magician had crawled half-way up the wall. In his arms he held Larissa with a grip that threatened to smother her to death.

"Help me, August!" The words came out choked at best. Larissa wiggled and struggled to get away.

"Shh, dear. You're so sweet and pretty." Svapada licked down the side of her face with one of his long red tongues. "But you're so very naughty when you help that ogre kill my men. Not very nice." He slipped a hand inside her ripped blouse. "I could just take one of these as repayment, maybe both. That would be quite fair, a small price to pay, don't you think?"

He latched on to one of her breasts, squeezing and thumbing the nipple. "Mmm, succulent." He nuzzled against her ear.

Larissa screamed.

August shot out a streak of lighting so strong it knocked Svapada of the wall. Larissa hit the floor with a blinding thud.

"You might have gotten away with that other unfortunate soul, but you'll not touch her." August charged toward the Devoratrix.

"Oh?" Svapada smiled. "I just did." He placed the small lump of flesh between his fingers inside his mouth and chewed. "Mmm, delightful."

August spoke the words. Svapada slipped into a wet mess on the floor. The Devoratrix leader rose right up in a second, sending August sailing across the room.

"Try all you want, Hawthorne, but you'll not have me. Unlike my men, I know special antidotes they don't." Svapada came toward him, his eyes turning yellow with rage. "I know who you are, where you come from, and you're not that clever." He held out a hand, sending a thick boiling stream of water crashing against August's chest. "You like it hot, don't you?"

August cried out in pain. In retaliation, he sent out a deluge of fire shots, which singed several areas of Svapada's skin. The Devoratrix winced in pain but shook his head, nonetheless. For several minutes, he and August engaged in a game of cat and mouse. Every time August seemed to strip the Devoratrix leader of energy or landed a formidable blow, Svapada countered and skittered to the walls, moving up and down with astonishing speed.

With one last move Svapada landed August on the floor, drained and nearly addled with fatigue and confusion. "There my boy, it's time for you to go home." He grinned down at the young man. "Guess what I have that you have too?"

August lay gasping for breath and drenched in sweat, unable to move.

"I, too, have your Grandfather Jove's secret recipe." He laughed. "I like to save the best for last." He lowered his hand toward August, "*Acidum . . .*"

Svapada's head sailed across the room. Behind him stood Larissa holding a sterling silver sword. Once the deadly stroke performed the final deed, it slipped from her hand, hit the floor, and disintegrated into oblivion as if it never existed.

August dropped back down on the floor, groaning. "Oh, please tell me we're done, that none of them are coming back."

"I think we're done, and none of them are coming back."

"How in the hell did you manage to decapitate that bastard? I thought we were nearly done in."

"We were," said Larissa, and somehow I found that sword lying next to me. I don't know how it got there. I don't remember . . ." She stopped talking.

August sat up. "What, Larissa?"

She looked down at her blouse. Dried blood covered the right side. The young woman sat down and sobbed.

Without a word, August gathered up a last-minute burst of energy and crawled forward, cradling her in his arms.

"Go away! Don't look at me," she wailed.

"Larissa, you have to face what happened. If you won't look, I will." He had barely lifted the torn blouse for a peek when she struggled free.

"You'll do no such thing." Larissa wiped her eyes. "I'll look."

The young man said nothing but waited patiently.

She turned her back toward him and opened her clothing. To her amazement, nothing was wrong, except for a circular scar that glowed a nasty angry red color.

"You okay?" August called out.

"Yeah, I'm good actually."

"Let's get that odious head and go.

***

"Ah, what a tale to tell," said Tiberinus, gazing out at the pair from behind his desk. "And thank you for such a trophy. I will be the envy of many a magical for this."

The three gazed at a table against the wall. Mounted on a golden stand was Svapada's two heads. The eyes had been cast in the evil glinting yellow showing the remnants of his rage.

"I don't know how I got the sword to kill him," said Larissa. She shook her head.

The Lord of Lakes smiled at her. "Think about it hard enough, and you'll receive the answer, my dear. The same one who delivered that sword healed you as well. But you'll always bear the scar as a reminder of your triumph."

"And now it's our turn," said August. He pointed toward the amoire.

"I would never forget my end of the bargain for such a splendid piece you two risked your lives to get." Tiberinus opened the armoire and pulled out the velvet bundle. Carefully unwrapping it, he pulled out an item that looked much like a toy top, one that a child might spin on a table, watching as it popped right side up on its spindle.

"This, my friends, is a Numeromancer. It divines numbers. Anytime you need to calculate something or need a combination code that involves numbers, here is your tool." He handed the bundle to Larissa.

She and August admired the piece, gazing at the gold surface. A quartz crystal window would show the divined numbers.

"How clever," said Larissa. "This will be most valuable on our quest."

Tiberinus bowed his head in agreement. "I should think so. Guard it well, for only a few Magicals own such a piece as this.

***

In France, Ciana sat glaring back at the angry man pacing her cell.

"You did it again, didn't you?" He whirled around and marched over to her, placing his face within inches of her own. "If you didn't have something I wanted so badly, I'd destroy you forever."

"You can never destroy me because of what I am. So get over yourself." She looked away. Secretly, she wanted to scream for joy.

"Allowing your niece to destroy one of my most valued allies?"

Ciana said nothing. She didn't wish to anger the man further. She could only supply the tool, and that feat took some work. It was up to Larissa to use it with what little time was left. From what she glimpsed, August would have gone down the same path as the Devoratrix he slaughtered earlier. And her niece. Ciana cried bitterly when it happened, when Svapada violated that precious girl. She had gained barely enough resources to heal the tender skin, but not enough to remove the scar, the horrible reminder of how it got there.

"You'll do wise to stay out of my affairs and concentrate on helping me." The young man turned away and left the room.

Ciana moved to a consecrated corner of her room. She eased herself onto a giant cushion, sitting in a lotus position. Closing her eyes, she willed herself into a neutral state, allowing the divine to fill her with energy. She'd never abandon her family. Nor would she ever abandon Clement's.

Chapter Seventeen

"You may encounter some leakage in the tunnels as it runs under the lake. There has been some erosion these past centuries." Tiberinus, the Lord of Lakes stood on the bank, watching as his guests prepared for the next part of their quest. "I trust you won't be so unlucky as to have it collapse before you traverse it and end up in the forest."

"Indeed," Larissa said. Concerned, she looked down the hole in the cavern floor. Rock walls surrounded it, and only a ladder-like stair remained on one side in order to descend into its depths.

"What about my boat?" August asked. He didn't care if he sounded rude or not. "It was a gift from a dear friend, Greta Marvo." To his consternation the Lord of Lakes threw his head back and streamed out a hearty laugh.

"Ah, it's good to know Greta is still humping every notable witch, young and old, in the Magiverse. I've had her a few times myself. And she does have a reputation for being generous, if you know what I mean." He winked, thumping August on the back. "Young Hawthorne Heir, you can either take it with you, or I will keep it safe here. I don't think it will fit down the shaft to the tunnel that runs under the lake, however."

August nodded, though the Lord's reply did not settle well with him.

He and Larissa thanked their host properly and departed. August insisted on descending first so that if Larissa lost her grip, he might catch her. But she didn't, of course. They were a half hour into the tunnel, when August abruptly stopped and drew his wand.

"Why are you stopping?" Larissa asked. A scowl crossed her face.

"I thought I heard something," August said. "Keep your wand handy. And conjure some sort of light. I thought I heard something up ahead.

Larissa uttered a quick spell, materializing a bright orb at the end of her wand. The light lit the tunnel for several feet ahead.

It had been treacherous going. The walls and floor of the tunnel were slippery. Often water from the rock ceiling dripped on them. August waited as Larissa shone the light in front of them and behind them again for safety one last time. They made out nothing but wet rock as they walked in silence. When she aimed the light up ahead once again, it was a different story. They saw movement accompanied by a chittering sound.

"What are they?" August said, gasping in surprise.

As the creatures scrabbled closer over the rocky surfaces, he identified them as troglobites, true cave dwellers. They gave off a faint phosphorescent blue glow.

"Stygian Scorpions," Larissa said slowly, "though I can't recall if they are poisonous or not. And I don't for a moment think that we can outrun them, either. I believe we probably need to stand our ground and stay perfectly still. They're blind you know. And they don't eat flesh. With any luck they will run right over us and continue on their way."

August bit his tongue, resisting the urge to scream. He hated creepy crawly things. The idea of allowing them to crawl over him was abhorrent. On the other hand, he believed Larissa. That meant he didn't have much choice in the matter.

The closed-in environment amplified the sound of the creatures as they skittered over the rocks. Their strange locust-like noises filled the air with a horrific sound. The pair steeled themselves for the encounter. The first few ran over their feet, but when they began swarming in from the walls and dropping down from the tunnel ceiling, August let out something akin to a whimper.

Larissa, who stood beside him, placed her foot carefully over his, reminding him to stay still and quiet. Any undue movement or noise risked arousing the curiosity of the scorpions. The incident seemed like an eternity before the last stragglers of the herd bustled off.

August shook violently as he rubbed over his body and through locks of hair. The last thing he wanted was one of these nasty creatures accidently left behind.

Larissa, though she wasn't shaking like a leaf, also brushed off her clothing and smoothed her hair. "That was interesting," she remarked. "My Aunt Dorenda was right. Sometimes the best thing to do is nothing."

August groaned, "Easy for you to say. Most of your sensitive sexual apparatus is tucked inside of you. I'll be reliving the sensation of having them crawl over my balls tonight when I sleep." He shuddered with disgust. "Ugh, that was terrible! Fuck! Fuuuck!"

"You're such a little girl. Stop being so loud, or they might come back." Larissa turned her head, hiding the beginning of a wide smile.

The encounter with the Stygian Scorpions hadn't been a picnic in her estimation, either, but she had never been a whiner. Jove's grandson was certainly used to the soft life, spoiled and sort of a creampuff. As fond as he was of his grandson, Larissa rather suspected it had been part of Jove's plan to send August on a quest, hoping he'd toughen up.

August sighed and squared his shoulders. "I hope we haven't too much farther to go," he said. His tone of voice reflected the pout on his face. "I'm getting dreadfully hungry."

After a few more yards, they felt the tunnel's incline. Moments later, fresh cool air blew around their faces. The tunnel ended at the mouth of a small cave tucked into a hillock. They found a clean patch of ground under an ancient elm tree and rummaged through their packs for cheese and bread. Larissa opened a can of kippers, two apples, and pulled out two small bottles of ginger water she had been hoarding.

The humble meal seemed like a feast. They munched on their food, feeling a moment of contentment while they looked around.

"I don't know these woods," Larissa said, "but I'm sure I can get a location on my WTP. We'll be trying to find the columbine tree next. That's the name Tiberinus gave us before we left, I believe."

Reaching into a pocket of her pack, she retrieved a Witches Temporal Positioning device. Unlike a regular GPS, it had the ability to show positioning on the nearest six realms.

The model she really wanted showed a traveler's position on twelve realms, but Aunt Dorenda said those were much more expensive, and she would have to wait until Christmas for it.

"I thought columbine was a plant with colorful flowers in rows along the stem," August answered. "Is there really a columbine tree?"

"The short answer is yes." Larissa fiddled with her WTP. "Surely you are familiar with the legend of how it came to be."

"Why don't you enlighten me, Princess Know-It-All." August stuck out his tongue.

Larissa let out a long sigh. It was a pleasant, temperate day. She wanted to wait for their lunches to digest before starting out once more, so she leaned back against the tree and began.

"As the legend goes, there was a warlock prince who fell in love with a completely ordinary village girl. She was pretty but not overly so. It was her purity and kindness that attracted him. He happened upon her one night while he was practicing his druid shifting skills. She was standing on a balcony on the topmost floor, watching the moon. He was in owl form, so he lit upon the edge of the balustrade to get a closer look at her.

"Being a lover of nature and all animals, she approached him, speaking quietly and stroking his feathers. He was completely smitten with her and pulled out his most beautiful striped feather as a gift. He badly wanted to reveal his human form but, not wishing to alarm her he decided against it.

"When she told her overprotective father of her encounter with the owl, he became alarmed and forbade her to go out on the balcony at night. The warlock prince returned night after night but never saw her until one evening when she was returning after nightfall from a village fête.

"As she passed with a group of partygoers, he called out to her. She saw him on the branches of a tree in a field of columbine. She loved the flower so much that she had fashioned a crown of it to wear in her hair. She quickly excused herself and walked over to him. He saw that she had attached his feather to a necklace so she could wear it.

"Encouraged by what he had seen, he quickly transformed into his warlock prince form. To his dismay, she was immediately horrified, turning and running from him when she recognized that he was a magical being. In his mind, she must have thought and believed that he possessed evil and unnatural powers. In her haste, she tripped on a tree root and struck her beautiful head on a stone.

"The warlock prince knelt beside her still body and wept. He knew immediately that she was dead. When her body was found, she was buried in the field of columbine, where the warlock prince made a tree grow over her grave, a tree unlike any seen in the region. Columbine flowers magically grew on its branches, perpetually and regardless of the season. The tree was a symbol, a declaration of love that the Warlock Prince had secreted in his heart. And that, my dear August, is the story of the columbine tree."

"So basically, we are looking for the grave of a girl so uncoordinated that she tripped and died senselessly," August said. "I mean, of all the ways to go, who the hell dies like that? Do you really think that that story is true?"

"Oh, my god!" Larissa exhaled with disgust, moving her eyes in a show of frustration. "Must you question everything? Don't you have a romantic bone in your body?"

"Of course I do!" August retorted. "And I'll gladly show you where I keep it, if you like. It was right here under my belt buckle last time I checked." He laughed at his own quip, barely dodging an empty ginger bottled tossed at his head by a bemused Larissa.

"Never mind, you idiot. Last time I'll waste my breath telling you a lovely bit of folklore. At any rate, the portal we are looking for is in the columbine tree. And as for your 'romantic bone', you can keep that to yourself."

The trek to the columbine meadow was uphill, at a steeper incline than expected. Though Larissa was in the lead, several times she nearly lost her footing. It rankled her pride having August for support to avoid falling.

August had a lot of questions but decided to keep his own counsel, especially since Larissa seemed to be in one of her moods. The more he thought about it, she was always in a bitchy mood. In his mind, he thought that she must be sexually frustrated due to the strait-laced upbringing by her Aunt Dorenda.

Moments in each other's arms at Gamal Emara's had failed. The time in bed while retrieving their youth did no better. He was sure that being laid the good old-fashioned way would do wonders for her disposition. Given the opportunity, he wouldn't mind volunteering for the task. Despite her grumpy old troll disposition, she was high-spirited and competitive, two qualities he admired in his sexual partners. She was also beautiful in a completely unselfconscious way that puzzled him greatly.

She had, from what little he'd managed to see, beautiful breasts. She was very curvy for being slender. The natural curve of her hips, when she lay on her side away from him at night, was fleshy and taut, which caused an erection at the mere thought of mounting her.

He would never understand why she wasn't all over him. He was handsome, rich, clever, funny (although she didn't seem to appreciate his kind of humor), and obviously endowed. He considered his huge penis one of his best features. While growing up, he had noticed that when the men in his family, including his father and grandfather, bathed in the sacred pools, most women found this trait hard to resist.

The blinding sun and a broad desert plane stretching in every direction was not what they expected when August and Larissa stepped through the portal in the sacred columbine tree. In unison they shaded their eyes and scanned the horizon in every direction.

They saw nothing but glistening sand far and wide. In one direction, it seemed to be pink sand. In another direction, a light ochre color.

"Damn," August said. He fumbled inside his vest and slipped on a pair of expensive-looking aviator shades, "I hope you brought sunblock, Larissa. I tend to burn, being fair like all the Hawthornes."

Larissa glanced over at August's burgeoning backpack with a sneer. "I've often heard it said that those more skilled in the magical arts are able to travel light." She sniffed. "I've already conjured up lenses that hover over my eyes to protect them from the sun's damaging rays and a spell of protection to prevent my own fair skin from burning, thank you very much."

"I'm rather hurt that you didn't include me, your erstwhile traveling companion, in your spells and charms," August retorted. "Seems to me that it would be a common courtesy to include your comrade in this quest."

"Ah, but you told me before you were prepared for anything, August." Larissa smiled. "I always take a man at his word."

August flushed and cleared his throat. He'd been about to apply sunblock but after her disparaging remarks, he didn't feel like doing it in front of her. He regretted not bothering to learn more De Auras spells, ones that conjured things out of thin air. It had worked with the mirror in his hotel room, but his skills didn't extend much beyond that. It was too late now to learn something on the fly.

He would just ignore her snippy jabs. They only reinforced his opinion that she needed to get laid, and by someone who knew how. Himself, for instance. He was convinced that she would exhibit a much sweeter side of her personality after a few turns in the sack, legs high in the air. Girls always did.

He did however look over with envy at Larissa's eyes, where a pair of iridescent protective lenses hovered without benefit of frames.

"So," he said, changing the subject, "Which direction do you suggest we travel in Miss Know-it-all? Any preference?"

Larissa's brows knitted together as she contemplated their surroundings, noting that the only shade to be had was their shadows. When the words came to mind, she spoke in a voice that rang with authority and assurance:

Grant life to our shadow selves
To guide us now and lead us well
To those who may give gifts and rest
To further us upon our quest

"Okay," she shouted with excitement, "there they go. We must follow them."

Astounded, August watched as their shadows took off before them, sprinting across the endless expanse of sand. It was difficult to keep up, and the pace was dehydrating in the arid heat of the desert.

"Can't you tell them . . . to slow down a bit?" August uttered the words in between breaths. "I swear . . . it seems as though . . . they are trying to escape . . . and leave us behind for good. Then what . . . would we do? I haven't seen one tree or rock . . . or anything that . . . could provide shade. Not even a cactus." He gasped a few more times. "If we cast a shadow . . . we might take turns . . . sitting in it . . . to get out from under . . . this relentless sun. As it is . . . I believe they are . . . purposely trying to ditch us."

Larissa laughed lightly. August thought he might have been attracted to such a lovely musical laugh if it didn't belong to such a bitchtress.

"I wouldn't blame your shadow if it took off and never returned," she answered, seemingly amused by the idea. "Considering how insufferable you are. However, shadows are designed to be our servants, so I don't believe they would desert us."

As soon as she finished speaking, her face clouded over. "Look at the horizon."

August lifted his gaze slightly. Through his dark sunglasses, he made out something that seemed to be forming above the distant sand, dark and purplish, like thunderclouds hovering low to the ground. Whatever it was, his instincts told him to run in the opposite direction. Their shadows, which had been moving steadily before them, suddenly stopped.

Making a quick decision, he turned to run back in the opposite direction. But Larissa caught his wrist in an unexpectedly firm grip.

"Wait!" she said in a loud whisper.

Filled with trepidation, they froze. The rolling mass moved closer. As though they, too, were perplexed and frightened, Larissa and August's shadows backed up until they had rejoined their rightful owners. When it seemed the rolling morass arching overhead might overwhelm and devour them, it dissipated at once, fizzling out. Sand fell like rain around them.

August and Larissa spit sand from their lips and wiped their faces. As they squinted through burning eyes, they saw a line of fantastic beings standing before them. None stood less than two and a half meters tall, from Larissa's reckoning. They were majestic and exotic figures. Some were entirely humanoid. Others seemed to be part animal.

Both knew they stared into the faces of personages who were at least demigods, if not gods of the desert realm.

August, impetuous as ever, opened his mouth to speak, shutting it when the being at the center of the chevron-shaped line spoke.

"We know who you are, heirs of the two most powerful houses of Magicals. Hawthorne and Strondovan. We also know what you are seeking, mayhap better than you do yourselves. You are brazen to seek us out. The one who sent you more so for having suggested it. We decided long ago to remove ourselves from the affairs of men. Our druidic magic, thus shielded from all the negativity of the Earth realm, has only grown more powerful.

"Much has been written about us, although our own lore, which is the most authentic, has been passed down in oral tradition. You think that you have come here for what gifts, blessings, or further direction we can give you. That may happen, but you should be aware of three things:

Each thing contains its opposite.

That which you seek also seeks you.

This meeting will not be the most important between your houses and ours.

"There will be a meeting to decide the fate of the entire world, and you will seek our intervention at the proper time, for we alone are the only religious and magical sect capable of preventing that which prowls the earth, ever restless and seeking to devour all that sustains life."

Larissa found herself mesmerized by the druid's speech. As she turned her head slightly, she was horrified to see August stifling a yawn. She jolted him to attention with a swift kick.

"Come with us now. You may call me Prince Elek. We will give you shelter and allow you to tell us of your mission."

Both Larissa and August nodded. Elek looked perfectly human, except for his long sleek fur-covered thighs and tail. He turned and motioned with his hand. In an instant, the pink sands of the desert swirled upward, forming a spiral staircase that disappeared into a thick, shifting mist forming a canopy over their heads.

"Come," Elek intoned again, stepping aside.

The pair of travelers stepped forward. August made a sweeping gesture and stepped back, indicating that Larissa should go first.

She narrowed her eyes at him. He either remembered his manners, or a case of anxiety consumed him. Her decision alighted on the latter. A doubtful expression showed the young man that she knew all too well the reason for such a gallant display of behavior. Larissa planted her hands firmly on the banister. To her surprise, her fingers met with cool brass. Instantly her body returned to a comfortable temperature.

After climbing a half dozen steps, she gazed through the white mists, unable to see any further than the next half dozen steps ahead. The sands below were no longer in view. Somehow she felt no fear. Aunt Dorenda had told her many stories of the Druids and their history, including why many of them had chosen to leave their original forests and caves and seek shelter in the arid climes.

She reached the top of the stairs and stepped through an arched gateway, finding herself in a high-ceilinged cavern strewn with thousands of blue stars resembling the galactic swirling of the Milky Way.

On closer inspection, Larissa identified the swirls as glow worms. She and her Aunt Dorenda had seen some when visiting the caves of New Zealand. They were as beautiful here as they were there. The short walk through the cavern opened on a meadow surrounded by giant trees. A temple built of white stone stood in the center. She stared with wonder. It appeared that these druids ingeniously brought their homeland with them.

Chapter Eighteen

When Elek spoke, she jumped. She had assumed that August was on her right side the whole time, but now she didn't see him anywhere.

"Where is August Hawthorne?" she asked Elek.

"They are bringing him now," said the stately being. A hint of amusement filled his voice. "Apparently he has an issue with heights. Flendra, the tigress shifter, is bringing him now."

Larissa viewed a goddess. She bore a human face and the ears and mane of a tigress. Effortlessly, the wondrous creature carried August in her arms. As they approached, August recovered and struggled against being carried.

"Put me down." His voice trailed out like one belonging to a peeved child. "I told you I can walk on my own. I got a little dizzy, that's all."

Flendra complied with his request, gently placing him near Larissa. After a few faltering steps, he seemed to regain his composure.

"What? You think it's funny?" he said to Larissa in an accusing tone. "For your information, it's called vertigo, quite common in my family. Hereditary and nothing to be ashamed of. So you can stop smirking, Larissa Strondovan."

Larissa ignored him and turned to Elek. "Is this your temple? It is very lovely. What's it made of?"

Elek beamed at her question. "This structure was built of hand-hewn blocks of moonstone. It took over a century to build, and it was built at much expense and sacrifice. Or should I say, many sacrifices."

Larissa cringed. She knew from her aunt that sacrifices had been part of druidic culture in certain locales and in certain sects. August could have benefitted from such instruction and history. She wondered what Elek meant by his remark but feared the answer if she asked.

According to Aunt Dorenda, some things were best left unsaid. For a moment a pang shot through her heart. Larissa tried keeping her emotions under control but found herself missing her aunt terribly. Most likely there was no WIFI signal in the halls of the druidic temple. Metaphysical communication would take a little more preparation and effort.

As the party entered the building and traversed the huge hall, several veiled figures stepped from the adjacent hallways to the arched stone entrance. Larissa assumed the hallways led to living quarters. Her imagination ran wild as she viewed the magnificent architecture.

Prince Elek turned to her again. "Ah, I see that you are interested in our abode, Heir Larissa North Strondovan. I see the questions in your mind. How wonderful it is to engage in telepathy. This may well serve you in the immediate future of your quest.

"The spoken word is powerful magic in and of itself. It can cause lovers to leap to their deaths, grant absolution and peace to the tortured, and not only start battles raging but cause them to cease, as history of both man and Magicals has proven.

"I discern that you have many undiscovered gifts. I do not believe even your beloved and well-respected aunt is aware of some of them. Part of my gift to you will be to help you hone them for the next part of your most important quest.

Nine beautiful females stood waiting for Prince Elek, their eyes downcast and heads bowed in deference. Translucent pastel-colored veils with glistening diamond-like ends obscured their faces.

"May I introduce to you the Gallizenae, our sacred druidic priestesses. Their dedication and focus on the arts of druid sorcery has increased their magical prowess, of course. Not only are they able to summon the wind and the sea, but they are adept shapeshifters with the ability to transform not only themselves but also others into different forms. They can cure any disease, even those thought to be incurable."

Larissa felt compelled to curtsey out of respect, noting with satisfaction that August followed suit. Apparently he wasn't too proud to follow her lead in some social situations. He had started out strong in the beginning of this venture, but lately he had caused problems when speaking first. She wondered if stress wasn't beginning to take some toll on her companion.

"May we approach the heirs?" The priestess in the center position asked the question. Like the others, she wore a woven crown of mistletoe on her head, reminding Larissa of Christmas festivities. She decided, except for their lack of wings, they could all have been angelic yuletide beings.

Prince Elek nodded his assent, and all nine of the Gallizenae floated en masse to where August stood, several feet away from Larissa. August was the better part of a foot taller than most of them, and Larissa heard their soft murmurs as they touched him lightly, speaking among themselves and ignoring Larissa completely.

Once again she looked to Prince Elek, her eyes full of unspoken questions.

He shrugged. A smile twitched at the corners of his mouth.

"They are enjoying his scent," he told her in a soft voice.

Both quietly stared at August, who clearly enjoyed the attention of the Gallizenae.

Elek continued, "It does something for them, because he is fully human, and they have not encountered a fully human male within these walls for a century or more. His presence has awakened their desires, which are usually dormant. Normally humans are not allowed, unless scheduled to be part of our ceremonies.

"Of course, being that he is the Hawthorne heir, and a magical, we have granted an exception to our ordinarily strict rules. The Gallizenae will undoubtedly be drawing straws to see which of them will keep him warm tonight."

Larissa kept her composure but inwardly fumed. She changed her opinion of the Gallizenae immediately, deciding that she didn't care for them, after all. They were supposed to be sacred and knowledgeable beings, but obviously their taste in males was up their asses. They treated August as a celebrity, almost like a demigod. She found the vision of it all positively nauseating, not to mention galling. And August would never let her hear the end of it, no matter how long their quest took.

Extracting the eager crowd of Gallizenae from around August was not going to happen without some sort of intervention. After a few more minutes, which were insufferable for Larissa, Prince Elek cleared his throat.

Immediately the druidesses peeled themselves away, looking back longingly over their shoulders as they departed. One politely came over to Larissa and bowed, speaking in an ancient language. Larissa caught the gist of the meaning, which paid homage and recognition to the Strondovan Clave. At least it was something.

"The Gallizenae will escort you to your rooms," Elek announced. "You will be bathed and given robes of the finest material so that you may be comfortable for our meeting. We have much to discuss, and the hour is growing late."

Larissa thought Prince Elek winked at her near the end. She was beginning to like him. At least he had paid attention to her. Communicating with him was effortless because he was able to read her mind.

She and August followed their Gallizenae caretakers down a hallway lit by elaborate sconces set high on the walls. Along the bottom border of the walls were the same tiny glowing creatures casting an ethereal bluish light so that their path was amply lit.

Hers and August's rooms were opposite one another. When it came time to go their separate ways, the single druidess who had spoken to her earlier motioned for her to follow. The rest of the priestesses ushered August into his room. Larissa's dislike of the Gallizenae grew stronger. Most of them acted like August's personal entourage.

The space was beautiful, even though it lacked windows. There were plenty of orbs sitting on top of sconce-like holders against the wall. The top of the room was domed and painted. The paint also gave off a glow as though it were lit. The scene on the ceiling depicted females cavorting with centaurs in a lush forest of flowers and fruit trees.

Some were engaged in various sexual acts. Two of the horned creatures suckled the breasts of a buxom woman while a third licked between her lily-white thighs. The look on the woman's face was that of pure ecstasy.

"Here is your bath. Please tell me if it is to your liking. I will be your lavandi raritate, your bathing assistant, if you please."

Larissa immediately stiffened. As much as she was dying for a bath after her dusty travels, she didn't particularly want to disrobe in front of a stranger due to her innate modesty.

"I assure you that I am perfectly capable of bathing myself," she said to the druidess. "Please feel free to join your sisters in attending to the many narcissistic needs of my traveling companion."

While she had been talking to the druidess, Larissa had been shucking off her garments. Quickly she strode over and, stepping into the steaming water gingerly, lowered herself into the bubbling eucalyptus-scented water. She let out a sigh of sheer sensual pleasure as the silken water caressed her skin.

"Please, let me help you," the Druidess said. She glided over to the marble tub, immediately sitting down at the side of the basin. With her dainty fingers, she grabbed a natural sponge from a basket along the side of it. "My name is Alma. I am a longstanding admirer of your line. It must be extraordinary to be the actual heir to the Strondovan line of Magicals. I can't imagine the glory or the responsibility of carrying your line forward."

Larissa almost wanted to laugh. She never felt like any sort of royalty. Her practical Aunt Dorenda, though she spoiled her at times, still made her take out the trash, clean her room, and do homework.

Nevertheless, she felt reasonably comfortable with Alma, grateful for someone in the world who admired and appreciated the Strondovan legacy. Against all her misgivings, Larissa complied with Alma's suggestion that she just lean back and let herself be washed. There was something therapeutic about relinquishing her control and letting the beautiful druidess stroke her body with a fragrant sponge lathered with a finely milled soap that strangely reminded her of childhood. She didn't even mind when Alma deftly cleansed her genital area.

Alma also worked a sweet-smelling shampoo into her scalp. Having her head massaged felt so good Larissa had to stifle a moan. The sensory stimulation, warmth, fragrances, and being touched reminded her that she missed being caressed by one of her boyfriends.

Larissa had been taught to have high standards, but if she'd had her way, she would have forfeited her virginity a long time ago. It was the fear of her Aunt Dorenda's disapproval that had served to keep her many admirers in line.

By this time, she was definitely horny. Just as Alma was rinsing her hair, she thought of Prince Elek. Apart from being almost freakishly large and tall, he was muscular and handsome. His dark hair had a strange whitish streak in the front, a lock that made his handsome face seem more mature.

"May I have a few minutes alone, please Alma? Thank you so much. I just need a little more time to relax and sort out my thoughts."

Alma smiled. "Of course. I will be right outside, Larissa North Strondovan. Please call me when you are ready to be dressed."

As soon as Alma left, Larissa closed her eyes and let her thoughts drift to the druid prince. What would his lips feel like against hers? She parted her thighs, imagining him stroking her sex and his strong fingers finding her clitoris. The tiny bundle of nerves throbbed and stiffened. Waves of pleasure radiated from it. She desperately wanted her nipples sucked and bitten.

She wondered what it would feel like to have Elek on top of her, the crown of his cock plunging deep inside her, stripping away the last remnants of virginity.

She gasped as her fantasies yielded to a hard, delicious climax. Her face and chest flushed with both pleasure and the heat of it. Before calling out to Alma, Larissa allowed herself a few minutes to bask in solitary pleasure.

***

The banquet hall was smaller and more intimate than she'd anticipated. August was already sitting there, looking refreshed and so happy that Larissa's first impulse was to walk over and slap the beatific expression off his face.

He was in a rapt discussion with Prince Elek, who rose when she entered the hall, acknowledging her with a half bow and gesturing to a seat on his right. He appeared to have lost his tail and was dressed in pants and boots.

An exquisite robe trailed from his shoulders. Larissa assumed he had shifted back to his fully human form, but somehow she hadn't minded him in his animal form. The real surprise came when she viewed the person seated next to her.

"Micah!" she cried aloud, unable to contain her excitement.

The young man immediately got up and met her halfway, picking her up in his arms in an exuberant hug. "Larissa!" His enthusiastic response echoed hers. "God, you're more beautiful than ever."

Both faces showed a light flush of excitement. Micah Gloria was one of her former beaus. His odd last name was due to his gypsy heritage, and the Gloria Clan was known for their conjuring skills. He escorted her to their seats.

Micah was a handsome ginger, with a cleft in his chin. The last time Larissa had seen him was at the coming out party hosted by her aunt after completing a rigorous course of study and testing. He had been clean-shaven then, but she found his well-groomed short beard equally to her liking. It took everything in her power to resist temptation and not run her fingers over it.

Immensely satisfying to Larissa was watching August's reaction after Micha's greeting. The over-the-top display of emotion succeeded in wiping the silly, self-satisfied expression completely off his face. He now wore a dismayed, almost pouting look.

"So tell me," Micah said, "how is your wonderful Aunt Dorenda doing?"

"Quite well, the last time I communicated with her. She's undoubtedly concerned for me and my traveling companion." Larissa answered simply, finding it difficult to avoid losing herself in Micah's honey brown eyes. "And we have had many unusual experiences on our journey. In fact, it's been a good mix of the pleasant and the dangerous."

Micah nodded and held a large Desert prawn dipped in butter sauce up to Larissa's lips "You know, if you were meaning to keep your quest a secret, I'm afraid the proverbial jig is up. Your journey is the talk of the global magical community. There's not a child nor witch born that hasn't heard of it. It's also the source of much speculation. No one seems to have the skinny on what you two heirs might be up to." He reached out a finger and delicately wiped away a drop of butter slipping down her chin. "So spill."

Larissa couldn't help but laugh. "I don't even know where to start, except that we're learning as we go. We've learned more skills, gained more weapons, and used more spells than one could count in a lifetime.

"The magical artifacts we've handled would take your breath away. Everything we have will be used at the right time." She shrugged and sipped from her goblet. "Other than that, Micah, we're no more knowledgeable than anyone else. And, as the old saying goes, 'I'd tell you more, but then I'd have to kill you'

"My quest partner and I have had much revealed along our travels, but again, nothing is totally clear at this time. We've had our moments of suffering, and we've been granted many pleasures. That is all I know."

Micah moved in a bit closer, until they were nearly touching noses. "I want to ask you something that I have no right to ask," he said in a sultry voice, "but if you will give me permission, I will ask it anyway. May I?"

Larissa nodded. "Go on."

"Please tell me that you haven't hooked up with the Hawthorne heir. It's none of my business, but he has a reputation. In my worthy opinion, he isn't fit to lick the bottoms of your shoes."

Larissa laughed again, lightly waving him off.

"As if," she answered. "No. Politics make strange bedfellows, and the truth is I loathe him."

"Good," Micah said.

He quickly looked around and surreptitiously placed a kiss on her half-open lips. Underneath the table he squeezed her hand. The display of amorous affection heated Larissa in all ways. In that moment she would have preferred other parts of her erogenous anatomy squeezed by Micha's able and nimble fingers.

"Can we go for a walk later, on the terrace? It's not a full moon tonight, so no thorny devil lizards."

"Oh, I think they're cute," Larissa said. "Aunt Dorenda and I used to play with them in the Australian Desert. Are you afraid of them?"

"Yes, and I'm not ashamed to admit it," Micah answered, a serious note in his voice. "In the half-enchanted realm, they are as big as alligators, and wicked quick! Not to mention ugly as the devil."

Just then, Prince Elek raised his glass to toast his guests, and everyone followed suit. Larissa didn't recognize the liquor that her flute held. It was a magenta color and tasted of honeysuckle. The flavor was exquisite.

Several trays filled with different, exotic desserts were passed around. When everyone enjoyed their fill, Prince Elek motioned to both August and Larissa to join him in his study.

As was the rest of the environment, it was a nicely decorated and comfortable room with furniture that looked as if it were crafted of rough stone, with cushions covered in a shiny ecru material.

"Sand," the druidic high priest and sorcerer said aloud to Larissa's unspoken question. "All of it through a process unknown to the Earth realm. What the famous George Washington Carver did with the lowly peanut, finding that it could be used to make many of life's necessities, we do with sand.

We have found that it can be melted and shaped into art and dishes, which you already knew. But it can also be liquefied and spun into cloth, used to form furniture and utilitarian objects, and also be used as a fuel in proper combination with other substances.

"Please have a seat, because it is later than you think. In fact, as much as I would prefer to keep you as my welcome guests for the next few days, for clearly you are exhausted, I am afraid you must leave tomorrow."

As Prince Elek, August, and Larissa sat comfortably in three armchairs gathered around a table, the center of the table opened, and a lit globe rose up through it. Rather than crystal it was murky and opaque, as if it had an atmosphere of shifting clouds boiling within it.

"I think it will save time if I show you first, and then explain afterwards."

August and Larissa leaned forward, their attention focused on the globe. As they watched, eventually it cleared, and they made out an aerial view of a craggy stone pass that looked vaguely familiar. Through the pass marched what looked like a small army of cloaked and helmeted soldiers wearing dark grey cloaks. A saffron insignia was imprinted on the back.

As the bird's eye view closed in on the line of travelers, Larissa noted more clearly the image on their cloaks, a saffron-robed warrior holding an upraised sword in triumph. In his other hand, he held up a severed head by its hair.

An immediate chill shot through her.

"That can't possibly be the Royal Order of the Chevron," she said, recoiling in horror. "Where did you come upon this image? How? I have never seen an actual image of their members. Some in the Magiverse believe their very existence to be folkloric, an old wive's tale."

"Oh, they exist, I assure you," Prince Elek said. His eyes met hers. "And these particular images we owe to a genius blend of modern technology and invisibility spells. These images are taken by drones, under order of the Glanarium Supremo, the GS, if you will. It allows them to keep mercenary factions under surveillance. The images are transmitted through the atmosphere to our visual receiving device, the Hollowell Globe that you see here. The technology is quite cutting edge."

"I believe I recognize their location," August commented. "We were there several days ago." He glanced up at Elek. "Are you telling us we are being tracked by the ROC?"

"Precisely!" Elek replied, smiling and pounding one of his fists into the other hand.

"You don't seem worried," said Larissa. In her opinion, he seemed much too enthusiastic. She was inwardly contemplating this unwelcome piece of news when something occurred to her. "The ROC has a reputation of being mercenaries for hire to the highest bidder," she said, "so this means someone is intent on preventing us from going forward on our quest?

"I don't understand. Even August and I are not quite sure of everything, yet. We are just following clues as it were, hopefully acquiring information and weapons as we travel."

Larissa looked over at Elek. "Why would they be stalking us? Do they want to murder us by beheading as in the early days? Do they seek to overpower us and hold us hostage?"

"All good questions, Larissa North Strondovan. Alas, I have no immediate answers for you. But I can offer you one favor that may only be used a single time in a single circumstance." He smiled at her. "I am sure you are aware that the Desert Druids have the reputation of being able to stop any battle, causing both sides to turn away in retreat. How we accomplish this is our secret and has to do with a blood magic so ancient that it requires sacrifice.

"I'll be honest. I have grown fond of you, and I wish to provide aid. There is no doubt that your task is enormous, maybe impossible. But I want to ensure the continuation of our druidian line and have something that benefits us. As it is, we are willing to gift you one favor.

"You may call upon us through a secret incantation, and we will come to your aid. But only once. Think of it as a "get out of jail free" card, like in the Earth game of Monopoly. A good game, that one. Even druids get bored from time to time and crave games of skill and chance. They are so like life, aren't they? Every day brings new challenges.

"Again, you both will receive the incantation, but it can only be used once. You do understand that, don't you?"

Both August and Larissa looked at each other and nodded.

Larissa frowned. "Can't you give it to just one of us? What if we are in a dire situation and get separated from each other? We wouldn't know if the other had used the incantation, would we?"

"Ah, that would be a risk you will have to take," Prince Elek said, rubbing his short beard. "But under the circumstances, it would be an insult to off this rare incantation to one of your houses and not the other. I cannot risk insulting either the House of Hawthorne or the House of Strondovan.

"And with that, I must bid you good evening and allow you to repair to your chambers. I wish to speak privately with the Strondovan heir, if I may." He held out his hand to Larissa, smiling. "Come with me, Larissa. For you I have a special gift before we part."

Chapter Nineteen

The pair weren't on the next leg of their quest for very long before they ran into trouble. It was Larissa who sensed they were being followed. At first Prince Elek's warning about the Royal Order of the Chevron came to the forefront of her thoughts, but then she remembered the smell of a creature she was only familiar with through her many educational travels with Aunt Dorenda.

It was in Peru where she, her aunt, and their host at the time had visited an abandoned monastery that sat high on a nearly inaccessible rocky mountain ridge. Regardless of their extreme isolation and strong faith, the order of monks that had originally used it had been invaded by sorcerers and slaughtered. Their souls were harvested, and their bodies were brought back by the darkest of magic to an insidious half-life.

The new beings were something between wraiths and monsters. They had physical substance, fangs like poisonous serpents, and a venomous bite used to change their prey into the vile creatures they were themselves. The sorcerer who had captured their souls kept them in a glass jar, where they fluttered like so many grey moths, endlessly beating their wings against the glass in vain.

That was how the lore had it; thus, how it was presented to Larissa and Aunt Dorenda. Their guide at the time made a brief stop at the original monastery. The thing that struck Larissa the most was the smell that permeated the structure. It was the scent of stone, dust, and decay, of rotten meat and smoke.

When the wind shifted, she recognized the same odor. Somewhere on the trail below, they were being tracked. Larissa wasted no time conveying her fears to August, and the pair took shelter behind a high promontory of rocks that overhung the path.

"Give me your panties!" August whispered to Larissa. "I have an idea."

Her eyes narrowed as she reluctantly complied, reaching up under her skirt, pulling them down. "Here."

He hurriedly stuffed them in his back pocket. Leaping out from behind the rock, he flattened the vipermonks with a single incantation. Larissa was impressed. There had been five of them. Their crushed corpses lay bleeding out in a spectacular fashion on the rocky terrain She looked down at August from her high perch. "What did you need my panties for?" she asked.

August grinned back at her, his lips pulled into a wide smile. "Oh, I just wanted them."

Ichor Barony was their destination, and the trek wasn't an easy one, like it hadn't been easy during any of their travels to various places as they searched for aid, allies, and additional magic with which to arm themselves. Larissa reflected further. Gaining information on what to do next had been the most frustrating at times.

"I'm not going to stop asking you about Prince Elek and why he needed to speak to you in private. Oh, so secretive he was," August said, continuing to be optimally annoying. He hadn't shown any care that his companion was already miffed at him. "I have a sense that whatever he said might impact our quest, so I must ask you to spill the beans."

"Really, it's none of your concern," Larissa answered. She grinned, remembering Prince Elek and his handsome face. "But if you insist, I will tell you, I suppose."

"I do insist," August said, glaring at her. "Both as your questing companion, and also because I am curious as to what a royal druid shifter might have to say to the Strondovan heiress. What was it that had to be said in secret?"

Larissa smiled and locked her gaze on August's eyes. "He asked me to marry him. He fell in love with me at first sight and wanted to offer sanctuary, protection and his undying loyalty. Not to mention, I would become the Princess of the Desert Druids. I would be royalty and rule beside him, as nearly his equal. He would teach me the arcane and nearly forgotten stronger magic of the Ancient Ones also."

August's brows knitted together in a frown. "And what did you tell him?" he asked. "The animal shifting Druid Prince of the Sands? I really liked his goat legs, by the way. Just stunning. And the hooves, of course. Simply divine."

"You're just prejudiced against Prince Elek because he is rich beyond measure and also powerful." Larissa scowled. And by the way, he wasn't half goat. He was half horse."

"I think I know goat legs when I see them," August said, laughing. "And he probably had goat balls too. The guy is an abomination, Larissa. An absolute walking freak show, in fact. I wonder what your Aunt Dorenda would think about you rolling around in the hay—and I'm sure it would literally be hay—with a man who is half beast? And I'm pretty sure there are laws against that in most countries."

Larissa turned up her nose, waving him off. "I'm sorry he causes your insecurities to rear their ugly collective heads all at once, August." Her eyes filled with a mischievous glimmer. "And for your information I am considering his offer."

They trudged on in silence until they reached a point in the path that opened to an incline that was wider and not as overgrown.

August thrust his elbow sharply into Larissa's side. "Look up there," he whispered, ignoring her protest. "What do you see?"

Larissa raised her eyes and looked. At the crest of the path stood a silhouetted figure wearing a cloak that came up to a peak on the top. Other than appearing tall, it was impossible to discern if the person were male or female. Nevertheless, they continued resolutely toward the figure. August, his eyes fixed ahead, silently retrieved a dagger.

When they got within ten feet or so, the figure called out to them. "Halt! Who comes now? Announce yourselves."

"We should offer the same greeting to you," August shouted back, fearless. "Stand aside stranger."

To both their surprise, the stranger let his hood fall back, revealing a youth of about August's age. The man wore thick brown hair that flowed to his shoulders. In his hand he held a longsword.

"Fair enough," he said in a milder tone, "Your grandfather Jove has been unsuccessful in getting any of the War Pigeons to find you for communication, so he sent me to track you."

The stranger stepped back, bowing deeply. August frowned, picking up something rather mocking in the tribute.

"I am the Wizard Willem. You may have heard of me."

"Can't say as I have. Sorry," Larissa said, speaking up at last.

August continued squinting, sizing up the stranger from top to bottom. "You say Jove sent you, but to what purpose?"

"Glad you asked," the stranger replied, smiling. Although he'd seemed rather plain at first, his smile transformed his face into a handsome one. "I have a unique set of skills. He sent me along as insurance for your journey, especially given the fact that he is well aware you are being pursued by the Royal Order of the Chevron. They are bent on disrupting your quest!"

"Ah," Larissa replied, "but how do we know that you are not one of them, sent to join up with us on the pretext of giving aid and then murdering us in our sleep instead?"

"Well, actually you make a point, except for the fact that I seem to know a lot about you, that I was able to pinpoint your exact location, and—oh wait—I have this."

He shoved his free arm forward, and August's jaw dropped open with surprise. There was a tattoo on the inside of the forearm, just below the wrist, that was instantly recognizable. It was an oak tree with a fork of lightning going diagonally through it, the symbol worn by the Secret Elite, his grandfather's special Guard.

Yet why didn't he recognize this soldier or remember ever having seen him? August saw movement in his peripheral vision. He was taken aback on seeing Larissa holding a bow, aiming an arrow at Wizard Willem.

"I don't trust this wayfarer," she said tersely, nodding in Willem's direction. "I can tell he fancies himself a charmer. All his explanations seem convenient at best."

Willem's face had blanched with fear. He gulped and gestured toward her bow and arrow. "Isn't your aim a bit low for my heart?"

"I'm not aiming for your heart." Larissa smirked. "Now hand that sword over to August for the meantime until we can truly ascertain who you are."

August sidled over to Larissa, saying in a stage whisper, "O Impetuous One, did you not see the tat he was showing us? It's kind of a credential or ID card, if you'd care to know. It's a mark conferred on those sworn to protect Jove and all his heirs with their Mortal lives. It has import. Significance."

"Tattoos can be duplicated. Now grab his sword and carry it." Larissa responded.

August reached for the longsword and abruptly handed it to Larissa. "It's heavy as hell. You wanted it? Great. You get to carry it." I am not your beast of burden, Larissa!"

"I know. I know." She sighed, placing it in a sheath behind her left shoulder. "You're just a beast. How could I ever forget that?"

Ignoring her, August launched into a conversation with Willem while Larissa brought up the rear. Even though she was positive she'd never seen Willem the Wizard before, there was something disturbingly familiar about him, as if she should know who he was.

For the time being, she was sure that they should watch his every move, though August was bonding with their unwelcome visitor already.

But that was guys for you, she thought, brooding. Always forming their twelve-year-old bromances with each other and leaving the serious business to whatever female was close at hand.

The path got wider, dustier. Though their surroundings had changed little, they heard the Falls before they saw them. The deafening roar of gallons of water descending from great heights filled their ears. They headed across a short meadow. Looking ahead, they discerned a sylvan path in the distance that obviously obscured their noisy destination.

Once they ventured back into the forest on the other side, the sound was so pervasive that they had to shout to hear each other.

And then it appeared: a massively powerful waterfall that looked for all the world like someone had transplanted half of Niagara Falls right there—with one difference: They were unmistakably red in hue. Not pink, not rose, but a color deep and bright as freshly shed blood.

Even at her age, Larissa had seen plenty of it before.

"It's not really blood, is it?" August shouted above the din. "I mean, how could it be?"

Willem smiled. "I'm kind of a hobbyist on arcane and inexplicable geographical global features, so I can explain this phenomenon well. This isn't the only Blood Falls."

August and Larissa strained to hear, barely catching every other word because of the background noise.

"There is a Blood Falls in Antarctica also," said Willem.

"Would you speak up?" Larissa shouted. She feared her voice would go hoarse if they talked much longer.

Willem repeated his last statements louder and continued, "Huge ones like these are caused by iron-rich waters hitting the air and instantly rusting. When this happens, the water takes on the color of fresh blood."

"Looks like the hillside is wounded, and the massive cut is pouring blood," August added.

Larissa had to grudgingly admit that it was a spectacular sight. But now she wondered which direction to go next. Looking about, she saw no dwellings of any kind. Though she may have had questions, it looked as if one of the party had a clue.

Willem turned and trudged up the much-narrowed path that seemed to circle closer to one side of the falls. Shading her eyes from the sun, Larissa discerned something sticking out of the pebbled lakeshore where the crimson-tinted waters lapped.

It looked like a crude shelter constructed of cloth. A tent, perhaps? It was a dark greenish color that almost camouflaged it against the scrub forest backdrop and the exposed overhanging dirt wall. A solid half hour of walking brought them close enough to see that it was indeed a tent-type structure, but not the usual style. Larissa guessed it might be a yurt.

They stopped and looked at each other. Willem smiled shyly at her, but Larissa quickly averted her eyes. She still wasn't sure about him, and her anger remained steadfast at August for refusing to carry Willem's sword. In her state of mind, she determined a remote possibility that Willem might have to die by his own sword if he so much as twitched the wrong way.

In the middle of their confusion, the yurt opened as if by magic. Willem gestured for the other two to follow. The interior was huge, basically round. Torches blazed along the walls. The space seemed sparsely furnished, with just a few benches set along the perimeter.

The focal point, however, was the huge hole in the center. Larissa stared at it in wonder. It seemed like a vast oversized rabbit hole.

"Ah, you've arrived!"

The booming voice behind them belonged to a female clad in chainmail from the top of her head to her booted feet. Through her hood, fashioned in the same style as her garment, a few blond curls peeped around the sides.

"Heirs of the light, please follow me," she said. After looking Willem over, she added, "And your manservant may come also, if you wish."

She strode briskly to the edge of the hole. "You will need to ride the spell-enhanced will o' the wisps all the way down." Her orders came, loud and abrupt. "If you miss one, you will descend rapidly enough so that your bones may shatter. So please time your descent carefully."

The lady turned and smiled at her three guests, "I will, of course, descend first to demonstrate. My name is Magnhild. See you at the bottom."

Everyone watched, open-mouthed, as Magnhild jumped fearlessly into the large hole. They ran to the edge and peered down. At once they perceived the glowing orbs rapidly moving and appearing at intervals. They reminded Larissa of seedling dandelion tops, except these were made of light.

"See how huge the will o' the wisps are? They may appear insubstantial, but they are very strong," said Magnhild. "Don't be afraid. Jump on one when it comes close to the edge. But you have to be quick!"

Though she was a large woman of great height, the vessel of light seemed to hold her weight. The remaining three watched the top of her head as it continued down the hole, disappearing from sight.

"That seems sketchy at best." August remarked. A frown covered his face. "Do we need to discuss this?"

"Are you afraid, August Hawthorne?" Larissa asked, tilting her head to the side, "You seem nervous. Obviously we are expected!"

"You go first, then, and show us how it's done." August squared up his shoulders and crossed his arms.

"Oh, I get it. Ladies first, right? But only when you are fearful that you might break your neck! I swear, August, you seemed to have inherited none of the courage that your predecessors are renowned for!"

"Oh, would you two stop. We are wasting time," Willem interjected. A look of impatience covered his face. "I will go first, then."

The next spongy orb of light that floated in proximity to the edge, Willem took in a deep breath and jumped on it. He seemed to bounce for a bit, and almost fell over the side, but steadied himself with a whoop and out-stretched arms.

Both August and Larissa watched his descent.

"Now, your turn," Larissa snapped at August. "Go on handsome, show us how it's done."

August appeared nervous. Nevertheless, as a particularly beefy looking globe of light energy rose to the top, he jumped on it, uttering nothing more than "oof" before he floated downward.

Now it was Larissa's turn, and she found that she was more nervous than she'd thought. She actually choked when the first will o' the wisp ascended, though it was large. That would have been an opportune time to jump down on it. After a couple smaller looking ones rose, but weren't quite close enough, she received an intuitive thought that too much time was passing.

It was now or never. Too late to regret she hadn't gone before August. Too late for her stomach to avoid flip flopping. So she leapt. The sensation when she landed surprised her. It seemed that her body sank down into the orb and then bounced back up, as though she had buoyancy when in contact with it.

Stranger still, she sensed that the will o' the wisp had an intelligence of some kind. Why this thought crept into her mind, she wasn't sure. But it was pleasant, drifting downward. After an indeterminable amount of time, she saw brightness below, and squinted against the light.

She was in a city square. The oddest thing about it was a sky above filled with fluffy white clouds. Shops lined the streets.

She turned her head when someone clear their throat.

"I say, what took you so long?" August asked her, reaching for Willems sword. He removed it from her pack and tucked it into his own. "Sorry I left you with extra baggage. I didn't mean to do that. I'm glad to see you, though. I . . . we were starting to get concerned."

"Welcome to the Ichor Barony!" Magnhild said. She smiled, showing a charming gap between her front teeth. "Since you are expected, I will take you to your quarters right away. Master Whitelock will be waiting to meet with you."

"But what is this place?" Larissa couldn't help but ask. "I don't recognize it from any of my studies, either in the regular realm or the magical."

"It is one of the captured regions," Magnhild replied. "Part of the vast underground empire of cities owned by the wealthiest and most powerful magnates on the surface. These cities started as a getaway for the rich and influential, in cooperation with the most powerful beings on the planet, witches of course.

"Lately it appears that more and more of the elite are migrating here and making it their permanent home. Don't worry if you feel a bit overwhelmed, everyone does. You'll be meeting with Whitelock in his office. I'm sure he will be able to answer any of your questions."

Traffic was light. There were no emissions, so Larissa surmised that only electric vehicles or ones that didn't require fossil fuels were used in travel. That was another thing she noted as they walked along. The air smelled fresh and pure. Her head swiveled, taking in the unusual architecture. The sky overhead had to be artificial—they had to be underground— didn't they? It was all difficult to fathom.

The party crossed a walkway catty corner to the diamond-shaped island of land on which they'd been standing. The building they approached was at least ten stories high and appeared to be made of burnished silver metal plates.

When they arrived at the revolving doorway leading directly inside, Larissa stretch out a hand to one of the panels. Surprisingly, it was cool to the touch.

Facing them was a fountain tumbling over rocks. Magnhild deftly walked around it and down a hallway wide enough so they could walk five abreast. At the end of it stood a set of double glass doors with 'Whitelock Industries' etched on the surface. After speaking briefly to a secretary sitting at a round black desk, Magnhild motioned for all of them to take a seat on a bank of connected upholstered leather chairs.

August was uncharacteristically quiet, but Willem kept up a patter of conversation with Larissa, as if he'd forgotten that she'd nearly shot him with her bow and arrow.

"I love this place," he said. "I've only been here once before, with Jove and some of the other Elites. Did you know they keep the environment comfortable by utilizing geothermal energy and air exchangers that are run by a combination of solar and amplified telluric or underground current that exists naturally?"

"No," Larissa said. She raised an eyebrow in skeptical surprise at finding Willem so loquacious. "This is an oddly intriguing place, though. If I hadn't drifted downward to get here, I would swear it's just another city on the surface world. How long have you been working for Jove, by the way?"

"It's a family calling," Willem said, his voice filled with a note of affection. "My father and grandfather have served the mages through the ages—ha, ha, ha, that rhymes, doesn't it?

"Anyway, keep in mind that I will have you and August's front, back, and sides at all times. I have mad skills with a sword, and you might as well return mine because they won't do me any good unless I can access the battle instrument in question."

Larissa answered, "Perhaps you should ask August about that."

Looking thoughtful, Willem nodded and rose to change his seat.

A door opened. Someone wearing a grey nondescript uniform announced their names. They trotted down the hall behind the attendant, who ushered them into an office at the end of the hallway.

Larissa and August exchanged glances after looking at the woman's serious face. Were they in trouble?

"Greetings, Strondovan and Hawthorne heirs." The man behind the huge desk stood up and gestured to three chairs positioned at an equal distance around the half circular curve of his desk. "And of course, we have a member of Jove's Elite Corps with us. Hello, Willem. So nice to see you once more."

The man spoke in a pleasant enough voice. He made an instant impression on Larissa, with a head of shoulder-length wavy jet-black hair. It was the pure white forelock that captured her attention. He was not a huge man, medium build and well-muscled. Larissa was not used to seeing his type in the world of Magicals.

"Shall we take our seats?" he asked.

The trio sank gratefully down into their seats, while their host studied them.

"You all look dehydrated," he said after several seconds. "I have just the thing."

Getting up, he turned around to a credenza. On it sat a silver tray with a crystal decanter and a few small fluted glasses. He poured a deep red-violet liquid into three of them and distributed the drinks to his guests.

"This should help revitalize you," he said. "Questing is very onerous work, and I'm sure that you could use an energy boost."

August shot Larissa a warning look, questioning if she was merely going to drink. Larissa held his gaze, raised the flute to her lips, and took a sip. At first her sips were tentative. After the third one, she downed the remainder of the liquid with gusto.

"Very nice," she said, placing her glass on the edge of Mr. Whitelock's desk. "What is that, exactly? It has a rich berry taste yet tastes different from any kind of berry I'm familiar with."

"It's one of your Aunt Dorenda's favorites." Whitelock chuckled. "And I must say you remind me of her when she was a girl. Very much so. She was a beauty as well. To answer your question, it is made from a berry that only grows in the Tibetan Autonomous Region of China in Motuo County. The land there is so unstable that no human who is not a slave to the vampire master resides there full time. I have it flown in, because apart from medicinal qualities, it is known as 'Verum seri'."

"Truth serum?" August said. He blurted out the question loudly, before Larissa had any time to respond. "Why are you drugging us?"

Whitelock leaned forward over his desk. "Because we will be discussing matters of great import, and I have no time for foolishness." He furrowed his brows. "This way there will be no hemming and hawing. Do we have an understanding, young heirs?"

Larissa merely nodded in response. There was no other choice but to agree. Her face was as flushed as August's. Despite the ire that Whitelock's actions had raised in them, she recognized that they had better keep their outrage to themselves. At least for the time being.

"Now listen to me, Heirs of the Light. You many not yet know the full import of your mission, but you must hasten to your next appointment. Where it is and when it will take place will be revealed to you at the proper time, the way much of this mission will unfold as you continue.

"Though you have allies, you don't readily know them at first glance. Therefore, trust no one in the beginning. I know that you no longer trust me because I have given you a potion, and it doesn't matter that you don't trust me personally, for I am a friend of the Light. What I am about to give you will be the most important and helpful weapon in your arsenal.

"Other entities—witches, mages, and wizards—will try to get you to open this before the appointed time. No matter how close you feel to them, no matter how kind they are to you, refuse to open it. Ignore everything they say. Some will say what is inside is dangerous and will kill you. Some will try to convince you that this gift, this weapon, will bring you to your destruction.

"Listen only to what I tell you now. It can save a life, but only one life. And if you ask that favor it will take a life in return. You will have no choice in the matter. Now, I have a few questions. Which of you can I trust to carry it, keep it hidden, and not discuss it with anyone?"

Larissa and August both glanced at each other and said in unison,

"Me!"

Whitelock chuckled. "That was kind of a trick question. "I know both of you sincerely believe that you are the best candidate to accept it. You are both being truthful. But I need to know who is the most vested in protecting the other, so let me ask this."

He turned his gaze directly to August. "Do you care for Larissa enough to die for her?"

"Yes!" August said.

Larissa sat, stunned at her companion's affirmation.

Whitelock nodded and turned to Larissa. "And you, Larissa Strondovan," he said, "Would you sacrifice your life for August Hawthorne's?"

"No," Larissa heard herself say. She cringed inside, never wishing to have uttered such a truth. But it was the truth. She couldn't deny it. But what a callous admission, just the same.

"Ah," Whitelock said. His shoulders relaxed at Larissa's admission. "August Hawthorne, sir, I believe this is yours." Without hesitating any further, he handed August a small box that looked like a miniature puzzle box attached to a long chain.

Larissa knew without looking directly that August was pleased with himself. She sensed the triumph fairly oozing from his being. Her gaze remained steadfast on Whitelock.

"What is the chain for?" August asked. "And why is it so long?"

"An excellent question," Whitelock responded. "Probably because it is best if you wear it around your waist. You won't lose it that way."

"But what about sex?" August blurted out. He was still very much under the influence of the draught Whitelock had given them.

"Well, I think abstinence would be the order of the day," Whitelock said, waving him off. "Now, my friends, you must go. Hurry up, or you'll be late." He pulled out a gold pocket watch and muttered, "And so shall I."

***

"I don't give a rip what Whitelock says." August huffed and fumed as the trio left the building. "I'm not wearing this thing around my waist twenty-four hours a day, seven days a week. I don't want to. Period." He turned to Larissa. "You can carry it around for all I care, Larissa."

"But he gave it to you," Larissa said back in rebuttal. "And I expect for a very good reason. It may not be convenient, but you should think of it as an honor because you were chosen. Doesn't that mean anything?"

"I'd rather be unchosen. Seriously, can you help me with this? I can't even remember what it contains or why he chose me."

"That's funny, I can't either." Larissa knew she was fibbing.

She did remember, but the conversation leading up to Whitelock handing the puzzle box over to August had been rather confusing. The man never said what was in it, only how it worked. She did have one unexpected takeaway from it. Under the influence of the liquor Whitelock had served them, he had asked her if she were willing to sacrifice her own life for August's, and she had said no.

She knew that she had answered truthfully. August was the antithesis of everything she had ever admired about men. He was spoiled, self-serving, cocky, and a male whore as far as she was concerned. She had no idea why a wise mage and magical such as Jove seemed to dote on August.

Larissa also remembered that when Whitelock had posed the same question to August, he spoke a very different answer with no hesitation whatsoever. His response puzzled her, but it was such a revelation. All he did was taunt and tease her and ask her for favors and expect her to do his share of any work to be done. Though he had come through on the rare occasion, she determined that he was not carrying his weight in their quest.

So why would he be willing to sacrifice his life to save her? Nothing in his character hinted of the sort of altruism such a sacrifice would entail. The memory of what occurred on the steps to the cave entrance at Endor still haunted her. Yet she had to assume that he answered honestly.

The whole subject didn't have easy answers, she decided. It was probably best to stop trying to figure it out. Was there something she was missing? Perhaps there might be a little more to August's character than she had assumed thus far.

They hadn't ventured far up the wide avenue when a wall of individuals formed directly in their path. Up ahead a group of armed soldiers wearing the insignia of the Chevron had formed a line across the street, blocking their way.

"I thought this place was heavily warded," August said with irritation.

"It is for the population," Willem answered. "But we are strangers and not afforded protection under the current warding spells. Given all that, I suppose we are in for a fight. May I please have my sword back now?"

Without hesitating, August drew it from behind and offered it to Willem. "One false move, and I will end you, of course." He stared young Willem in the eye.

"I wouldn't have it any other way." A big smile crossed Willem's lips.

It was Larissa who lunged forward and struck the first blow, landing a nasty gash on a soldier nearest the trio. Blood gushed from his shoulder, spilling onto the ground. Seeing the Order of the Chevron close up was disconcerting. They fought in chevron formation with the leader taking the initiative. As soon as he was injured, another stepped up from behind, taking his place.

They also wore hideous masks of leather and bone to conceal their faces. To Larissa many of the styles were reminiscent of the macabre bird-like masks the doctors wore during the time of the plague centuries before. Some were vaguely reminiscent of animals, everything from tigers to horses. Some depicted birds with long wicked beaks. Others seemed like boar heads. Larissa had a vague notion that if she could cause confusion by disrupting their Chevron formation, they might be off kilter enough to defeat.

"Divide and conquer," she murmured.

Lifting her hand, she conjured up a fireball as big as a cannon ball and propelled it to one side of the group. She hadn't had a clue whether her magic would be effective in this strange realm, but to her great satisfaction, it exploded into the tight line of soldiers, blowing the first into smithereens and blasting the arms off the soldier immediately behind the first.

Encouraged, she sent another fireball into the opposite wing of the Chevron formation. The results were more spectacular than before.

"Bravo!" August shouted.

He and Willem stood in the background, engaged in face to face combat with others in the troop who had disengaged from the back of their formation.

Larissa kept up her volley. To her dismay, the particular conjure spell associated with pyrotechnic phenomena was energy-draining, and she was wearing down quickly.

When a few members of the Chevron soldiers remained, the leader gave an order. They retreated and dispersed, leaving behind a smoke screen thick enough to obscure their escape route. Larissa felt like the skirmish had taken no more than a scant few minutes. She wouldn't have believed that it had transpired at all, except for the irrefutable evidence left behind.

Blood spattered on the formerly pristine pavement. Though Larissa didn't want to examine the detritus too closely, she detected what looked like body parts. Willem the Wizard came up to her side. His chest heaved from exertion, but his face showed an expression of triumph.

"Jolly good pyrotechnics, Larissa Strondovan." His voice reverberated with enthusiasm. "Hat's off to you. I doubt I could have done any better, though I am familiar with that particular conjure."

Larissa glared at him. "Then why didn't you help me? I'm sure it would have ended the battle much sooner!" She knew her tone came across bitchy, but she didn't care.

"I apologize, Strondovan Heir," Willem said. He bowed deeply in deference. "I got carried away. I wanted to fight alongside the Hawthorne Heir. It's quite a bragging point in our corps. And who can resist a chance at live-action swordplay?"

Larissa's eyes bulged with anger, but she said nothing. August had joined them after wiping his sword down.

 "I don't like this," he said, showing them the cloth he'd used. "Look at this. Some bled like humans, and others seemed to have blackish blood running in their misbegotten veins."

"What does that signify?" Larissa asked.

"Some were full on human, and others, if I'm not mistaken, were some human-demon hybrid. I don't like it. That is very dark, and I think a bad portent."

"You worry too much," Larissa answered. "We got them, anyway" She pushed past him and surveilled the street for a moment. "I need a bathroom like two hours ago!"

Chapter Twenty

They found their way back to the Elevation Shaft, the name in that realm for their accommodating will o' the wisps, and rode upward. When they exited the deserted yurt, they discovered that the scenery had changed—and in no small measure, but spectacularly.

Gone was the deafening roar of the Blood Falls, or any other of the easily recognizable landmarks they had seen on their trek to this mysterious place.

Instead they found themselves surrounded by a huge hedge stretching upwards of thirty feet or more. It cast a large cool shadow over them as they stood silently craning their necks.

"I don't like this." August said at once. "Let's return to the tent and inquire about what's going on."

To his chagrin, he glanced back, noting that the tent had vanished, leaving an empty, arid-looking meadow that seemed to stretch behind them for miles. Larissa detected that the temperature had dropped at least thirty degrees.

"We could go in the opposite direction," Willem said, "but I rather get the impression that no matter which direction we chose, we would end up in the same spot, don't you?"

August whipped out his compass. It was a high end, Lensatic compass, touted as the most accurate under any set of circumstances—except their present circumstances. August mused, watching the needle spin endlessly around and around without stopping.

"Look at this." Larissa pointed to an area of the tall, impenetrable, seemingly endless hedges. "I think we may have found a way out." She walked over and inspected the opening closer. "Or we may have found the entrance to . . ."

"Stygian Labyrinth: Flying Prohibited." In unison, the trio read the words on the sign that had sprung up. The words sparkled in changing colors of garnet and onyx.

"Fuck me!" August said loudly in disgust. "I was just about to suggest we fly over it."

"Why don't you try, anyway?" Larissa suggested. Her lips pulled into a sly grin. "I know that's what the sign says, but you always seem up for a good challenge. If anyone can do it, you can." She crossed her arms, eyeing her companion." August could be goaded into anything, she knew. And a wicked curiosity to see the outcome burned inside her.

"I wouldn't if I were you, Hawthorne Heir," Willem said nervously. He ignored Larissa glaring at him. "I'm sure the Labyrinth is warded from anything flying above it. Witches notwithstanding, I'm sure the sign is meant for drones also."

August didn't bother commenting, but Larissa watched with heightened interest as he muttered an incantation. He rose several feet in the air. After reaching fifteen feet, he hovered for a moment. His lips still moved, but despite the magical spell, he couldn't rise any further.

A few seconds later, he lost his temper and made a decisive run at the huge opening in the bank of greenery. He bounced off. The force of impact propelled him backwards about twenty feet, where he skidded to a stop, landing squarely on his buttocks.

"Sir! Are you okay?" Willem rushed over to August.

Larissa, after covering her mouth, gave up all pretense of trying not to laugh and doubled over in gales of mirth.

Willem busied himself brushing fronds of grass off August's clothing. Larissa saw that he, too, was hiding a smile. August, sensing it, kept turning and glaring at him suspiciously.

"How did that work out for you, August?" Larissa asked, smiling. She couldn't resist the question. "Are you convinced, or do you want to give it another go?"

August glared at her but kept silent.

"There," said Willem. He brushed off the remainder of grass. "I think I got most of it."

Without a please or thank you, August trudged toward the entrance of the labyrinth. The other two stared after him. He yelled, "Are you coming or not?"

Willem and Larissa scrambled to catch up.

"So you think it's a good idea to enter a labyrinth at this hour?" She tugged on August's sleeve when she caught up to him. She pleaded her case with one last complaint. "I am exhausted, and I know Willem probably is too."

"I don't see how we have much of a choice," August responded, waving her off. "You can see there is nothing left outside of this place for us to travel to. And this labyrinth seems different. Anyway, I think someone must live in the center of it. Look." He pointed.

Although it hadn't been visible when the trio had been standing on the outside, Larissa looked over to where August was pointing. Ahead of them, a single turret flew a bright green flag with an emblem on it. But how to get there was another consideration.

August continued his argument. "There appears to be a building up ahead, if we can keep going in the right direction to get to it. And where there is a building there is generally shelter and perhaps something to eat. If we get famished in the meantime, we can snack on whatever we have left of the supplies that Prince Elek gave us—the dried fruit and those tasty little cakes that remind me of mincemeat."

Larissa fell silent. They wouldn't starve, but all the same, she felt so depleted, almost numb. She had hoped to rest more than anything.

"You are weary, Strondovan Heir," Willem said, coming up beside her. "I, too, would appreciate a rest. But if it would take your mind off things, I will gladly sing. I know a lot of tunes from the elder days. One is by Talinman. I think he might have been a long ago relative of yours."

Larissa smiled at Willem despite her creeping fatigue. "Go for it," she said, shooting a frown at August's back. August had seemed out of sorts since he'd gotten repelled by the hedge. She felt his mood was affecting the entire group. Anything that served to bring up the energy level would be welcome at this point.

"Alright, then," Willem said in a pleased tone, "I shall start with one of my favorites."

He began singing in Welsh. Though her Welsh was a bit rusty, Larissa was charmed by the words of the song.

"I found her under a willow tree.
The fairest in three counties was she.
I asked what I must do to win her hand
She said, "All I ask of any man
Is to bring me the Grail and the Sacred keys
So we can have Immortality."
Well, I traveled long, and I ventured wide
Till I heard she became another man's bride,
Who ventured for nothing but kissed her lips
And dandled her with his fingertips.
So I no longer search for grail or key
But for a truer maiden to marry me."

Larissa was enchanted by Willem's singing. He had the lilting voice of a troubadour and flushed with pride when she broke into applause at the end of his song.

"I'm glad my singing pleases you," he told her. "And if I might, I would like to tell you that I believe you yourself are the most beautiful lass in twenty counties, Strondovan Heir Larissa!"

"Thank you," Larissa said automatically.

She found herself enjoying Willem's company and companionship, even more so since August seemed to be in a snit. She also noted that August had stopped walking and turned to the side. He appeared to be speaking, though she couldn't imagine with whom he was conversing, since he was speaking to the hedge.

When she and Willem caught up with him she had to step back for a moment. In the hedge a face protruded, comprised of the same greenery as the hedge but nevertheless a face that included discernable features, including eyes, brows, nose and mouth.

The features were refined, as though it were a woman's face, and it was speaking to August.

"Yes, two turns. One will appear at first to be a dead end, but if you use an unveiling spell, it will seem as though the hedge has parted to let you through. You must be on your toes, however, for it will open but one time and then be sealed. Do not think that you might return to the entrance, either, because it is forever sealed until the time when the next visitor is selected.

"Ivy, the Mistress of the Hedgerows, will escort you the last quarter mile in. If she asks that you come into her cottage, you must accommodate her, or risk her wrath. Be not surprised nor dismayed at anything you might see, however strange. You will not be harmed, I promise you. Be sure to heed every word I say, for if you become lost, you will be lost for all eternity."

Willem's eyes had grown large in his face, watching the exchange. When the face, which was at least three times larger than a normal human face, had ceased speaking, it withdrew back into the hedge, making only a slight rustling sound.

August looked as though his mood had improved. "Well, I got directions without even asking for them." He chortled with glee.

"Good thing," Larissa said wryly. "Men never ask for directions. You might have broken a record or violated a longstanding tradition."

"How hormonal of you, Larissa. Now, if you are finished being snarky and Willem is finished butchering the music of our ancestors, we need to get going. It will be dark soon. Who the hell wants to be in a labyrinth after dark? I'll leave that to the overachievers, I think!"

August whistled merrily as the three continued on. He deftly chose a direction to follow at every juncture as though he were certain of their trajectory. Larissa was highly suspicious of his sudden elevation in mood. It didn't make sense unless . . .

Of course. That was it. August was thinking he was going to get laid. The talking hedge face had hinted that he might be of service to Ivy, the Mistress of the Hedgerows. If that turned out to be the case, she and Willem could look forward to milling about outside of wherever the caretaker resided, waiting for August to get his rocks off. Spectacular.

As they walked, a wave of longing swept over Larissa. She keenly missed having her Aunt Dorenda to bounce off ideas, join her in making fun of men in general, or just listening to Larissa's problems and woes, offering up practical advice.

She hadn't even run into a female that she could relate to, really, except for Greta Marvo. And even she seemed to have her issues, with thoughts running along the same lines as August. They didn't suspect her of knowing what they did that night in the cottage, but she knew all too well when she heard footsteps leading to Greta's bedroom. Her sleeping spell was firm, but not to the point that it knocked her out cold.

It simply wasn't fair. One reason why she'd been so intensely proud to be a witch was that witchcraft and magic put women on equal footing with men. Magic was the device, the great leveler, that enabled women to aspire to the same heights of power as their male counterparts.

It all came down to respect. On this quest, with rare exception, many seemed to know of August's reputation, yet he seemed to be afforded the same respect, without having earned it. She, on the other hand, felt like she had to prove her worth over and over again.

Whatever happened, she was positive about one thing and one thing only. After they had accomplished their mission, their task, she was never having anything to do with August Hawthorne again.

She glanced over at Willem. It was odd that he hadn't exhibited much skill in the magical arts since he appeared. She made a mental note to ask him about that, as well as ask more about his background. She was finding that she liked him more and more. His easy-going disposition was a welcome relief from August's overbearing one and (though she hated to admit it) from her own moodiness.

Willem wasn't as handsome as August, but he was definitely cute in his own way; she wouldn't mind kissing him.

The group hurried on with August leading the way, until he suddenly stopped dead in his tracks. They had come to a dead end, it seemed.

"Stand back," August said. His former buoyant mood dissipated. He pulled his prized short collapsible wand from the inside of his jacket pocket. Flicking it open, he recited a familiar spell that Larissa recognized as one she'd learned in second grade.

She and her Aunt Dorenda had always referred to it as the Open Sesame spell. But nothing happened. Just as August's face reddened in frustration, the seemingly impenetrable wall of fragrant boxwood whirled open in kaleidoscope style, creating an opening large enough for them to pass.

Standing on the other side was a young woman of exquisite beauty, gesturing them in frantically. "Hurry, all of you!" she cried. Her tone resounded with panic. "This one is very twitchy. Once it closes, that's it!"

The three managed to scramble through just in time. Larissa's little finger of her right hand was sliced along the edge as the hedge spun itself back together.

"Here let me see that." The young woman marched directly to Larissa, who dutifully held out her bleeding finger. Before the first drop could fall, the Mistress of the Hedgerows wrapped a few leaves from a cypress hedge around it as a dressing.

As she tended the wound, she told Larissa, "Blue cypress is great for minor wounds and burns. Should be healed in a jiffy." Her eyes sparkled with satisfaction.

"Thank you." Larissa told her. She meant it. To her surprise, she found that she had instantly liked the Mistress of the Hedgerows. This was a rare time on their quest that she had been recognized before August.

"Well then," the young woman said, "I am Ivy, Mistress of the Hedgerows. I know that two of you are the heirs, but I think we should all introduce ourselves properly."

Larissa, on viewing the woman close-up, guessed she was in her early thirties. "I am Larissa Alexandra North Strondovan, heir of the Strondovan House. I am honored to meet you, Mistress Ivy. And thank you for nursing me."

"You are most welcome," Ivy said pleasantly. Turning to Willem, she asked, "And would you be the Hawthorne heir?"

Larissa saw August bristle with indignation and had to catch herself from laughing aloud.

"No, Mistress, begging your pardon. I am just a bodyguard sent to aid and protect the heirs on their long journey. My name is Willem. Most refer to me as 'Willem the Wizard', and I was thrilled to have been chosen by Mage Jove Hawthorne for this assignment." He bowed in respect to Ivy. "I trust you know that I am at your service as well and appreciate your hospitality."

Ivy winked at him. "You are quite welcome, Willem. She turned to August. "Ah, at last by process of elimination, I believe I am face to face with August Eugene Perceval South Hawthorne. I am honored to meet you as well."

And I, of course, am equally honored." August's voice came out smooth and ingratiating, as always when he wanted to present his best side. "I hope we are not inconveniencing you, Mistress, but my companions are very weary and in need of accommodations. We are, and have been, most grateful for your assistance since arriving here."

He held out his hand for hers, which Mistress Ivy extended, giggling when he brushed his lips over it.

"We are a scant quarter mile from the citadel. You must keep close, because the closer the path gets to it, the more likely for changes in direction or a complete circle around. The other reason you must stay close to me is that my children are very hungry this time of day. If you stray too far, they might snatch and eat you. They are frightfully quick. So be forewarned, travelers."

All of them believed Mistress Ivy and practically tripped over each other in their efforts to stick closely beside her. She was a pleasant and talkative hostess, telling them that the Stygian Lord would be happy to meet them at last, and that tales of their prowess and grand heritage had preceded them.

Surely enough, as they rushed past the immense walls of hedges, they saw hideous faces peek out at them momentarily, only to vanish back in place once they leered with a hungry look. Once a huge bearlike paw with fearsome claws swiped out at Willem when he got too close. This was followed by a terrible roar that shook all members of the trio to their feet.

"Oh, that's just my Joshua Simon. Don't mind him, Loves. It's just been days since he has eaten," Mistress Ivy said.

The last few yards Larissa noticed, as did the others, what seemed like human bones scattered along the edges of the wide path, shiny as though they'd been polished. Several grinning skulls lay in place, too, their bony mouths agape as if in agony.

Larissa assumed that these were visitors who either hadn't kept up with Mistress Ivy or had veered too close to the hedges as they made their way to the Citadel.

"Ah, home safe," Ivy said with a wide smile lighting her face. "And look, it's as though all the lights have been lit to welcome you."

Directly in front of them the trio saw two structures. One was a high fortress with several turrets. The other was a quaint cottage set to one side in its shadow.

Mistress Ivy walked to August's side, taking his hand. "I will be taking August with me for the moment," she told them, smiling. "Larissa, you and Willem can go on into the Citadel, where I am sure you will be well taken care of."

The suggestion took Larissa aback. She opened her mouth to say something but noticed that Mistress Ivy's hand had found its way to August's crotch and now openly massaged a growing bulge through his clothing. The lady's expression hadn't changed one whit.

"Oh, okay. Fine," she said. "We will see you both later, I suppose?" Larissa's face showed an expression of disgust. Turning to Willem the Wizard, she added, "Come on, we will be the first to greet the Master of the Citadel, you and I."

The way into the Citadel was a huge gate, but it was open, and so were the interior doors to the first building they encountered. As they entered, it took a moment for their eyes to adjust to the dimness within. Larissa stopped for a moment and listened. From somewhere further in the interior of the building, she detected the tapping of footsteps as they echoed through the halls.

"What do you think that signifies?" Willem asked, pointing upward.

Above them was an arch where a strange language had been carved into the structure. "It's not an 'Instant Death' curse or anything is it? I shouldn't like to die today. And you know this place must be heavily protected by magic to have no armed guards about."

Larissa looked up. Nearly fifteen feet above her head were indeed words written in Sanskrit.

"Adityas," she murmured. Her voice faded off into a whisper as she read what had been carved there in the Egyptian marble and gilded so that it might be easily read. Although her Sanskrit was a bit rusty, she was able to make most of it out.

The darkness will descend like a shroud upon the earth.
And demons will embrace it, for it heralds the birth

Of the age of endless night, and as such it will empower
All the ancient evils from the dawn of time
Within a single hour.

"What does it say, Larissa?" Willem asked. His voice held a tone of anxiety. "Is it something good?"

"Not really good," Larissa told him. "And I am not sure how accurate my translation is, but it is difficult to ascertain who it is meant for. It is addressed to 'ADITYAS', but that could mean anything, from the literal progeny of the wife of a pharaoh to meaning descendants in general."

"I'm not so well acquainted with the Ancient Egyptians as you are, Strondovan Heir," Willem said, "but weren't the children of Kasyapa Muni's wife born demigods?"

Larissa shot Willem an approving look. Even though he might be a flunky for the Hawthorne Clave, he was cute and apparently well-educated.

"Yes, as a matter of fact." she answered.

"Well, then, I guess whatever it says it is meant for someone other than us." He smiled. "That's a good thing."

A scent reached their nostrils, a sweet aroma, a conglomeration of honey, rice, and raisins. Being hungry, their mouths watered. As another strong waft from the fragrance filled the room, a tall figure swept into the entranceway.

"Very pleased to see you made it here," the individual said. "I know one of you is helping our Mistress of the Hedgerows at the moment, but please follow me and the other servants. We will get you situated, hmm?"

The person escorting them was a lad in a hooded caftan of black and gold silken material. As they walked through marble halls, the beauty of the surroundings overwhelmed Larissa and Willem.

What puzzled Larissa the most was the inability to discern the sex of their greeter. More puzzling was the appearance that all the servants were clones of the first.

The host led Larissa and Willem down another hall and stopped. "My guests, it has been brought to my attention that you need refreshment. You will be bathed and fed. Please follow the attendant who will care for you. Again, welcome to The Citadel."

Larissa luxuriated in a hot bath filled with aromatic water, sinking down into pure bliss. After her experience at Prince Elek's bathing rooms, the presence of the unusual attendant didn't bother her in the least. Afterward, the attendant brought her a silk emerald-green caftan and invited her to indulge in the food placed on a silver tray.

She wasted no time in donning the clean clothes and filling her mouth with dates, cheese, almond-stuffed olives, and honied pastries. The attendant and other servants watched closely, ensuring every need was addressed. Just as she pushed a fresh pair of emerald stud earrings into her ears, Willem appeared at the door. He had been nothing but dusty and dirt-smudged since she had met him, and his appearance stunned her.

"Willem," she said, "you clean up nicely, I must say! I hardly recognized you."

"You look beautiful, but then, you always do," Willem answered. "Astonishingly so. Do you know if August ever made it into this Citadel?"

"I assume he has. I would think if he is servicing the Mistress of the Hedgerows, he would have been directed to bathe and so forth." Larissa brushed and pulled part of her hair back in a bun, leaving the rest resting at her shoulders. "When do we get to meet the Lord of the Labyrinth? Do you happen to know?"

"One of the servants told me that they will meet us at twilight in the Moon Room for victuals. Apparently there is not only a Lord but also a Lady of the Stygian Labyrinth. But fair warning, I get the impression that they are not entirely human. Haven't you noticed the portraits?"

No, she hadn't. Taking the time now, her gaze rose, scanning the walls. There were no discernable human faces, though the individuals in the portraits were attired as human nobility, wearing cloaks with ornate gold and jeweled fasteners. They had the heads of minotaurs. Larissa was grateful that Willem had pointed out the obvious. It diminished another surprise, allowing her to conduct herself properly in this environment.

Within a few minutes another attendant led the way to an indoor maze where they walked through a series of winding passages until the hallway opened up and spit them into a grand room with a domed ceiling. In the middle of the room sat a long table filled with glassware, dishes, and trays of steaming food.

Larissa was glad she had pigged out on the stuffed rolled dates and olives. She wasn't at all sure of what minotaurs ate. Somewhere in her subconscious, old legends spurred the memory of them as ones who ate humans.

Their hosts sat the head of the table. Somehow they looked right at home, like they belonged here. Though their heads and horns were large, they didn't seem as fearsome. August and Ivy sat at the right hand of the male minotaur, looking relaxed and happy as if they dined here every day.

An open spot remained on the right side of the female minotaur. As her own eyes met the creature's, Larissa noted how kind they were, like the eyes of a gentle dairy cow.

"Welcome, Strondovan Heir," the male minotaur bellowed. "So glad that you are able to join us. This is my co-ruler and queen, Yezper. I am Bello, king of the Stygian Labyrinth, keeper of the Aronzanule Treasures.

Larissa curtseyed bowing her head in deference. She noticed that King Bello was looking at Willem the Wizard with a rather strange expression.

"Willem?" he announced. "Willem Wyndom Wiles. I never expected to see Gunther Wiles's grandson within these walls. I apologize for your loss and hope that you do not think ill of us. What happened to your grandfather was a tragic accident that has never been repeated in over half a century.

Willem drew himself up to his full height, and Larissa acknowledged for the first time that he was nearly as tall as August.

"I continue as my forebears did in the service of the all-powerful Hawthorne Mage Jove," he answered, bowing low. "And I have no ill will toward any Stygian in this realm.

I know that my grandfather wandered too close to the Titanboa nest and was never seen again. I do not blame his hosts for the unfortunate accident. He was a brave Guardsman. None of my kinsman bear any ill will toward those of the Stygian Realm."

"Very good then," King Bello said, smiling. Larissa guessed that it was a minotaur version of a smile, though it looked more as though the King were grimacing.

"Hello, Larissa, Strondovan Heir," Mistress Ivy said, popping up out of her seat. Larissa could see that the bosom of Ivy's dress had been laced up too hurriedly, and that Ivy's lips had a swollen look to them, as if she and August had gone about the business of sexual intercourse with a sort of violent urgency.

Immediately she flushed. Why should she care what August Hawthorne did with his prick and who he shoved it into? He was disgusting. Turning to Willem, she ignored the lady, deciding that she didn't like her, after all. Larissa concentrated on Willem, who had surprised her with his wit and charm.

Their eyes met. They kissed. In her peripheral vision, Larissa saw August's smug expression change to dismay. The kiss came as a total surprise, though she didn't deny it had been mutual. It wasn't a deep kiss by any means, but it left her feeling buoyant. She also noted that August nearly burst with wanting to say something about what he'd seen but could barely contain himself.

"Certain of these dishes you may want to avoid," King Bello said. He gestured to the trays set directly in front of himself and the queen. "As you know, minotaurs in the past required the sacrifice of nobles to be fed. Seven noblemen and seven ladies of the nobility. We still have a taste for it, but it need not concern you. Although the heirs qualify as the nobility among Magicals, we prefer locally grown sacrifices. Still a tidbit here or there, either stewed or in a fricassee, I always welcome."

Larissa was chewing when King Bello made his comments, and she quickly glanced over at the trays from which she and Willem had served themselves. One contained prawns, the other escargot, and the third looked like vegetables in a savory butter sauce.

Confident that she had not been unknowingly indulging in cannibalism, she relaxed and swallowed. Near the end of the feast, when guests awaited dessert, Larissa excused herself, intending to look for whatever came close to a bathroom. She hated the thought of having to go back to her room. It was a long way, and she feared getting lost.

A voice sounded from behind. When she turned around, she saw Mistress Ivy speeding down the hall, trying desperately to catch up.

"Strondovan Heir," she said called out breathlessly. "I hope you're not angry that I slept with your boyfriend. I do not desire to wed him or anything. But it has been too long since I was bedded, and he is so handsome that I could not resist."

Larissa stopped in her tracks. "Oh, he is not my boyfriend. I don't give a fig of a damn what he does, as long as he carries his weight on this quest. You do not have to apologize to me."

"But I sense that you are put out with me, and that makes me sad," Mistress Ivy said, resting a hand on Larissa's arm. "I was hoping we could be friends. Real friends. I think I might be of help to you and August on your quest." The lady frowned a moment and pulled something from her gown. "By the way, this was left at my cottage. He took it off, saying it made him uncomfortable. I stuck it in my pocket so I wouldn't forget to return it. Do you know if it is something important?"

Mistress Ivy held out her hand, displaying the carved puzzle box and attached chain. Larissa's eyes widened. How scandalous that her companion had carelessly cast aside such an important gift and then egregiously forgotten about it completely.

"Thank you so much, Ivy," she said grimly, taking the artifact from the older lady. "I can't imagine what he was thinking, but then I never have been able to figure him out. I am sure that he was so overcome by your charms that he thought of nothing else."

"That's very nice of you to say, but I think he just wanted to fuck," Mistress Ivy told her solemnly. "Really, I think he would have fucked anyone. I could feel horniness wafting off him like smoke. And of course, I have been horny lately, too, so it was a spur of the moment invitation. This is why I always say that it is a woman's children that she lives for. In the final analysis, they are what matters most. Men are merely conveniences when you have an itch to scratch and background noise. He is dreadfully good in bed, though, I must tell you. He satisfied every part of me, and he has stamina as well."

Larissa stood still with an open mouth, resisting an impulse to run from the information overload from Mistress Ivy's revelations. The last thing she wanted to think about was how good August was in bed.

"Is your friend Willem good in bed?" Ivy asked. "I saw you kissing him. Is he good at fucking?"

The two ladies turned their heads toward the sound of heavy leather boots coming up from behind. Ivy immediately broke into a grin at the sight of August hurrying toward them.

"Mistress Ivy, if you don't mind, I need to have a word with the Strondovan Heir," August told her in a serious tone.

Ivy nodded and politely took her leave. As soon as the lady was some distance down the corridor, he turned furiously to Larissa.

"Just what was that I saw at dinner with the minotaur king and queen?" His face colored red with irritation. "Is there something you want to tell me about you and Willem?"

"Absolutely not!" Larissa shot back. "What I do is my business. And may I add that that's a hilarious question coming from one who will literally fuck anything that bends over in front of him or grabs his willy." She stood, hands on hips. "Have you no self-restraint whatsoever?"

"Whether I do or I don't is off the subject, okay? All I want to know is are you fucking Willem the Wizard?"

"None of your business!" Larissa said. She had no desire to give him the satisfaction of her denying the accusation. In her mind, August was such a narcissist that if she denied it, he would probably think she was saving herself for him.

She stuck out her chin and pushed him lightly away, but he caught her arm and spun her around.

"I bet he can't do this!" he cried.

August planted his lips over hers, smothering Larissa with a deep kiss. There was a moment of confusion. Never in her wildest dreams had she expected August to do that. In response, Larissa pushed hard against his chest and ended with slapping him soundly across the face.

"Don't you ever do that again," she railed. "I knew those exercises Gamal Emara had us do would give you ideas, but here's a clue. The tantric exercises were designed to bring us together in a way that would benefit our quest. Nothing else."

"Pity," August said. He ruefully rubbed his reddening cheek. "This quest would be ever so much more pleasant if you would allow yourself to release some of that sexual tension that you are always giving off. You should take a few tips from Mistress Ivy. Did you know she has three teats and two . . . well, you know. Very unusual. How could any man ever get bored with that?"

"Oh, I'm sure you'd manage!" Larissa said. Her voice held the bitterest tone.

"Whatever. But here is my point. If I can satisfy a woman with three breasts and two vaginas, one in the front and one in the back, I should certainly be able to satisfy one sexually neglected Strondovan Heir, don't you think?"

Larissa narrowed her eyes in rage and shouted at him. "You are impossible!"

At the sound of her voice, attendants came scurrying forward from several directions.

"Oh," she said, getting her breathing under control, "can you please escort me to a restroom? I seem to have gotten lost."

After the feast, Larissa's nerves pounded with dread when King Bello asked to speak with her alone in his private chambers. Not August, just her. She wondered if he were going to hit on her or even ask her to join his harem. According to lore, minotaurs had multiple wives. Prince Elek was one thing, but marriage to a minotaur was out of the question.

He sat on the opposite side of a desk, keeping a professional distance after the door was closed and they were in private.

"You mustn't think badly of Mistress Ivy," King Bello told her. "She was married off far too young to a monster and then gave birth to even more of them. I should know, for one of the monsters was my brother Ferox. He was the worst of all minotaurs ever born. He pillaged villages and ate children alive.

"The labyrinth is warded off from him, but when you leave, you will not be so protected. He had chosen to follow the darkest of dark masters, and if I ever see him again, I expect we will be fighting on opposite sides."

"I am sorry to hear that," Larissa told him sincerely, "Do you have any advice for us?"

"I can tell you that this won't be our last meeting, for we will meet again on the battlefield at the End of the World," he answered with a sigh. "In the meantime, I believe you have a puzzle box that was given to you by Mr. Whitelock," he continued. "May I see it, please?"

Larissa thought she should have been more reluctant to hand the box over to King Bello, but for some reason she found that she trusted him.

"Hmm," he said. The king turned the box over and over in his hands, studying it. His monstrous biceps, each of which was bigger than a man's head, flexed as he did. He looked up at Larissa. "And what did he say about it?"

"He gave us a truth serum. When he asked about August's and my feelings for each other, if we would die for the other one, I said no. But August said yes."

"Were you surprised at his answer?" King Bello asked, staring at her in earnest.

"Yes, of course I was. It didn't make sense to me."

"Hmm, maybe it would have if you knew what was in it." King Bello said. "And for the time being, I believe you should keep it with you. The Hawthorne Heir will undoubtedly lose it. You may return it to him perhaps at a later time."

"Do you know what it contains?" Larissa asked.

"Oh yes, yes. Most assuredly I do. Minotaurs have the most supernaturally developed olfactory nerves of all creatures who roam the earth. I can smell its fragrance through the puzzle box. But unfortunately, I cannot reveal its nature to you, Strondovan Heir. It would change things. Suffice it to say that all men and most supernatural creatures would kill you without hesitation to have it all to themselves." His eyes sparkled with kindness. "Keep it with you and guard it well, my dear."

When Larissa awakened the next day and prepared to leave the Labyrinth with Willem and August, she still thought about a vivid dream she had during the night. Whether it was Miss Ivy's questions or August's hateful ones—or something more subconscious—she didn't know why the dream had occurred.

In the dream she and Willem were making out in her bed. Willem told her that he had fallen madly in love with her at first sight and begged to kiss her all over. She remembered finding Willem's confession of love endearing and gave him permission to kiss her. He asked for her to close her eyes before she felt the first press of his hot mouth on her flesh.

When he kissed her breasts, she wanted very badly for him to suckle her nipples. She was about to tell him so, but in her dream he whispered, "Only kisses, with one exception my beautiful Larissa."

By the time she felt his lips and probing tongue between her legs, she realized how starved she was for sexual attention. The orgasm she had was so real that it awakened her, and she realized that her own fingers had found their way between her legs, rubbing her clitoris furiously until she orgasmed.

She had sat up, panting and flushed, for a moment and wondered if any of it had been real. Before the trio stepped off the terrace leading back into what King Bello referred to as "the short end of the Labyrinth', she caught Willem's eye. He grinned at her.

"Sleep well, Strondovan Heir?" he asked.

"Yes, very well," she said, calmly. "And you?"

"Yes, after a while," he told her. "I had very vivid dreams. Must be something about this place."

"I had vivid dreams too," she confessed.

Willem didn't say anything more but tilted his head to the side and smiled at her. She thought he was about to say something else, but all he said was, "Good."

Chapter Twenty One

The three of them stood before the Labyrinth, ready to leave. August frowned at Willem. "And how did you come to know where we need to go next? King Bello didn't say. Neither I nor my companion have been informed." He glanced at Larissa.

Larissa said nothing, gazing at Willem for an answer.

"The reason I mentioned Derestney Downs earlier, sir, is because that is where we will learn more about our mission."

August stood rooted in place. "That's all fine and dandy, but I still demand to know how you gained this information instead of us." He crossed his arms, resolute."

Willem restrained a look of exasperation. "Sir, it came by way of a War Pigeon. Unfortunately, the sender didn't reveal himself—or herself. I found the parchment paper in my bag this morning before we left the Citadel. I thought now would be a good time to know our next destination."

Something in Larissa's gut told her the wizard was right. She didn't question it further. "Lead the way, Willem." Larissa walked closer to the Labyrinth exit. "Let's just pray we make it out of here alive so we can reach Derestney Downs."

King Bello told the truth. The trek out of the Labyrinth took less time leaving than coming in, but they made a run for it several times, dodging the phantom hands reaching out for them. One grabbed August's hair, nearly pulling him into the hedges. Larissa and Willem fought fiercely to free their companion from such a nasty grasp. Their own cloaking and protection spells were weak at best.

It also hadn't gone undetected by Larissa the quick view of seeing Mistress Ivy landing a sloppy kiss on August's lips and cupping his balls for added good measure when they said goodbye.

Despite some of the happenings in this realm, she strongly believed that their venture here yielded intriguing revelations, especially the inscription over the huge arched marble entrance to the hall where she and Willem first entered.

For all his penchant for dining on human flesh, which she supposed he couldn't help, Larissa rather liked King Bello. She especially liked him because he had indicated they would be fighting side by side at some point in the future. Didn't all great quests end with one final epic battle?

All the one's she'd heard about certainly had. She prayed that when the time came, she, August, Willem, and whomever else was destined to join them, would be ready with a few tricks up their magical sleeves. Larissa also fervently prayed that she wouldn't be on her period when that occurred.

At the first rest stop after clearing the Labyrinth, she and Willem left August sitting up against an old elm while they walked off to sit on some hospitably comfortable large flat rocks overlooking a stream. The edges of the rocks were close to the water. They spent several minutes splashing water on their faces, at each other, taking a sip, and dipping their tired aching feet into the cold depths.

Larissa looked over a Willem. She had splashed him so much that his shoulder-length hair was dripping wet with droplets coursing down his handsome face.

"Tell me, Willem the Wizard, she said in a teasing tone, "since you are a wizard and all, what kind of magic do you do exactly? I find it odd that we haven't seen you access your mad wizarding skills on this journey so far. I am wondering why you are so shy about showing us what you've got."

Willem plucked a strand of grass growing between the rocks, cupped it between his two hands, and blew so it made a shrieking sound. "You're absolutely right when you say you haven't seen me performing magic." He looked at her and smiled. "The truth, I am not a showoff like some other Magicals we may or may not be traveling with. I don't find a need to call attention to myself constantly."

Larissa looked perplexed.

The young man sighed. "So what I am trying to say is you have seen demonstrations of it, though you may not have known it. For example, didn't you find it curious how easily August and I fought off so many soldiers in the Order of the Chevron?"

Larissa shook her head slightly. "Sorry. I wasn't paying attention. Mostly because I noticed that my conjured fireballs tore them to smithereens. Um, what exactly was your contribution again?"

"I cast a Supresso spell," Willem said. He modestly lowered his gaze toward the water. "It slowed their reaction times. Because of that, August and I gained the upper hand in the sword fighting. It's a handy spell in battle, unless the enemy is very heavily warded against it. From what I could tell, it provided an advantage."

"Okaaay," Larissa said slowly. "And what else did I perhaps miss?"

"I am versed in Elemental Magic, and I kept the falls from reaching out long tentacles of water and dragging all of us under before we could reach the tent." Willem's gaze locked onto hers.

"In case you didn't know, those falls are enchanted. They are not simply a natural feature. Those falls are more intelligent, predatory, and alive than they appear to be. Everyone they drag under gives them more power to do the same to any other unsuspecting traveler. Entire armies have disappeared beneath the waters.

"It is not only the iron that gives them their red color. Did you notice the pretty pink clouds of foam along the edges? That is caused by the blood of the drowned."

"Oh," Larissa answered, embarrassed by her own arrogance. Willem certainly turned out to have more depth than she had surmised. "Anything else?"

"Yes. I have dream spinner skills. I can send dreams, all sorts of them, when I focus on a person. Pleasant dreams, dreams of glory, even nightmares featuring their deepest fears, and prophetic ones also."

Larissa's breath hitched in her throat. She still remembered the dream of her and Willem the night she slept in King Bello's citadel. Stunned, she said nothing, staring down into the bubbling, rushing waters of the stream. Her heart pounded. Had he had sent that particular erotic dream to her, expressing his true feelings?

Willem's fingers intertwined with hers, an affirmation of her suspicions. She also sensed in the gesture a warmth and kindness mixed with shameless acceptance of their feelings and needs. Larissa knew in an instant that she need not feel uncomfortable, and that he had sent the dream when they truly needed it most.

The young man quickly released her hand and walked away, heading back to where August sat. Larissa used the brief solitude as an opportunity to address nature's calls. She carefully slid off the rock, using several smaller ones as footholds. With no one looking, she could take a bathroom break.

No one had warned her that this quest would be like camping. Going to the bathroom outdoors wearied her at this point. They all still had far to go. For now, she supposed she would have to endure it. But the sensation of Willem's fingers lingered on hers, along with a strong ache between her legs as the dream replayed itself in her head. Larissa crouched low, ensuring nobody saw her. With a middle finger placed on her clitoris, she stroked until her hips rocked with a strong, delicious orgasm.

"Willem tells me that you were able to read the inscription over the arch at the Citadel." August glanced at her as they tramped through the forest on a barely discernible path. The forest seemed more like a tangle wood, something from a fairytale. It wouldn't have surprised her at all to come upon a princess laid out upon a flower-covered bier.

"Yes. It was in Sanskrit, so I am not certain of what it said word for word, but it was a very dark-sounding prophecy. That much I could tell. It had a funny title at the very top. I think it translated roughly to 'Descendants'."

"That sounds interesting. I wonder what 'Descendants' it was referring to. Too bad it didn't say 'Heirs', right? Then we would know that it might have been meant for us."

"That's what puzzles me too," Larissa answered. "Because as far as I know, there is no word in Sanskrit for 'Heirs'. It might have been meant for us, for all I know. I memorized it, anyway. I have a kind of photographic memory. And I will make sure to commit it to a page. Perhaps we will come across someone that can verify it's meaning or make more sense of it."

"I'm sorry about last night," August told her. For once, he sounded sincere. "I apologize for everything I said. I know that I had too much to drink, but that is no excuse, and I know that if your Aunt Dorenda were around, she would likely geld me." He grinned a little. "I have no idea what came over me. That's all I have to say. And I am sorry."

Larissa chuckled and tossed her head. "Nothing you do or ever will do surprises me at this point. But you would do well to watch your drinking if it makes you ruder and crasser than you normally are. I think all of us are growing weary of it."

"Okay, that's fair," August said, "I will make a mental note not to drink so much." He paused a moment in thought. "But maybe you can explain why you were in a lip lock with my servant, Willem the Wizard.

Willem is sworn to serve any and all members of the Hawthorne Clave, not the Strondovan Clave. I know that he is here to protect both of us, but that doesn't include making passes like he was on our social level. What do you think your Aunt Dorenda would say?"

"I think she would say that whomever I show affection to is strictly my business," Larissa sniffed, "and maybe you should do some soul-searching before you pass judgment on anyone else. Willem has been nothing but helpful and accommodating to both of us."

August looked as if he'd like to reply but decided the better of it. "All I'm saying is, we don't know him that well. He could be a spy. We have no way of verifying beyond a shadow of a doubt that he is who he says he is. Perhaps he is just playing along until he is sure we have our guard down so he can murder us in our sleep."

"May I remind that you mentioned that possibility before, August," Larissa said. "If you want to remain hyper vigilant and lose sleep over that improbable scenario, that's fine. As far as I'm concerned Willem has more than proven himself."

Willem, who had been walking in front of the couple, just out of earshot, stopped and waited for them to catch up. "I think I know a faster way to get to Derestney Downs," he said. "A way that will save both time and effort, if both of you are willing, that is."

Along the way the trio of travelers fell into a conversation about ancient artifacts.

"What gets me is that if you do even a little bit of homework on the subject, you discover a plethora of them," Willem said. His voice sounded off with unrestrained enthusiasm. "Every major and minor religion mentions them. Lots of legends and lore surrounds them that tells tales of their being found, lost or destroyed.

"What keeps me up at night is wondering which ones still exist, waiting to be found or recovered. Even though we practice magic at a high level, there was never a lasting spell for protection or ongoing power or immortality. If there is, I have never heard of it."

"Eternal youth," August said, musing. "I think most of them promise immortality or eternal youth. Our druidic ancestors had the Grail of Immortality and the Sacred Keys, both rumored to have originated in the lost city of Atlantis. Ever heard of them? Do they actually exist anywhere? Who owns them?"

"I thought the thirteen Sacred Keys were a blueprint for how to live life," Larissa commented. "Not physical keys. They were supposedly divine laws that gave a blueprint on supplying power to cities and the like."

Willem chuckled and shook his head. "Who can know? I am sure your Aunt Dorenda might be able to clarify some of the most well-known ones from lore, but just recently I came across a few more mentioned in ancient texts.

"The Cuff of the Eternal Sun, for instance. Its existence supposedly dates back to the War Scrolls, some of the Dead Sea Scrolls, plotting and depicting the battle of the Sons of Darkness versus the Sons of Light in the Book of Enoch. It is said that even some of the scrolls themselves have power, particularly the copper inscribed ones.

"Then of course you have the Philosopher's Stone as detailed by Sir Isaac Newton, concocted from a mythical formula and purported to be a philosophic mercury compound having several amazing properties, not the least of which was turning lead into gold and aiding humans to achieve immortality.

"And you have the obvious ones, like the Elixir of the Gods, that supposedly was created in a fixed quantity, secreted away and employed by a few of the most famous warriors and leaders throughout history to assure their victory in battles.

Of course you also have other more arcane artifacts, everything from magical rings to garments to the sacred cloth, golden cloth spun by fairies from grain or straw. Some even say by the wind."

Larissa made an odd noise, followed by a fit of coughing.

"Are you okay, Larissa?" Willem asked anxiously.

"Yes. Sorry. Something caught in my throat," she said.

"Hey, by the way, don't some covens of witches spin on spinning wheels?" Willem asked. A smile lit his face. "Is that part of the Strondovan legacy? Do you happen to know how to spin straw into gold for instance?"

"Actually, no," Larissa answered. She was glad that Willem had bungled the question so deftly. At least she answered him honestly. Spinning was one thing, the kind of magical spinning that her Aunt Dorenda had taught her while telling tales and legends. She only wished it had included more of her family and what it was the way she knew it before everything horrible happened.

The sacred cloth—the conjuring cloth—it was that powerful a magic, more so because few could actually create it. Those who knew of its existence, knew very little. Over time, the tales etched in the memories of those who had ever witnessed it died along with them. Now the stories were few and had been altered by the many retellings.

That was all for the best, because the product of the witch spinners was at the least an advantage and at most a powerful weapon, so knowledge of it should be in the hands of the few who were the remnant of the once powerful and illustrious Strondovan Clave.

***

On the other side of the world, in a space that was not on any map nor cited in any historical accounts, a legion of creatures amassed.

They slithered out of holes in the earth, emerged from caves, trekked downward from lofty glacier-covered citadels and journeyed across arid deserts.

Some of the larger more impressive ones convened at the black bottom of ocean abysses, at fathoms so deep that they all had been overlooked by the huge plate shifts in the earth's crust. They could not venture to the surface of their watery domain but relied on their shared hive mind to be updated on their predestined mission.

Even the most hideous in form, even those resembling genetic mosaics of plant, animal, and human had intelligence and a will to serve the Darkness.

In an underground city three miles below Washington, D.C., a meeting convened inside a hotel reserved for politicians, government officials, a few well-chosen celebrities, and foreign dignitaries who still had embassies along Embassy Row in the nation's capital.

The first to speak was the President of the United States.

He began, opened his arms, and gazed with satisfaction around the huge oval table. "My distinguished friends, I have heard from many of our global contacts, and I am receiving more word from others as we speak.

"All of them unanimously support our glorious initiative to restore power once and for all into the hands of those meant to wield its reins. We must take seriously our sworn mission to eradicate all our opponents who hide their shallow weakness behind their so called 'Humanitarian' agenda. To allow their existence is to also allow all the despicable characteristics of lesser men and women to carry on their ineptitude.

"We have not only the carnal weapons and innovations of warfare on our side, but also the powers of the Ancients, also known as 'The Magicals'. Their tribes have pledged allegiance to us, and we have found that wherever they convene to cast the spells we request, the oppositional Humanitarian force is defeated.

"Even I myself am astounded by what they are able to accomplish. Whereas it took the Military Corps of Engineers at least thirty-six hours to create weather phenomena, a high-level dark conjurer can summon extreme weather and use it as a weapon of warfare in an instant.

"Working with some of our Nobel Prize-winning physicists and scientists, they have developed the 'Nightbloom' phenomena, a ground zero targeted weapon tested a few years ago in a remote village in the UK, that was able to target and annihilate populations silently and effectively. To date, it has been one of our greatest achievements, and they are yet working to further expand its reach and programmability.

"Our Agenda is vast, but as our resources increase, we have every confidence that it will be achieved. You, my friends, are the elite of this millennia, and you will live far longer than your predecessors. How is that possible? By virtue of the huge underground cages where the dispensable human beings—the unintelligent, the imperfect, the undesirable—will be farmed so that their organs will prolong your lives.

"Now that we have perfected the genetic blending enzyme that eliminates organ rejection issues, you can expect to live a full century and beyond! Truly we have much to celebrate, but we must also continue to work toward our common goal. In the next few days, we will have even more extreme weather, and to be fair, some of it will be coming to the East Coast of the United States.

"There will be cyclones offshore and tornados inland in places that have never seen that particular weather phenomena in centuries. We had considered sparing the Capitol, but that might cast suspicion upon our nexus of operations. Some of you might be forced to evacuate. Some will certainly lose their homes if they find themselves in the path of destruction.

"I regret the inconvenience, but I am warning you in advance so that you can warn your inner circle and move your friends and family underground for the duration. Not only are we well-situated to accommodate you all, but we will have no shortage of anything you may require. Now, any questions?"

As soon as the President finished speaking, several hands shot up. The President's gaze swept over the gathering and selected an attractive blonde woman from one of the most celebrated and illustrious families of American Industrialists.

"Bonnie? A question?"

"What about our very close friends who live in the same area? Should we prewarn them?"

"Great question," the President answered. "Look, whatever happens will happen fast, and if it gets bad enough so that you need to evacuate, it will be over in twenty-four to thirty-six hours maximum. So feel free to bring a party. Have a hurricane party, for all I care. Your stay will be brief."

There were a few more questions. The President wanted to chuckle, because he could tell that everyone he had gathered felt themselves to be apart and protected from what was coming to claim most of humanity. They couldn't have been more wrong. They were only privy to stage one of the Divine Agenda, which was to eliminate the riff raff of humanity in favor of the Elite.

But they were completely unaware and ill-informed when it came to stage two. Stage two would move on to eliminating ninety percent of humankind, leaving a few breeders and a scant handful of the Elite. Most of the remaining would be clones, aliens, or high-ranked Dark Magicals.

The President wasn't sure what stage three would involve, but he wasn't taking any chances. He had volunteered for the genetic enhancement early on so that he might be an asset to whatever was in the works. He knew that this coming conflict might end mankind and establish a new order that would destroy the old. He would either be in or out. He prayed that he would be in.

***

"I haven't heard you sing anything at all since we first started journeying together." Willem complained mildly to Larissa. "August and I are singing constantly, but never you. Why?"

"Probably because she can't carry a tune in a bucket," August said, jumping into the conversation. "I can't imagine the Strondovan Clave is much for singing. The Hawthorne Clave is renowned for their songwriting, especially as an ongoing historical tradition."

Larissa's expression showed disgust at the jabs by August. "Do you know the folksong *The Room*?" She turned to Willem, who was making sure that the strings on the lute he had been playing were in tune.

Willem nodded. He was sensitive to Larissa's moods but couldn't resist teasing her at times. Her pouts were adorable.

"Play it then," she said in a commanding tone.

Willem strummed the opening notes. Larissa sang:

A room awash in blue and gold,
His heart was warm, but his hands were cold.
Two lovers in strange circumstance
Giving Love a chance.
They knew that they might live or die
And so together they would lie,
Each precious kiss a benediction
Lost in passion's friction.
That night would be their first and last.
As soon as crest of morning passed
Soldiers seized them where they lie,
And one of them would die.
She could not bear it when they said
The wicked King would take his head.
She would join him in death as well

And threw herself from the Citadel.
She'd see her father King in Hell.
She'd see her father King in Hell.

By the time the last strains of the song faded, both August and Willem sat with expressions of incredulity.

"Wow!" August exclaimed. "I never knew you could sing, Larissa. You have a beautiful voice."

"I agree." Willem smiled and nodded with enthusiasm. "You should sing more often, Strondovan Heir. Bravo!"

"Thank you," Larissa replied primly. She smoothed her skirts and brushed her hair back from her shoulders. "My aunt arranged for voice lessons at an early age.

"Wait," August said. "Listen. Do either of you hear music?"

All of them remained silent, including the deafening noise of the cicadas that had kept up an intermittent hum. The piping sounds of calliope music drifted in on the breeze from some far-off location.

"Looks like our destination is having the first of their Autumn Festivals," August remarked. "And I'd have to say that I am in the mood to see common folk and drink harvest ale." He looked at Willem and Larissa. "What say you both? Shall we make haste?"

Chapter Twenty Two

The buoyant calliope music was enticing. Mesmerized, the trio gathered their gear and, trekking across the open field, headed straight toward it. Within minutes, they saw a spectacle of gaily colored tents, flowing pennants, and milling crowds of young and old. They had reached the outskirts of Derestney Downs, a town none of them were familiar with but that sounded quaint and homey.

Laughter of the faire goers reached their ears. They sniffed the air, inhaling the enticing aroma of roasted turkey legs, buttered corn on the cob, and a variety of meat and fruit pies. Their mouths watered. Larissa whipped out her purse and paid for all of them to eat.

They had been wined and dined by all their hosts, but an outdoor celebration, indulging in food under the dining area of a large tent, was what they enjoyed most. Every succulent bite surpassed every delicacy they had been offered on their quest.

"Mmm." August gnawed at A huge turkey leg, savoring the tender meat dripping with juices. "This is a superb feast. Thank you so much, Larissa."

"I thank you as well, Strondovan Heir." Willem chimed in after swallowing a generous mouthful of meat pie. "This is truly wonderful, and the honeymeade is sublime. I have eaten far too much. Still want to keep eating." He swallowed another bite. "But I don't think we should get too far off track. We must be close, but we need to get to Derestney Downs before darkness falls."

"Do you know whom we are to contact there? Or where we are supposed to meet?" August said. He frowned in Willem's direction.

Larissa stopped in the middle of biting into a tiny lattice-topped apple and currant pie. She gazed at Willem, waiting for an answer.

Willem stared at the two, speechless. He looked up, right, left, and back at Larissa and August. "The parchment. It told me where to go. To Derestney Downs." He snapped his finger. "I remember seeing something on the back. Some names." He wiped the back of his neck, clearly panic-stricken. "I know I read the names." He stared at the ground, embarrassed. "I don't know."

Larissa spoke up. "No, I think you must be under some kind of forgetfulness spell. An Obliti spell, as it were. I wonder who did this? Perhaps the Order of the Chevron sent it your way after their defeat at our hands. "But you have the parchment in your bag, right?" She clapped her hands in glee. "Just check your bag, Willem."

Willem did as she commanded, reaching in his bag and pulling out the slip of parchment. He handed it to Larissa. As she unfolded it, the men leaned in, curious to see what was written on it. But to their collective surprise it was blank.

"I don't believe it!" Larissa gasped. "What kind of Obliti spell does that?"

She heard a fluttering noise behind her, turned, and ducked, narrowly missing a War Pigeon that had aimed for a landing on the top of her head. Instead, it landed on the crude wooden table where they ate.

"Uncle Jove!" August exclaimed. "I'd know our War Pigeons anywhere!" While the pigeon eagerly pecked at crumbs from their feast, he removed the message from its ruff, unrolled it, and read aloud:

Greetings. I trust this missive finds you all well, and that you are now in the company of my fine and loyal guard Willem the Wizard. As soon as I became aware of your increasing peril, I sent him to aid you.

He is pledged to protect you both with his life, but the longer you can keep him alive the better, for he is a crack wizard and knows a great many conjures and spells.

I am aware that the Forces of Darkness are constantly casting spells your way meant to confuse and impede your progress. I want you to find the shop of our ally Cosmo Caster. He will have a task for you that will further empower your quest.

All my regards. Travel safely,
Jove
PS-Cosmo's horse Arion can speak, so do not be surprised.

"How timely," Larissa remarked, "At least we finally got confirmation after the fact that Willem was sent by Jove."

"I believe that this is not the first War Pigeon that Jove sent, Rissa," August said in a serious tone, "I think he sent at least one or two previously, but they were intercepted. The Order of the Chevron themselves have trained falcons to attack our War Pigeons and carry them and their messages back to the Order so that they might be intercepted."

"Nice to be validated." Willem teased Larissa. "But admit it, Strondovan Heir, you were finding that you liked me anyway."

"I think 'like' may be too strong a word," Larissa scoffed. "I was getting used to you. I was finding you useful. That sort of thing."

"As you like," Willem answered mildly. His response held an amused tone.

Much to her consternation, Larissa found herself flushing. She did like Willem, but she would be damned before either admitting it or allowing their business relationship to get personal. She had become increasingly aware of her need for affection and closeness, but since becoming engaged in this quest, choices had been limited to old lovers that had shown up at their various destinations, that self-indulgent horror of a Hawthorne heir August, and Willem the Wizard.

She was growing weary. More and more she wanted to be back with her Aunt Dorenda, young and carefree as she had been before all this hopping from one place to another had begun.

With difficulty she pulled herself out of her reverie and noticed that August was staring hard at a figure standing just outside the perimeter of the food tent. As the War Pigeon kept pecking at table crumbs, waiting for Willem to scribble a response to Jove's letter, Larissa followed the direction of August's gaze. The view didn't surprise her in the least.

It was a gorgeous young woman, tall, dressed in emerald green velvet, with dark hair flowing past her waist, and huge dark eyes. From looking at them, they were captivated with each other, their gazes locked on each other like tractor beams.

"Hey!" Larissa said. She rudely snapped her fingers in front of August's face, "Take a picture. Or go over to meet her. I can't believe that you are staring so hard!"

"Sorry," August replied. His tone was uncharacteristically mild. "But I think I just found my future wife. In fact, I am virtually sure that I have. I have never seen such a glorious creature in all my days. Excuse me, would you?" He rose from his seat and hurried over toward the young woman.

Larissa noted as soon as he left the bench and was introducing himself that the woman was taller than he. But then again, she was wearing heels. Larissa reasoned with herself that it was impossible to tell because she was wearing a long dress too.

Biting into an apple, she waited until Willem had finished writing a response note, rolled it up tightly, and attached it to the foot of the War Pigeon. The bird seemed to have gotten bigger after having gorged itself on the leftovers from the trio's impromptu picnic.

"What do you make of that?" she asked Willem. "August caught sight of that girl over there and seemed instantly taken with her."

"She is attractive, to be sure," Willem said, "but I think there is something off about her. What do you think, Larissa?"

"I have never been able to make any sense of anything August Hawthorne does, but now that you mention it, she does seem odd. She is unusually tall, for one thing. Not to mention the fact that we are on an important quest, a mission, and as a rule we probably should eschew strangers."

"Good point," Willem said in agreement. "And I will remind him if he ever pries himself away from her company. He almost seems entranced."

Larissa snapped her fingers. "Exactly. I think that's what we are both picking up. It seems that he is under a spell. I think we need to intervene. I think I know just the counter spell." She turned back to where August and the girl had been standing, but they seemed to have disappeared. "That's odd. Where did they go?"

"I think I saw them go inside the small tent marked *Storage*, Willem muttered. "Should we follow them? Though I'm sort of afraid of what we might find if we do."

"We have no choice." Larissa squared up her shoulders. "It's kind of our duty, now that we have agreed August is under an influence of some sort. Follow me."

Both walked over and ventured cautiously into the tent. It was dim inside, but both their heads turned when they heard a groan to their left. Over against one corner of the tent, the young woman sat half reclined against the canvas with an unlaced bodice, her breasts exposed. August was shirtless and had wrapped one of his arms around her, supporting her languid body while he suckled one of her nipples.

"This has to be quick," Larissa said. "August would never do that in public, even though he is a libertine and has always flaunted his ribald sexuality in private. She has cast a spell on him, and I am going to break it."

"Do you have a wand on you?" Willem whispered. "Might go easier."

"Of course I do," Larissa answered crossly, "but Aunt Dorenda always taught me self-reliance in magical practices. Wands are great for focusing and conducting energy, but on a quest like this, they may be impractical at times, since we have zero time for wand maintenance.

"It's not like in those silly popular movies you know. Wands must be recharged after multiple uses. You can't just throw them back in your pocket and expect them to work without being recharged by crystals and the light of the sun or the moon."

"Fine. I get your point." Willem raised his voice in defense. "But if you don't do something soon, they are going to be fucking each other, Strondovan Heir."

Larissa called on the silver white energy of the universe to descend and flow through the top of her head to the tip of the index finger on her writing hand. She stated the words, *"Revelare, revelare, revelare."*

As both stared, the appearance of the girl August held changed. Her face morphed into that of a wizened hag. Her body didn't look exactly human, either. Peeking out from the lacy hem of her dress appeared to be the tail of a large serpent. What was more appalling to gaze upon was the fact that August was unaware that he was playing tonsil hockey with a crone.

He continued to kiss her, bending his head occasionally to take the teat end of one of her wrinkled flaccid breasts in his mouth as if it were a thing of beauty

"Oh, dear." Willem breathed anxiously, looking on in dismay.

It was obvious to both that the spell on August was stronger than they had imagined.

"I need your help," Larissa said. "Willem, repeat the Confractus spell with me. And use your wand if you have it handy. I believe it will take both our skills to break August from this grip."

Willem nodded in agreement and dutifully pulled out a small, smart-looking wand of almond wood. Larissa noted with satisfaction that it had the sacred word 'Raidho' carved into the handle end of it—a good omen, since seeing through illusions was exactly what was needed at the moment.

They recited the reversal spell in unison. It worked. August's eyes widened as he quickly jumped up and gazed down, horrified, at the true harpy that was the hybrid of a crone and a snake.

"What's the matter, my sssweet?" the hag hissed "Lost your desssire?"

As he bent to pick up his shirt from the ground, August noticed Larissa and Willem and ran toward them. He seemed both embarrassed and relieved. All three exited the tent. A great glass of Honeymeade seemed to return August to his former self. All of them avoided speaking of what had just transpired, except for August thanking them both in as awkward a manner as possible.

"I don't know what came over me, but I am glad that you two knew the magic to release me from my delusion. Thanks for that." He finished, draining his glass.

Thinking about the event later sent Larissa in a fit of giggles, laughing until her sides ached and tears ran down her cheeks. She would never forget the exact sound August made when he realized that he was making love to a half-naked and toothless crone with stringy hair and saggy breasts. It was a noise that was a cross between a pig squeal and a cat that has had its tail stepped on.

"I'm all for heading out now for Derestney Downs," Willem said solemnly. "I'm not sure this carnival is what it appears to be. I am picking up undercurrents of deception and illusion."

"But my friend, isn't that what carnivals are all about?" August responded, "Isn't that the allure? It is supposed to be a world of the extraordinary, one that you enter at your own risk."

"Easy for you to say now that you've been pulled back from the brink of madness by Willem and me," Larissa said.

August winced. Her scolding tone grated instantly on his nerves.

"I think Willem must be right," she continued. "I think we should leave while it is still daylight."

"But Larissa, my sweet, you simply can't leave until you have consulted with Madame Haruspicem over yonder." August turned and pointed at a purple and gold tent. The sign positioned in front of it seemed to have appeared from out of nowhere. "And how about this music? We simply must have a dance before we depart. "Come with me, Strondovan Heir. You really must have fun before you leave this place." He gallantly stood up, holding his hand out to her.

Larissa hesitated briefly and, for reasons she didn't understand, took his hand, accompanying him to a space before a tiny stage on which musicians were playing.

Willem had pulled out his lute. After briefly speaking to one of the musicians, he joined them in making merry music for the dancing crowd. They played the song "The Fickle Damozel", one of Larissa favorites. She hummed and twirled as she and August joined the revelers.

Uncommonly pretty, but poor as a mouse,
I coaxed the pretty Damozel from her house.
Her hair full of ribbons, her smile was sublime.
She was alone so her parents not mind.
She was fetching and shy and curious about men.
I showed her where to hold on, and so it began.
She rolled up her skirt, and I rolled up my big sleeve.
And what happened hence you would never believe.
She wanted to tarry and stay close to me,
But after we were done, I couldn't agree
With giving her either an oath or a ring,
For she'd given for free what was worth anything.

Larissa was laughing and breathless by the time the song ended.

"See? See how happy you are, Larissa North Strondovan?" August teased her, smiling. "I say three more dances you will be walking on air."

The fact that August was such a good dancer surprised her.

"One more," she said, conceding gaily. "And then I want to visit the soothsayer. Then we should be on our way."

They danced again. This time it was a slow and soulful song about star-crossed lovers and the treacherous full moon that had sealed their fate. Larissa found that she was surprisingly comfortable with her head resting just below August's shoulder. More surprising was that she didn't object as before when the song ended, and she felt his lips brush the top of her head for a brief kiss.

Her thoughts quickly reverted to the moment he held her after the slaying of Svapada. He'd seemed genuinely concerned. Why had she revolted from his touch then when all he wanted to do was truly comfort her? And she was frightened when that horrible serpent could have sent August to his death. It had been a brief awkward moment when they both noted that she'd wrapped her arms around his as if they did it as lovers do.

Willem rejoined them as they walked toward the purple tent of the soothsayer. When they reached the entrance, August remembered his manners enough to step aside and allow Larissa to go in first.

The interior of the tent was dimly lit by a few strings of colored light bulbs. Through the opening of a thick gold curtain, they saw a short older woman wearing a bejeweled headdress, many rings of multicolored cabochon gemstones and huge gold hoop earrings.

"Welcome," she said. The woman greeted them with a slight nod. "I have been waiting for you. Are all of you here for a reading or only the Strondovan Heir?"

Willem cleared his throat, bowing back to her. "I'm not here for a reading. I am just their bodyguard, Madame."

"Ah, I see," she said. Turning to August, she added, "And you Hawthorne heir?"

"Depends on how much time it takes," August told her. "Really just Larissa for now, Madame."

"Very well." The old lady nodded. She immediately motioned for Larissa to sit in the vacant chair across from her. When August and Willem attempted to follow, she held up a hand.

"My readings are private. You must wait for her outside."

August's eyes met Larissa's. She nodded to him that she was okay with the soothsayer's request. Willem and August headed outside the tent where they dropped their packs and sat on the ground cross-legged, waiting.

Inside the tent, Larissa gazed at the small round table, which held a huge crystal globe in the middle of it. The soothsayer waved her hand over the sphere. It glowed with a light from within.

She spoke, "How far into your future would you like to see, Strondovan Heir? And that will be twenty-five dollars paid in advance, please."

"I'm not sure." Larissa was taken back by the question but rooted around in a quaint embroidered change purse for the money. "I'm not sure how it works." She pushed the crumpled bills across the table to the soothsayer.

"Very well. How about if I show you the birth of your first child? All young women love to see their future children."

The light within the crystal faded for a moment and returned showing a hospital scene. Larissa watched her future self crying out. She also heard the cry of a baby.

"It's a boy!" A masked doctor behind a tented sheet made the announcement. Even though the image in the crystal was distorted like a fisheye lens, Larissa saw that he held up a red-faced squalling infant with a light fuzz of curly golden hair and a tiny penis.

Nothing prepared her for the impact she experienced on gazing at the image. She gasped; her eyes filled with tears. Abruptly, the image faded.

"But whose child am I having?" Larissa asked, dabbing at her eyes.

"That cannot be revealed at this time," The soothsayer's voice seemed to come not directly from her but from behind. "What would you like to see next?"

"I want to see my Aunt Dorenda in real time. I miss her, and I want to see what she's doing."

"Very well," the soothsayer said.

Immediately the crystal globe brightened, momentarily dimmed, and brightened again with an increasingly clear image that didn't make immediate sense to Larissa.

When it cleared enough to make out the image, she saw the buttocks of a naked male on top of a woman who was moaning in pleasure as he thrust repeatedly into her. The woman's legs were over his shoulders and she wore a gold ring on one of her little toes. All of her toenails were painted in a color of deep crimson red.

Larissa averted her gaze. She was sure that the woman was Dorenda because her aunt always painted her toenails red and wore a gold ring on one of the little toes.

Apparently her aunt wasn't missing her as much as she'd thought. She'd certainly found a few diversions since Larissa had been away.

"Whoops! Awkward moment." The soothsayer chortled, obviously amused. "Oh well, it will give you something to laugh about when you return home. Now, one more time, I will ask you. What would you like to be shown?"

"Show me the end result of our quest," Larissa told her. "Show me whether we will be successful or fail."

"Very well." The soothsayer sighed again, waving her hand over the globe, muttering as it faded and brightened, this time to an incandescent glow that was almost too bright to view directly.

Larissa leaned forward anxiously, not concerned about the brightness of the crystal globe making her eyes smart. Suddenly it cleared. It was a view of the earth from satellite, apparently. She saw darkness cover it like the shadow covering a moon as it goes through various phases. First just a small portion of it was in darkness, then more and more until only a sliver of the earth globe remained visible.

In a blinding flash, it reappeared as it originally had, with no darkness shrouding over any portion of it. As the image faded, Larissa determined that she couldn't make any sense of what she had seen.

"What was that?" she asked, startling at the loudness of her own voice. "What was that I just witnessed, Madame Haruspicem? I can't understand any of it."

"I don't give interpretations, my dear," she answered. "I promised to show your future, and I have. Unless you would like to fork over another twenty-five dollars to see more, your session is over."

Larissa rose stiffly and thanked the woman, feeling more confused than when she'd entered. At this point, she wanted to get as far away from the carnival as possible. On exiting the tent, Willem and August rose from their places. Madame Haruspicem poked her face through the curtain one last time.

"Hawthorne Heir," she called out, "I have something to tell you."

August was immediately interested in a freebie. "Yes?" he asked.

"Your son will be born in August two years hence, in the month of your name."

"Madame, you must be mistaken," August replied. "I'm not married."

"Yes, but you sow a great many wild oats," the woman said. Her lips turned up with a smirk. And with that comment, she disappeared beyond the gold curtain once more.

They left the sprawling carnival and crossed the meadow. Nearing the woods, they heard a loud noise so deafening it sounded like a sonic boom. The trio had hurried away, fearful of looking behind. Now they couldn't help but look back on the amusement that had first seemed so welcoming and friendly yet had grown darker the longer they tarried there.

It had all vanished. The three sighed in unison, glad to be rid of it, agreeing that the diversion hadn't claimed any more of their time than it could have.

Not far into the forest, August threw his pack down in a small clearing encircled by elms.

"I am exhausted," he declared. "Too tired to go another fifty feet. And since we won't make it to Derestney Downs before nightfall anyway, the shops will likely be closed until morning won't they?"

"More than likely," Willem answered. He also dropped his own pack to the ground. "What say you, Strondovan Heir?"

"I suppose you're right," she said. Larissa still had a clear image of the creature who had cast a spell on August. Though she had a hearty laugh in private, the incident now seemed more sinister than amusing.

"Willem, can you make a fire? We can sleep here, I suppose. August, can you help me with the tent?"

But August didn't answer. He had already passed out, using his pack for a pillow. Hours later, he awakened with a start. The Honeymeade in which he'd indulged much earlier left him a bit disoriented. He sat up, inhaled deeply, and tried to clear his head.

Thoughts slammed into his groggy brain, tumbling in one after the other without ceasing. All the truths he refused to recognize during the light of day had found him in his sleep, and he felt a grip of panic and sense of urgency as he confronted them. For the first time the reality of his feelings stared back at him with full force.

He didn't hate Larissa. All the energy he had spent taunting and even tormenting her, trying to drive her away, were part of his refusal to admit that she had gotten under his skin.

He was in love with her.

It was a damning admission to face and would more than likely have damning consequences. His heart pounded with new energy in his ears as he looked across the burning campfire and saw that Larissa's furs had been cast aside. She was not there.

August staggered to his feet, calling out her name. She didn't answer. The light from the cold full moon poured into their hideaway, and wearing only his breeches, he stumbled forward, thinking that she had left their camp to relieve herself. When he stepped farther away, a chilly mountain breeze nipped at his skin. He looked around carefully. The moon glow emerged from behind a trailing scarf of cloud, and August saw them.

They were standing under a single massive elm, whose heavy bare lower branches formed a bower above them. They were silhouetted perfectly against the backdrop of the huge moon, and he recognized Larissa's profile immediately.

But who in the name of the gods could she be with? August continued watching as the taller figure, obviously male, bent down and planted what suspiciously appeared to be a lingering kiss on Rissa's upturned face. A short gust of wind brought the low murmur of a deeply masculine voice to his ears.

His heart sank to the soles of his feet, immediately replaced by a burning and rising anger. August moved his hand automatically to the jeweled dirk at his side, walking cautiously towards the couple.

Just as he advanced a few steps, a blow caught him from behind, sending him to his knees. He pitched forward into the dirt and slipped into oblivion.

End Book One

Introduction:
Hour of the Witch Spinners-Pendulum (Spinners: Book 2)

Larissa, Edouard, and a couple of his henchmen gazed down upon August's body. Light from the full moon illuminated what could be seen of his handsome face, and he seemed for all the world as though he were sleeping.

"I hope your guard didn't hit him too hard," Larissa murmured.

"Just hard enough. Don't worry," Edouard said, quickly reassuring her. "And I have so much to tell you. But as you know, August Hawthorne has always been a maverick and a wild card, and I need to get him contained and get both of you to safety as quickly as possible.

"The Order of the Chevron has discovered your location and is riding here as we speak."

He pulled her closer to him. Larissa could smell the scent of clean leather mixed with something more exotic.

"I have thought of nothing but you since we last met. Come now, your safety is of the utmost importance, my love!"

About the Authors

Scarlet Darkwood: Scarlet Darkwood wields a mighty pen, or at the very least, delivers mighty punches to the computer keys when she's typing furiously on a story. She likes dark and twisted, and the weirder, the better.

Always preferring avant garde themes, her stories take the reader on unusual adventures, exploring the darker parts of the human psyche as she whips out cunning prose wrapped in provocative themes. Sometimes she veers from her beaten path and takes a happy-go-lucky romp in the brighter sides of life, kicking up her style into sharp, snappy dialogue and clever descriptions.

Writing in several genres unleashes her imagination so she never grows bored. From a young age, she's enjoyed writing and keeping diaries, but didn't start creating novels until 2012. She's a Southern girl who lives in Tennessee and enjoys the beauty of the mountains. She lives in Nashville with her spouse and two rambunctious kitties.

You can visit her BLOG at: www.scarletdarkwood.com Follow her on MeWe (Scarlet Darkwood), Instagram (scarletdarkwood), Facebook (Scarlet Darkwood Author), and Twitter(ScarletDarkwood)

P. Mattern is an Amazon #1, top 100 best-selling and award-winning author. Born with a stylus clutched in her tiny hand, she's been producing stories since she was in utero and hasn't looked back. She is the author of the Strident House and Full Moon Series, as well as other entertaining novels, short stories and novellas. Always the weaver of enticing plot lines, she wrote stories to entertain classmates in elementary school and won awards for fiction and poetry in college. After being laid off from her professional job in mental health, she began writing down all the stories she had carried in her head and made outlines in earnest for her vibrant characters.